PRAISE FOR *FORBIDDEN*

"Sure to appeal to fans of Ilona Andrews and Patricia Briggs."
—*Library Journal*

"I was captivated by the magic of this world. I was also amazed by the social dynamics of Luna Lake. Recommended for . . . fans of strange and beautiful magic."
—*The BiblioSanctum*

"Clamp brings us shifters, secrets, mind control, and romance as we race to catch an unknown predator. One hell of a sexy ride!"
—*The Lovely Books*

"Electrifying. Thrilling suspense."
—*Literary Addicts Book Community*

"I *loved* it. I had no idea who the bad guys were until the end of the story. I have to applaud her talent for suspense!"
—*Coffee Addicts Book Reviews*

"Cathy Clamp is a name I love to see on a book cover. She delivers a p_____nce, characters you r_____some surprising twis_____

_____less Zine

TOR BOOKS *by* CATHY CLAMP

THE TALES OF THE SAZI: LUNA LAKE TRILOGY

Forbidden

Illicit

Denied

BY CATHY CLAMP *and* C. T. ADAMS

THE TALES OF THE SAZI

Hunter's Moon

Moon's Web

Captive Moon

Howling Moon

Moon's Fury

Timeless Moon

Cold Moon Rising

Serpent Moon

BY C. T. ADAMS *and* CATHY CLAMP

THE THRALL

Touch of Evil

Touch of Madness

Touch of Darkness

Writing as CAT ADAMS

Magic's Design

THE BLOOD SINGER NOVELS

Blood Song

Siren Song

Demon Song

The Isis Collar

The Eldritch Conspiracy

To Dance with the Devil

All Your Wishes

LUNA LAKE • BOOK THREE

Denied

Cathy Clamp

TOR

A TOM DOHERTY ASSOCIATES BOOK
NEW YORK

This is a work of fiction. All of the characters, organizations, and events portrayed in this novel are either products of the author's imagination or are used fictitiously.

DENIED

Copyright © 2018 by Cathy Clamp

A Tor Book
Published by Tom Doherty Associates
175 Fifth Avenue
New York, NY 10010

www.tor-forge.com

Tor® is a registered trademark of Macmillan Publishing Group, LLC.

The Library of Congress Cataloging-in-Publication Data
is available upon request.

ISBN 978-0-7653-7724-1 (trade paperback)
ISBN 978-1-4668-5462-8 (ebook)

Our books may be purchased in bulk for promotional,
educational, or business use. Please contact your local bookseller
or the Macmillan Corporate and Premium Sales Department
at 1-800-221-7945, extension 5442, or by email at
MacmillanSpecialMarkets@macmillan.com.

First Edition: August 2018

Printed in the United States of America

0 9 8 7 6 5 4 3 2 1

DENIED

CHAPTER 1

*S*tep. Jump. Pull. Toss. Every shovelful exposed unburnable dirt, and added to the hope of stopping the fire before it could reach town. The smoke blown in on the wind stung Anica's lungs, made her eyes water nearly uncontrollably. She could feel, could smell, the panic of the people around her rising as the heat increased. Every person's distinct and individual scent of sweat and fear erupted from their layers of protective clothing in bursts of sharp unpleasantness. Along with charred bark and grass, the odors painted themselves on her skin; she desperately wanted to find a stream and scrub away the stench. But there was no water here, just fire.

So she concentrated on the clean smell of the dirt that rose from the ground as she dug, breathing in the sweet, thick scent of life under the roots, letting her sensitive nose find some relief. The crackling of bark was audible now in the distance, making her work harder. Her heart was pounding and so was her head; her muscles ached. *This would be easier in bear form.* She was a strong digger. But not everyone shoveling beside her was a shape-shifter. Some were professional firefighters . . . human residents from neighboring towns. Nobody could know that her kind lived among them.

A tap on her shoulder made her turn. Peering through the smoke, she made out the shape of a man, definitely human, wearing a gold insignia on his helmet. He touched her shovel and yelled over the noise of the helicopters passing by.

"Petrovic! Take a break! I'll take over!" He handed her a plastic bottle of water and waved her toward a truck that was pulling up along the makeshift road that wasn't much more than beaten tracks through the tall grass. Anica stepped aside, yielding her place in the fire line. Looking back, she saw a wide path of bare dirt behind her. It made her feel proud.

When she reached the truck, Rachel Washington reached down to help her into the cargo area. Soot was smeared in patches on the woman's warm brown skin, and her eyes were red from the same smoke that marred her natural sugary scent, like a frozen treat made of cherries that made Anica's raw throat wish for ice. Ash rained down on them, sticky and gray. She sat down on the truck bed next to her new friend. "Wow! You rocked that fire line!" Rachel's voice cracked.

Confused, Anica frowned and shook her head. "No. No rocks. I moved rocks so no one is hurt walking."

Rachel smiled and shook her head. "'Rocked' means you did a good job."

"Oh! Yes, thank you." English was such a difficult language. So many words had more than one meaning. "Did you also rock your dirt?"

Another smile. "Yeah, I did." The other woman's smile faded as more sirens filled the air. "I don't know if it's going to do any good, though. The fire just crossed Highway 21. If we have to evacuate, we'll have to go east, or north into Canada."

Anica shook her head and stared out at the smoky landscape as the truck jounced through the forest. Ash, dirt, and pine needles rained onto her borrowed jeans, and she carefully brushed off the debris before it could stain the fabric. When she and her family had come to Luna Lake for a mediation between her family's bear sloth and the neighboring one, she'd brought only a few clothes, and most of them suited for the negotiating table, not physical labor. Her family had intended to stay for only a few days. During those few days, her life had changed, possibly forever.

With the help of people she'd met in Luna Lake, she'd been able to root out slave camps back in Serbia and free many children taken captive by the evil snakes. But some of the bad men had not been found, and Anica knew they would be looking for those who had ruined their plan. For *her.* Serbia could not be her home, not now. Fortunately, her father had been asked by the Sazi council to become the new Alpha of the town and Anica would stay with him, at least temporarily.

As for her mother . . . she had stayed behind to care for the new bear shifter cubs they'd rescued from the snakes. *Stayed behind.* It was what Papa had told her and her brother, but Anica knew it was a lie. Mama had betrayed the family, and Papa had cast her out. But Anica knew everything that had happened was actually her fault. She had been weak. After she had been kidnapped and turned, she had turned the rest of her until-then entirely human family.

Her other brother, Samit, had gone insane and tried to kill her. Poor Samit was dead now. . . . Her cousin, Larissa,

another betrayal, another attempt at murder. Luna Lake and
the people here had saved her. This place was all the Petrovics had now—Anica, Papa, and Bojan.

Anica opened her water bottle. Her throat was so sore
from smoke that the water actually burned going down. She
grimaced, then took another drink. The pain eased a little. By
the time she'd finished the bottle, she could almost swallow
normally. They picked up Dalvin, Rachel's fiancé, a few
moments later, at the next fire line.

The truck turned slowly onto an even bumpier back road,
passing other groups of diggers, working side by side with
the trained firefighters, before swerving to the side of the
road and skidding to a stop. A shower of soot blanketed
them. Anica tried to dust it off, but it smeared into the fabric. A line of green and brown camo-patterned trucks sped
by. To Anica, the uniformed men inside looked like soldiers.
"The army comes?"

"National Guard," Rachel replied, speaking close to her
ear. "They're civilians who volunteer for military duty. The
governor must have called them in, which isn't good. The
fire must be getting worse. But they'll have better equip-
ment, and more of it." Rachel touched her hand. "Don't
worry about the jeans. They're yours. Consider them a gift.
But I'm afraid they're going to get dirtier before this is over.
Maybe with the Guard here, it'll be over quicker."

Anica nodded gratefully before her eyes returned to the
line of trucks disappearing into the smoke. "Thank you." She
didn't have a good feeling about soldiers being involved, but
Rachel didn't seem concerned, so she would wait and see.
She'd learned that her friend was very suspicious of authority, much like she was herself, so she trusted the other
woman's instincts.

The truck neared the edge of a boggy area that smelled of bugs, frogs, and thick algae and made her mouth water. She liked bogs. They always had berries and roots that were succulent and sweet. She was so hungry after working hard all morning. Anica sniffed deep, trying to memorize the smell so she could come back later. In human form, her nose wasn't as sensitive. She'd learned how to inhale and hold the air in while her mind sorted the scents. But what she smelled now wasn't food; it was *danger*.

She jumped to her feet and began to slap on the roof of the moving truck, trying to make as much noise as possible. "Stop! We must stop!"

The exhausted volunteers became instantly alert. The truck stopped so sharply that Anica had to hold on to the grating covering the back window to keep her balance. The driver's door opened and the head of the local owl parliament, a man named John Williams, exited and asked, "What's going on? What's wrong?"

Anica pointed ahead of the truck, to the treetops. She tried to think of the words, in English. It was always harder when she was stressed. "The fire, it smells different. Hotter than before. The trees burn . . . inside. Not bark. We must not go further."

The others in the truck lifted their noses and inhaled. Rachel was an owl. Others were wolves, wildcats, eagles. But Anica was a bear. Her nose was better than theirs. As she watched, the smoke ahead grew darker, passing through gray to black; a roaring sound filled the air. The trees were too close to them. There was no way to turn the truck around.

"It's crowning!" John's eyes got wide and he jumped back behind the wheel. "Hold on, everyone! We're backing up, and fast."

The world turned orange. Fire raced across the tall trees overhead, which began to explode. Anica jumped out of the truck. "Come! We must get wet!"

"Anica, wait!" Rachel called. "Don't get out of the truck. We'll outrun it."

"Truck is not fast enough!" she shouted back, heading for the bog. "We must get to safe wet!"

Thankfully, the man in the passenger seat of the cab, a wolf—who, she remembered, was a firefighter from Seattle—agreed with her.

"She's right. C'mon. It's coming too fast."

Anica leaped into the water. It was only waist deep, so she took a deep breath, dove under, and started to dig, covering herself with thick, mossy mud. "Come! Mud will help." If the fire lasted too long, even the mud wouldn't be enough. It would turn scalding hot. But treetop fires often passed over and burned only a little. She'd grown up near other woods, with different trees, but fire was fire, and she'd been through this before.

A wall of red began to spin, turning into a tornado made of fire. As the others jumped into the water and dug down into the mud beside her, Anica smelled a bear. Not a natural one, a shifter like her, She also smelled blood. Both scents came from the other direction . . . not from the truck. The others wouldn't be able to smell it, she knew. She had no choice.

Jumping out of the water, the mud stinging her eyes and the smoke making her cough, she raced into the woods. Bits of burning leaves and branches rained down on her, quickly extinguished by the thick layer of wet mud. It would soon dry in this heat, so she had to move quickly.

At last she saw the source of the scent—a large brown bear,

who smelled of exotic spices that in another age would be reserved only for the tables of royalty. Rich and luxurious, the odors filled her nose and then her whole head, making it hard to concentrate. But she had to: he was unconscious, pinned under a massive tree, and bleeding from his side. His fur was smoldering as the tree began to burn. Coughing, her lungs stinging from the heat and smoke, she tried to shield her nose and mouth with the kerchief she'd been using earlier, while digging. But it too was coated with mud. She quickly slapped it against her leg until it was cleared enough to breathe through. It still stank, but the algae coating the cloth blocked the spicy smell of the injured bear.

The tree was too big for her to try to lift, but it was already badly damaged by fire. Working quickly, Anica dragged a large rock close to the tree and tore off one of the branches to make a pry bar. While strong, she wasn't very heavy, and the trunk did not move. She needed more weight. There. A rock. She strained to pick up the stone that was as big as her torso, then set its weight at the high end of her lever. Instead of lifting, the tree broke in two where it was most charred, freeing the trapped man. She gingerly lifted the smaller piece of trunk and branches off him, careful not to drag it over his injuries. She winced at what she saw. One of his back legs was visibly broken. There was no way he'd be able to walk. But she was so tired and the smoke was so thick. . . .

I cannot leave him here to burn.

She shook his head hard, tapping on his nose, which always woke her, even from the soundest sleep. But he was limp, unresponsive. Squatting, she grabbed handfuls of the bear's coarse brown fur and heaved his weight up until she could wrap his front legs around her shoulders. Anica leaned into the task of dragging the unconscious shifter to safety. She'd never known a shifter who could both shift off the moon and retain his form after passing out. But being an attack victim, she didn't know many bears outside of her family and the neighboring sloth. Did that mean he was more or less powerful than her?

It took every ounce of her strength to pull the massive bear forward; he probably weighed close to four hundred kilograms. Her leg muscles began to cramp as her lungs starved for oxygen. But there was no clean air to be had in the burning forest, so she did her best to only take small sips through the cloth.

A cracking sound above her nearly made her drop her burden. As a tree limb broke and fell, Anica took a huge breath and threw herself and the injured bear to one side. The gasp she sucked in was full of ash and soot and she began to cough uncontrollably. She dropped to her knees to find clear air near the ground, as her father had taught her when she was a child.

Smoke and ash swirled around them; her eyes were streaming with tears. Unsure of her way, she felt the world narrow as she tried to smell the bog through the fire. The bear started to rouse, instinctively digging his claws into her shoulders. She fought to keep his claws from breaking through the cloth. Yes, she would eventually heal if he mauled her, but it would take time and energy she didn't have. "Do not fight me!" she yelled, hoping he heard her over the roar of the blaze. "I know you are burn, but I am take you to safe place!"

Now fully awake, the big bear tried to pull away. She had to dig her hands into his fur to keep him tight against her. He bawled in fear and pain but didn't speak. That confused her. Maybe he was a three-day or a rogue who could not speak. Maybe he didn't speak English. She tried her own language, Serbian. There were many brown bears there. "Ovde sam da pomognem." *I am here to help.* Simple and, she hoped, easy to understand.

He bawled again, clearly in pain. His skin was blackened with burns and his foot pads were raw and bleeding. She kept her grip tight in his fur. Frustrated, she returned to English. She had to immerse herself in this language if she was to live here, since few people she'd met spoke more than one language.

"You must be strong. Please try to walk. I know a safe place." He struggled for a moment, but when she refused to let him go he finally stopped trying to get away. He put a little weight on his one good foot, pain in every line of his body. He would have to stand it, like she had to. She stood. The soles of her boots were beginning to overheat—the rubber becoming tacky and sticking to the leaves. Even her hard hat was smoldering. It wouldn't be long before her clothing caught fire.

"Anica! Where are you?!" Rachel's voice came through the smoke to her left.

She adjusted position and called back, "Here! I have wounded bear. Help me!"

Another crashing sound from behind her made her turn. A massive pine tree, red-hot and crackling, had broken into pieces and then exploded in mid-air. Fiery logs began to rain down on them!

CHAPTER 2

*T*he plan had backfired. Badly. Tristan could kick him-self for letting it go this far. But he'd honestly planned to be found easily when the trucks came by, and he hadn't planned for the whole forest to burn down around him. When the small, mud-covered woman appeared out of nowhere, looking for all the world like a diminutive bigfoot, and grabbed his fur, he was too much in shock to respond. He'd also in-haled far too much smoke. It felt like his lungs were buried in ash. She was right that they had to get out of the forest. If she knew a safe path, he would gladly follow. She spoke broken English and a language from somewhere in central Europe. He didn't know all the languages there. For some reason, he trusted her, even though he didn't want help. Well, *actual* help, anyway.

But she wouldn't let go, even though he tried to pull away. Another woman called out a name from somewhere inside the smoke and his rescuer answered. His savior's name was Anica. She was pretty, and her scent was amazing—like nothing he'd ever encountered. He had no time to process it, though, because the sap inside the tree next to them boiled and then exploded. Massive chunks of wood began to fall, causing even more limbs to come crashing down.

Yet she didn't abandon him. For someone so young, that was astounding. She couldn't be much older than her teens, but she had the depth and strength of people a century older. He couldn't decide whether that made him happy or sad. Anica used surprising strength to quickly drag him close to the base of a massive old pine twice the diameter of the others, and covered his body with hers—spreading open her heavy fire-resistant jacket to try to protect him.

He couldn't let her take the brunt of the damage. She was a shifter, of that he was certain, but she wasn't very power-ful. He could barely feel her magic pushing against his. It was time to throw off the charade, at least for a moment. The victim needed to become the rescuer. Searing pain drove through him as he rose to three legs, lifting her right off the ground. Hell, he'd actually wounded something in his leg when he crawled under the tree. She was coughing hard now, unable to catch a full breath. *And I'm not in much better shape.* Wheezing heavily, and trying not to take too deep a breath, Tristan hopped on his three good legs, avoiding the bouncing pieces of burning wood, toward the people crashing through the brush who were calling her name.

Then hands, covered with slimy mud, were reaching for him. He couldn't tell who was male or female through the thick, wet slime, but the mud was cool and wet. They half pulled him through the trees to where the ground gave way to water. When the people pulled him underwater, he was grateful. He let himself be covered with mud and dug his claws deep into the muck for more. He got a mouthful of stale water each time he came up for air, but he didn't care. Water was his natural home, no matter how foul. The mud took some of the sting out of his burns, and even the pain in his hands and feet eased to a throb. He shifted to human, hoping the shift would help heal his burns and cuts. It was hard to tell under the mud, but maybe it worked, at least a little.

The water in the bog heated as the fire soared all around them, but stayed below the temperature of a hot tub as they waited out the flashover. When the fire finally moved on, leaving behind an eerie stillness and the scent of scorch, eight pairs of eyes rose from the water like a military assault team.

"Okay," said an older man who smelled of owl, "I think we're in the clear. Watch for hot spots and let's head back to the truck and get our tools."

"If the truck hasn't burned to a crisp too," a woman said wryly. Judging by the natural kinked hair under the soggy kerchief, she would have dark skin under the coating of muck. The others pulled out of the pond with wet, sucking sounds, using their hands to scrape down their skin and clothing, flinging mud back into the water. It was just him and his rescuer left.

Anica stared at him with amazingly large, expressive eyes. "Can you speak? What is your name?"

"Ris—Tristan." He'd nearly given his real name without thinking. *Idiot!* Why would he give her a name, much less an identity, that he hadn't used in hundreds of years? At least he could avoid giving his last name until he had a story put together in his head.

She nodded and held a tiny hand toward him. Everything about her was tiny, except those eyes. "Anica. I am glad you are safe. How is your leg?"

How *was* his leg? He was lying on his side in the water,

holding his weight on one elbow, deep in the mud. He tried to straighten his leg—big mistake. Sparkles blazed to life in his vision, and flaring pain made him mutter curses. "Pretty sure it's broken."

She frowned, pursing rosebud lips in concern. Anica was cute, which wasn't really a good thing. He seemed to have a weakness for those brown eyes, which weren't really brown, but a hundred different shades of gold. "I am sorry. But we have healer at camp."

He recoiled at the word. "I don't use *healers*." That would be bad. A true healer would see right through the lies he was going to have to tell to get through this investigation. "But I'll need to see a doctor."

Anica nodded. "Yes. Doctor is healer. Healer is doctor. She fix your leg."

Time to change the subject. "Where are you from? You can't be a local."

When she smiled, her whole face lit up. "I am from Serbia. New to America. You are also not local. Your accent . . . where are you from?"

He needed to shut up. Now. He shifted his position as though his elbow had slipped. His leg hit the muck hard and he slid under the water, coming up sputtering. "Motherfu—" It was loud enough to bring the others.

The dark-skinned man came to the edge of the water and offered his hand. "The truck survived. Let's get you out of there and get those cuts healed."

"His leg is broken, John," Anica said. "Please, we should help him to walk."

John nodded. "We have a stretcher in the truck. Wait here."

Really what Tristan needed was for all these people to leave so he could get back on the job. Tristan twisted his lips a little to get the trace of his native Indonesian out of his voice. It had taken five dialect instructors and a hundred years to remove his natural accent, but one beautiful woman later and—"Actually, I'll be fine. Why don't you guys go on ahead?"

Out of the corner of his vision, he watched Anica's face grow confused as his words came out with a very midwestern American accent.

John looked bemused as he handed Tristan a blanket to cover himself. "Leave you here? With a broken leg in the middle of a forest fire? I don't think so. C'mon. We'll get you back home, wherever that is. Grizzly, right? Are you part of the National Guard? What sloth are you with? We'll call your Alpha . . . let him or her know you're okay."

For as casual as the words came, the questions were very probing. And his eyes. Those unwavering owl eyes were even more piercing than a falcon's. "I don't really have a group. I was an only child. Grew up in Kansas."

"Got the truck fixed, Dad." The woman who had called through the smoke appeared next to John. "The fan belt melted, but there was a spare in the back. At least the tank didn't blow."

"Full tanks don't generally explode," replied another man who appeared just behind the woman and put a possessive hand on the daughter's shoulder. What a nice, happy bird family.

"Our new friend was just about to tell us about himself."

"Tristan," Anica said, touching his shoulder, "do not worry. They are friends. You can trust them."

Trust? No. There was no trust when he was working. But he smiled anyway. Worked to get his scent lighter. "Okay, sure. I guess I could use some help. My leg probably should be set, even though it'll likely heal next time I shift. But I need to get my clothes and pack." He pointed behind him. "They're back that way. I'll get them and meet you at the truck."

"No, no," Anica said with a cheerful, helpful note in her voice. "You go. Get leg fixed. I will find clothes. I have very good nose. Is not far back to meet place."

John touched his daughter's shoulder. "Rachel, you and Dalvin stay with Anica. Put out any hot spots you find. I'll leave shovels and a foot pump and bucket. You can use the bog water on smoldering trees. Try to protect any rare plants that might have survived the fire. Rachel, you know the ones. Meet us back at the lake."

The lake. Had he finally made it to Luna Lake? He couldn't afford for anyone to find his pack, if it had even survived the fire. But sure, it would be good to have his leg set. It would be hard to finish the job while limping. "That sounds great. Thanks for your help." He turned to Anica. Those wide eyes sucked him right in again. So deep and expressive. "And thank *you* for saving me. I'd be a pile of charcoal if you hadn't found me." He pointed toward the edge of the mountain. "I stashed my pack in the rocks that way. It would really help if you could find it."

Again, her face looked confused, but she nodded. "I will."

The three new acquaintances left in the direction he'd pointed, as John and two other men arrived with a portable stretcher. "So," John said conversationally as he walked into the knee-deep water and lifted Tristan as easily as if he were a child. "Tristan, is it? Welcome to Luna Lake. Tell me about yourself."

He went with the story he'd planned to tell, with a twist.

"Not much to tell. Like I said, I was born in Kansas. I'm the only shifter in my family . . . apparently a recessive gene. And a big, dark family secret. I was sent to live with my uncle in Canada. I was just heading back home to see my family when the fires started."

He paused, waiting to see if he'd made the story believable. It wasn't just the words that came out of his mouth when talking to other shifters. Everyone could smell lies.

John didn't respond for a long moment, and when he did the response gave Tristan no indication whether he believed the lie. "Okay, then. Let's get you back to town and get that leg looked at."

"That would be great. It hurts like crazy." It did, so no lie there either.

As they bounced down the dirt road, he did his best to ignore the pain in his leg. He watched the scenery so he could find his way back to this place. The random pattern of the fire was like the aftermath of a tornado. One stand of trees would be charred to sticks, while just a few feet over the trees were untouched. Soon he began to smell the fresh scent of water and green grass. Slowly his coughing turned to cautious sniffs of smokeless air and then to deep breaths that made his head finally stop aching. After a week of hitching rides and walking through the fire zone, he'd forgotten what it was like to be able to think clearly.

Tristan lifted himself onto his elbows so he could see out of the truck bed as the road smoothed out. As they rounded the next corner, an opening in the woods revealed a small town. The buildings were either log cabins made of what appeared to be native pine or prefabricated metal buildings. Rows of single-person tents were scattered in every open space available. Firefighters, black with soot, slept on the bare ground or sat at picnic tables, their eyes glassy and half-closed, shoveling food in their mouths as fast as they could chew.

The truck came to a stop next to the police station, even though there were plenty of open spaces around other buildings. If the goal was to intimidate him, it wouldn't work. Better than this lot had tried.

In fact, that kept him focused on his goal. If he succeeded, he would be righting a great injustice by capturing a serial killer.

CHAPTER 3

*R*achel patted the back of her shovel on the dirt she'd just dropped on a smoking patch of grass and then leaned her weight on the handle. "So, are we going to get this guy's pack or what? I'd really like to get back to town and get some lunch . . . or dinner. Whatever time it is. Where did he say it was?"

Anica turned in a circle again. This was absolutely the place she'd found Tristan. *Tristan.* It was an interesting name, because it didn't match his appearance at all. The name seemed so French, but he looked Asian, or somewhere close to that part of the world. His hair was very black, like hers, but his eyes were an odd gray-green, like where the faster river met a still pool. Even his accent when he first spoke didn't match how he'd later spoken to John. Something was very wrong, but he didn't feel evil. She knew what bad people felt like. He seemed both lost and confident, if that was possible . . . like when Bojan was forced to work on cars when he would rather be in the kitchen. He could do the work, but it took much concentration. More than chopping and seasoning food.

She could smell the direction he'd come, but it was no-where close to where he'd pointed that he'd left his pack. Anica wanted to find that pack. Somehow she knew the mystery of him would be solved inside. She pointed to the mountain, toward the fire. "That way." Anica shook her head. "But it cannot be."

Dalvin Adway took the kerchief from around his neck and used it to wipe his face. "Why can't it be? Wouldn't he know where his own pack was?"

She poked her shovel blade into the soft muck and let it stand on its own. She tried not to be frustrated with them, but they just didn't understand. "You are owls. You fly and you *see*. Very good eyes. But I am bear. I *smell*." She held up a finger. "One drop of blood, one *tiny* drop, I can smell, kilo-meters away. I smell the bugs and worms under your feet where you are standing. Right now." She pointed at the ground. "This dirt, it tells me a story." She took a deep breath and sneezed before pinching her nose and sneezing again. "But smoke up here, it fools my nose. I must have my nose down there with dirt. Then I can find pack." She couldn't help but sigh. "But Papa is fighting fire, and Mama is back home. They cannot help change my nose."

Dalvin shook his head. "Wait. Are you saying all you need is for someone to shift you so you have your animal nose? Heck, I can do that."

Anica felt her jaw drop open. The smoke painted her tongue. "But I am *bear*. You are owl. How can that be?"

She looked at Rachel, who only shrugged. "Don't ask me. I don't have any idea how it works. But the town Alpha for years was a bobcat and he shifted me every month, so I pre-sume it has nothing to do with the animal you are."

"Why would you think—" Dalvin began with a bemused

look on his face like her brother Samit used to have when he would mock her, but Rachel held up her hand.

"Dalvin, we've already had this talk, remember? It's a privilege thing, which isn't just about money. *Cultural* privilege sucks. People like me and Anica . . . we don't know *shit* about the Sazi world. We've lived in a knowledge vacuum." She put her finger in the air, twirled it in a circle, and then pointed it at Dalvin with her other hand on her hip. "Don't judge."

Anica didn't understand exactly what conversation they'd had before today, but she did understand that knowledge was power and not to judge people who didn't understand. "Yes. Rachel tells truth. I do not understand many things."

Dalvin let out a slow breath and then walked over to Anica and touched her on the shoulder. He squeezed lightly and smelled sad. "I'm sorry. I keep forgetting you're attack victims. You came into this life the hard way. I'll try really hard to answer questions when you have them."

She patted his hand and nodded. It was good to have friends in this new country. "Thank you. So, it is not just my alphas who can turn me during the full moon?"

"Not at all." Dalvin backed up and leaned his shovel against a tree. "It's easier for your own Alpha to do it, because you're tied to them. But any Sazi with alphic abilities of sufficient power can help you shift forms."

"Or force you to," Rachel added with anger in her voice, turning to look at her. "We've already met a lot of those."

A shudder of revulsion crawled up Anica's spine, because she knew exactly what Rachel was talking about. The nightmares still happened too often. "I would like not to talk of that."

"Of course," Dalvin said. "Part of the problem is that it

used to be a high crime to attack someone and turn them into a shifter. Nobody dared to risk bringing Wolven or the Council down on them. It was so ingrained in our society that it didn't happen often. But then Sargon started his *camps* and now the world is flooded with new shifters who don't understand the process or our history." He let out a frustrated screech that seemed like it came from the wrong kind of owl. It echoed through the trees and made her flinch. "We don't even know how many there are. And I know it's not your fault. I *know* that. But it makes me so mad that you had to go through that hell. Shifting should be natural, a treasured part of you. Not something to be embarrassed about or feared."

She paused to think before speaking. "I do not fear my bear. Not now. At first, yes. Yes, I feared the pain and the not remembering. But when my family become like me, there is no more pain and they remember for me." She knew now that following Papa's command to make them like her was wrong too. But they'd all agreed. Or so she'd thought. Yet, even now, months after his death, Samit made her heart hurt. Dead, and she had blamed him for causing it. "I think they all agree, Rachel. I truly did."

Her friend smiled sadly. "I know you did. I was there. Remember?"

"Yes." She had been, and through Rachel's magic, along with their families, the other woman had seen into her mind . . . her heart, and helped locate the caves where she had been held captive and turned into a bear. "But I should have thought more . . . about how *their* lives would be not good. Samit would still live; my parents would be together."

Dalvin waved away wispy smoke hanging in the air and used the inside of his jacket to rub one eye. "I wouldn't bet

on that. One of the things I've learned since working in Wolven is that it's not the animal at fault . . . well, hardly ever,
anyway. The animal inside doesn't want much. Food and
water, shelter, sleep, and family. People are what screw it up.
That's when you get greed and hate and the wrong kind of
pride involved. You wanted your family. That's all. You were
afraid and your parents wanted you safe. What better way
to keep you safe than to be like you?"

"Yes." Anica nodded in agreement. "This is true. Papa told
me not to fear. He would make it right, keep me safe."

"From everything I've heard since Samit died," Rachel
added, "he had some mental problems before, when you
were kids."

"The cat doctor, Amber, she ask me about this. Samit was
a quiet boy. I was younger, and girl, so I do not play the same
games. But I did not like the boys he plays with. They hurt
other children, younger ones. Samit, he does not. But he
also does not stop them. I never liked that—that he would
just watch the others hurt little ones." Rachel and Dalvin
frowned. *Maybe I should have said something to Papa or
Mama, the things I saw. But I never considered Samit dangerous. Just a little odd.* Anica started walking toward the direction her limited human nose told her to follow, and the
others picked up their tools and fell into line behind her. "I
like to think that Samit got sickness. Others have gone
rogue who were not bad people, so maybe Samit is not
either." She wasn't really talking to her friends, more to
herself. But Dalvin responded.

"There's really no clear answer on why Sazi go rogue. All
the healers and seers have tried to find some connection. But
other than the moon magic becoming chaotic and driving
the person insane, there's nothing the people really have in

common. Not race, or geography, or kind of shifter animal.
It just . . . happens. So, yes. Maybe Samit was a good person who just got sick."

Anica stopped, her nose so full of the smell of smoke that
she couldn't go any farther. She pulled a cloth kerchief from
her pocket and blew her nose to clear it. The tears she
blinked back had to be from the smoke as well, didn't they?
"Thank you." The lump in her throat said perhaps not. With
a catch in her voice, she said, "Could you maybe make me
bear now? My nose is stuffy. I cannot smell so good."

"Sure." Dalvin's voice was gentle; Rachel's face and scent
held sorrow, wet and soppy, like just-rinsed laundry. He
pointed to a still-standing group of bushes. "Why don't you
undress over there? I don't need to see you to shift you."

Oh! She hadn't considered that possibility. "Yes, that
would be good. Papa would not be happy." In fact, she had
gotten to know Rachel because Papa wouldn't let her stay
in the same house as the unmarried school headmaster
during the mediation between the sloths—even though all
the rest of her family were living there. Papa meant well,
she knew. She was his only daughter. But even though she
was twenty-four, he didn't think of her as an adult, which
was frustrating. She was far more adult than he imagined.
There were many things Papa did not know about her. She
undressed quickly, feeling very human. There was no pull
from the moon at all. Was Dalvin's magic really strong
enough to make her a bear not only days before the full
moon, but in full daylight?

"I am ready!" she called out, staying behind the bush. She
wasn't sure what she expected to happen, but the warm sensation that coaxed the bear from inside her was very different from how Papa turned her. This felt like climbing out

of the pool after a swim, versus jumping over a stream and landing hard on the other bank. Both got you to the same place, but Dalvin's way was refreshing.

She shook her head to orient herself and then shook her whole body, not really believing she was in her furred form. "Oh, Dalvin! You must teach this way to Papa! It was so smooth."

Rachel let out a little chuckle as she picked up Anica's clothes to tuck into her backpack. "Yeah, my boy is a smooth one, all right."

Dalvin reached out one of his long legs and gave her bottom a light tap with the toe of his boot. "Who says I'm your boy?"

Rachel bumped his shoulder with hers and laughed. "You do. Every day."

He smiled broadly in return. "Damn straight I do."

"This is why I like you both. You have such joy together." She would smile if she could, but pulling her lips back only bared teeth. Luckily, they understood. "I hope to find someone to love someday. Perhaps now that we're in America, Papa will allow me more freedom as well."

"Your dad's pretty cool," Rachel said as they walked where Anica's nose was leading. "I'll bet he'll ease up. He's really proud of you for having the guts to go take down that snake nest. He told me so."

It had been very hard to go back into the cave where she'd been held captive, but she'd done it and saved a lot of children. Her papa had never said much about that, so to hear that he was proud of her made her heart warm. She stopped and looked at Rachel. "He never tells me this. He only tells me his worry, but not his pride. So thank you for telling—"

A scent caught her attention and forced her to concentrate ahead of them. The spicy scent of the bear . . . intense and dizzying. There was no doubt it was Tristan, in an area directly opposite where he said he'd come from. She put her nose to the ground, nuzzling through the light coating of ash, and inhaled deeply. She could smell his footsteps, the scent of his . . . *blood*? Had he been bleeding this far from where the tree had fallen? But there was more. Another person had followed him, walking exactly in the footsteps of the bear. This was also a Sazi, but not one whose scent she recognized from town. And over that was another odor, something *odd*. Sweet but pungent and earthy. It was familiar, but she couldn't place it . . . thick with some strange chemical she'd never encountered before. She began to sneeze, over and over, in a fit like she'd never experienced.

Every time she caught her breath, it would be stolen away by violent sneezes that made her eyes water and her nostrils swell nearly shut. The first few were normal, much like when she was hunting for mushrooms. The spores would tickle her nose and she'd sneeze and be done. But now she couldn't shake them; the sheer force, over and over, was making her chest hurt and it hard to even stand.

Anica shook her head and tried to blow out whatever was affecting her, but she couldn't get enough breath to do more than move the scent to different parts of her nose.

"Anica, are you okay?" At first Rachel and Dalvin had waited for her sneezing to stop, but now they were noticing her discomfort. But she couldn't respond. All that came out of her mouth when she opened it was a yelping noise that was cut off with another sneeze.

She had to open her mouth now, because her nose had swollen shut, and with every sneeze it felt like her eyeballs were exploding. "Dalvin," Rachel said, "we have to get her back to town. Something's really wrong. She can't breathe at all."

Chest burning with the need for air, the sneezing had turned to coughing and it felt like when she'd slipped on rocks in the river while escaping the caves and inhaled water into her lungs.

"You're right," Dalvin replied with concern in his voice as Anica struggled to stay on her feet. "I'm going to turn her back. Maybe that'll help."

"I'll get her clothes." Anica didn't see her leave but felt the ease of magic into her skin that pulled the fur inside. But even though she could see her hands and feet turn human again, the magic hadn't cleared her lungs. In fact, with her smaller mouth and nose it was even harder to get air.

Dalvin quickly shifted into a large brown owl that he'd called an eagle owl. Once Rachel had helped her back into a shirt and her pants, Dalvin fluttered into the air just above her and wrapped massive talons around her upper arms. Sensing that he planned to fly her to town, she reached up and did her best to grab on to his feathers so he didn't have to worry about dropping her. "Meet us back at town, Chelle. You know the way."

"Will do. I'll see if I can find the other bear's backpack while I'm here."

Anica would have responded if she could have, telling her where she thought it was, but forcing her lungs to pull in what little air they would was all she could focus on.

CHAPTER 4

Tristan sat on an exam table in the town's small medical clinic, sensing all the people who came and went through other rooms and past the building outside. So far, he hadn't felt any evidence of the criminal he had been sent to find.

Ahmad al-Narmer was nothing if not careful, so Tristan fully understood why he'd been sent here. Regular Wolven agents wouldn't be of any help. There were only a handful of their kind left in the world who would recognize Ur-Lagash, the feared lion cupbearer for Sargon of Akede. That Ahmad had even tasted his scent was nothing short of amazing. He'd spent little time around Lagash, and the ancient assassin was cautious. After the fall of the city named for him, Lagash had become one of the high priests of Marduk, caring for the needs of his new master. Palace intrigue was his speciality, along with torture and death. Tristan felt a shudder pass through him. The sharp ache of his broken leg would be considered nothing back then. He would have been required to *crawl* on it, to beg forgiveness for whatever petty sin had brought about the torture.

The whisper of an alto voice and a familiar sensation made him look up sharply. The white door set in the peach-painted frame opened inward. Amber Wingate, wife of the Chief Justice of the Sazi, wearing blue hospital scrubs covered with tiny yellow ducks, walked in. She looked harried as she swept into the room, not even glancing at him. When she did look up, she dropped the clipboard from her hand and slammed the door shut behind her with wide eyes. Her voice lowered to a harsh hiss that better suited her cat form. "Risten? What in the name of . . . well, pick your deity, are you doing here?"

"It's *Tristan*, if you please," he responded in a similarly quiet voice, keeping the midwestern accent in his voice. "Tristan Davies. I'm a traveler, from *Kansas*, who got caught in this sudden forest fire. My leg is broken." He pointed down at the borrowed clothing, now spotted with blood. "It really is broken."

Her eyes narrowed, but she flared her nostrils and he felt a tentative lash of magic in his direction. She realized he wasn't lying, but it wasn't enough for her to taken even a step closer. "Who could possibly break *your* leg? Why are you in America? You haven't set foot outside Indonesia in a hundred years."

"Two hundred, actually." Staring at those angry eyes reminded him of the first time he'd seen the French healer, weighed down under a dozen yards of heavy black fabric and her ever-present medical bag. She had glared at him just like this while they argued about a Sazi taking a political stance in the human world right after Napoléon's army decided Ris's native Sumatra should become a French "colony." The army brought the scourge of cholera to the invasion party and Amber, then known as Nurse Yvette, had been trying to save the French as hard as he had been trying to kill them. He'd been far more successful. She'd never forgiven him for that.

"And not a who. A *what*. A burning tree fell on me. Knocked me cold. A pretty little bear found me." He crossed his arms over his chest and raised his brows. "So? Heal me."

She made a rude noise, somewhere between a laugh and hacking up a hairball. "First, stay away from the townspeople. They're innocents. Why are you in America?"

"Visiting family, not that it's your business. My mother's family are dragons. I've been paying my respects to my . . . for lack of a better term, *niece*, Asri, and her clutch." Once again, he pointed at his knee. "The leg? Unless, of course, you want to explain to the *innocents* why you're letting a simple traveler suffer."

"I could tell them the *truth*. That you're not who you claim and it's why I'm not healing you. You're slightly less dangerous and easier to fight with a non-working leg."

She stared at him, defiant, and he stared back. After a few long moments, he realized he was being silly. The only reason he'd come to the medical station at all was to assess the townspeople. But many who were needing attention were humans or barely Sazi. Those stronger in magic were likely healing themselves. And . . . the doctor was in the room with him, with a closed door. . . .

Not taking his eyes from hers, Tristan reached down and felt for the lump in his calf where the bone had separated. Grasping the leg below the break with one hand and above it on the opposite side with the other, he pulled and pushed sharply and felt the edges of his bone scrape and crunch. White spots appeared in his vision from the pain, but he pushed the hurt aside by taking a deep breath and letting it

out in tiny bursts. He called power from deep inside himself and forced it to his purpose. This wasn't healing magic
that would soothe the damage and heal. It was raw power
that blasted through the wound, leaving the nerves raw but
mended in the wake. While he'd rather not have had to
waste the power, he had no plans to share the reasons for
his mission.

He smiled but had no doubt there was anger in the baring
of teeth. "Why, thank you, Doctor." He let his voice rise so
it would carry. "What an amazing gift you have. It's like it
was never broken."

She snorted. "You're an ass."

Swinging his legs off the table, he stood. A shock of
protest from the nerves was quickly silenced with another
assault of magic and then the leg was repaired. Not easy or
neat, but done. He walked toward the door, which was being
blocked by the powerful healer. He had no illusions about
Amber. She was a powerful foe. But she was also primarily
a pacifist. He threw out a lash of power intense enough to
hold her momentarily still and silent while he grasped her
shoulders, picked her up, and moved her aside. He whispered in her ear while she struggled against his power in
vain, "Make no mistake, Amber. I will not tolerate any interference. Do not speak my name, or of my presence, to
anyone or you can easily disappear. You know full well I
do not fear your husband or any of the Council. When my
business is done, I will leave and nobody will likely even
know I was here."

She'd gone still, not trying to fight the pressure on her.
But the sensation that enveloped his skin and rose in her
scent said she was annoyed. Not furious, likely not even
angry enough to attack, so he loosened the hold on her

enough so she could speak. Her voice was calm, precise. "Is there a good reason why you're here? Enough for me to keep my mouth shut and not tell Charles and the Council?"

"It's possible they already know. But yes."

"What about Bobby?" She waited, and her anticipation told him she was baiting him—waiting to see if he was telling the truth that the man really was his nephew-in-law.

"He knows."

She relaxed the rest of the way. If Bobby Mbutu knew he was here, Amber knew to trust the reason. While the python shifter could deceive and had done so before for his own purposes, the purpose was usually noble and reason enough to lie.

"So Lucas finally recruited you. I've been wondering when he'd start to bring in some of the older Sazi."

That brought a choking laugh from his throat without warning, and he released the remainder of his hold on her. "Hardly. The trials and tribulations of your kind don't interest me. The concepts of right and wrong change as often as the borders of countries. Bobby is welcome to make those distinctions. I'm only here because nobody else *can* do this."

The curiosity of her cat rose to pulse against his skin, but she held it down in her voice and scent. "If the townspeople are in danger, I need to know. I was planning to leave this week, once the fire is out. Most of the residents are magically weak. They wouldn't be able to heal themselves without me."

Tristan shrugged. "If it goes badly, no amount of healing magic will help, so it doesn't really matter. Go. Stay. Your choice." He didn't wait for her to respond, just opened the door and left. Amber didn't follow.

The waiting room was full of people who were coughing

and covered in soot. One man, who smelled of burnt flesh, held a wet cloth against his arm. No doubt respiratory issues and burns would be most of what the healer would be working on today.

Before Tristan could reach it, the door swung open and the dark-skinned man who had stayed to search for Tristan's backpack raced in, holding the little bear. Anica was struggling to breathe, eyes wide and panicked, hands clutching her throat. She reached out, grabbing at his sleeve as she went by. Something was very wrong with her. This was no ordinary smoke inhalation. He found himself following behind, calling for the woman he'd just left. "Doctor! We need your skills!"

Amber raced out of the room where he'd been, her eyes taking in the scene. "This way!" She guided the man—
Dalvin. Tristan remembered the name suddenly. He followed her into a different exam room, identical to the one he'd just left, but painted a pale green instead of peach, with all the cabinets and the sink on the reverse wall. Amber was about to shut the door when he found that he had put a hand on it and followed them inside. She raised her brows a tiny bit but let him come in before shutting the door.

"It's not smoke." He said it without realizing.

Dalvin nodded. "No. It's something Anica smelled on the ground. She was looking for your backpack. I changed her to bear form. She said it would be easier to smell that way. We were talking about her father and she leaned down and sniffed around, like a bloodhound. She apparently smelled something interesting but then suddenly couldn't breathe. She couldn't even tell us what it was. I shifted and flew her here as fast as I could. It's only been a few minutes since it happened."

Amber was using a lighted instrument to look up Anica's nose and down her throat. "Everything is swollen. It's an allergic reaction to something. There's no magic to fix this. Dalvin, see if they have any EpiPens in this place. Check with Marilyn. Ris—I mean, Tristan, I need to do a tracheotomy to help her breathe. Hold her still."

Dalvin raced out, calling the other woman's name. Amber turned and started digging through cabinets and drawers until she found a sealed plastic kit of some sort. She ripped the top open with her teeth while Tristan put his hands on Anica's shoulders and held her firmly. Those impossibly large eyes locked with his, and what he found in the depths of them was . . . trust. It unnerved him a little, because people didn't trust him. He was used to suspicion. But to have her trust his touch, even though she couldn't breathe, and put her tiny hand over his made him *happy*.

If Amber noticed, she didn't comment. She extracted several items and laid them out on the table, then went to work making a small incision in Anica's throat with a scalpel. When blood welled up, Amber made the second cut and picked up a set of forceps to open the skin and muscle. He could feel the little bear's pain press against him, felt her hand clutching his. But she didn't move. It made him smile at her.

"Okay, got it." Amber put the end of a syringe against the tube and pressed the plunger. There was a tiny popping sound and then a ragged breath expanded Anica's lungs.

He squeezed her shoulder. "Good girl."

"Where the hell is Dalvin with that epinephrine?" Amber let out a small snarl and stalked toward the door. "Keep her breathing and don't let her move around."

Tristan nodded and Amber left them alone. Anica had her

eyes closed, doing her best to stay calm and keep breathing
through the small tube. Now that he had time to concentrate, he flicked his tongue, finally catching her underlying
scent through the blood. She smelled of sunshine—that
nose-tickling scent of dusty warmth when the sun is shining
hot, wrapped around a freshly turned pasture. He couldn't
pin down a particular grass. It was a blend of sweet, healthy
growing plants and rich soil. He squeezed one shoulder and
those golden eyes opened, her lips parted slightly even
though she wasn't using her mouth. "So, little bear, let's try to
find out what happened to you."

She opened her mouth and he put a finger against it.
"Don't try to talk. Just blink those big brown eyes at me.
Once for yes and twice for no. Okay?"

She blinked once.

"This didn't happen because of smoke, did it?"

Two blinks.

"Was it something burning, maybe a chemical?"

Two more blinks.

"Did it feel like an attack, like it was intentional?"

Her eyelids dropped once. It was obvious she wanted to
talk, to explain. Her expression grew frustrated and her
breathing was getting more ragged as she struggled to make
him understand. "Wait. I could use my magic so I could speak
directly into your mind, and you into mine. Would that
help?" Instead of blinking, she nodded, which nearly dis-
lodged her breathing tube. He pushed her head back onto
the table with a light touch of his finger on her forehead.

It had been a very long time since he'd slid into another
person's mind. The last had been a criminal who had refused
to reveal where he'd sold a friend's wedding ring, when Tristan
lived in Jakarta. Recalling it now, he remembered the man

hadn't actually survived that intrusion. He should probably be more careful this time.

Tristan let power flow to his hand and lightly put it against the side of her face. Her skin was the exact same temperature as his hand. That was fairly unusual, because he was cold by nature. "Are you getting enough oxygen? Let me see your hand."

Her brow furrowed and worry brushed his face. She lifted her hand and he inspected her fingertips and pushed on the skin to see whether they were white or blue. The fingertips were the right color and returned to pink when pressed. It was worth a try, in case she didn't make it through this. Lagash was well known in Akede for his mastery of poisons. If it was a direct attack, there was no way of knowing what he'd used.

It wasn't difficult at all to ease into her mind. The surprising part was how *normal* it felt. Whenever he'd tried it previously, it was like reaching his hand through broken glass. It was sharp and harsh and he had to be careful not to get cut. But this was like sliding his hand into bathwater. No resistance, no bottom, just unending depth and warmth. Anica's eyes were locked on his. The expression on her face was close to amazement.

Amazed. Yes. It is like when Papa turns me. He speaks to me like this. But it feels very different.

Tristan wasn't used to having his private thoughts overheard. Normally he could control the mental conversation. **You're hearing what I'm thinking without my actually talking to you?** Her eyes confirmed it before she even spoke into his mind. **Yes. Of course. Is that wrong?**

Well, it wasn't so much wrong as unusual. The door to the exam room opened just as he was deciding how to respond.

Amber strode forward with purpose. "Back up. I need to get this in her."

He stepped back at the same moment he realized he shouldn't have. Anica reached for him, grabbed the tail of the plaid shirt he'd been loaned. **Don't leave. Please.**

You'll be able to talk in a minute. No need to stay attached. He slipped out of her head like normal, and began to pull his magic back inside himself. Keeping it tightly bound in a ball in his core was the only way for others around him not to realize how powerful he was. But as easy as it was to sink inside her mind, getting out was proving to be more difficult. He kept swimming to the surface of the magic to break free, but the more he pulled away, the deeper he fell.

When Amber administered the medicine by stabbing a prefilled syringe into her thigh, he felt a rush of . . . *something* flood through him. In sheer self-defense, he cut the tie cold. His heart was racing, making his head pound. He fell back against the counter, spilling a tray of plastic containers of cotton balls and swabs. The clatter caused Amber to turn her head. "What the hell is going on with everyone today?" He saw her turn away from the table, saw Anica try to rise up from the table, and was only able to point to Anica to get Amber's attention. The pounding in his head was making it hard to think straight.

Fortunately, Amber realized what he was trying to say and turned just in time to push Anica back down on the table, like Tristan had just done to her. Her eyes began to glow and Anica's body went still. Amber then came to his side. "What's happening to you, Ris? Can you breathe? Talk? Is this contagious?"

Amber held out her hand and helped him to his feet. Her skin was hot, fevered, from the power she was using to heal

Anica. "Talk to me, Tupo. Any chance whatever she reacted to is the cause?"

The healer putting Anica in a magical hold was enough to sever the last tie to her. He sat down on the floor heavily and tried to catch his breath. "Stupid of me. I did a mind link to try to find out what happened to her. Couldn't break free and got feedback from the drug. I guess I'm out of practice doing this sort of thing."

He paused and then added, "But I would really appreciate, *Yvette*, if you would watch your tongue." It was important to remind her that prior identities shouldn't be used. She'd used both the first and last name of a person he wasn't anymore. He hoped calling her by the name she'd discarded more than a century ago would work. Every older Sazi in the world had gone through things they'd like to forget, had done things that couldn't ever be revealed in the current world.

She winced, like he'd hoped, and her face blushed almost to the color of her hair. "Point taken. My apologies." She held out her hand. "Amber Wingate. A pleasure to meet you. And you are?"

"Tristan Davies. From Kansas."

She nodded. "You said that earlier. I was just surprised and apparently not listening. I must have mistaken you for someone I used to know."

"Apparently." He said it wryly, but it was important to say out loud, just in case anyone had been listening. After all, most everyone in town was Sazi. Some had exceptional hearing. That wasn't one of his own gifts, but he'd known plenty of wolves who could hear a fish jump in a different lake.

"Where is Anica?! Doctor!" A booming baritone shout rattled the walls. "Dr. Wingate!"

"Oh, lord. It's Zarko. Anica's father." Amber put a hand on his chest on her way to the door. "You stay here with her and keep her held. I'll calm him down."

She didn't wait for him to agree. Tristan looked at Anica, still doing her best to stare at the ceiling and breathe through the tube. He wrapped a light magical hold on her. But her anxiety was obvious. He could feel it press against him like a second skin. He was starting to wonder whether her anxiety was about the medical condition or seeing her father. He couldn't help but turn his attention to the door, wondering when it was going to burst open. The way Zarko was yelling at Amber in the next room made him wonder what sort of relationship the father and daughter had at home.

Papa worries. But he means well. Do not worry for me.

Tristan's head turned sharply. Anica was staring at him with those so-patient eyes, her pale pink rosebud lips closed and the breathing tube still in place. "How can you be talking with that tube in your throat?"

She touched her head and her voice appeared like magic in his mind. **We talk in our minds, like you say.**

He responded in kind. **But I disconnected that link. How are you still using it?**

Her brow furrowed, causing tiny lines between her eyebrows. **Why do you not answer? Are you angry with me?**

"I did answer you. You can't hear me in your head?" She shook her head. Well, that was odd. "But you can speak to me?"

Yes, of course. I can feel you hearing me, like an echo in my ears.

Interesting. And worth talking to Amber about once they had a free moment. The door burst open just then and a large bear of a man filled the doorway, blocking any view of what was behind him. No doubt of his identity when he spoke. "Anica! You are hurt? There is blood. Who has done this to you?" The glowing eyes turned Tristan's way. The twin emotions of anger and suspicion hit him in the face like a club just before the man pointed a finger at him and began to stalk toward him. "You. *You* did this."

CHAPTER 5

*T*ristan didn't back up at all as her papa stalked toward him. He was either very confident or very foolish. Even when her father grabbed the front of his shirt and pulled him very close, his face remained calm. "What have you done to Anica? Who are you and what are you doing in my town?"

Anica tried again to sit up and this time was able to push away the sensation of a rope around her that felt like one of her brother's wrestling holds. They had wrestled often as children, before she began to look too much like a woman. She was very good at slipping away from him. The swelling was down in her nose, and if not for the tube in her throat she would be able to breathe normally.

"My name is Tristan Davies. I was helping the doctor so Anica could breathe. See?" He pointed toward her and Papa turned to see her fiddling with the tube in her throat. "She wasn't getting any air."

The doctor walked through the door and let out a great sigh, much like Mama would do when Papa would argue with Samit over politics. Amber's eyes began to glow with golden light, nearly the same color as the ducks on her top. Anica's father began to slide backward across the tiled floor. Tristan stood still even as Papa's grip pulled his shirt until it ripped. "Zarko! What did I say? I said, *don't* overreact. Anica will be fine. The medicine is working on the allergy. I can heal anything else," Amber said. She took a few steps and then pulled him by force of magic alone to the edge of the exam table. He watched, his eyes glowing bright blue as he fought against the power of the bobcat healer, to no avail. She was a very powerful shifter. He was forced to watch without talking as Amber examined her again. She flicked a gaze toward Tristan. "Okay, the swelling is down. She should be able to breathe on her own again once I get the tube out. Keep her still a few seconds longer, Tristan."

Did she not realize he wasn't holding her anymore? Shouldn't she be able to feel that? But she had to let the doctor do her job, so she remained still. Tristan came to stand beside Zarko and winked one eye at her and curved his lips in a slight smile. His scent was amused, as though he found the fuss over her funny. She struggled not to smile back, because it hurt her throat. Tristan put a hand on her shoulder again as the doctor pulled the tube from her throat. It hurt. A lot. Both Tristan and Papa noticed, but it was Tristan who eased warm magic into her that made the hurt go away.

The warmth flowed deep into her throat and a tingling spread into her chest. She could suddenly breathe again and took her first inhale with her nose and mouth since smelling the soil in the forest. She risked talking. The first words came out as a croak. "It feels . . . good . . . to breathe again."

"I'll bet it does," Amber said with a smile. "Let me get you some water. It'll help with the pain in your throat."

"That would be good. I would like to get back to the forest

very soon to find that spot again." Already she could picture
the spot, knew just how to get back there. It must be soon,
before too many other scents covered or mixed with it. She
wasn't very good yet at sorting out layers of smells.

There was sudden silence in the room and Anica found
that all three people were staring at her with varying levels
of shock on their faces.

The doctor spoke first. "Whatever's out there nearly killed
you, Anica. I don't want *anyone* going out there until we can
find out if there's a toxin out there."

She shrugged, not really understanding the concern.
"Dalvin was not sick. Or Rachel. Now that I know the scent,
I can avoid breathing too deep."

Papa added his own concerns, with a low growl that always told her he was worried. He put a hand on her shoulder, tried to push her back to where she was lying down
again. "There is no reason. You will stay here, in town, where
I can make sure you are safe."

She pushed his hand away, suddenly annoyed, and swung
her legs off the table before standing up, feeling nearly normal from the healing of Tristan and the doctor. "Papa, stop!
I am grown. *I* decide what is good reason. Not you." She
pointed at Tristan, who had furrowed brows but was saying
nothing. "This man is a guest, and he is in danger. Someone
is following him, stalking. We need to know who. Others
could be in danger."

Her statement made Tristan's scent change abruptly.
Where before he was slightly amused but not concerned,
now he was suspicious and alert to her every movement.
"Why would you say that? Who would want to follow a simple
tourist?"

She didn't mean to, but when she blew out a frustrated

breath it sounded much like a rude noise. She touched her papa's arm again. "Please, do not lie. There is no reason, you understand? This is my papa. He is Alpha of whole town. The doctor is important person in Council, but you know this already . . . yes? I have seen your mind, your heart. You are not tourist. Whatever your reason for coming, it is good, honest. If not me, then you can trust them with your reason." She touched the side of her nose, even now smelling the turmoil of scents that came off everyone in the room, including the overwhelming scent of his lie. "But I can smell, you see? Very good. You have enemies. Someone knows you are here, but not why."

Papa tapped his finger on the edge of the exam table and then turned slightly and poked it in Tristan's chest, his scent and face full of suspicion. "You will come with me. Doctor, you as well. And Anica—" He growled again. "You will stay in town. Rest. Do *not* leave again until I say. If you are grown, and you will not listen to your papa, you *will* listen to your Alpha. Yes?"

She had to work not to roll her eyes. That would be disrespectful. "Yes, Papa. For a little while. As you say, until I'm rested."

He turned and stalked out, muttering under his breath in Serbian, "Gospode daj mi snage." Asking the good Lord for strength to deal with her seemed a little overreaction. The doctor struggled not to smile and followed him out. Tristan made no such attempt and winked at her again as he left.

The air filters quickly cleared out most of the emotional scents. She'd noticed that the buildings in town were very good at that. It was probably a wise thing, since so many different animals lived so close together. She didn't really care for the scent of the cats. The musk was sharp and unpleasant. But then again, she'd heard the same about bears, which she didn't understand.

She swallowed, and the pain was much less. Touching her throat, she found there was little left but a tiny ridge of scar and some itching. It was still so amazing to her what the Sazi could do. Even the least of them seemed to be able to do so much more than her. The only benefit she'd received was a strong nose, and what good was that really? Smelling only caused more trouble.

Opening the door to the exam room, she walked down the short hallway without meeting anyone she knew. But out in the main waiting area, Dalvin and Rachel were waiting for her. "Hey!" Rachel said with a smile. "We saw Amber and your dad come out a minute ago and they didn't smell worried, so we figured you were all healed up. What happened to you?"

"They say it was an allergy. I used to be allergic to berries as a child. So I suppose like that. It did swell my tongue and throat like then. But it wasn't berries."

Rachel looked at her oddly. Her scent was a burst of something close to limes. "You were allergic to *berries*? But you're a bear. That would suck. Like me being allergic to mice." She made a little face. "Which I actually wouldn't mind. My owl wouldn't like it, but I sort of hate them."

"But I didn't eat it. It was just a smell. Can that be?"

Dalvin shrugged and held the door to the clinic for her and Rachel. "Sure. Some people are allergic to perfume or car exhaust."

That made Anica nod, remembering something. "This is true. I remember my uncle Baku—it was not his real name, but what we called him—he would sneeze whenever it rained. Papa said it was because of the moss at the river, even though we were far away."

The breeze was blowing in from the mountain as the sun lowered behind the tops of the trees. The smoke was a little less thick in the air now, giving way to the scents of people and cooking food across the town square. "The fire goes the other way tonight. That is good. Maybe we sleep safe." She could also smell the route that her father and the others had gone. She could nearly see their trail as a shining path with her eyes, but she knew it was her nose that could "see" the three scents. It was easy to sort scents in the air. Even the wind didn't diminish the scent. It shifted it, but whole, like blowing a leaf from place to place. But with the leaf, she could always find the tree.

"It's going to be dark soon. Want to get some supper?" Rachel looked almost too tired to chew, and so did Dalvin. Their eyes, so red, and the skin was puffy beneath. She was a little surprised they wanted to stay with her instead of going home to sleep.

Her hand went to her hip with mild annoyance. "Did Papa tell you to keep me in town?"

Dalvin's face was blank, but Rachel shrugged, admitting it. "Yeah. But I'm hungry too." And the moment Anica thought about food, her stomach rumbled impatiently. She sighed. The forest and its intriguing scents would have to wait.

"Yes, we should eat. I've missed too many meals today. My bear is not happy." Anica knew there would be hamburgers, ribs, and sausages, along with fruit and salad, at the food station. She swallowed and felt a sharp pain, reaching up to touch her throat instinctively. Not unexpected after the wound, but annoying. "My throat is sore still. Perhaps something cold first?"

Rachel agreed by scent alone, but Dalvin added words. "Ooo! Cold sounds good to me too. Dessert first it is. Polar Pops?" Dalvin held out his arm, crooked at the elbow, and Rachel tucked her arm around his. The dark-skinned man held out his other arm. He was so much taller that Anica had to reach up to rest her arm on his.

It was only a few blocks on the dirt roads to the ice cream shop owned by an odd falcon named Skew. It wasn't her real name, which was Sensabille—a very pretty name. She re-minded Anica of a parakeet her grandmother had owned. It was a tiny yellow thing with a spotted chest and always seemed to flit this way and that around her small house. Skew was the same in human form. She *flitted*. Her attention changed as quickly as her eyes moved. She was nice, and friendly, but it was hard to carry on a conversation with her. Anica hadn't known any other shifter falcons, but it didn't seem like they should act that way. Falcons in the wild seemed so intense and intelligent. Yet, sometimes, Sensabille seemed almost normal. It was as though she was two halves of one whole person, with neither half knowing the other existed.

Even before they entered, they could see that the shop was busy, with nearly every table taken, inside and out. Anica had found that even in the cold months some of the people in town liked to sit outside. "I think I see a table in the corner," Rachel said over the bright ringing bell as they entered, pointing to a small, round table with two chairs. "I'll go grab it. Order me something simple, like a chocolate sundae. But—"

Dalvin continued with a pat on her shoulder, "No nuts. I know. You never did like peanuts with ice cream. I'll go brave the line. You two sit down. See if you can find another chair somewhere. What would you like, Anica?"

Rachel made a face, confirming the statement. "Yuck. Peanuts aren't good for anything other than peanut butter. How about you, Anica? Do you like nuts with ice cream?"

She couldn't think of anything she didn't like with ice cream. "I like everything. So many different flavors." Anica looked up at the menu board posted high on the wall above the front counter where Skew and two helpers were scurrying around, making sodas and shakes and towering sundaes. Everything was bright and happy here. The white walls with bright spots of colors and the painted cartoon polar bear that took up one whole wall, they all seemed to add to the festive feel of the room. She'd been coming to this shop every few days since arriving in Luna Lake and had yet to find anything she *didn't* like. So many different kinds of bars and cones, some with nuts and others with sauce or sprinkles or even tiny bears made of soft fruit. It was all wonderful! She'd been trying everything on the menu, each in turn. Today, she would have . . .

"I think I'll try the Happy Birthday Surprise today. I was saving that one for my actual birthday later this month, but today I am happy that I am alive."

"Your birthday is this month?!" Rachel let out a little squeal. "That's great. We'll have a big party! One thing Luna Lake does well . . . the only thing really, is parties."

She tried to wave off Rachel's enthusiasm. "There is no need, truly. In our femily, most birthdays aren't much different than any other day."

"What sort of things did you do back in Serbia?"

"Oh, it was nice. When I was little, Mama would make a white sugar cake. White sugar had to be bought in the city, so we didn't have it often. But once Bojan got older, he took over the baking. He is such a good baker, and he made pies that neighbors would come from all over to buy. He never needed white sugar. He would use fruit for the sweet, but you would never know the sugar was missing.

"For my sixteenth birthday, which is one of the special birthdays, when I am officially woman, he make me a black cherry torte that I can still remember." She remembered back, fondly, feeling a smile pull at the corners of her mouth. "That was the same year the femily gave me hope chest. Papa and Samit carved it from a great dead tree from the forest. They must have spent the whole year making it. It is so beautiful, with patterns and a beautiful deer carved on the lid.

"Mama filled it with linens she'd embroidered, for me to start my own femily. I'd never even seen her pick up a needle, so it was a big surprise." She could see it in her mind, at the foot of her bed, covered with a thick crocheted blanket that she would pull up over her feet for cold nights. "It's still in my room, waiting for me to come back."

Rachel's voice grew soft, and the other woman's hand touched hers. "You miss your life back there, don't you?"

Anica pulled her attention back to the present and the tired laughter of the people around her, some new friends like Rachel, others strangers. "Yes. But also no. My life isn't what I'd planned when I was tiny. That birthday, it was both happy and very sad, because even though Mama and Papa were trying hard to make it happy, they knew I could never have the life they would hope for me. I could smell their sad.

"We cut ourselves off from most of our friends after the attack. Nobody courted me, I could not attend parties in the village. I could never marry someone from the village. We couldn't risk people dropping by near the full moon. Samit and Bojan were too aggressive and I could change at any time. It was a lonely time." She looked around her again, and there were only smiles when people met her eyes. "But here, nobody stares or moves their eyes away when I walk by. I know I made people afraid in Serbia. People couldn't help themselves and they didn't understand why, I don't think. But they feared us."

Rachel didn't seem to know what to say, but Anica could smell her sad. Dalvin arrived at the table just then, carrying a metal tray with one . . . *large* mountain of color that had burning candles and even lit sparkling sticks of metal that smelled of gunpowder! He smiled. "I told S.Q. this really was for a birthday, and she sort of went over the edge. When I saw her piling on the scoops, I figured I'd skip ordering for the rest of us."

Even Rachel was a little stunned. "Wow! That is . . . impressive!" She pulled out one of the burning sticks as Dalvin stole a chair from another table. "Have you ever played with sparklers?"

Anica shook her head, a little nervous about Rachel waving one around. "They are very pretty. But do they explode?"

"Nah. You just wave them around and make patterns in the air until they fizzle out. Little kids play with them on the Fourth of July—Independence Day here in the U.S. We didn't have any this year because of the burn ban. But normally, we have a big fireworks display over the lake and the kids run around town with these." She plucked the other one out of the ice cream and handed it to Anica and showed her how to write her name in the air. The letters appeared golden for a moment and then disappeared. It was gaining attention from people around them, and soon there were more such sundaes leaving the front counter and the whole room was lit up with sparklers. It felt very festive.

Dalvin noticed and gave a little smile, his teeth snow-white against his dark skin. "Everyone is tired and scared right now. Nothing like sparklers to lighten the mood a little." He took a spoonful of a scoop of ice cream that was slightly orange. "Mmm, peach. I do love homemade ice cream."

"Yep," Rachel agreed as she dug into a scoop of chocolate on the other side. "Skew makes most of her own product. She buys the toppings and bars, but the ice cream is all hers."

"Hey, you guys!" Anica looked up with a mouth full of strawberry topping and some sort of green ice cream that tasted of nuts. Scott Clayton was waving from the door where he and her brother, Bojan, were just walking in the shop. The man with the waist-length blond hair with a streak of white that matched his owl feathers had quickly made friends with her brother since they'd arrived. Bojan cooked and Scott hoped to one day open an herbal medicine shop. Her brother was teaching the other man cooking, while Scott was helping Bojan find edible natural foods in the forest. "It looks like you could use some help with that before it melts."

Rachel nodded. "Absolutely. Find some chairs and some spoons and dig in. There's no way we'll finish this."

Anica took another bite. "Oh! There's cake in here too!" Bojan sat down next to her, smelling happy for the first time she could remember since they'd arrived in America. It made her smile at him and he smiled back. "Try some of the green. It's interesting."

Bojan took a bite. "It's a sort of nut, but I don't know what sort."

Scott replied, "It's green, so pistachio." He pointed with his spoon. "I used to work here. The orange is peach; the caramel color is either black walnut or—" He dug at it with the spoon. "Yep, black walnut. And, wow, she even threw licorice in here. Brave woman! Try the black, Anica."

She'd been sort of avoiding that scoop but tentatively put a little on the spoon and sipped it off the spoon. She grimaced and shook her head. She had finally found something she did not like here. "No. I do not think so. That flavor should not be with ice cream."

Dalvin noticed and aimed his spoon right for it. "Ooo. I love licorice ice cream. I'll take that one off your hands." He turned the whole plate so that it was right in front of him.

"Please," Anica agreed. "I will try some other colors." She liked the berry-flavored ones, so moved to a pink scoop with obvious chunks of strawberry. It quickly got the harsh taste of the licorice out of her mouth.

Rachel pointed with her spoon at Scott's clothing, which was surprisingly clean. "*You* have not been on the fire line. Slacker," she said with words of scorn, but the words didn't match her scent, which was warm and playful.

"True. We've been on the food line instead. Gotta keep the troops fed. Man alive, are there a lot of extra people in town. We're cooking our fingers to the bone. We just came over here for a quick soda on our break, but this is even better."

"With practice comes skill, Scott." Her brother, like Rachel, sounded stern, but there was happy in his scent. She liked the smell of happy—bright and citrusy, with oranges and lemons and something musky.

Rachel nodded and then motioned at Bojan with her chin. "Bojan, Anica was telling us about the black cherry torte you made her for her sixteenth birthday and how good your pies are. What made you start baking?"

Bojan finished another mouthful of the green pistachio

ice cream before answering. "It start with raspberries. We have a large farm, very big, and we would lose many berries that were overripe. Once they're picked, we must sell them very quickly. If we cannot, they spoil."

Anica nodded. "But they do not spoil so quickly if we cook them into syrup. Mama would cook the juice down to syrup for days. You started helping her when you got so sick, yes?"

He nodded. "Not sick, but it was a bad cough. I was ten or twelve, I think. Before Anica went missing. It would not go away. The doctor said I was not a sort of sick that there was medicine for. But I could not work in the fields, or go to school, because they would send me home, afraid I would make others cough. So I helped Mama stir the juice. It would turn bitter if we didn't stir it often. The cough was not so bad in the kitchen. Mama would be so tired stirring that I would help cook the meal at night. Papa and Samit would be very hungry, so I had to make a lot of food. Making the food made me happy. At first, it was not very good. But I got better. Mama helped me learn how to spice and use different pans."

Anica felt her eyes roll and she smiled. "He lies. He was always good cook. Even at first. It was better than Mama's, and she knew it."

"So what was the cough?" Scott asked. "I haven't seen you cough here, even with the smoke."

Anica laughed, nearly spitting chocolate syrup on Dalvin across the table. She covered her mouth with a tiny paper napkin and cleaned her lips. "Sheep."

Bojan's face flushed pink and smelled of embarrassment, but he nodded. "Sheep. It was allergy. We had sheep at house, but there were no windows in kitchen. There were sheep in pasture near school. Always there were sheep. I thought *sneezing* was for allergy, not coughing."

Dalvin raised his brows. "No wool sweaters for Bojan for Christmas, I guess."

"No," Anica responded. "Not wool. Actual *sheep*. Bojan would help shear and would cough so bad it scared the animals. Papa would send him inside. But when the wool was brought in to wash—" She raised her hands. "—nothing."

"Is true," Bojan said, dabbing at his mouth with a patterned cloth from his pocket. He hated paper napkins. He always carried at least two cloths—one cotton and the other silky. "The doctor could not explain. He was sure it was the fleece, but it was something else. We still do not know what. We sold sheep at house, and fifth-year school was not near sheep. I am happy there are not so many sheep here too."

The door opened again, accompanied by the bright bell ring, and the breeze carried something inside that the bear inside her couldn't ignore. She lifted her nose, turning so sharply to trace the source that she nearly hit her nose on Scott's elbow. *Blood.*

An image appeared in her mind with the scent. A kitchen she didn't recognize, spattered with red. She could see a hand with nails painted nearly the same color as the liquid that dripped onto the floor. A wide gash, ragged and raw, had opened the wrist and traveled upward out of her line of sight.

Bojan noticed the scent at nearly the same moment. She could see him as a faint overlay of the kitchen. His happy scent went metallic and serious. "Someone is hurt."

But Anica knew it was more than that. "No. Someone is *dead*."

CHAPTER 6

Stepping carefully on the tiled floor to a place where he could squat down and survey the murder scene, Tristan tried to think like an investigator. It wasn't what he was trained for, but the scent he was chasing definitely came in this direction. He flicked his tongue out repeatedly, trying to capture the person's smell again, but the coppery blood overpowered the trail.

He pulled a cell phone from his pocket, purchased at the airport when he realized his international phone wouldn't work in this area. He dialed a number he knew by heart and waited as it rang. "Hey, it's me. I need a favor. How soon can you get to Washington?"

The response in an amused baritone nearly made him drop the phone. "Already on the way. I'm about an hour away from town. It *was* a half hour until I got detoured around a wildfire."

"What?! Why?" A part of him was insulted; while another part, relieved.

"I started thinking when you left here—which is always a mistake. You're like another friend of mine: a hunter, not a cop. You tend to *cause* the aftermath, not try to figure it out." One thing about Bobby . . . he was a realist, and didn't judge. "And, you're a little out of practice, even as a hunter. If he-who-can't-be-named really is there, like Ahmad claims, you'll need help. Even Ahmad did, if you recall."

"So what should I do now? I have a dead body in front of me, and a town full of helpful humans who are fighting the fires."

A pause. "Crap. Forgot about the firefighters. There's probably military roaming around too. Is the dead person Sazi?"

He flicked his tongue in the direction of the woman again. She was in the late twenties, maybe early thirties, and— "Yep. A she-wolf. Mauled by claws. There's too much blood for me to chase down what sort of claws. Your tongue will know better."

"Okay, first, let me rule out the obvious: Did you kill her?"

It was barely worth a response, but he'd asked for Bobby's help. "No. I've never seen her before. I just got here and she's probably an hour dead."

"Then secure the scene. Don't touch anything, and keep anyone else out until I get there. The blood scent will start to draw a crowd. Are there any townspeople you can trust?"

A strange feeling came over him, sort of a fuzziness that made it hard to think, or respond.

"Ris?"

He shook it off after a moment. "Yeah, sorry. Amber is here, and the town's Alpha seems the law-abiding sort from the lecture he gave me about keeping away from *his* people. That's where I was an hour ago."

The blurry edge in his mind persisted but didn't get any worse as Bobby chuckled into his ear. "Well, can't beat that for an alibi. Get out of the house now, before you accidentally touch something."

Tristan stood and retraced his steps backward out the small living room to the front door. He stared at the door for a moment and swore. "Of course, now my fingerprints are on the doorknob. Should I wipe them off?"

"Don't bother. I doubt your prints are in the system. And anyone with a decent nose will know you were inside. Did you touch the body? Even a little?"

"You know I did. I was following a trail, trying to get a scent."

"Let it go. Just secure the scene and keep everyone out until I get there." The call went dead, leaving Tristan with nothing to do but wait by the small house in the woods.

Breaking of branches in the distance said Bobby was right about the scent of blood bringing the crowds. The first out of the brush was a small bear, nose in the air following the scent. A second, larger bear was right behind, followed by the pretty black girl and her boyfriend, Dalvin. He licked his lips, catching the scent of sunshine and meadow from the little bear who was apparently Anica's animal form.

Dalvin, barely out of breath from what Tristan presumed was a run from town, stepped past the others toward him and pointed at the door. "Davies, right? I'm going to have to ask you to step aside. I have reason to believe someone is injured inside that house."

"Long past injured, I fear," Tristan said with a shrug. "But I can't step aside, I'm afraid."

He took a step closer. "I'll ask again. I'm Wolven. Step aside before I make you."

Tristan sat down on the step, centered between the wooden pillars that held up the porch, and planted his feet solidly two steps down. He couldn't help but chuckle. "I can assure you that won't happen. I was asked to secure the scene. Nobody gets past me until the person who gave the instruction arrives." He pushed magic out in a bubble, blocking the door. He pressed it outward until it touched Dalvin's rising power. He kept it there, just letting it hover, from earth to sky, letting Dalvin taste the immensity of what he could bring to bear but hadn't.

To his credit, Dalvin didn't falter in the face of impossible odds. The man locked eyes with him, arms crossed across his chest, and raised his own power up a few notches. Nothing aggressive, just a reminder that he was chosen for the law enforcement branch for good reason.

But the others couldn't know what was happening, unspoken. They were lesser Sazi, and only felt the sting of magic that swept across their skin like biting ants . . . much like Tristan himself had felt in the presence of Lagash, or his master, Sargon. But that had been long ago, and Tristan was very young. Over the decades, then centuries, his own power had grown, until he was a likely match of Lagash, if not Sargon himself.

"Please, do not fight!" Anica stepped forward, slicing like a knife through both of their power, and planted her tiny bear body between them. "We need no more death today. Use your magic to help this poor woman find peace instead."

Dalvin, his scent as surprised as Tristan felt at Anica's intervention, stepped forward and touched her ear. "Anica, don't worry. We're not going to fight. I'm sure Mr. Davies is going to be reasonable about this and let me investigate whatever happened inside the house." He paused and then looked at the little bear. "Wait. How do you know a woman who died is inside?"

The larger male bear shook his massive head and let out a noise that could only be derision. "Do owls have no nose at all? Even I can smell it is a woman, and a wolf, who died. *Anica* can probably name her brand of lip paint."

If a bear could blush, Anica was. She lowered her head shyly and scuffed the dirt with one paw. The wide claws seemed almost delicate, the way she moved them in a circle. "Bojan, please. I do not smell *that* well. But I do know she has not been dead long. We should be looking for who in town smells of blood before they can wash it off."

"Are you freaking kidding me?" Dalvin slapped his forehead with his palm. "Yes. Yes, we should be doing that."

Rachel leaned against a tree and let out a little laugh. "I was wondering when you men were going to stop bumping egos against each other and think about Paula. That's who lives here, by the way. I would imagine that's who's dead inside."

Anica let out a little cry of surprise and pain. "Paula? The waitress at the diner? Oh, no! She was so nice. Who would want to hurt her?"

Rachel rolled her eyes. "Nice? Pfft. Well, maybe to paying customers."

Tristan had seen that cold, calm look before, and knew what it meant. He raised his voice to reach to the tree. "I take it you're not sorry she's dead."

Another snort from the woman covered in soot. "Nope. She was a flaming bitch. And I'm not the only one in town who thought so. I can think of a dozen people who would have been happy to pack her bags for a vacation in a hot place down south. Waaay down south."

Dalvin turned to his girlfriend with an odd look on his face. "You been packing any suitcases lately, Chelle?"

She responded with a look that was a little surprised and a lot insulted. "No! What the hell, Dalvin? I've been with *you* today, if you remember. And if I'd wanted her dead, do you really think I'd have waited this long? Or done it with Wolven and Council people in town?" She turned her face to stare at Tristan, rubbing her arms and letting a tiny slip of fear show past her bravado. "Because, dude, if you aren't Council, I'm betting you're who keeps them awake at night."

He didn't respond. There was no need. Anything he could possibly say either would not be believed or would only confirm her statement. Anica followed Rachel's steady stare and cocked her head as she looked at him, as though she wasn't quite sure what to make of him.

Before anyone could say anything further, he heard the high-pitched whine of an ATV motor coming up the narrow lane that served as a road to the house. He rose to his feet as the branches revealed the occupants as Bobby Mbutu, Amber, and the town Alpha. None of them looked particularly happy.

Amber snarled as she got out of the front seat. "Really? Less than a day since you arrived and there's a dead body?"

Anica's father pointed at Tristan as he brushed the dust from his faded blue jeans. "Take him with you, Agent, and be sure he pays dearly for the death of my resident."

It wasn't the first time he'd been accused of a death that wasn't his kill. Actually, he couldn't remember a time he'd been accused of a death he'd actually caused. He tended to be more careful than that. It seemed redundant to say, but he supposed it was necessary: "I didn't kill her. She died sometime when I was with *you*, in your office, getting a lecture about avoiding contact with your residents."

Bobby started walking slowly toward the door, licking his

lips constantly. "I have to agree. The smell says an hour, maybe two."

Anica padded up to the python shifter, her scent suddenly excited and curious. "Excuse me? You are police? How do you know? I mean . . . *know* that, just by smell? I try so hard to know, but there are so many smells. It . . . " She seemed to struggle for a word. "Muddies. You know? Dalvin changes me so I can smell better, and I can smell tiny things, all things. But I cannot . . . " She let out a harsh breath. "Pull apart. Is like big knot in my nose."

Instead of dismissing her like Tristan had seen him do with a hundred other people, Bobby stopped and regarded her seriously. Instead of answering, he reached up and pulled a trio of leaves from a waist-high shrub next to the house. He flicked out his tongue and tasted one leaf and then pulled it off before putting the remaining two in front of her nose. "Tell me about this leaf. Everything you can."

She blinked oversized eyes at him and snuffled around the leaves, smelling them front and back. "The shrub, it is healthy and makes fruit. Not sweet, but not hurt stomach."

He shook his head. "What else?" Nobody else said a word while he stared at her, so intense was the look in his glowing eyes. "Don't look at it. Close your eyes and let the scent tell you a story."

She closed her eyes and flared her nostrils. She began to sway just the tiniest bit and Tristan nearly swayed with her. It was like some mysterious dance as her eyes began to glow around her eyelids and her head moved to music only she could hear. "The woman touched these leaves often when she walk by. A man's scent is on top of hers, but lightly, like he only touched once but she many times. He was angry; his scent is bitter, burnt."

"Do you recognize the man's scent?"

She opened her eyes, as though surprised by the question. "No. But I do not know many people here yet and there are many new people in town because of the fire."

"You didn't mention the fire. Why not? Is there no smoke on the leaf?"

The whiskers above her eyes twitched. "Everything smells of smoke. It wasn't a *different* smoke, if you understand. So to tell that was . . . not important."

"What perfume was she wearing?"

A pause and then she nodded just a touch, her nostrils flared wide. "I have smell this perfume before. In city when we arrived. I see it on poster in airport, named for celebrity. Pretty blond singer. I cannot remember name. But if I saw poster again, I would know it."

Bobby nodded sagely. "Would you remember the man's scent if you smelled it again? His perfume, his sweat, his anger, if you smelled the person?"

She paused. "No anger. He was not angry. I know that scent very well. Like hot metal. I remember smells very good. But sometimes, I do not know what the smell is."

"Close your eyes and turn in a circle. Use your paw to point to two other bushes like the leaves, without looking."

She quickly did so. "There are many more than two. But these are first two."

"Good," he replied. Amber and Anica's father opened their mouths, almost simultaneously, as though to ask what he was trying to accomplish. *He's teaching her to use her gift.* Bobby held up a dark brown hand and shook his head, asking for continued silence from the onlookers. Rachel seemed very intrigued by what was happening. Dalvin looked a little bored.

"Now, you know what the woman's blood smells like, yes?"

"Of course," she said, and started to open her eyes. He put his hand over her eyes.

"No, keep them closed. Now, find her blood *outside* the house. Let it find you. Ignore the overpowering. Concentrate on the lost bits that match."

Her whole body stilled when she realized what he was asking her to do. He was asking her to track the killer's path away from the house. "He was careful." She said it out loud, but not really to them. "He slink away, sneaky, low to ground." Her nose went to the ground also, and she started to make little snuffling sounds, like a pig after truffles. "He steps on beetle here, but picks up and takes. Why would he want bug?"

Bobby followed her as she stepped into the brush, her nose moving back and forth across the ground. "Careful indeed."

Without warning, Tristan felt a sensation of panic press against his skin just as Anica let out a cry. "No! Not bad smell again! What is this?" Then she was gasping for breath again, like in the hospital. Bobby moved forward and pulled her bodily away from the patch of forest. Tristan found himself moving to her side to help lay her down. She looked up at him, her eyes wide. But her scent wasn't so much scared as frustrated. He heard her voice in his head once more.

I was doing it, Tristan. The policeman was helping me untie the knot.

"I know." He said it out loud, since she couldn't hear him last time. "We'll get you fixed up again. Just rest and try to breathe."

Amber swore. "I didn't think to bring another EpiPen

with me. Damn it! We have to get her back to the hospital, and I hope to God that the EMT from the National Guard has another one in his bag."

"I've got her." Tristan lifted her easily and carried her to the ATV. For a bear, she was light as a feather, and molded into his arms as though made to fit. The others gathered around, hands reaching to offer comfort as she struggled for air.

"What the hell *is* that?" Bobby's voice cut through the murmurs of sympathy and the ATV's engine as Zarko turned the key and Amber crawled in beside him and Anica. "Wait. I *know* what this is! Stop! Stop. Don't leave. I can fix her."

Amber turned to him and blinked. "I know what it is too. It's an allergy and we have to get the swelling down."

Bobby reached his arm between them to a bag that was on the floorboards of the ATV. "Oh, it's an allergy, all right. One every Sazi shares. She's just extrasensitive to it." He pulled a clear plastic bottle from the bag and started to unscrew the wide lid. He put the opening to Anica's nose. "Inhale this."

Even Tristan could see that her nose was completely swollen shut. "She can't breathe it in, Bobby. That's sort of the point."

"Well, shit. You're right. I need a straw of some sort." He started digging in the bag, obviously looking for tubing, and Tristan suddenly understood what he meant.

"You need to blow in the powder. Got it." He slid out from underneath Anica's head and pushed aside the paw that reached for him. "No, just stay still. I know what he's trying to do."

Tristan looked around the thick undergrowth until he saw what he needed. A tree that had some new growth, close to the house where it got shade and water. He ripped off a slender branch and used his fingernail to score the bark. Then he peeled it away from the center, creating a flexible tube from the outer bark that was relatively dry. He walked back and handed it to Bobby. "Not the most sterile, but it should do in a pinch."

"I have *got* to start carrying more stuff in my pack. But this should work." He motioned to Amber. "Lift her head and keep her still."

Amber lifted Anica's head and used her magic to hold it steady. But she motioned to the plastic container. "What's the powder?"

"Remember back in Chicago a few years back, when you poured a witches brew down my throat to save *my* life? Same stuff, but with less rotting meat."

She blinked and then her jaw dropped. "Are you *serious*? Here? In the forest?" She started to look up, into the tree-tops, her movements sharp and nervous. Tristan smelled a scent he didn't think the powerful bobcat was capable of.

Fear.

CHAPTER 7

The dark-skinned policeman began to tap the side of the plastic container, and the white powder fell into the bark. He blew it out onto the ground and then started the process again, opening the tube to look inside. She suddenly realized what he was doing—drying it out so the powder didn't clump.

"Stop playing with tube and save her!" Papa was worried. She hated to see him like that, but the policeman was not worried, so she was not. The reaction to the smell wasn't nearly as bad as before. But the scent wasn't so strong as it had been. She could still get a little air into her lungs by opening her mouth, so it was closer to when she'd had a bad cold as a little girl. Her nose and sinuses were like a solid mass, but she could breathe through her mouth if she concentrated.

Tristan was petting her head. She didn't think he knew he was doing it because he was busy watching Bobby, but it felt nice. His hand played with her fur like it was hair, and that relaxed her. There was something about him that she trusted, even though a part of her knew he was a very dangerous person.

He held her nose in the air as the policeman finally was ready to do whatever he planned. He gently opened one nostril and inserted the tube inside. He looked into her eyes with his dark brown ones. He blinked then and her heart skipped a beat. He blinked *up*, from the bottom. She couldn't struggle but wanted to. *Needed* to. He was a *snake*! No longer calm, her breathing became labored and she fought against the magic that held her. Snakes brought death and pain.

Even as she thought it, he said, "This is going to hurt. Sorry."

He put his lips to the bark in her nose and puffed his cheeks. The powder entered her nose like flame and stung like salt in a wound. She tried to pull away, began to panic as pain shot up her nose. He quickly did the same with her other nostril and all she could feel was fire burning the sensitive skin in her nose and then bleeding down the back of her throat. She let out a bawl of pain and Tristan tightened his grip in her fur, keeping her steady. "Shhh. Trust Bobby. Let the medicine work."

"What are you doing to her? What is that?" Papa snatched the bottle of powder away from the snake policeman and sniffed it. "Salt? You blow salt into her nose?"

The snake named Bobby shook his head. "Not salt. Sodium bicarbonate. Baking soda. It neutralizes the poison."

"Poison?" Rachel exclaimed. "Someone poisoned Anica? What the hell!? Is that what happened to Paula too? Or did she find out someone was putting out poison and they got rid of her?"

"That's actually not a bad guess," Tristan said. "I could see that scenario happening."

"Why would someone poison my little one? She would not hurt a fly." Papa smelled both outraged and confused.

Wait. Smell. She could smell again! And she suddenly realized she could start to feel air through her nose.

"I can smell again." She coughed, not hard, and then pulled in more air. Already the swelling was going down as the doctor's magic released her. But no. Not the doctor. It had been Tristan's magic holding her. She could feel the difference now. She looked at the policeman with anger rising. "You are *snake*. You are not policeman."

The dark man sighed. "I am a snake. *And* I am a policeman. I've been a Wolven agent for many years, since before the attacks on you. I never supported Sargon or his goals, or the sort of camps you were taken to."

She could smell he wasn't lying, but she couldn't help but laugh, a harsh sound, even to her. She backed away from him, across the laps of both Tristan and Amber, who didn't try to stop her, until she was on ground again with the cart between them. "You say 'camps.' I say 'prison.' Snakes make prisons and steal children to attack. Snakes are evil. I do not trust *any* snake."

Amber let out a sigh. "It didn't used to be this way, Anica. The snakes used to be integrated among the Sazi. They are no more evil than any other animal. Some *people* are evil. Animals aren't evil by nature, and the type of animal we happen to shift into doesn't make a person evil or not evil. Bobby is not evil. He is well respected as an investigator and a chemist. You can trust him. I promise."

Tristan was looking at her very intently but didn't say anything. She could feel the weight of his eyes, as he thought about what she said. It gave her a funny feeling in her stomach, both comforted and nervous. So she asked him instead. "You are bear, but you know this snake. You trust him?"

He glanced at the other man, casually, like there was no

real decision to be made. "Like I would my own brother. I have known him his whole life. I've never questioned his honor or loyalty. You could learn much from him."

She had backed up even more and found herself next to Rachel and Dalvin. Rachel would understand why she feared and hated snakes. "What kind of snake are you? You don't smell like a cobra." It was Rachel asking, but Dalvin answered.

"Python. There are lots more kinds of snakes than just vipers, Chelle. Bobby's sort of a legend in Wolven. Top of the Academy and a fairly famous chemist, even in the human world."

Amber waved her hands in the air, trying to break the tension and finally throwing out a burst of magic to get everyone's attention. "We need to get back to the problem at hand, people. Bobby's not the problem here. We have a dead body, and a spider to deal with."

"A *spider*?!" Dalvin and Tristan both said the words, nearly simultaneously, and with equal amounts of alarm. She wasn't sure why a spider would make such powerful men feel afraid. She thought spiders were pretty. Most she had found would not bite if not provoked.

"Yes, and no," Bobby replied. "Yes, a spider. But not actually here."

Now Amber stared at him, her brow furrowing a little in confusion that matched her scent. "Wait. You said it was spider venom. You said it was the same as Chicago."

He nodded, once. "I did. It is venom and it's why the little bear had the reaction. She has a very sensitive nose. With training, it could be the equal of my tongue. But the spider isn't here. The venom is either powdered, used to throw off our noses—like a skunk can be used to blind a bloodhound—

or diluted and used for some other purpose. Possibly it's intentional poison, to try to kill. But I'm thinking it's a smoke screen to hide a trail."

"Then the man plays the fool, yes?" The more Anica thought about it, the more foolish it seemed.

They turned to look at her and the snake policeman raised one brow, like her uncle Petar could do, and then licked his lips. His scent turned sweet and syrupy, but like he was not something that should be eaten. "Interesting. Go on."

Anica took a deep breath and sat down. It was difficult to describe. "The man wishes to kill Paula. I do not smell angry smells or romance in air. No emotion at all. Even she has no emotion. So surprised, I think, by a man who intended to kill." Tristan nodded his head and suddenly smelled of the *palačinke* Mama used to make, filled with raspberry jam, cheese and cloves sprinkled on top. So many emotion smells she still didn't recognize, even this many years later. "He wishes to have nobody know he was here, so he sneaks away on his belly, but then leaves behind something that is sure to have notice? It is foolish."

"Hey, yeah," Rachel agreed, and moved to stand next to her. "That *doesn't* make sense. Why not use a skunk for cover, or start a fire or something? Nobody would notice that with the wildfire nearby. Why use something that spooks even Sazi cops? Now, I don't know what sort of spider freaks you guys out, but I guess it's not a local one. Is it one of those big Australian kinds?"

"It's a spider *shifter*." Tristan's voice was calm, but there was an underlying tension that told Anica he'd encountered one before. "They feed on other Sazi. We're *prey* to them."

Rachel's reaction was immediate and echoed what was going through her own mind . . . a horror almost too big to think of. "Oh, *hell* no!" She looked up in the trees and around to the suddenly sinister forest, and started rubbing her arms like something was clinging to them. "Spiders with *brains*? Are you kidding me?!"

Anica wanted to crawl underneath a log and not come back out. "Are spiders size of people?"

Amber nodded her head, her arms tightly wrapped around her body. "My husband, Charles, has told me stories about hunting down the spiders with two other men. They'd eaten all of the Sazi where they lived in what is now South America, and had started to move out into the bigger world. Charles and his friends tried reason first—they are part human, like us. But their minds work so very differently. The human half was their sin, their shame. They didn't want to live with us, among us. They wanted to hunt us, even after they knew that hunting us to extinction would mean their own death."

Anica wanted to take her mind off the thought of a spider the size of people, so she tried to shake it off by getting back to Paula's death. The pretty waitress had always been nice to her. She didn't know why Rachel didn't like her, but Paula had never done anything to make Anica think badly of her. In fact, she'd always greeted her with a smile and even asked what sort of foods she used to like back home. After Papa made Mama leave, she had the cook make a passable *musaka sa krompirom*, a baked beef and potato supper that made America feel a little less frightening. "Then why use something to bring attention to Paula's death? Does this person *want* to be catched?"

"Caught," Tristan corrected, almost automatically, but he was nodding, moving closer to her, and squatting down to stare into her eyes. "That is a very good question, Anica. Why indeed?"

Then he slid inside her mind, his eyes still locked with hers, making her brain fuzzy and the people around them fade into the background. **Something is causing you pain. What is it?**

Telling him seemed so easy, like whispering with Bojan behind the house at night after everyone had gone to bed. **Paula was good woman. Her killer should not escape. I must help find him.**

He's a dangerous man. That doesn't frighten you?

A snort burst out of her nose. "*Life* is dangerous, often frightening. It does not change what needs be done." It was something that needed to be said out loud, not hidden inside her mind like a shameful thought.

"Interesting non sequitur." Dalvin let out a little chuckle. "But true. So what now?" He wasn't asking her. When she glanced up, he was looking at the snake policeman, deferring to him. If that was to be, and he was honest, she would try to trust. But she would watch for deceit. Snakes could not be trusted. Tristan's face took on a small frown, as though he heard her. But he was bear, so he should understand. He stood up and stepped a few paces back, to give her room to stand up.

"Now," Anica said, and stood back to all four feet. "We track him. He makes one mistake. Maybe more mistakes inside. We must go look and smell, find who he is so he can be punished."

Papa let out a low growl. "Not you. Anica will go back to town. What is inside is nothing a child should see. Or smell."

"I am not a child, Papa!" She was growing ever frustrated

with this insistence that she couldn't stand on her own, think for herself.

Amber let out a little noise that was part embarrassed cough and part hiss. "While I dislike his *opinion*, I have to agree that Anica isn't a trained investigator, or part of Wolven. I don't know that her presence is more than a distraction. Probably she *should* go back to town with Rachel and Tristan."

"But—!" *How could the doctor say such a thing?* "Why should *you* stay then?" The cat turned to her with a look close to anger. Very well. If the doctor wished to strike her down, then so be it. "There is nothing left for you to heal. *My* nose can find killer. I have to help!"

Amber ground her teeth, her magic rising but not stinging like it normally did. She looked to Bobby and Dalvin. Dalvin shrugged, leaving the decision up to the snake shifter. Her heart sank. Why would the snake help her?

Tristan was tapping one finger on the windshield of the motorcart thoughtfully. He tapped loud enough, slowly at first, but increasing in frequency and intensity every time that the snake opened his mouth to speak, but would have to yell over the noise, that the snake let out a loud sigh and turned to stare at him. "What?"

He shrugged, fluid, elegant. "You said her nose needed training. Her father said she shouldn't see the scene. The killer *does* need to be caught. How about this? We cover her eyes and Bobby leads her through the scene. She doesn't see, she does smell, and she gets training from one of the best. The rest of us go back and just the two of them stay."

Papa frowned, his whole body voicing his disapproval before he ever spoke. His voice was even deeper than normal.

"I do not like this. Alone in woods. I do not know him. No. Doctor will stay to watch."

The doctor let out a laugh at nearly the same time as the snake, but it was the snake who spoke. He gave a small bow to her papa. "Alpha Petrovic, I do understand your customs. But I am happily mated with six children and my wife is a Komodo Dragon shifter. I assure you I am not willing to risk the wrath of the very dangerous woman inside my head right now."

Her papa's eyes nearly showed the amusement his scent gave away, but he didn't laugh. Instead, he held his ground. "Then would it not be better to give her no reason to fear? Let the doctor guide her while you teach."

The doctor let out an annoyed sound that was like a housecat hiss. "Zarko, while I appreciate your concerns, I simply don't have *time* to babysit your daughter. There are still people back in town who need healing. The fire hasn't suddenly disappeared, and more people will be coming after the next shift."

Rachel lifted her arm. "I'll do it. I've seen plenty of blood and guts. I can do it one more time, I guess." She lowered her voice a bit, and hot metal frustration made her continue. It was one of the things she liked best about Rachel. She didn't fear speaking her mind. "But Zarko, if you don't think Anica has already seen enough horrors to last a lifetime, then you're deluding yourself. This is one dead woman. Yeah, there'll be blood, but the pain is at least gone. You saw the cave in Serbia, what the children looked like. You *know* the things she saw."

His eyes flicked away. They'd never talked about her time there. Never. Even Mama couldn't ask her of the things she'd experienced. A sharp, bitter scent came from his pores, over a dusty smell that she'd learned was shame. Why would he feel shame? "She escaped. My little girl escaped."

She stepped toward him and bumped his hip with her head. She didn't want to open that tightly bound box deep inside her now, not in front of all of these people. But she had to at least admit the box was there. She *had* been a little girl then. So little and afraid. The things she saw, smelled— "Yes. I escaped . . . after eight *months*." Eight long months, filled with days and nights of screams, blood. Fear was the first scent she was able to put a name to, even before she became an animal. He looked down at her then and there was a look she'd never seen on his face before. A pain, a *haunted* look of anguish. He reached down and touched her ear, her *fur*. She wanted to lean into his touch, accept the comfort of her father, but to do that would admit she was still what he claimed. "I haven't been a little girl for a very long time, Papa."

He coughed, then held his head up and pushed past to bury his emotion, yet still unwilling to let go, even a little. "Rachel will stay and guard."

Now the frustration scent was her own. Anica's friend rolled her eyes. "Goody." She reached in her pocket and removed a key ring, holding it out to her fiancé. "Dalvin, do me a favor and run back to my place and get something out of my closet that blood won't ruin. I think there's some old sweats in the back." He nodded and took the keys, tucking them in his front pocket. Then Rachel snapped her fingers. "Oh, and get something for Anica to wear too, when you shift her back." Yes, she would need clothing. Rachel paused and looked down, meeting her eyes. "Wait. Can you hold her in animal form if you leave?"

Oh! She should not change and be naked in the forest with strange people. That would be very uncomfortable.

Especially if Tristan was still here. Why that would be worse she didn't know. But Dalvin only shrugged, his scent betraying no alarm. "I'm not holding her *now*. I presumed it was Bojan who shifted her."

But her brother shook his head, his scent confused and surprised. "No. I am not good at shifting another, even with the moon." He looked at her then. "How *did* you shift?"

The sensation of shock that raced through her made her head fuzzy. "I . . . I do not know. I thought Dalvin—" She tried to feel for a presence of magic, like the last time Dalvin changed her. Even though it had been smooth, she could feel the sensation, like being in a harness with a taut rope, pulling. But she couldn't remember the moment when the change happened. She didn't feel anyone's magic holding her. There was no tension of her animal wanting to slumber inside her, even though the moon was not close. She was a bear and it felt like she had no rope around her at all.

Amber pushed out her own magic, touching gently. "As far as I can tell, nobody is holding her now."

Papa stared at her with an odd expression. "You change *yourself*? But you have never—"

"No. I have no magic to make change. Dalvin must have. He was there, in the soda shop with me. Just me and Bojan, and Scott, and Rachel."

Amber didn't seem to think it was interesting enough to be concerned with. "One of you must have, and Zarko is probably holding her without realizing it. She's his sloth and could be drawing on that unconsciously."

"Truly, Doctor—" She had to speak up, because something important was happening, and she didn't understand it. "I feel no tie. I do not think of it until now, but there is no pull to keep animal out."

That made the doctor rear back a little, and then her face grew thoughtful. "Okay, new theory. There's a lot of powerful magic in a very small forest. Maybe it's like a Council meeting, where weird stuff happens. Too much magic in the area can have odd effects on weather and lesser Sazi. Usually, they sting or burn, but I suppose it's possible there's enough loose magic that she's able to draw on it to hold herself."

It made sense. Ozone filled the air like just after a lightning storm as the others agreed. The snake nodded. "Been there, seen that. I do recall at a couple of Council meetings that there were spontaneous shifts. At least two of you guys could qualify for the Council if there weren't already-filled spots." He didn't say who, but she knew Papa was likely one of them. He was a very powerful bear . . . equal in magic to the one who held the title now. She was always proud of that one thing to come from her attack: Papa had grown more powerful and more respected.

The snake looked at her, and the look was almost *kind*, which startled her. "Anica, when everyone leaves, all that magic will go away and you'll likely change back, suddenly and probably painfully. Do you want me to hold you in form so you can stay as a bear and have your best nose while we go through the house?"

If the doctor was right, then . . . but he was a *snake*. She was torn. Rachel had little magic too, so she couldn't help. She looked at the house. No. She must be strong. Paula deserved better. She was not a little girl to fear help, even if she didn't trust. "Yes. I will allow." She was going to stop there, but Mama's chiding came to her mind—*Manners, Anica! Do not be rude.* She dipped her head in his direction. "Thank you."

He dipped his head in reply as the others squeezed into

the ATV. Papa changed Bojan back to human and let him appear to wear clothing for his dignity. As he started the engine, Papa took a deep breath, still uneasy, as the snake's magic flowed over the top of her with a sensation of stinging. It was not painful, exactly, but it was like running her hand over a nettle bush. She didn't feel any different than she had. The bear inside seemed not to mind where the magic came from, which still seemed strange. Papa watched her for any sense of discomfort, but there was none, so he said, "I will be back soon. We will seal area like before hunt so nobody comes to interrupt."

The snake nodded. "Thank you. That'll help me concentrate and not waste my own magic."

Once they were gone, the snake spoke. "Okay, look. Bullshit aside. Are you guys really okay with going into a crime scene? 'Cause it won't be pretty in there. I can smell the amount of blood and there's a lot."

Anica already knew that. Her head nodded before she even thought about it. "There is much blood smell. But I have seen arms and legs ripped off, watched bears feeding on people who did not survive. They are not things I try to remember, but the pictures come in my mind at night. I often wake after."

Rachel let out a small shudder but agreed. "Yeah, I've seen bad shit too and still get nightmares. All I smell is blood here. Like Anica said, no pain, no fear, or sweat. It's the pain that's the worst. This is pretty clean, as smells go."

The snake turned without digging into those memories. "Great." He walked to the porch of the little cabin, expecting they would follow. "So, let's get to teaching. First, a little about me. Like I said, I'm a python. I have a great tongue for scents. But I'm also a trained chemist. I hold a doctorate in organic chemistry from an Ivy League university. The reason I went to college is because while I could smell things with my tongue, I didn't know what the smells *were*. I had no names for the smells."

"Yes!" Anica couldn't help but shout it, and it made Rachel laugh. "I have this same trouble. I smell emotions, but don't have names. I smell plants and have no names. It makes my head crazy!"

The snake, Bobby, let out a chuckle. "I have a friend who was also an attack victim. I knew him before, as a human, and he dealt with smells afterward differently than I'd ever encountered. I was born a Sazi, so I've just always *known* certain smells, like emotions, because my parents explained them as they happened. But for Tony, he had no frame of reference other than matching food and things around him with the smells. He started matching emotions to things he already knew, and the more I thought about his comparisons, the more I realized they played out."

Rachel was leaning against one of the porch pillars, not really unwilling to go inside, but clearly in no hurry to either. "Such as?"

"You mentioned pain and fear. He always said that fear smelled like hot and sour soup from a Chinese restaurant, and pain was like Worcestershire sauce—the scents made the back of his jaw tighten and his mouth would drool. He discovered he'd started eating his steaks with extra Worcestershire sauce after the change. That bugged him a little at first, after he put two and two together."

Anica found herself liking this snake, despite her best effort. "Yes, I see. Is like when people laugh. I smell oranges. Mama says I am silly. But I know I smell oranges from their mouths, no matter what they have eaten."

"Hey, yeah," Rachel agreed. "And I can spot right away when people are lying to me. It smells just like a pepper grinder. The bigger the lie, the stronger the smell. When they're telling a real whopper, I start sneezing."

"It is true!" Anica found herself finally telling someone what she'd been thinking for years, without embarrassment. "Back in Serbia, when Mama and Papa were sitting in yard, I could smell cakes and cookies. There was cinnamon and sugar and nutmeg, and I knew they were happy, in love. But after they fought and Papa sent Mama away, he smelled cold and wet but peppery . . . not like lies, but like Mexican spices, and I knew he was sad and angry with her."

"Well . . ." Rachel tried to figure out how to say something, and Anica knew she was trying to be tactful. "Your mom did sort of betray you all and nearly got you killed."

It was true, but—"I want to believe she did not know Larissa's intention. I can't believe Mama planned for me to die."

Rachel didn't comment, just tipped her head and shrugged. There was a long moment with no sound, and then Bobby cleared his throat. "So, anyway. Scents. The more you can expose yourself to names of things, the better. The leaves I had you smell were from a Black Hawthorn, also known as a Douglas Hawthorn. You've lived here for a month. You should have known that. Buy field guides to plants. Go on nature walks everywhere you travel. It's not only okay around humans; it's actually encouraged to smell things. Start opening food and smelling it. Stand in the produce section and sniff the vegetables. Again, perfectly natural and nobody looks at you strange. Same with the meat department and seafood. Then smell fresh versus frozen, then various stages of rot. Bananas are great for that. They go overripe fast. Make soup from scratch and smell each spice

as it enters the pot and the quantity. Smell the final product and remember the quantities that created the whole.
Then compare it to pre-canned. You'll smell the chemicals
they add right away—the artificial flavors and preservatives
that aren't natural. But without knowing what each chemical smells like, it doesn't help."

He opened the door, and the powerful scent of blood,
which had been more muted with the home sealed, burst
into Anica's nose. Her animal wanted her to snuffle in the
scent, wanting it to be food. It made her cringe. "How do I
stop wanting to roll around in smell? It is not . . . *right* to
want this. It offends my heart."

"Yeah, smells get the best of me too," Rachel admitted.
"When I used to smell a dead mouse in the wall as a kid, I'd
wrinkle my nose and leave the room. Now when I smell it,
my arms shake like my wings would flutter in my owl form,
and I want to rip into the wall to find it . . . to *eat* it, and it
makes me sort of sick."

"That's another tough one," Bobby agreed. "Same with my
friend. He had a bad spell once, and wanted to chase down
a jogger. He's a wolf, and chasing down prey is natural. He
had to fight for control, which is critical as a three-day. I don't
have any easy answers for that one. Control is your friend.
Avoid first, and when you can't, have a buddy system. Let
other people keep you away from the temptation. We're
humans first, and we get to control how we react. That's why
murder is illegal, even with our kind. We not only have the
ability but the *duty* to control ourselves."

Anica touched the doorway, getting accustomed to
the smell of death. "I will try." She looked at Rachel as she
climbed the stairs to the porch. "You will help me not roll?
I will stop your arms flap too."

"Sorority sisters, girl. You know it." She smiled, but it was shaky.

Bobby raised that one brow again. "You were in school together?"

Rachel shook her head and laughed as she pushed away from the post. "Just an inside joke. Anica and I, and another girl in town, Claire, were all prisoners in the caves. Claire and I were together in Texas." She shrugged. "Sorority sisters."

Bobby's face darkened. "Sargon was a sick bastard. Taking little kids, doing that to them . . . " He couldn't finish, but Anica could smell his outrage without even looking at his clenched fists and face twisted in anger. He was truly offended at what had happened to them, and suddenly he didn't seem as much like a snake. Like Ahmad. Even though Ahmad was Sargon's son, he was filled with hate for his father. She had seen that hate in his eyes when they had met here in Luna Lake, and again back in Serbia when he had helped rescue other captive bears imprisoned by his father.

"Okay," Bobby said after a few moments, "let's start to process the scene like investigators until your friend comes back with more suitable clothing. We start by looking at the outside of the house. Was there forced entry? Anica, you mentioned it *smelled* like the woman—Paula, did you say?—was taken by surprise. Can we prove or disprove that by looking with our eyes and smelling more carefully?"

They started walking around the building with Bobby, his tongue flicking almost constantly now, and he began to point out small clues that Anica hadn't noticed before because of the overwhelming blood smell. The branches of one bush were ripped and blood spattered across the remaining bark. Bobby explained that the man may have used the leaves to wipe the blood from his hands. But where did the leaves go?

He stood back, pulled a small tube of wax from his pocket, and rolled it around his lips, encouraging her to match the two scents, the pungent blood and smoky leaves, and find them again, and she did! The bloody leaves were buried under a mass of pine needles a dozen meters away. "So, he wasn't so panicked at the death, at what he'd done, that he couldn't take the time to try to hide his tracks," Bobby explained. "Pine is a great hiding place in most cases. It's why humans use it as cleanser and for animal bedding and cat litter. It hides scents. But if we focus our noses, we can sort through and find his trail."

"So, we go chase him now? Make him pay for her death?" Anica felt almost excited at the prospect, even though the man obviously was willing to kill.

Bobby let out a little chuckle at her excitement. "No. That comes later. There are times when a Wolven agent has to punish. We have that authority—sort of like a spy having a license to kill from his government. But it's not our primary role. We are investigators first. We gather evidence sufficient to take it to our version of court . . . the Wolven chief or the Council, for *them* to act. The Council members are the real authorities. An order of death is a serious thing. We don't take it lightly, and there is a process."

Anica turned her head as an engine sound approached down the worn path through the trees. Dalvin was alone in the ATV and had a bundle of clothing on the seat next to him. "Sorry it took so long," he said as he parked and turned off the engine. Anica was a little surprised at the comment, because she had been so busy she hadn't noticed much time passing. But when she looked up, the sun had definitely moved. The house was throwing shadows deep into the trees. Dalvin's movements were hurried, rushed. "Another load of firefighters arrived. The fire turned again. It may be headed this way. Word out of Republic is they've raised the warning to voluntary evacuation of the county."

Bobby let out an annoyed sound. "Then we have two jobs. First, investigate. Second, clean up. We can't have the human authorities discover this. There are too many fire volunteers here who might be police in their day jobs. We can't allow them to take samples of our blood. That's the second primary role of Wolven, ladies. Keep the secret. It might be considered the first role."

Dalvin nodded as he handed a long-sleeved gray sweatshirt and pants to Rachel. "I do consider it the first role. Investigation comes out of someone having broken the secret, like this death. Someone has lost control of themselves to leave the body of a Sazi for anyone to find. That has to be punished . . . it's actually a larger crime than the murder itself."

"At least equal to it," Bobby agreed. "Sometimes the animal half does get the better of us and the death is accidental. But leaving the body and not informing Wolven or the local Alpha raises the level. Now, sometimes they don't remember doing it and just wander off. That can happen with lesser Sazi."

Anica felt a low growl rise from her chest, which made the others look at her in surprise. "I am sorry, but I dislike this word very much. I hear often, and it offends. *Lesser* Sazi. I am not powerful, it is true. I am a little bear with little magic. But I am not *lesser*. People say it and wave their hand as though I am not worthy of existing." She shook her head and slapped a paw against the pine boards underfoot, struggling not to dig her claws in and give her frustration a vent.

Rachel looked down at her and nodded, a similar metallic scent of disapproval joining in the air with her own as she pulled the sweatshirt down over her springy dark hair. "Yeah, that pisses me off too. It was bad enough when I was little and I just had to worry about the color of my skin being accepted. But now it's my animal, or my level of magic. It never fucking ends. It's like alphic is the gold standard and the rest of us are broken somehow."

Dalvin raised his hands, his scent apologetic, but he didn't really know what to say.

Bobby crossed his arms over his chest, the tan cloth stretching tight over large muscled arms. "Historically, that's sort of true. Long ago, *all* Sazi were alphic. We couldn't have survived, as a species, without the ability to change at will or, more important, to change *back* to human form. But like all species, the more you breed outside the pure line, including attack victims, the more watered down the magic. I'm not saying it's *right* to use the term. I'm just saying that it's where the term comes from."

Rachel had sat down on the first porch step, pressing against Anica's side so she could pull the elastic of the pant legs over her shoes. "Well," she said, "you know what happens to *pure* lines in animals? Inbreeding. Bad hips, health problems, *temper control* issues. Paula was alphic, and she was a bitch. Sargon was an alpha, along with all of his followers, and they were homicidal meglomaniacs. Our former town leaders were alphas, and were *insane* meglomaniacs. So maybe it's one of you gold-standard alphas who went nuts this time too."

Dalvin gave an annoyed hoot, his hands on jean-clad hips. "Chelle, don't go off on an *us-versus-them* theme. People are people. Some are racist and classist bastards, but most of us aren't."

"—Intentionally," was her only response.

They glared at each other for a few seconds, and Anica wasn't sure what to say. Bobby finally intervened. "I have to admit, it is usually the alphas that go off the reservation and commit crimes. A *lot* of alphas truly believe they're better. Alphas better than non-alphas, Sazis better than humans. It's where the plague came from . . . the *cure* that made Luna Lake come about. The human family members rose up and reminded us that we *aren't* better. Out of frustration for being slighted, ignored, and abused, they turned into terrorists and killed thousands of our kind. But Sargon killed hundreds of humans in his quest to make Sazi the dominant species on earth. Maybe thousands. We don't truly know how many he killed. So, who's better? More special?" He kicked the edge of the step for emphasis. "*None* of us. We all have the capacity to be monumental asses. Assholery and violence seem to be the two things we all truly have in common."

Anica had no response to that, and it didn't appear that Rachel or Dalvin did either. The pause grew uncomfortable quickly, but what made her look up was the sudden influx of fresh smoke. "We should go inside now?" Talking about something that couldn't be fixed would not find who killed Paula, and the fire was definitely moving toward them. "We have little time, yes? The smoke, it is new . . . not old trees from far away."

Bobby licked his lips, his tongue flicking out like a snake, but she wasn't thinking of him that way anymore. "Yeah, we need to get to it." He turned and stepped through the doorway, crooking his finger for them to follow.

"I may keep my eyes open? No blindfold?" She didn't want to disobey Papa, but she wanted to see the crime scene. She wanted to learn this so badly. It was something she could do better than others. Like Bojan could cook, and Samit could work with engines.

Bobby shook his head. "I doubt you're skilled at lying . . . Your father would know and I'll bet money he'll ask." But then his eyes began to twinkle. "Something just occurred to me, though. I really don't have a blindfold handy that would fit a bear face. Even money it'll slip up to your ears if you trip."

Her smile likely looked like she was angry, but the oranges' scent would give her away. "I will try very hard to not be clumsy enough for that to happen."

Rachel grabbed the blue and white bandana Bobby tossed over Anica's head. "I'll let you do the honors," Bobby said. "After all, you're her guard."

Anica tried to stand very still while she tied the bandana around her eyes. "Boy, you aren't kidding. It doesn't fit her face." She tried to tie it around her head, around her snout, and even around her ears, without success. "How about I just do this?" She placed the cloth loosely over Anica's head and tucked it around her ears. It was fairly thin cloth. Even in the shadow, she could faintly see. Not clear detail, but enough to walk.

"My eyes, they are covered. It is what Papa wanted."

"Works for me," Bobby said with a serious expression that didn't match his scent. "Long as your nose isn't covered. Let's go. Let the scents tell the story. Smell every surface you can."

Rachel stood by her side until they reached the doorway; then she let Anica go ahead. The kerchief blurred her vision

as she walked into the house. She could see light through
the windows and spots of light on the floor but most of
the furnishings and colors were muted or tinged with blue.
Rachel's voice was quiet and low when she spoke, as though
she didn't want to disturb the dead. "Ick. I'm glad you can't
see this, Anica. There's blood everywhere."

Bobby's voice came from deeper in the house in response.
"Ignore the blood, Anica, unless it's not the deceased's. Find
what eyes don't see. Focus on what the smells tell you."

But she wanted to see. At least where she was going.
When Anica looked down, she could at least see where she
was walking. The floors were wood but were covered with
scatter rugs. The one under her paws now was very like the
ones that she and Mama used to make . . . braided from
strips of old clothing, softened from years of wear and
washing. She leaned down and sniffed. She could smell Paula
mostly, the scent of a thousand meals served covering the
soles of her shoes. The famous-singer perfume soaked deep
into the cloth along a route that stepped over a very particular path. As she snuffled along the curved edge of the
braided cotton, other images came to her mind. A spilled
cola and drips of coffee dotted here and there, heavy with
chemicals that tried to pretend they were hazelnut. Then,
other footprints that were heavier, pressing dirt into the
fibers. "This is not Paula. It is the man."

Bobby walked into the room. She could see the tips and
feet of boots made from a lizard, which seemed odd for a
snake to be wearing. "Point with your claw to where you
smelled the man." She did and he put a bright yellow round
sticker on the floor next to the spot. "Okay, move on. Don't
get buried in the scents this first time. We don't have much
time."

Rachel smelled frustrated. The burnt-metal scent blended with the metallic blood so it almost seemed like Paula was still alive. "Shouldn't we be taking evidence with us? Fingerprints or trace evidence? Putting it in envelopes, like cops do? And what about gloves?"

Anica had wondered the same thing but didn't want to seem naive. Dalvin let out a small chuckle as he moved around the living room. "You watch too many crime shows, Chelle. The evidence we gather is in our heads. The sights, the smells, the taste. When we go before the Council, the seers dig through our heads, pull out the whole experience, and dump it straight into their heads. It's as though they were here with us. A strand of hair can't do that, or a fingerprint. We investigate at a different level than humans."

Part of Anica was intrigued, but part was horrified. "The Council has witches who can see my thoughts?"

Bobby patted her cloth-covered head. "Don't call them *witches* to their faces, or even think it too loud. A few of them, like my friend Tony, might find it funny. At least one I know wouldn't. She's a little sensitive about her gift."

Rachel shifted her feet so she was facing Bobby. "You said your friend was an attack victim, like us. How did that happen? Don't only the top alphas become seers?"

Now he laughed out loud. "All of the *rules* of the Sazi that everyone talks about? Tony eats them for breakfast. He doesn't conform to any of the rules. The ones he doesn't break outright he bends to fit his mood. If you're good enough at what you do, you can make your own rules."

His words struck Anica in the chest like a hammer. She reached up with her paw and pulled the cloth from her head. "This is what I wish to do. Make my own rules. So I must become very good. I cannot become good with blind."

"You go, girl." Rachel was smiling down at her, the same scent spilling from her as she had smelled earlier.

She flared her nostrils, trying to catch the smell, to remember it. "The smell, just now. Is emotion? What is it?"

Bobby seemed preoccupied, putting stickers on various surfaces, from the wall to the edge of a bookcase and the shade of a lamp, but he responded. "Pride. Sort of like cloves, but sweeter. Rachel is proud of you. Not the emotion I'd recommend, by the way."

"Yes. Like *palačinke*. I smell earlier, but did not know name." She had smelled it from Tristan, but she couldn't remember what she had said at that moment for him to react with pride.

Rachel approached him, touched his arm to get him to look at her. "Why wouldn't I be proud of her for wanting to get better?"

Not just his eyes met hers. Anica felt some of his magic leave her to surround Rachel, freezing her in place. He leaned in very closely, until their noses were almost touching. "Because you weren't proud of her for wanting to be good. You were proud of her for wanting to disobey her father and break the rules. Let me be very clear, Ms. Washington. My friend, who broke the rules? He had the ever-loving shit kicked out of him multiple times. Once was on my recommendation. He nearly died several times. I won't hesitate to do the same to you or Ms. Petrovic if you step on the wrong toes or break the wrong rule."

Dalvin sighed and moved closer. "Bobby, please. Rachel doesn't condone breaking the law. She's just trying to get her feet under her after a lifetime of hell."

Bobby lifted his chin until he was looking up at Dalvin. Rachel still seemed frozen, her mouth slightly open. Even a tiny spot of spittle shimmered, held in place at the edge of her lip. "I'm well aware of her past. I read the files of everyone in town on the way here. I also know several Council members have taken a personal interest in her. What I don't know is *why*."

Anica felt a tightening of his power around her, pressing against her fur until it was tight and uncomfortable. "*Don't* follow her example. Learn well; be strong. But don't break rules. You're not predator enough to pull it off."

He released his magic abruptly, standing up as he did so. Anica could feel the sensation like a slingshot against her skin. Rachel fell forward hard, but Dalvin reached out and caught her before she hit the floor. "Asshole," she muttered under her breath as she shook off the sensation. If Bobby heard it, walking down the hall, he made no comment.

What he said instead was directed to her. "Anica, get back to smelling, please. Adway, come help me with the victim." Dalvin took a deep breath, let it out slow, and moved away from Rachel to join Bobby in a room Anica couldn't see.

Rachel frowned. "I'm sorry, Anica, but I'm out of here. I thought he was cool, but apparently, he's just another jerk."

"Rachel—" Anica reached out, touched her leg with one paw. She wanted to say so much, but her friend had such anger, deep down. "You are like me. You wish to fight for all . . . those who cannot fight for themselves. You wish to lash out to those who hurt you. I wished that too. But Mama told me once that first step to fight whole world is to *forgive*. I asked her why forgive horrible people? She said there is often truth and pain inside horrible people and to forgive is to set the pain free so there can be trust. You must let go of anger. Learn to forgive."

Rachel snorted, her arms crossed over her chest defiantly. "Trust and forgiveness won't change evil. Only force will."

Anica nodded her head. "No, you cannot change evil. You can only contain it or destroy it. But whole world is not evil. Only little part. Trust and forgive are for those who *can* change. Those who are willing to live with rules for all." She pointed to the next room with her paw, her claws pulled inward carefully. "Snake policeman is not wrong. He wishes all to follow rules, which is what I wish and you wish too. Yes? No more hateful people, who steal children or force bad things on others. No people who kill people."

Rachel moved her head from side to side, lowering her arms and tucking her hands inside the pockets of the sweatshirt. "Yeah, I guess. But I *really* hate when people hold me with magic. It pisses me off. Makes me feel—"

"Powerless?" Anica finished. "Yes. I feel same. But in times we can control us, *we* control. You see? They cannot take what we control." She looked around the room. "And what we control today is search for killer. We look; we listen; we smell. You will help?"

Rachel let out a small laugh that made Anica happy. She reached down and ruffled the fur between her ears. "Yeah, I'll help. I didn't like Paula, but I'll help *you*."

"Good." She lowered her voice, motioned with her head for Rachel to bend closer. "I agree with you that we should have evidence to take with us. In case seers are not close. You have fingers. Take little bit where yellow spots are. What will hurt anyone?"

"Right under the agent's nose?" Her friend was whispering now, close to her ear. "What if he sees?"

"Then we stop. But perhaps he not stop us? I will say I

want to save for later, learn how to smell correctly. It is true, so no lie smell."

She nodded quickly. "Okay, you go sniff around in another room. I'll take care of it."

Anica padded across the living room toward an open door. The couch in the living room was old, threadbare, dirty, which didn't seem like Paula. She was always careful with her appearance. Uniform always clean, nice shoes. When Anica looked closer, she realized it didn't match the rest of the furniture. The other wood was pine and oak. The wood on the arms of the couch was red. She padded over to sniff the couch. It didn't smell like Paula, which wasn't right. She should have sat on it. It faced the television. There were magazines on the short table in front of it.

She decided it was important to tell the others about it. Halfway across the room, one of the boards underfoot bent under her weight, even though the others seemed sturdy. She heard a pop and the familiar scent filled her nose, making her heart start to race.

Anica yelled for the others, and started to run. "Leave! Leave the house. There is dynamite in couch!"

Rachel's head rose and she raced toward the scent of the blood. "Dalvin! Get out of the house! Anica smelled a bomb!"

Bobby and Dalvin came out from the back, carrying the bloody body of Paula. Anica watched as her head lolled to the side. Her eyes were open, her mouth frozen in a scream. Her throat had been torn to shreds. It was nothing more than shards of meat. "You must hurry. Please."

"Yep, I can smell it. The fuse is burning. No telling how much time we have." Bobby was swearing under his breath, pushing Paula's legs as Dalvin nearly ran backward with Paula's shoulders held as high as he dared.

Rachel held open the front door and Anica fled the building with the others hot on her heels.

Sound and motion seemed to slow and then speed up as an explosion from behind caught them, threw all of them up and forward to land at least three meters away. When Anica hit the ground, she was in human form. Not a surprise Bobby couldn't hold her during the impact. She turned her head to look at the house. Fire and debris shot into the sky but hit a container of magic and flowed out and around, trying to escape. But the magic was stronger. She couldn't tear her attention away as the building imploded in a collision of magic and dirt. It compressed inward, pushing the fire down onto itself. Deprived of oxygen, it collapsed, leaving nothing more than a pile of rubble that had been a house.

A warmth penetrated her in a wave and she turned suddenly, looking for the source. Tristan was coming up behind her, unfolding a blanket that he draped over her shoulders. She didn't feel cold, but Papa wouldn't like her being naked around all these men.

Tristan's mouth was moving, but she couldn't hear anything. The explosion must have made her deaf. She hoped it was only temporary. She shook her head and pointed to her ears. Seconds later, she heard his voice in her mind, echoing like a low bell.

Are you all right?

She spoke out loud because it seemed wrong somehow to speak in his mind with the others present. It was too . . . personal, even though she doubted it was to him. "There was bomb. I smelled it and we were able to get out." She turned to Rachel and the others and shouted in case they couldn't hear either.

"Are you okay?!"

Bobby was on his knees, shaking his head slowly, like he was trying to orient himself. Dalvin was on his back, just beginning to move his legs. The movement was tentative; then his leg twitched and she could smell his pain. He must have broken something. Rachel crawled to his side, rubbing the side of her head, where there was a flow of blood.

They didn't respond to her.

Tristan touched her shoulder. **I don't think they can hear. You stay here and rest for a minute. I'll go talk to Bobby. Don't worry. Nobody will have heard the explosion. I blocked the sound.**

It made her frown, but she couldn't get the fuzzy out of her head enough to ask him how he had done that, or how he knew to be here, just *after* the explosion.

Tristan walked quickly over to Dalvin and checked his legs. He frowned a little and put a hand on either side of his thigh. Anica felt a surge of magic expand outward, surround her, caress her as though it were his hands touching her skin. It made her feel giddy, like she'd just woken after a good night's sleep. She had no idea he was a healer, like the doctor!

Not questioning the assistance, Dalvin started to move his leg, testing the strength. He was on his feet in moments, stretching and surveying what was left of the house.

Then, without a word, Tristan put a hand on Rachel's head and the bleeding stopped, dried right on her skin. She touched her head, then her ear, and got an odd expression on her face.

Bobby wasn't injured, but Tristan offered his hand and Bobby took it, using the leverage to get to his feet. Tristan didn't touch him after that.

She looked up as Rachel came over and pulled off the gray sweatshirt and pants. Anica had forgotten she had other clothes on underneath. The owl shifter took the blanket and held it like a shield between Anica and the others while the little bear got dressed. "Thank you. I'm sorry they were damaged." The back of the sweatshirt had multiple burn holes. Likely only the hood kept her hair from burning. While Anica's skin felt hot, she didn't notice any actual burns when she was dressing. Her fur must have protected her.

Rachel let out a startled laugh and lowered the blanket enough to put her head over the top. "Are you kidding me? You saved my *life*, girlfriend! If you hadn't warned everyone, little bits of us would be splattered all over the tree line."

"How *did* you find the bomb, Anica?" Bobby asked from a dozen feet away. "I didn't smell anything, and I have a very sensitive tongue." Bobby walked their way, carefully averting his eyes until Rachel put down the blanket.

When Anica shrugged, the arms of the shirt fell down over her hands. She pushed them up again. "I did not smell either until fuse was lit. I think there was trigger in floor that I stepped on. I am very sorry." It was embarrassing, to have not noticed that.

"Don't touch her." Tristan had moved, so quickly she didn't even see it happen. He was right next to her, stopping Bobby's hand in mid-air as it reached out to touch her shoulder.

Bobby pulled his arm back, giving Tristan a curious look. "I wasn't planning to hurt her." He motioned with a finger for Tristan to follow him away from the three of them. Tristan gave her a long look and followed him. They stepped a dozen feet away and stood with their heads together for several minutes. She couldn't hear what they were saying and she didn't think Dalvin and Rachel could either, although both of them were very obviously trying, even though they were seeming to look nonchalant.

After several tense moments, Bobby threw up his hands. "All I wanted to know was what made her realize there was a bomb in the house." He walked back toward them and looked right at her. "What made you notice the couch?"

Tristan was only a step behind Bobby. He shrugged and looked to her for confirmation. "The couch was out of place. Right?"

"Yes." It surprised her that he would have noticed. Most men didn't think of design. "The couch was old and not right color for room. I went closer to see and smell, as snak—as Bobby told me. That is when I stepped on board that was weak. I heard noise and smelled cord burning. I have smelled dynamite fuse many times. Papa cleared rocks from land that way when we started farm."

Dalvin was closer to the house, stepping carefully through the debris to get closer to where the explosion started. "So we have a dead woman and either a killer who planned to murder the first responders or a murderer trying to cover his or her tracks."

Anica nodded. "I believe man plan to kill others. Too many careful plans. Old couch removed, new couch brought in. Trigger planted under floor and rug replaced. Bloody leaves buried. No. Murder is only to bring more people to kill. I see many times in Serbia during war. Kill man, wait for funeral. Kill whole femily when they grieve. This is act of hate, not just anger."

"I agree," Rachel said. "But then, whoever did it might not have targeted Paula specifically. Maybe it didn't matter who was killed first, as long as other people were caught in the trap."

Bobby was nodding. "Maybe the important thing is where she lived. This house is one of the furthest from the main part of town. The killer needed time to plan all this. And he probably needed help. I can carry a couch by myself, but it's clumsy. There were corners to get around. I didn't see any chips in the doorways where a couch hit on the way in or out."

"But was it to kill humans or Sazi?" Dalvin's question was wise. There were many humans in town. Explosives could be handled by either.

"Cops." Tristan sounded positive. "The bomb wasn't by the body. That would have been a quick kill with maximum damage to first responders. Paramedics and Good Samaritans go for the body first, not wander around the living room."

"They wish police dead," Anica had to agree. "Wolven police. Papa would not let human police investigate before Wolven, especially since they are in town already."

Bobby let out a hiss that would have made Anica shrink away if it were directed toward her. "Wolven or alphas. A bomb does head and heart very well."

"Head and heart?" Rachel asked what Anica had wanted to. She knew so little about how Sazi law enforcement worked. Of course, if she had known more earlier she probably wouldn't have brought her family over, made them like her. Maybe Samit would still be alive, and Papa and Mama still together, if she hadn't.

Dalvin answered instead of Bobby. "A high-level alpha, and many non-alphas too, can only be killed by taking out both the heart and head simultaneously. One or the other can be healed, but both can't."

A little hoot slipped out of Rachel. She covered her mouth like she had burped. "So I guess bombs are common assassination tools, huh?"

Her fiancé shook his head. "Actually, no. First one I've seen. Usually our animal would prefer to use tooth and claw to kill—whether it's for revenge or lust or anger. Bombs are human tools, for human results." He looked to Bobby for confirmation, but not Tristan. In fact, he hardly paid him any attention at all, as though he weren't there.

Nor was Tristan paying any attention to them. He was standing in the middle of the debris, staring at his feet. He'd taken his shirt off for some reason and just stood there among the smoke vapors rising from the collapsed structure. As she watched, he raised his arms and lifted his head, turning in a circle slowly. That's when she noticed he was also barefoot. Why would he be standing among the shards of glass, nails poking from broken boards and smoking embers?

"Tristan? You are ok—" She stopped when Bobby shook his head quickly, putting a finger to his lips. She must have looked confused, because he stepped closer and lowered his voice to speak next to her ear.

"Don't interrupt him. This is how he investigates."

That's when Dalvin and Rachel both turned to look at Tristan. "What the hell—?" Dalvin's voice was somewhere between amused and annoyed. He pointed at Tristan and tapped Bobby's arm. "He can't be doing that. He's compromising the crime scene. He's not Wolven."

Bobby let out a snort that sounded more like a pig than a snake to Anica. "No. He's not Wolven. Consider him a special investigator on loan *to* Wolven."

"On loan from where?"

The snake policeman shook his head. "Not from *where*. From *who*. And that's all you need to know. Let it go. He'll stay out of our way. We just have to stay out of his. Think of us as the local cops and him as the FBI. He's way above us on the food chain. We can have the collar, but we play by his rules."

Anica stared at his muscled back. He stretched his arms out and flipped his head from side to side. The popping sound of his neck joints settling into place was even louder than the popping of wood embers under his feet. She couldn't help but stare at him, examine every line of his back. His muscles were slender ropes under his skin, not at all like her brothers or even her father, who grew more bulk after they became bears. She took a deep breath, trying to find his scent over the burnt home. It was there, faintly, and her nose locked on, entranced. The exotic blend of spices could fill an entire marketplace. It was only sheer force of will that kept her from walking forward to run her fingers over his skin, to absorb the scent of him into her fingertips.

There was a pale blue tattoo of ocean waves on one tanned shoulder. It seemed an odd tattoo for a bear. Even though she liked the water, enjoyed finding sweet fish, she thought if she were to get a tattoo—which Papa would definitely disapprove of—it would be a ripe raspberry or maybe a pine tree or even a little stone bear totem, like she had seen in museums.

He turned his head, almost startled. He locked his eyes on hers and she couldn't feel the ground under her anymore. There was a weight in his eyes . . . of timeless power that was as deep as the ocean, and as callous. The depth seemed to suck her inside. She was falling into the waves, unable to catch her breath.

And she didn't care if she drowned.

CHAPTER 8

The heat of the smoldering wood underfoot helped ground him like he was meditating on the beach. Tristan opened his senses to the house, let the past soak in. After a few minutes, he realized that just exposing his feet to the scents wouldn't be enough. He stripped off his shirt and immediately a thousand smells flowed into his pores. His species was unique among the Sazi, which was why Ahmad had called him in. His entire body was like a nose. Every pore soaked in scents, so it was nearly impossible to hide a smell for long. He spread his arms, blocking out the chatter of the others behind him so he could unravel the truth.

The fire had released the scents of years past. He smelled the woman who lived here more clearly. She was lonely . . . no, she was *pining*. She was mated to someone who wasn't mated back. She was weary, struggling against the weight of her depression. He turned in a circle and the debris of the bathroom told more of the story. Her hairbrush was thick with oily residue that smelled of sweat and cooking smoke. She wasn't washing her hair, just brushing it and putting it up in a series of combs and bands.

Another turn and the living room hit him full in the chest. The explosive was hard to sort down through. It covered over so many older scents. But he sifted, flicking aside the bits of nitrates to get down to the scent of the people who had existed when the couch had been brought in.

Wait. No, he needed to know more about the couch. Where *had* it come from? This was a small town. There couldn't be a lot of used-furniture stores in town, much less Dumpsters filled with broken-down couches. The couch was little more than toothpick-sized shards of wood and cloth. But even those tiny scraps had memory. The couch had been thick with dust. So Anica was correct that it didn't fit with the house. It had been brought in from . . . he didn't know where. It smelled of the area but didn't as well. He'd recognize the combination of scents if he encountered it again.

An image flashed into his brain, raw and startling. It wasn't a sense of the past, but the present. He could see himself from the outside, as though there were a camera pointed at his back. But it wasn't just an image; it was a sensation. Want, brazen desire, hit his skin, both cloud and club to overwhelm his senses. He turned, startled at the intensity, and saw those eyes, golden and wide with what could only be lust. Anica's pale pink lips were parted, glistening in the fading light. He could almost feel her hands on him, sliding along his skin, her touch both curious and demanding.

He shook his head, trying to force his mind away from continuing that fantasy, to slipping the oversized, shapeless shirt over her head, revealing the slender figure he'd already seen, even if only from behind, then turning her around, pulling her close. Would she sigh? Whimper? Or growl?

No. She wasn't anything like him or his kind. What she saw, sensed, was just an illusion. But he couldn't remember the last time he'd been this attracted to a woman. Decades ago? Centuries?

He had to force his gaze away from her, but he managed. With effort. She seemed almost embarrassed as he slid on his shoes and walked past her, carrying his shirt. "I need to spend some time in town to find the source of some of the scents I got."

Bobby nodded. "It's probably time for all of us to get back. There's not much more we can do here for now. I think I can hold active aversion magic on this area for the night, but we might have to post a guard to watch for people with no sense."

Rachel motioned to the ground, where the body of the house's owner lay, facedown, lifeless. "What do we do with Paula? I mean, I didn't like her, but she doesn't deserve to just stay out here for the animals to eat. She didn't have any family I know of locally. We can't just carry her back to town. There are dozens of humans roaming around."

Anica furrowed her brow, carefully avoiding looking at him. But then she smiled like sunshine breaking through a cloud. "Polar Pops!"

He didn't know what that meant, and Bobby didn't either. But Rachel reached up a hand toward Dalvin, who slapped it.

"What is Polar Pops?" Tristan and Bobby asked nearly in unison.

Rachel answered before Anica could. "The ice cream parlor. They'll be closing for the night soon and there are plenty of coolers and freezers in the basement. We could put Paula in one overnight until we can figure out how to bury her. Although," she continued, sticking her tongue out with obvious distaste, "I don't know how Skew will feel about a dead body sharing space with her ice cream. Not very sanitary."

The more Tristan thought about that, the better he liked it. "Actually, just the basement may be sufficient. I haven't had a chance to check her wounds out for the scent of the killer. This was a personal kill—so teeth or claws. But he'd meant to destroy the body in the explosion—along with our bodies. Probably he would have then set another wildfire to cover the explosion."

Rachel shrugged. "You can't check that here?"

He and Bobby shared a look. "It's a messy process. I doubt you'd enjoy watching and it's difficult to protect the body in the process." That was an understatement. Unlike just sniffing, he had to bury his hands in the body, let what humans now knew as DNA soak into his pores to reveal the killer. At least he didn't examine the body the way Bobby did—cutting the wound apart and rolling it around in his mouth in snake form to taste the flesh, inside and out.

He heard a small noise and looked left to see Anica staring down at the deceased woman's body, looking a little green. "Are you all right?"

She looked up, her face stricken. "Please do not do that to Paula? Her body deserves respect." Anica paused and then shuddered. "Digging around? No. That is not right."

Wait. How had she known that? He stared at her and she stared right back. The thing was, she didn't seem concerned by hearing his thoughts, while he definitely was. It had been years since he'd had to put up shields. Not since his mother was alive. But he still remembered how. Whatever magic Anica had used to slip past his defenses would end here.

"Let's get the body . . . *Paula* . . . to the shop. And I will be respectful."

Bobby picked up the woman like he was carrying a toddler and put her in the back of the ATV. Tristan felt a press of magic from the python shifter that would make the bloody body appear to be something innocuous to passersby. Likely he'd pick a form that would make sense, like a sack of laundry, so nobody would stop to ask questions as they drove through town.

There were too many people to transport in the vehicle. Bobby motioned to Rachel to sit in the back to keep Paula upright and lifted his brows, asking without words who Tristan wanted to walk back with. At this point, he didn't want it to be Anica. That was the path to temptation. "Agent Adway, could I speak with you for a moment?"

Dalvin seemed surprised at the request. He looked at Bobby and then Rachel for their opinion. They both shrugged. So he got out from behind the wheel of the ATV and moved closer to Tristan. Bobby smiled at Anica and opened the tiny half door to the front seat. She got in, shooting a confused and disappointed look at Tristan. Tristan could feel her frustration, yet at the same time, her relief. So, perhaps she was also bothered by the connection.

After Bobby got in the driver's side and the vehicle left, Dalvin held out his hands. "What did you want to talk about?"

"How long have you been in town? I need to know more about the people here—from a Wolven perspective."

The owl didn't answer at first. He crossed his arms over his chest. One long dark finger tapped on the opposite sleeve thoughtfully. "You're not Wolven. Who are you?"

It was a fair question, but he couldn't answer. At least,

not entirely. It really didn't make any sense to pretend to be a tourist anymore. If he wasn't specifically a target of the bomb, at the very least, his presence with Amber Monier and the town's Alpha, as a colleague instead of a prisoner, would have been noticed. "I would appreciate it if you would keep my presence here as quiet as possible. I was sent here by Ahmad to find someone we both thought was long dead. If he's here, the entire town is in danger. Everyone in the world is in danger."

Dalvin swore under his breath. "I *knew* it. I knew Ahmad was looking for someone when he sent us hunting through every house in the town before the peace talks. He wouldn't take *no* for an answer . . . just kept sending us back into the woods, all fucking night long, looking for a ghost that he wouldn't even give us a description of."

"He would have if he could have. It's been a thousand years since anyone has seen him, including me. He could look like anyone by now." That was the frustrating part. He really could be anyone in town. His illusion magic was immense, second only to Sargon's, and he was very skilled at keeping his magic low-key. Even Sargon didn't realize just how powerful he was for years.

Dalvin had an odd look on his face but shook it off after a few seconds. "Well, he's a snake. That's what Ahmad had us looking for. You can't hide that, and there wasn't one in town . . . and not counting Bobby, there isn't one now either." Dalvin seemed so confident, so sure of himself. It nearly made Tristan laugh. The other man noticed and was annoyed. The press of heat against his skin wasn't strong, but it was there. "You think something is funny?"

"No." It wasn't, really. "But you have a lot to learn about power and illusion." The darker man frowned, so it was probably time to change the subject. "Who's the most powerful original resident, someone who's been here since the camp was formed?" Perhaps there was a way to network to get more information about the townspeople. "I need some more information about how the townspeople were vetted."

Dalvin thought for a moment. "Probably the Williams family and the Kragans. They're all owls. There are actually a bunch of birds in town, which is sort of unique. Maybe they know why."

The last name Kragan rang a bell, but he couldn't remember why. "Okay, which way to get to where they live? It doesn't matter which I start with."

"What about Paula? We need to get to the ice cream shop."

It was time for a harsh life lesson for the young Wolven agent. "There isn't anything I can do to bring her back, Agent, and she's not going anywhere. Her death is what Wolven is here for. So, please, go investigate her death. I'm here to investigate what you can't."

Now the agent seemed angry. But his scent said he was merely suspicious. "You said *you* hadn't had the chance to check her wounds. Are you not planning to follow through?"

"Not until everyone is long asleep, Agent. I still have to find out what . . . or, more precisely, *who* I'm looking for."

"I'm sorry," Dalvin said with an expression and scent approaching a sneer, "But I just don't buy that any Sazi can change his or her entire persona. I mean, if an alpha shifts into a owl maybe . . . *just* maybe, he or she could convince strangers they're an eagle of similar size or coloration, at least for a few hours. But you're talking about a *decade*, living in a small town with a hundred people who see you, smell you, shift with you, hunt with you, every day." He shook his head. "Nobody could keep up such a complicated lie. Just the scent of a lie alone would be enough to have someone notice."

"Really." It wasn't necessary to say more. Yes, he could prove his point, but how would it help? The young agent would learn, just as Tristan had learned. There was so much more that magic could do than simply shift you or make you faster or stronger. "So I suppose it would surprise you to learn there are more snakes than just Bobby in town?"

That widened his brown eyes. "One of the volunteers you encountered? I haven't met them all yet."

Tristan shrugged and ran fingers through his collar-length black hair, almost ironically. The weight of it, the texture. All perfect. A perfect lie. "Your job to figure it out. Not mine. I'm just here looking for a ghost . . . remember?"

"Anyone tell you you're an ass?"

He couldn't help but chuckle. "A few people. Ahmad, for example."

There was silence for so long that Tristan had to look up. The shocked expression was priceless. "*Ahmad* thinks you're an ass?"

Tristan's only response was a quirk of a smile. "Oh, and the lovely doctor, earlier today."

It took Dalvin two tries to wrap his lips around Tristan's words. His forehead was furrowed so deep it was surprising he could see from under his eyebrows. "How are you not dead?"

It was a good question. There was a really good answer. "There are only two things that keep an ass alive, Agent. Being that good, or being that *bad*."

CHAPTER 9

She looked so . . . damaged. Paula's skin was white, turning to blue, so the red stain that used to be her neck and chest seemed almost garish. She was fully clothed, which was at least a small dignity. Anica looked around and realized she was the only person in the cool basement who was mourning the woman. Bobby was very carefully sniffing around her neck by flicking his tongue. After what Tristan had thought, she was fairly certain he was being careful for her benefit, not Paula's.

Rachel was searching through the storage area that took up a large section of the room, looking for something to raise the body up from the floor so the blood didn't stain the concrete. Skew had told Anica, during one of her visits to Polar Pops to sample the ice cream, that this building had been used as a storage shed when the town was first set up. It was only in the past few years that the mayor had opened the ice cream shop and put Skew in charge—around the same time the refugee camp had become a formal town, with a post office and a jail and everything.

As a new resident, Anica didn't feel comfortable going

through the cartons and piles of stored items; after all, all these things technically belonged to people who lived in Luna Lake, many of whom Anica did not know at all. Rachel had essentially grown up here and had undoubtedly visited the storage area more than once in her role as the town's Omega, searching for something someone needed. So Anica had asked her friend to find something to protect Paula's body. But she could tell that Rachel's heart wasn't in the task, that she was only looking so she didn't have to stare at the body.

Skew had at first objected to the body in the basement, seeing them enter the empty store and racing to put herself in their path with a shouted, "No, no! Not safe!" But when Bobby had simply pushed past her with magic and brute force, she'd relented and meekly followed them down the stairs. Now she looked like she normally did—not really in touch with what was happening, in her own little world. Her head bobbed and jerked as she looked around the room, as though seeing it for the first time.

"Hey!" Rachel called out from within the path through the ceiling-high boxes, crates, and furnishings. "Found something. Anica, give me a hand."

Anica followed her voice until she could see Rachel trying to pull what looked like a green cot out from among the boxes. "Wait. That box above your head is about to fall!" She rushed forward and stood on tiptoes to steady the rattling carton. It was fairly heavy. While it probably wouldn't kill Rachel, it would have given her a bad headache.

Rachel looked up just as the cot came free from the jumble. "Eep! Thanks. I didn't even notice that one." She had apparently seen one of these types of cots before, because she immediately began to open it up, snapping the legs into position with practiced ease. "I knew there had to be at least one left back here." She set it on its end on the floor. "We all slept on these when we first got to town. They dumped us off the buses in what's now the parking lot at the lake. I just remember everyone being scared." She leaned forward and sniffed the sturdy woven green fabric. "Take a sniff. It still smells like scared kids. That scent never comes out."

Anica didn't smell it. She didn't need to. "I remember scared smell. I could not get out of my nose, off my skin. Weeks after I escape, it won't wash off."

They made their way back to the main room. Skew turned around as Rachel set the cot on the floor with a small clink. Her eyes seemed to clear, as though a fog was passing. She pointed a finger at them. Her voice turned from the regular singsong soprano to a confident alto. "Girls to the left. Boys to the right. Stay in line, kids." She made shooing motions with her hands. "Pick up sheets on the first table, a towel . . . only one per person, on the second table, and a toothbrush and soap on the third. Report back to your cot and wait for someone to talk to you."

She saw Bobby kneeling next to Paula and went over, put a finger aside Paula's neck, and shook her head with a sigh. "This one didn't make it. Pity. Pretty thing." She raised her voice, calling to someone only she could see, "Robert! We need a stretcher." Putting a hand on Bobby's shoulder, she patted gently and said softly, "We're cremating the remains. I hope you understand. We'll do our best to get all her ashes back to you."

She looked squarely at the wall and shouted again. "Robert! C'mon! We have to clear the space. If you can't find a stretcher, get a blanket!" She raced up the stairs, still shouting for people. At least there was nobody to find upstairs and the front door was locked.

Bobby moved his head closer to them. "What is up with her?"

Rachel was shaking. Anica reached out and touched her and the woman's eyes were tearing up. "Rachel?"

Her voice was a whisper, her scent wet with heavy sorrow and the tang of anger. "She's reliving the first day. I remember her like this—back before she turned into sweet, flaky *Skew*. She was a town leader, directing the whole operation. Dozens of buses, hundreds of orphans and frantic adults, looking for their families. And she handled it all. I haven't seen her like"—she pointed at the ceiling—"*this* since . . . since that first day."

Anica stared at the stairs and thought about the little parakeet she'd known for only a month. Skew had stopped yelling. It sounded like she was cleaning, moving chairs around. "What happened to her?"

"I don't know." Her voice was sad, confused. She stared at the stairs. "Is there any way to find out?" She looked at Bobby. "Can she be fixed?"

He took a deep breath and let it out slow. "If she can be, Amber's the one to do it. Nobody better at sorting through mental scars. Honestly, if she's met the woman, I'm surprised she hasn't already healed her."

Anica leaned against the concrete wall and nodded. "She has met Skew. Amber and I ate ice cream together here before the fire got so close. She did not mention healing her."

Bobby reached his arms under Paula and waited until Anica and Rachel got the cot situated under her, then gently draped her on the cot, crossing Paula's arms over her chest.

"Okay, let's get the walk-in cleaned out so we can put her inside. You're right; we don't want to have any food in the same freezer."

Anica's fingers were going numb by the time they finished clearing out the big freezer and her nose could only smell death mixed with fruit pops, which was very strange. All of the smaller freezers had been rearranged and were completely full. As she was coming out with the last few boxes, she saw movement and heard a tapping on the small window at ground level. She couldn't see very well, so she went closer. "Dalvin? Why are you crawling on ground?" She reached up but couldn't quite get the lock on the small window open.

Rachel came out from the freezer, broom and dustpan in hand from sweeping up the remains of boxes they had to open to arrange things in the small freezers. "What are you doing, Anica?" As Rachel walked closer, she saw her fiancé on the other side of the window. "Here, let me get that." She reached above Anica and unlatched the window, using the dustpan to push it up to open it. "Where have you been and what in the world are you doing? Tired of using the front door?"

He let out a snort. "Long story, and have you *seen* the front door? A tank couldn't get in there."

Rachel looked at her, then at the stairs, and then motioned behind. "Go get Bobby. I'll help Dalvin inside. I think we need to go upstairs."

Getting Dalvin through the window took all three of them. Feetfirst hadn't worked at all, so he had to come in headfirst. When his belt got caught on the window frame, they had to push him back out to take off the belt and then try again. While they were waiting, Rachel walked up the stairs. Moments later, she called back down, "Oh, you guys *need* to see this!"

Anica and Bobby looked at each other and then started up the stairs. But Dalvin's voice stopped them. "C'mon, guys. Get me inside first, huh?"

Rachel bounded down the stairs, past them. "You need to see this too. Get on in here."

So back they went to the window. This time, without the belt holding him in, Dalvin easily slipped through the window. "Thanks, guys," he said once he was inside and putting on his shoes, which he'd taken off and tossed in ahead of him. "I'm really wondering what it looks like from the inside. Because from outside, it looks like a pawnshop during a riot."

Anica had no idea what that might look like, so she was very curious. When she got to the top of the stairs, she could only stare in disbelief along with the others.

The entire main floor had been cleared of furniture. Tables and chairs were all piled up in front of the front door. The plate-glass windows with painted cartoon ice cream cones frolicking at the edge of a crescent-shaped lake had disappeared behind heavy metal grates that Anica had no idea existed.

"Look at all the mousetraps!" Rachel's voice was somewhere between amused and disturbed. The traps were set only inches away from one another on the black and white tiled floor, leaving not even enough room to walk. On top of each set mousetrap was a pair of twisted nails. Anica could see that if a mousetrap was set off the nails would pop into the air and embed themselves in whatever was close. It was a very effective trap. "How long did this take to set up?"

Bobby looked at the watch on his wrist. "We've been working on the freezer for about an hour. She moves quick."

Rachel tiptoed into the room, trying not to set off the traps. "Skew? It's me . . . Rachel. Can we talk?"

Anica nudged Rachel and pointed to where Skew, now in falcon form, was perched on top of the white board menu, staring at them. She flapped her wings hard and fast, sending a burst of wind to push her back. It made all the traps vibrate but not pop. Her beak opened and an earsplitting screech filled the room, followed by shouting: "*Snake!* Hide the children!" She said it over and over, sounding for all the world like the alarm in some cars Anica had heard in the airport parking lot.

"Uh-oh," Bobby said. He reached out and pulled Rachel back through the door and backed up a pace so they could all stand together on the top two steps. "If her head has slipped back in time ten years, me being here isn't good. Every snake was a suspect, a threat. I had to go underground for weeks until I could prove myself all over again to the hierarchy."

Rachel shook her head, her scents a muddle of emotions. "She wouldn't hurt you. Skew wouldn't attack a fly."

Bobby sighed. "And I don't want to hurt her. But if her mind is in the past, where all snakes are dangerous, she won't listen to reason."

Dalvin poked his head forward, both surprised and confused. "I didn't even know she was alpha enough to shift before the moon."

Rachel just shrugged. "I can't say I've ever seen her shift outside the moon. But there really hasn't been any need, except for rogue attacks, and those have always been handled by the mayor and sheriff, or the Williamses. The town is pretty close to humanity, and the forest is popular with tourists. We don't tend to shift unless there's good reason."

Anica saw movement outside the thick steel grate over the windows. Tristan was outside, looking in. She heard his voice in her mind: **What's happening in there? Are you okay? I heard screaming.**

Skew is upset. She thinks Bobby is here to hurt the town's children. Her mind . . . it's not stable. Can you—She tried to think how it might be done. **Use your power like at the house? Pop all the mousetraps but keep them from hurting anything?**

She could tell that popping the first mousetrap would set off more. It would be like another bomb exploding. She saw Tristan put his hands on his hips, look over the room. **Yes and no. Yes, I can, but not with all of you inside and not without damaging the building. Magic doesn't trump physics. If you can get the falcon downstairs, I think I can handle the rest.**

Anica turned her head and then ducked back into the stairwell to be heard over Skew's screams. "Tristan is outside. He said he can help if we can get Skew down here with us."

Rachel cocked her head and sounded suspicious. "How do you know that?"

Anica pointed at her head. "He talks to me here. When I couldn't talk with my throat swelled up, he asked if he could. I said it was okay."

Dalvin looked at Bobby with a questioning look. "Is that possible?"

The other man nodded. "Sure. I'm a little surprised he would with a three-day, but he's got the ability. I've talked to him that way myself." He looked up at Skew. "I could put her in a hold, but if she's alphic she'll feel I'm a snake and could fight to the point I have to hurt her. I don't think Dalvin is strong enough to hold her." He mused for a moment, rubbing his thumb and forefinger at the edge of his mouth. "Y'know, most psychotic episodes end by themselves with the right trigger. Anica, could you go get Mrs. Williams? She's been here since the first day. You're the smallest and can get out the window easily. Maybe seeing someone else from that same time could end this quickly."

He stared at the doorway for a moment and Anica could hear the echo of his voice in her head: **Ris, I'm sending Anica to get Asylin Williams. She should be able to reach the falcon's brain. If you need to talk to someone from the early days, she and her husband are two of them.**

Anica nodded. "Yes. I will. Dalvin, could you give me a boost?" He nodded and she turned briefly to Bobby. "Have Tristan meet me around back and I will show him way to house. I would tell him, but my head, it hurts from the mind talking."

She bolted down the stairs with Dalvin right behind her, but not before she smelled a burst of surprised scent coming from the snake agent. She turned her head to see why, but his face was a blank slate. He just stared at her with pleasant ambivalence.

Dalvin locked his hands together into a stirrup that she put her foot in. He lifted her and she crawled through the transom opening. Tristan was on the other side and took her hand to help pull her through. An electric charge ran through her when he did, making her stomach tight and her head almost too clear. Night had fallen completely and the breeze that came from the north held the threat of ice. Not fluffy snow that she could romp through, but heavy, blue ice that would stick to her fur, weigh her down, and cut her feet to ribbons.

Tristan shuddered as the wind raised hair on his bare arms. "You do not like the cold?"

He shook his head. "I come from a warm climate. I haven't seen snow in years."

She motioned for him to follow her. Even with little light to guide her, she could find her way. The Williamses were owls and their home always smelled of freshly killed rodents. It wasn't a bad smell, exactly. It was like a meat-cutting shop. The product was fresh, but it smelled of meat, not fur and life. "This way."

He followed without question. The pine trees that towered overhead created a familiar path. They traveled at an easy jog. She often ran through the forest in the mornings, letting the morning dew soak into her socks and shoes. It made her feel alive. After that, she would dive into the lake, a little farther each day, to catch her breakfast. Of course, she would still go back home and make a real breakfast for Papa and Bojan, but more often Bojan was doing the cooking and Papa was going to the office early, leaving her to eat alone.

"You seem to know the forest well. You jumped over a rock you couldn't have seen."

She smiled, feeling a strange flutter in her chest at the sound of his voice from the darkness. "I have been this way, but I smelled the rock. I don't know how I can tell the height of things from the smell, but I can."

"I understand. I can too." There was a pause as the light of the Williams house came into view. "Do you hate all snakes?"

The question startled her. "Of course," she replied with a light laugh. "They are evil. Even Bobby, I think, is probably evil. Or can be."

Tristan's reply was thoughtful, his scent an odd mix of emotions. "Yes, he can be. But can't bears be evil too?"

That stopped her short. She turned to face him. "Of course. It was bears who stole me, took me to the snakes. It was bears who turned the children. But it was *snakes* who put them up to it. Either for money or for fear." She stared at him, willing him to understand. He seemed angry, but she wasn't sure why. "You understand, don't you?"

"Strangely," he said with a sigh, "I do." He pointed to the porch of the large log cabin ahead. "Is that Mrs. Williams?"

It was. Anica leaped into a sprint again. "Mrs. Williams!" Asylin Williams turned and saw them running. Her eyes immediately became alert and she came down the stairs.

"Anica, right? What's wrong, sweetie?" Her eyes had gone golden and shining and the power that surged from her was protective, like a mama bear sweeping a cub under her body for protection.

"Skew has had an attack. She is at the Polar Pops and has set traps all over the floor. She thinks the Wolven snake agent is attacking children. Rachel said she was saying words like from the first day the town was started. But now she is screaming, 'Snakes!' and made traps."

"Oh, lord. I was afraid this would happen one day." She shifted so quickly that Anica's eyes couldn't follow the change. One minute she was a nice dark-skinned lady, and the next a large white owl. "Okay, you and your bear friend stay here. *Don't* go back there. I'll take care of this." She fluttered into the air and circled once. "Do me a favor. Knock on the door and tell John where I've gone. I might need his help too, so I need him to lock up the house."

Anica nodded and Tristan trotted up the steps to the front door, starting to knock even before Asylin had soared out of sight over the treetops. A tall, slender dark-skinned man answered the door. "Yes?"

Anica came up to stand beside Tristan on the wide pine porch that smelled of a hundred different animals and happy memories. Tristan stuck out his hand. "Mr. Williams, I don't think we've met. Tristan Davies. I was sent here by the Council for an investigation. I'm hoping you can help me with some information."

That was not what he was supposed to say. Anica stepped in front of him. "Asylin asked us—"

Tristan cut her off with a grasp on her upper arm that surprised her with the intensity. "Asylin had to run an errand. She asked us to tell you she'd be right back. Can we come in?"

Anica had heard Rachel tell of Mr. Williams's suspicious mind. But she didn't notice it here. He opened the door wide and stepped back. "Of course. But I don't know how much help I'll be."

She walked in, followed by Tristan. John walked past the darkened living room. The television was on and she could smell Tammy, the cougar shifter about her own age, and the Williamses' two younger children, both future owl shifters. In fact, she smelled too many owls in the room. She turned around, looking for another person, but saw only Tristan and John. That's when she realized it was *Tristan* who smelled of owl. But he was a bear! How could he smell like an owl? Yet that same exotic spice was now buried under the warm fluff of feathers. How was that possible?

John led them down the hallway by the staircase to the kitchen at the back of the house. He sat down at the head of the table and held out his hand, offering chairs to them. Her chair was also made of the same pine that surrounded them, making it hard to know if her nose was smelling right. There was so much pine around. She had to close her eyes, to sort as the snake agent had told her. While she inhaled, matched scents, Tristan began to speak.

"When the town was first formed, how were the refugees selected?"

John let out a laugh that had a brittle edge. "*Selected?* I doubt there was any sort of process anywhere. We took all comers. If a bus showed up, from anywhere in the country, we off-loaded them and gave them a cot. We had every species, every age. Everyone was scared and cut off from their families."

Tristan nodded, tapping his finger on the table. "Okay, then, how about after . . . once the dust settled and some families had reunited? Who decided who stayed and became a permanent member of the town?"

The other man shrugged. His fluffy green sweater stretched, showing just how muscular he was under the knitted wool. "I suppose Van Monk probably made the final selection, although it just sort of sorted itself naturally. We only have so much land here, just fifty acres, so we're limited on the number of houses we can build."

Tristan's voice was soft and conversational: "And a lot of people didn't want to live in such close quarters?"

"Not everyone is suited to living here. That's true. People from big cities who were used to malls and Wi-Fi on every corner found it difficult to live in the wilderness. Those families left early on. Orphans tended to stay. Asylin and I raised them as our own."

"I'm looking for single males in the thirty-to-fifty age group, but alphas, so they might be older."

John leaned back in his chair, thinking while tapping a

single finger on the edge of the table. "The school principal, Nathan Burrows, is single and an alpha bear. But he moved here later, probably five years ago. The Kragan brothers are both single, and so is their sister, but they're ancient. Several hundred years at a minimum."

Anica suddenly realized what Tristan was looking for, but he was going about it wrong. "Were there any newlyweds? Anyone who seemed more involved with each other than the snake crisis?"

She saw Tristan glance at her and smelled *palačinke* again. Bobby had called it pride. That was nice. John shook his head, his scent just owl, no emotion at all. "Not that I can remember. But it's been ten years. I'll think about it more and talk to Asylin."

Tristan still smelled of owl, which frustrated her. He must have noticed it in her scent, because he put his hand on top of hers and patted it. "Thank you. And I would appreciate it if you would keep this low-key. If the person I'm looking for is here, there's some danger involved."

The front door opened and closed. Anica recognized the scent and voice of Denis, Alek Siska's younger brother. "Man, I can't believe you watch that crappy fashion show." The words were harsh, but the emotion behind them was warm. He came through the door and stopped cold. "Oh. Sorry, Dad. I didn't know you had company." He smiled behind a curtain of golden hair that fell down over his eyes. "Hey, Anica. How you doin'?"

Denis had been very nice to her ever since she moved to town, just like his older brother. "Hello, Denis." She motioned with her hand. "This is Tristan. He's new in town too."

Denis pulled his attention to the side and the smile crumbled, fell away like dust. "Hey. You here fighting the fire?"

"Just passing through." Tristan's voice was a little deeper, his scent not aggressive, but not friendly either.

"That's cool." The smile was back, a little fragile, but there. "'K. I'm gonna head to my room."

John looked up at him, then tapped him on the forearm. "No video games until your homework is done. I want to see that term paper done *before* it's late, for a change. Remember our agreement."

Denis gave an exaggerated sigh. "Yeah, okay." When John cleared his throat meaningfully, he added, "I mean, yes, sir."

"Better." He winked at his foster son. "Don't forget to give the kids a kiss good night."

"'K." He pushed open the swinging door and called out, "Hey, Mom. Just headed up to do my homework!"

"Well, my goodness!" Asylin's voice was pleased from the hallway. "What a nice surprise. Thank you." Anica could feel warm maternal magic flow through the doorway that made her heart twinge a little. She missed that feeling when Mama hugged her, like a warm, fluffy blanket in front of the fire. Moments later, Asylin pushed open the door and let out a short laugh. "Well, no wonder he was so cooperative. You already gave him the nightly lecture." She ruffled John's hair. There was a warm flow of magic between the two of them . . . an unspoken conversation that no one else was part of.

She looked at Anica and Tristan. "Problem solved. Did you tell John yet?"

Anica shook her head. "Not yet."

Addressing her husband, Asylin shook her head. "Poor Skew. Her mind is really going. She slipped back to our first day here this time."

"Oh, no. Including the snake?"

She nodded and addressed the explanation to the two of them, instead of John. "There really was a snake that first night—a viper who had wrapped herself around the gear-box of one of the buses. She went for one of the elderly cats, not realizing the old girl was actually pretty tough." Asylin shrugged. "Just now, I just told Skew that Abigail killed the snake and everything was fine. That's what really happened, back then, so there was no lie to smell. Skew snapped right out of the past."

"What about traps? They were everywhere."

John winced. "She did the mousetrap thing . . . with the nails? Ooo. Ouch. That's going to be tricky. They'll scatter everywhere and impale the walls. Plus anyone standing in the way."

She sighed. "I haven't really figured that one out. I'm hoping I'll think of something overnight."

"I actually did have one idea. I thought of this when I saw Skew perched on the signboard," Anica said.

John opened his arms wide. "Shoot. I'm open to ideas. I can't even imagine the mess over there, but I'm betting I'm going to be stuck fixing the walls if those nails start flying."

Anica took a deep breath. It was refreshing to be able to speak her mind without Papa interrupting. "It will take several birds working together, but if they all fly up the stair-case with a large tarp, like the one on the ground by the food tables in the center of town, and all drop at same time, all mousetraps will go off at once—"

Tristan finished the thought. "But nothing will get past the tarp because of the weight. A good idea."

Asylin smiled brightly. "We'll have to trim it to fit so the counter doesn't throw it off-balance, but it should work. We'll do it first thing in the morning, before the store is supposed to open. Thank you, Anica. That was a very good idea." She leaned down and kissed her husband on the cheek. "I'm going to get the kids up to bed. Don't stay up too late."

Anica stood as well. "We must leave too. I must go home to get Papa's dinner ready."

John showed them out the front door. The town was easily visible because of the blinking red and blue lights. Fire didn't sleep, so neither did those who fought it. She blinked several times and struggled not to rub her eyes, because that just made it worse. "I am tired of my eyes burn from the smoke."

Tristan put his fingers on her chin and turned her face into the light. A nice tingle made her neck warm like in a hot bath. "They are fairly red."

It made her laugh. "You use red light to tell me eyes are red?"

He twisted her head a little more, and then smiled. "They're red in the blue light too."

She couldn't help but smile at his twinkling eyes. She couldn't tell whether the blue glow was from the lights or from his magic. "And yours are blue in red light. We are pair, yes?"

The smile stilled and his voice lowered, grew softer. "Yes." He leaned forward and she didn't stop him as his lips brushed hers. The taste of him was like his scent: rich, exotic, something that she should not be able to afford to indulge in. Her blood heated in her veins, made her heart race. When he wrapped an arm around her, pulled her close to him, and opened her mouth with his, she couldn't seem to breathe. Not her first kiss, by any measure, but it was fast becoming one of the best. She leaned into him, feeling dazed, her eyes closing because her lids were too heavy to keep open.

A whimper escaped her throat and it urged him on. He let out a small growl and ate at her mouth, now moving one hand to slide through her hair, letting it fall through his fingers before clutching it possessively.

Her skin seemed to vibrate from the weight of his magic pressing against her. She needed to touch his skin. The fascination that had held her transfixed at Paula's house became a command she couldn't ignore anymore. Her hands slid under his shirt and his moan filled her mouth. His fingers dug in just as his tongue found hers and began to twirl and dance.

She couldn't move, couldn't think past the growing heat that filled her belly and spread between her legs and then through her body. When his hand lowered, cupped her bottom, her breasts tightened, felt heavy and hot. The boys she normally dated were clumsy, their foreplay rushed or rough. But Tristan's touches were both confident and knowing. Every contact was clearly intended to heighten her arousal. She knew then he could do anything to her and she wouldn't be able to stop him . . . and wouldn't try.

"I almost hate to interrupt you. Almost." The baritone voice came with a blast of heat that felt like touching a hot poker in the fire. Tristan looked up sharply, saw the face of a man, and sucked in a harsh breath. He instantly pulled her behind him, shielding her from the magic that should sting but didn't.

"So Ahmad wasn't wrong. You are still alive, Lagash." The man he'd called Lagash was tall and bald, with skin the color of Ahmad's, from the Middle East. He smelled like a railroad. She couldn't think of a better way to describe it. It was oil, hot metal, and the bitter scent of wooden railroad ties bound to the rails. The heat in her body from Tristan's touch turned cold and dangerous. The cold was his normal temperature. She knew that now. The overwhelming scent of anger filled the air, and she wasn't sure who it was strongest from. She didn't know what their past was together, but they definitely had one.

"Oh, I'm most definitely alive. I find it amusing Ahmad couldn't find me, right in plain sight, and that you haven't either. You've passed right by me, several times. Of course, you've just arrived and have been a little . . . *busy* with the locals, haven't you?" He let out a low, dark chuckle that made Anica shiver.

The look he gave her was predatory. It was the same look she gave fish in the stream. *Run. Hide. But you will still be dinner.*

Tristan's power was flaring up, the blue from his eyes expanding to become a flame that surrounded him. It should burn her skin, should make her run screaming. Lagash didn't raise his power, but she could feel it press against them both. Tristan's voice was low, dangerous: "You do realize I've grown up, and outgrown you."

The other man let out a low chuckle. "You're still a little worm, barely capable of squirming under my feet. But just as a reminder—" Lagash swept his hand sideways and a burst of wind came from nowhere. It lifted them both off their feet and threw them through the air so fast and far that it felt like she had been shot from a cannon. They hit the second-story wall of the Williams house with such force that it stole the breath from Anica's lungs and made stars appear in her vision. They dropped to the ground and she couldn't seem to get up.

Tristan was immediately on his feet, as though only a light breeze had passed by them. But the one he'd called Lagash was gone. He'd melted into the blackness of the forest, leaving no trace behind. Not even a scent.

"Damn it!" Tristan shouted in frustration. Anica was trying to get her feet under her. Everything hurt, like she had after she'd escaped the cave. It had been many years since she'd hurt this much. Tristan was immediately at her side, helping her up. "Are you all right? I'm very sorry, Anica. I shouldn't have involved you."

"But you did not. You didn't bring me to him. He came looking for you." She truly believed that. Tristan meant no danger to her.

"Yes. He did. And I need to find out how he knew where to look."

CHAPTER 10

Why had he gotten distracted by a slip of a girl? He had Lagash in his sights. He could easily have fought him, killed him, and eliminated the threat. He could be headed back home by now. If not for protecting the girl.

Why was he even protecting Anica? Spending precious time with her he could be using to search? Yes, she was an innocent, but many of those here were. They were damaged, fragile. But that wasn't it.

What was it about her?

She let out a huff of air. "He is very angry. If he has been successfully hiding for so long, why be angry?"

That was a very good question. "Because I could end his game?"

She shook her head, staring at the part of the forest where he'd disappeared. "No. That is not it. He was *successfully* hiding. He brags about it. You see? Peppers is wrong smell. He should smell of *palačinke* or oranges."

Tristan tried to wrap his head around that. "*Palačinke?*

Isn't that a cheese dessert, like a blintz? Why would he smell like cheese?"

She was animated, excited by some sort of revelation. "The snake, Bobby, he tells me of emotions that smell of food. When you are proud of me at house, it smells of *palačinke*. Bobby says it is the cloves, but it is more than just cloves. It is the sweet, and the rich too. And happy is oranges. Bobby says it is because I am human before Sazi. I compare scents to things I know."

He was starting to realize why he liked talking to her. She thought very logically, but in a way that was totally unique. "So Lagash doesn't smell proud or happy. He smells angry." He needed to think about that. What would cause anger after a decade alone in a small town . . . one that he could have left any time he wished? He could have moved any-where. Couldn't he have? He could have even moved *home*, back to Akede, or even the city named for him, Lagash. It was Iraq now, but he would be accepted there. The language had changed, but only a little, and his skin color was cor-rect. "Let's get you home to clean up. I need to do some thinking."

"But you have nowhere to sleep. We must find you room first." She paused and turned around to stare at the house, putting her hands on her hips and cocking her head to the side long enough that her shining hair fell down to cover one eye. "Why did no one come outside?"

"Excuse me?" But then he thought back. They hit the side of the house with enough force to likely knock items off the wall—and on the upper floor. "Why *didn't* they come out?"

"We must ask." She trotted around to the front of the building.

Had the wave of magic been powerful enough to have knocked out the residents of the home, or even killed them? If it had been, perhaps Lagash had lost some of his power, or his own power had increased to the point Ahmad didn't need to fear him anymore.

"Come." She grabbed his hand, heading for the stairs, and the shock of electricity that had made it so easy to kiss her flowed up his arm again. "We will talk to Mrs. Williams. She will know where you can sleep. If she does not, Papa will know."

Her father? Oh, that would be a bad idea. "And have him smell that we've been kissing? After that scene at the woman's house?"

Realization came to her face and faded to a horrified expression that rose into her scent. "Oh! What do we do? Papa will be furious!"

"We need to see if you can shower first, and then I need to go back to my hunt."

Her pretty face fell into confusion and a sad scent rose from her in a misty cloud. "Why must you kill this man? Why can he not live his life in peace?"

Peace? Lagash had never been interested in peace. How could he explain this to her in a way that would make sense? She was so very young. "Did you ever read about modern dictators in school? Stalin? Hitler?"

She nodded. "Yes. Of course. They were very bad men."

"Yes, but more—they were men on a mission. Certain people were in the way of their mission, and they needed to be eliminated. No matter who they were or whether they were innocent. They were eliminated because they were inconvenient. Long before those other men existed, others like them also had missions. Lagash and his master, Sargon, intended to rule the world. They were very good at it. Sargon was smart . . . truly brilliant, and powerful, both magically and physically. He created an empire. But he was heavy-handed and in time evil, because it was so easy to be—like Stalin. People feared him. In the times he was not bad, he was a great leader, so people followed him, but warily, always watching for his next evil. Lagash, on the other hand, was charismatic, like Hitler. He could tell people exactly what they wanted to hear, and made them believe that being bad was acceptable. They followed him because they believed he was *right*. Which is worse?"

Anica was listening, really listening. "I believe Hitler is worse."

He nodded, knowing that she was understanding. "Why?"

"Because Stalin create horrors, but people recognize the evil and know he need to be stopped. Hitler make people think horror was okay. They allow it, ignore, and choose not to see, so it spread."

"Exactly. Let me show you something." He touched her face, and when he slid into her mind she didn't fight it. It wasn't often he showed his memories to someone, let them live a bit of the past he'd lived through.

He remembered the day so clearly. It was the day he knew he had to leave Akede forever. It was the day he met Ahmad, the youngest son of Sargon. Torches lit the hallways into the great hall. He hated coming to the great hall because he had grown to detest the smell of creosote, which was Lagash's trademark. Ris could still feel the sting of the lashes to his back for daring to speak up against the killing of a cook for bringing Lagash's dinner late. But Lagash was the cup-bearer, the second in command of temple affairs. The cup-bearer had the right to kill a mere cook for the oversight.

Why Ris was spared death for his arrogance in speaking against Lagash he never found out.

A crowd was milling around the audience hall, which smelled of fresh plaster and paint from the frescos that covered the walls from floor to ceiling. Brightly colored chariots raced across the walls on a pale blue and yellow backdrop, surrounded by predatory animals that mirrored the shifter residents of the town. Snakes, great cats, raptors, all shared space in the hunting scenes. Grand statues of the finest artistry filled the corners. The eyes of the snakes and lions glowed with gems that reflected the firelight and gave the appearance of magic spilling out from inside.

When Sargon entered the room in his shining white robes, followed by his children, silence fell. Their king did not brook idle chatter.

The children, dressed in fine linens and jewels that reflected their status, took their places behind their father's throne, while his consort, a spider shifter who had pledged her loyalty to Sargon, curled at his feet. There were no spiders on the walls. It was too uncomfortable a reminder that even their own kind was prey to something.

With any luck, the king would announce that the war had ended. Too many good men had gone to battle and had not come back. Too many women in the city had been pressed into service they were not suited for. Loading and unloading ships, cutting stone for the next great monument, digging troughs for water.

Instead of Sargon speaking, however, it was Lagash who stood from his smaller throne beside Sargon's. Excitement rose in the room, because he was always interesting to hear.

"People of Akede, hear me! The war with Nineveh is over! Our armies have spread the light to a new people! All hail

Sargon, king of Akede, overseer of Inanna, king of Kish, anointed of Anu! Sargon's benevolence will protect those who follow him."

The crowd cheered, including Ris, because it was long past time for people to come home.

"But there are still many who do not follow, who do not understand that those of us with the spirit of the animal inside were intended by the creator to rule. We are stronger, are we not?"

"Yes!" the crowd shouted back.

"Are we not blessed by Anu to rule over the lesser beast?"

"Yes!" roared the crowd.

"Too often," Lagash said, his voice full of barely contained anger, "those who have no animal spirit rise up. They rise up in fear and shame. They strike out at us to deprive us of what we have. To make *us*, we blessed of Anu, feel shame. Have you not felt the anger and hatred of the lesser beasts, the traders who come but won't stay? The citizens of other lands you may visit who run from you, or your mate, or your children, or hide their wares so you cannot buy?"

"Yes!" the crowd shouted again. Ris could smell their rising anger.

"It is time, people of Akede! No longer will it be a crime to bestow the gift of an animal spirit on the lesser beasts. To know the light, the life of Anu inside, to allow others to bask in the greatness of like beings, this gift, this *right*, must no longer be hidden away or forbidden."

There was a hush, while the people tried to understand what was being said.

"Do you not wish that all of your families could feel the joy of the animal spirit?"

A few shouted, "Yes!" But not all. There was a nervousness.

"Do you not wish that wherever you walked, you could know and trust the other man as a brother or sister of Anu?"

Now more people shouted, "Yes!"

"Then know that the blessing of Sargon is with you! Know that you, the highest of the high, the blessed of the blessed, may share your animal with all you encounter. If they are strong enough, if Anu wills, they will be turned and will come to understand the joy that we each know! The people of Akede will reign supreme. Go forth and take your families to the widest reaches of the world. Build your homes and share the spirit of Anu with all you encounter. Those who are not chosen by Anu will fall and you, as the blessed, will be entitled to what they leave behind. You will become more blessed with each life you touch, the riches you add to your own from those who Anu turns away from."

"Yes!"

Ris felt uneasy, seeing the growing fervor of the crowd. Was Sargon truly condoning the forcible turning of humans? Tristan looked past Lagash to the thrones—to see the reaction of the royals. Was this their wish, or just idle words from a Second? But no, Sargon was smiling, that dark smile that barely held back his fangs. The reactions of the children were mixed. A few smiled just as eagerly. *Encouraging* it— and telling people to take possession of the property of those who could not make the change? When someone was turned, there were only two options: change and survive, or die a hideous death. The more mercenary among the Sazi would surely target the wealthiest humans first. Undoubtedly, many would die.

"All of you may share the joy today!" At Lagash's gesture, Sargon's elite guard, wearing the golden snake headbands of their office and carrying heavy bronze spears, pulled four people, a man, a woman, and two children, into the room. The family—it was clear they were related—were cowering in fear, and no wonder. They were full human.

"This family is not of the spirit of Anu. They are from the newly protected city of Nineveh. We will share the light with them today."

Lagash turned into a massive lion. The humans screamed but the guards held them firmly. Lagash pounced, ripping a wide slash of claws across the husband's chest, leaving him barely alive. Even now, centuries later, Tristan couldn't erase the memory of fur and claws. But it was a lie—years later Tristan had learned the truth, that Lagash had never shifted at all. The "claws" had been knives, the lion . . . an illusion. Lagash was a cobra shifter, like his King. But back then, Tristan saw a lion, saw the blood paint massive claws. The screams of terror, the twin scents of blood and fear, made his pulse pound for the chase. Lagash fell next on the wife and then the children. Soon they all lay near death on the floor, their blood pooling in an ever-growing circle. "This is the proper way. They live. They breathe, and soon, they will be filled with the animal spirit . . . Anu willing."

Human again and covered in blood, Lagash said, "Guards, take them, but gently. Anoint them with healing herbs and allow them to rest until the spirit comes to them." He turned to the crowd. "Can you not feel the animal spirit inside you, longing to bring others to the light?"

Eyes all over the room were glowing with magic, the savagery of what they had just witnessed making the predator come to the front. "Yes!"

"Then go forth! Sargon blesses you all. Bring the light to others." Lagash dipped his right hand in the spilled blood and touched the faces of several people near him, leaving a red handprint behind. They turned away, leaving the throne room; Ris saw more than one person touch the mark, then lick the blood from their fingers. Soon a line had formed, Sazi eager to be anounted. Ris felt sick. Permission had been given for a massacre. There would be far more deaths than successful turns, and those who survived turning would be mentally scarred, perhaps completely unable to function.

He looked around the room, filled with too many scents to sort out, feeling overwhelmed by the fervor of a dozen emotions from a hundred people. He backed away, ducking into the hallway, cutting his own hand on the sharp edge of a stone so he would have blood on his face with the others. The guards would be watching to see who were believers. Those who were unanointed would likely never make it out of the palace.

As he watched, another man did the same thing. He was one of the children of Sargon, Rimush, the youngest, who often bore the lash and fangs of Sargon's enforcer, Nasil. Ris had seen him before, but always at such a distance that Ris had not been able to sense his emotions. They shared a glance and then more, as the younger man suddenly let down the magical shield that made him appear weak and fearful.

He was neither. Now Ris saw him as he truly was for the first time. Not only would Rimush likely grow to become his father's rival; he also was appalled at what he'd just seen. Ris wondered why the young royal would share such personal information with a lowly servant.

Just as quickly as the moment happened, it ended, and Rimush's horror and anger were replaced by his usual blank face and scent.

The image in Tristan's mind of the young Ahmad faded. When the forest reappeared, Anica's eyes were wider and more horror filled than before. But she didn't hesitate this time. "Is this true? It happened?"

He nodded. "I shared a memory with you. It was long ago, but I cannot forget the sights, the sounds, the smells of that day. Is it the same man you saw today? The same scent?"

She nodded. "Are you certain he still wishes this? Perhaps he saw the pain, the damage it caused, and now wishes for peace."

Tristan stared into her large brown eyes, filled with flecks of golden fire, and asked one question: "Then why anger?"

Anica frowned, her scent thoughtful. "I must think of this while we check on Williams femily." She reached forward and knocked on the door, very real worry filling the air between them like a cloud.

Muted footsteps sounded on the wood floor inside, and when the door opened it was the young man Denis. He shrugged one shoulder, almost embarrassed, and glanced down at his feet. Tristan hadn't noticed it before, but the teen was attracted to Anica, but too shy to say anything. A little part of him was amused, but a larger part wasn't. The boy could be a distraction he didn't need. He let out a small cough and then looked up, his eyes only on Anica. "Hey, you're back. What's up?"

"Are you okay?" Concern was plain in her face and scent. But the boy wouldn't know about the scent. He was full human.

But she would be able to smell his confusion. "Yeah. Why?"

"We—"

Tristan stepped forward, put an arm around her, effectively

taking over the conversation. Denis began to frown. "We saw something hit the house. It was pretty big and we wanted to make sure everyone was okay." It was more or less the truth.

Denis shrugged, trying to appear nonchalant. But Tristan didn't believe it for a second. "I didn't hear anything and I've been right here."

"Could you get your folks?"

The boy's lips tightened into a thin line. There was nothing worse than being reminded of parents when trying to impress a girl.

Anica nodded, oblivious to the clues Tristan was seeing. "Yes, please. I worry for them."

At her serious tone, Denis began to grow concerned. "Hang on."

Moments later, Tristan was showing John Williams where the *object* had hit the wall. "Good lord, would you look at that?" The flashlight revealed that there were deep cracks in the wood where their bodies had struck. Following the now-concerned Williamses inside, they climbed the stairs to the second floor.

Asylin Williams turned on the light to an empty bedroom. Two of the heavy pine logs were pushed inward, crushing the headboard into splinters. An outside breeze pushed past the grout that had sealed the space between the two logs. She touched her husband's arm, her fingers clutching the woolen sweater arm tight. "Oh, John! What could have done this sort of damage? Thank God Dani is away at college." She turned her head to explain, "This is my daughter's room. She always studies in bed. She's not a strong alpha. She could have been crushed."

Anica fidgeted, feeling guilty. He could sense it. But the guilt smelled very much like worry. It was likely the others wouldn't notice the difference. "I am glad you are safe."

Asylin released her husband's arm and wrapped Anica in her arms, so suddenly the young woman barely had time to react. Asylin was tall and the motherly concern bleeding from her pores made Anica sniffle and hug her tightly in return. The Williams matriarch kissed her hair. "I'm glad you are too. You could both have been killed by whatever that was. We're lucky it hit the house instead of you two. Things can be replaced. People can't." She let her go and ruffled her hair. "You should get home, Anica. Your father is going to be worried." She turned to address him. "You're welcome to stay here, young man. We always have room for visitors."

Tristan wasn't sure it would be a good idea to be surrounded by more people. They were just cannon fodder to Lagash. "I appreciate the offer. I might take you up on it." Might. Not will. "Let me get Anica home first."

Anica looked over at him. "Can you walk me to Rachel's apartment instead? I need to pick up my purse."

It was a good lie, if it was one. A purse was often an extension of a woman, like a wallet for a man. It was one of those items that people didn't willingly leave for long periods in the possession of another person—no matter how trusted. He nodded. "Of course. It's not far."

They started to walk together, the night feeling colder than it had just moments before. Tristan could feel her tension and could sense that she wanted to ask something. "Go ahead."

"Those people, from your memory. What became of them?"

He sighed. He'd wondered the same thing and visited Nineveh a few years after, when the riots started. "The parents didn't survive the change, nor did the daughter. The son did. He became a lesser lion and eventually moved back to Nineveh with a mate." She nodded silently, her scent sad and angry. It might well have been the end of a sad story, but what eventually happened cheered him a little. "The boy drove the snakes from his city and successfully pulled away from the empire. Sargon could see the writing on the wall. That's about the time he chose to 'die' and move away, leaving the eventual total defeat of his empire to his children's legacy."

She nodded her head, just once, and smelled . . . wasn't that the strangest thing? She was right. Pride really did smell like a cheese blintz with fruit and cloves. "That is good. Even the little ones can become great."

As they neared the house where Anica lived with her father, they saw Zarko leaving the house. Anica pulled Tristan behind a nearby tree and put a finger to her lips. "Papa is leaving. I don't have to go to Rachel's room if I can shower here. Clothing is Rachel's, but I will wash and return to her later."

When Zarko got in his ATV and started the engine, Anica tucked herself closer to Tristan to blend into the forest. The warmth of her body seemed to seep into him and push away the growing chill of the night. Her scent of sunshine and warm soil blended nicely with the thick pine needles underfoot, turning the darkness into day in his nose. If Zarko smelled them hiding there as he drove by, he gave no sign, which seemed amazing. How could anyone *not* be able to smell Anica a mile away?

"What about your purse?" He whispered the words,

because he was fairly certain that the Alpha of the town could hear them if he tried . . . even from a distance.

Anica waved that off with a quiet puff of air from her lips and rolled eyes. "Pfft. I do not own purse. Mrs. Williams is nice, but she fusses. Even more than Mama. I do not wish to live there, even for one night."

He couldn't help but smile. "You don't like people fussing over you?"

"No. I like to *do* fussing," she said, her scent mingled with frustration and pride. "It make me happy to cook for femily, or make pretty things to surprise them." She paused. "Do *you* like people fussing?"

Ris tried to recall a time when someone had fussed over him. It was so long ago, it was just a distant memory. "Nobody ever has, so I don't know. I don't think I would."

"I understand." She waited for a long moment, until they could no longer see the taillights of the little cart; then she tapped his arm. "We go now. Quickly."

Her version of "quickly" made him smile. It was nothing more than a trot across the dirt road in front of the home. "Thank you for walking me to house." She started up the steps.

"Let me know right away if you see Lagash again. I'll try to track him down in the meantime." She turned to face him and he realized they were eye to eye. He put a forefinger to her forehead. "Call me *here*. It'll be faster."

She nodded, then surprised him by putting her hands on either side of his face and kissing him. His body responded so strongly he could barely breathe past the waves of sensation rushing across his skin. Her lips were full and rich and the taste of her was like rolling in the grass under a hot sun. Which was exactly what he wanted to be doing with her.

The sensations sucked him under, as though falling into deep water, and he suddenly realized he'd pulled her tight against him once more. His mouth was sliding down the side of her neck, tasting her, while she clutched at his back and made small, plaintive noises that urged him on. His own hands were under the oversized top, gliding across her taut back muscles. When he shifted one foot, he became aware he was erect, almost painfully so. The throb of his need made him pull back harshly before he completely lost his mind. Her face was slack, her large eyes dark with the same need. "I do not have to shower alone—"

Tempting. So very tempting. "That would be a bad idea."

She nodded, her fingers playing with the back of his neck, kneading gently. "Yes, but sometimes bad ideas are fun."

It made him laugh, a deep chuckle that told her he agreed. But he still pulled away and she smiled too, teasing. "Your father could come back at any moment."

"True." A sigh slid out of her lips and she ran a finger down the front of his shirt. "A pity."

Yes. It was. "Go. Shower. A *cold* one, and I'll do the same. And remember . . . watch for him and let me know if you see or smell him. Anywhere in town."

"I will. Please . . . you will be careful?"

He stepped back, leaving her on the steps. "I wouldn't still be alive if I wasn't."

The farther away from the house he walked, the easier it became to walk at all. He didn't know what it was about her that was making him so distracted, but he had to avoid her or he wasn't going to be able to function.

A swim was what he needed right now—that always helped clear his mind. He quickly ran, using the real defini- tion of "quickly," to the little crescent lake, took off his clothes, and dove into the water, welcoming the cold shock as he submerged. He let his body shift into his true form: a krait. It wasn't the only form he could take, or *appear* to take, but it was his natural form. He swam smoothly, letting his eyes and body adjust to the temperature. The water seemed to get warmer as his heartbeat slowed. As he swam deeper, the pressure against his skin eased the tension in his muscles. Fish didn't turn out of his path, not even recognizing him as a predator.

His serpent body acclimated even more, until the cold lake felt almost like bathwater, allowing him to swim easily . . . all of the aches soothing away as he glided around, exploring the debris scattered around the bottom. Mostly logs, but a few seemed to have been sunk intentionally, as fish habitats—barrels open on both sides, with the openings covered with narrow panel fencing. Small fish could get inside for protection, but the larger fish couldn't. He counted four—no, five such barrels, along with some concrete blocks that were covered with a variety of underwater vegetation.

As he swam around one of the blocks, he became aware of a scent similar to mint. No, it was definitely mint . . . a mix of peppermint and spearmint. He tried to decide what could cause the scent this close to the bottom of the lake but couldn't find anything that would account for it. He'd have to chat with Bobby and have him come swimming with him. His tongue was better trained to identify chemicals. Tristan couldn't think of anything hazardous that smelled of mint and none of the fish appeared to be avoiding any area. He flicked his tail hard to catch up to a large trout that seemed to be circling the area, looking for an easy lunch. No, it wasn't a trout. It was a salmon. While it seemed perfectly at home in the lake, it couldn't be native.

Then he thought of the bears in the area, and it made sense. Given the option, the residents probably preferred salmon to trout. The salmon stopped in the water, then stared at him with wide, unblinking eyes. *Probably trying to decide if I could be dinner.* It allowed Tristan to get a good look at it. The eyes were clear, the scales even and shiny. Other than a few battle scars, it was a good specimen. He threw out a small push of magic to spook it and watched as it flipped its tail and swam away in the flurry of bubbles.

Should have eaten it, he thought, though he didn't particularly care for salmon.

The mint scent was increasing. He needed to get out of the area before it gave him a headache. It wasn't a large lake, but it was big enough to get some exercise. Picking the supports for the pier as a goal in the far distance, he put on speed. He was barely out of breath when he reached the heavy pine logs, so he decided to circle the entire lake at the same speed, back to the same point again.

As the first barrel habitat went by in a blur at the corner of his vision, he heard Lagash's voice again. *You've passed right by me, several times.* He couldn't get past the taunt. Was it a lie? He hadn't smelled any deceit, but he hadn't been concentrating on scents. He'd been watching Lagash's hands and feeling for his magic.

And yet . . . he hadn't seen the magic coming that threw them a dozen feet into a wall. It had been like a freight train at full steam colliding with him.

He'd nearly reached the spot where he'd left his clothes when he felt a tap at his mind. A politeness by someone of high alpha level before they intruded to talk. He opened his senses, rising close to the surface to feel if it was Lagash. Of course, he wouldn't have *tapped*. It would have been a full-out assault. But it was a man—Bobby.

Rising to the surface, he swam through the misty smoke that floated over the surface of the water toward shore. "Everything okay?"

Bobby squatted down in the muddy gravel, being careful to pull his pants up so they didn't drag in the mud. "I should ask *you* that. I got a call from Zarko, who had gotten a call from John Williams. It seems there was a little altercation at their house. Two people-sized dents in the wall of the second story. I have to assume one of them was you, since I've asked most everyone else. Who caused the second dent?"

It wouldn't do any good to lie to Bobby. His tongue was flicking so rapidly, he was probably smelling everything down to the level of mosquito pheromones in the air. But not answering wasn't lying. "I was with Anica, asking Mrs. Williams to help you with the falcon." Of course, Bobby already knew that part. "We talked to Mr. Williams for a few minutes. I asked him if he knew any single male alphas that didn't seem to fit in here."

Bobby's face took on an amazed expression. "Wait. *John Williams* did that to you? Are you kidding me?! Who was the other person?"

Tristan let out a short laugh as he slithered onto shore. "No. Of course not." He shifted forms, picked up his clothes from the grass, and shook them out.

Bobby reached forward and grabbed the shirt out of his grip, held it to his face, his tongue flicking fast, and then let out a bark of a laugh. "Ris, are you *insane*? You had sex with the Alpha's daughter? Do you have a death wish? She's barely an adult!"

He couldn't meet the disapproving look on his longtime friend's face. "No, I didn't have sex with her. It was just a kiss. A mistake."

Bobby held up the shirt. "*This* is not 'just a kiss,' Ris. There's heavy shit in this fabric." He threw the balled-up shirt at his chest. "You're damned right it was a mistake. You need to burn these clothes and then go shower with some peppermint soap before Zarko comes hunting for you with a silver bullet."

Peppermint. That reminded him. "I smelled peppermint a few minutes ago. Underwater. What would cause that?"

A low hiss rolled out of his mouth and his scent turned metallic. "Don't change the subject. Leave the girl alone. Now, who did this and who was with you? Don't make me pull rank on you."

Tristan couldn't help but laugh. But the sound was bitter, brittle. "While I'm normally happy to bow to your official position, this is different. You know why I'm here. I outrank you on my mission."

He crossed his dark arms over his shirt, his movements short and impatient. "So, what? You're saying *Lagash* threw you against the hou—" His voice stuttered to a stop with a gurgling in his throat. Tristan wasn't positive he could make that noise again if he tried. Then the words dropped to an almost whisper. "You're not saying that, are you?" The tone was a mixture of skepticism and horror.

Sitting down on the ground, he pulled on his shoes. "Not proud of it, but the blow came out of nowhere, Robart. And I was watching for him to make a move. That's what hurts the most. Well, that and my lower back."

"Ahmad was *right*? What are the odds?" Bobby sat down, and Tristan wasn't sure it was entirely voluntary. "Ur-Lagash, in modern-day America." He picked up a nearby rock and threw it, hard. It landed in the water with a small splash halfway across the lake. "And you and Amber didn't chase him because . . . ?"

"First, I was remembering how to breathe. Wait. You said 'Amber.' No, it was Anica."

Bobby's head snapped to stare at him so fast that Tristan heard his joints pop. "Anica? Holy hell! Where did you bury the body? We need to get our stories straight fast, before Zarko starts asking questions."

Spinning around to rise to his knees, Tristan brushed the dirt and sand off his pants before standing up. "There is no body. She's fine. I took her home. I shared a memory with her from Akede so she knows what he's capable of. Plus, she knows his scent now and she can talk to me mentally. If he comes anywhere near her, I'll know."

Bobby was staring at his lap, his chest moving in near-silent laughter. The scent of citrus flooded Tristan's senses. "What are you laughing about?"

"I've got to call Asri. She's going to laugh her ass off."

Asri had no sense of humor that Tristan knew of. Like him, she was Indonesian, a Komodo Dragon who was the enforcer of the Chicago wolf pack. She lived to punish, maim, and kill at the whim of the Alpha there, Nikoli Molotov. She loved her job. "Care to share the joke?"

Bobby looked up and his face was the picture of sunny good humor. "The joke is *you*, old friend. And it's even funnier that you don't know why."

He wasn't sure whether to be amused or angry, but Bobby was acting very out of character. "Apparently not. I just told you Lagash is in Luna Lake and nearly killed me and one of the locals. Dying is funny to you?"

"No. Not at all. It's the *nearly* part that's funny. Ris . . . Anica is a three-day. She can't even shift on her own on the moon. Don't you remember us discussing that just a few hours ago?"

"Sure. And . . . ?"

The answering sigh was deep and apparently supposed to be meaningful, but Tristan still wasn't getting the point. "Ris. We've been friends for more than a century. I know you cut yourself off from the rest of our kind, but surely you remember a little about lesser Sazi, don't you?"

He shrugged. "Of course. I've known plenty of them. Including your assassin friend."

"Then you know they don't heal for shit. About the same as humans, when it comes down to it. They have no control over their shifting. They have very little magic and, other than Tony, who is a rare exception, have no gifts at all."

Tristan nodded. Nothing he didn't already know.

"Then what are the odds, Ris that a three-day bear would *survive* putting a dent in a solid pine log?" A sick feeling started in the pit of Tristan's stomach. "What are the odds a three-day would be able to have a mental link to anyone other than their Alpha without their brain exploding . . . in very a literal sense?" The sick feeling rose to become acid that stung his chest and throat. "And finally, what are the *odds* you would just happen to be so physically attracted to that particular barely legal three-day that you don't seem to *care* that her father will likely track you down and kill you before Lagash has the chance?"

The bile flew into his mouth so quickly that he barely had time to turn and drop to his knees in the mud before it spewed out of his mouth, along with the meal of rabbit and crackers he'd had before he got caught in the forest fire.

Bobby patted his shoulder, adding insult to the injury. "For what it's worth, I feel your pain. I threw up a couple of times too when I found out I was mated. So did Tony."

Tristan wiped his mouth with the bottom of his shirt before pushing the other man's hand away. His throat felt raw and wounded from the acid. "I've had women mated to me before, Bobby. I'm an alpha. Have been for centuries. Dozens, if not hundreds, of women have been mated to me."

"Sure. Me too. But she's not still alive because *she's* mated to *you*, and your stomach knows it." He raised his forefinger. "She shifted on her own when she never had before and survived a blow strong enough to leave *you* with pain, meaning she's pulling enough power from you that you can't heal your own wounds." His middle finger rose to join the first in the air. "She can talk into your head with such ease that it felt normal to you." His ring finger rose to reveal the golden band of his own mating. "You even shared a memory with a three-day, which just isn't possible." Just having Bobby say it out loud caused his stomach to revolt a second time, littering the water with foamy yellow bile. "Face facts. The only way she's still alive is that you're mated to *her*."

CHAPTER 11

Anica reached her foot out of the water to turn on the hot tap again. She sank in the hot foamy water up to her neck and let out a slow breath. The pain had nearly subsided to tolerable levels and the minty bath bubbles had relaxed her head. She had to find a way to let go of the things she'd seen today, because the more she thought about the events of the day, the more terrified she became. She couldn't decide what had been worse: Paula's death, the bomb that had nearly killed them all, the madman in the horrible memory Tristan had shared with her, or Tristan himself.

The front door suddenly opened and then slammed shut hard enough to vibrate the pictures of salmon jumping out of a crystal blue stream that were scattered on the walls. Her heart began to race. Had Lagash come to find her? She turned off the tap and ducked down below the water level, leaving only her nose up, like a tiny periscope, and sniffed deeply. Her muscles had tightened so quickly that the sudden release actually hurt when she realized the person in the next room was Bojan. But his scent was accompanied by anger. He was furious, but there were many other scents muddled with the anger. He was conflicted about something. She called out to him, "Bojan? Da li si dobro?" Asking if he was okay in Serbian might ease his anger a little.

"Speak English, Anica. We are not in Serbia anymore." His voice was a sharp rebuke, for no good reason.

"Don't be angry with *me*, Brother. I've had a bad enough day. What is wrong?" She brushed the bubbles off her skin and hair and got out of the bath, grabbing a towel to dry herself.

Bojan stopped outside the bathroom door. "I'm sorry. I should not yell at you. It's Scott I'm angry with."

That made her sad. He'd been so happy earlier in the day. She wrapped one fluffy blue towel around her body and wrapped her hair in another and opened the door. "I'm sorry, Bojan." A quick sniff made her look down at his hands. His right hand was swollen and red, with the knuckles scraped and dotted with blood. "Were you in a fight?" She picked up his hand and he winced. "You should clean that." She pulled him forward into the bathroom and turned on the sink. She backed up so he could step in front of her. "Use soap so it doesn't get infection."

He stared at the water but put his hands on each side of the sink instead, flexing his fingers on the white porcelain until they were nearly the same color. "I punched him . . . and should have done worse." He turned his head. "He *kissed* me, Anica. On the mouth!" He wiped his lips with the back of his hand and then spit in the sink.

Oh. Oh! "He thought you are—" Scott thought Bojan liked men. In that moment, her nose unwound the muddied scents from him. The confusion of scents made more sense now. He was angry, yes. But under the top layer were other things, including cookie spices and the same oily, musky scent she'd smelled from Tristan earlier. The scent of passion. The more she thought about it, the more she wondered. "Are you?"

His head turned with such speed and anger that she nearly backed up, but she didn't—knowing that would be his reaction. *"No!"* He stared at her as though she'd suddenly shifted into a Psoglav, the demon with horse legs and a dog head. He slammed his injured fist down on the cabinet around the sink, causing a smear of red across the surface. "How could you even ask that?"

Calm and quiet was the best response to his outburst. "Because Mama always had to force you to choose a date for school events."

He rolled his eyes, his face an exaggeration of outrage. "The girls in school were more interested in finding a rich husband than dating a real man."

She couldn't deny that. All of her friends were looking for older men, rich business owners who would take care of them. But she countered his statement anyway. "Because when Samit would watch girls in the marketplace with his friends, you never found any of them pretty."

A shrug was his response. "They weren't."

"And yet," she pointed out with a gentle finger on his nose, "you couldn't name a single girl or woman you *did* think was pretty when Papa asked."

He turned off the water without putting his hand under and turned to face her, his arms crossed tightly over his chest. "Papa was trying to start an argument . . . again, and I wasn't interested in sparring with him." He let out a snarl of frustration, something the gentle, sweet Bojan didn't used

to be capable of. "Don't you think I would know if I was a
buljaš?" He used the Serbian slur, which made Anica let out
a growl.

"There is no reason to use a bad word. Just say 'gay.'" She
closed the lid and sat down on the toilet, giving him a little
room. "And no, I don't think you *would* know. All your
friends were anti-gay and so was Samit. Just learning to cook
caused so many bad, horrible words from Samit that I heard,
and heaven knows how many you heard alone with him, that
even if you had such a feeling, you would bury it so deep
down it would never see light of daytime."

He blinked. Then blinked again and his whole body sort
of collapsed. He leaned back against the sink cabinet. His
voice lowered to almost a whisper. "Is it bad thing to say that
I don't miss Samit at all?"

Anica knew there was no love lost between the brothers.
Samit was much like Papa. Bojan like Mama. It was a wonder
that Papa and Mama had ever found love. "Perhaps. But he
was hard on you. I'm sorry I couldn't have helped you more
when you would fight." She did miss Samit and was sorry
he had gone rogue and died. But she could understand why
Bojan wouldn't miss the taunting.

He sighed and his brown eyes were sad when they met
hers. His long black lashes had always been the butt of
Samit's jokes, including" 'joke" gifts of mascara each holi-
day and sometimes lipstick. "You couldn't have done anything even if Mama hadn't shooed you out of the room every
time. I just wish Papa would have stood up for me. Just once.
Samit would have listened to him."

She couldn't help but shrug, reaching to catch the oversized towel before it fell down. "I don't think Papa believed

there was real hatred in Samit. Papa actually doesn't think badly of gays. His friend Petero . . . did you know he became open just after you left for cooking school?"

Bojan's eyes widened and the shock of surprise floated over the minty steam in the room. "No! Really? I had no idea. They hunted together many times and they met in town for drinks."

She nodded. "Exactly, even after he announced. He did not talk much of it, but Mama patted his cheeks after one hunt, telling him she was proud of him for spending time with Petero. So many of his friends had faded away. But not Papa."

That interested Bojan. "What did he say about it when Mama said that?"

"Only little. He just shrug and say, 'He's still Petero. He still hunts. He still drinks. What has changed?'"

Bojan put his hands on the cabinet and hopped up to sit on it. He didn't say anything for a long moment. She spoke to fill the void. "Perhaps I should not say this, but Scott is a nice man. He is honest and kind and makes you happy." Her brother raised his head and stared at her with an emotion in his face she couldn't quite name, so she pressed on, wanting to get her point out before he left in a huff. "You were happier today at ice cream store than I've seen you since you are accepted at cooking school. I have watch you cook together and laugh and walk together and smile. If he kisses you, maybe it because he sees that same happy and thinks he is reason." She paused as his brows lowered and his expression took on a small amount of anger. But then she forged on, ready in case he reached out to slap her for saying it. "And maybe he is. You do dress better lately and comb your hair more. Your scent makes your words a lie. You liked the kiss, Bojan."

She could hear his heart pounding in the quiet room, louder than the popping of bubbles in the tub. When he spoke, it was to change the subject. "I don't know how you can smell anything over the mint in the room. Don't accuse me of having a boyfriend when you're hiding one too under all these bubbles. Afraid Papa will find out who he is and scare him away like all the others?"

She had to smile. Bojan was the one person she could talk to about her boyfriends. Papa had no idea she'd had men in her life, and her bed, since she was fifteen, but Bojan knew them all. He was wonderful at listening and giving advice when she was sad or happy or in pain. "He already tried. This one does not scare easily."

Now her brother's face had a shocked look. "Is it the dark-skinned snake? Or the blond bear? They are the only ones I can think wouldn't be afraid of Papa. But they are both *old*, Anica. Even for Sazis."

She gave him a little shrug and a half smile. "He has many mysteries. That is only one of them. I like mysteries. He showed me a past time, from his own mind, where torches lit rooms made of stone." And among his many mysteries was his appearance. What she saw with her eyes wasn't how he saw himself in his mind. Which was true? "He is also not blond and I am not positive he is bear."

Bojan laughed, both at having guessed right about Tristan and also for the thought of hiding his animal. "That's not a thing you can hide, Anica. You are bear or not bear."

"And we used to think 'you are human or animal.' Sazi didn't exist. *Both* human and animal wasn't possible. But we learn, Bojan. As things change and become truth, maybe nothing is what we believe now." So many things she thought she knew had changed in such a short time. "Maybe we only begin to know what is true."

He nodded thoughtfully, his scent matching the look at last. "Maybe."

The front door opened, making them both look toward the living room. Papa had come in, his scent and bearing weary under the layer of smoke and soot. He walked to the bathroom door, his face confused, but his scent filled with smoke and worry. "Anica? Bojan? Why are you both in bathroom?" He sniffed the air in the room and wrinkled his nose. "Mint again? I thought you had stopped using that soap. It always made Mama sneeze."

Anica got to her feet and pulled the drain plug in the tub before he could come in and possibly smell other things that neither she nor Bojan wanted him to smell. The scent of mint increased even stronger as the water began to swirl and spin down the drain. "It make the smoke smell go away. I thought since Mama wasn't here—" She didn't finish, not wanting to remind him of that. But she heard Papa sigh and his scent grow sad again.

She looked up, opened her mouth to ask how he was doing, but he waved her out of the room. "Go, go. I need to shower. And why do I not smell food cooking?"

Bojan slid out the door past the big man, keeping his eyes on the floor. "I'll start the fish. Anica, could you make a salad?"

She nodded but risked a look at Papa's face. He was alternating staring after Bojan and then at her. Worry was leaking out of him like air from a balloon. "Papa? What is it?"

He took a step and touched the side of her face, his face

full of warmth and love. "It is nothing, *jagnje*. Go dress and we will have dinner."

Now she was even more worried. He hadn't called her baby lamb since she was a small child. She still remembered the white knitted hood with fluffs of wool she used to wear that everyone said made her look like a tiny sheep. She would hide among the animals in the barn on their farm and nobody could find her for hours.

Dinner was nearly silent. Only the clinking of forks against the plates could be heard, and discomfort filled Anica's nose even more than the excellent-tasting fish Bojan had cooked. It wasn't until she was picking up the dishes to take in to clean that Papa spoke. "I talked to Mama today. She called the office."

Anica was halfway to the kitchen and nearly dropped the handful in her rush to turn. "How is she? Is she happy? How are the new bears?"

Bojan joined in, his questions rolling over the top of hers. "Has she been able to make it back to the farm? Are the horses well?"

Papa raised his hand, his face solemn. But his scent was conflicted. Happy but sad and angry, all balled into one. "She is well, still in hiding outside of Belgrade. The new bears take up much of her time. Their families rejected them. When the first family was told, they were horrified. Word spread and the children were told not to come home."

Anica's stomach grew sick. That could easily have been her own story. "Thank you, Papa. I haven't said that enough. You took me back and kept loving me."

He looked at her, his face stricken. But then he coughed and cleared his throat. "You are my daughter. Of course I did not turn you away. Nor would Mama. But that means

she must care for the other children, train them. She is trying to teach them farming so they can eventually go back to
our home. But the children . . . they are not farmers and
they have much sadness. Two already have jumped in the
river, from the big bridge."

Anica couldn't help but cover her mouth and let out a
small cry. Killing themselves wasn't the answer. There was
a life as a Sazi. It wasn't a bad life, even as a weak bear. "Oh,
Papa. I'm so sorry."

He cleared his throat again, his fingers tapping on the
table. "So you will both go back to Serbia and help Mama.
That is all. Pack your things."

Wait. What? She put the dishes on the counter. Bojan was
likewise stunned. He leaned over the table, hand flat on
the polished surface, staring at their father. "We have
barely become settled here. You said Mama would eventually come back *here* to live. I have interviews at restaurants
in Spokane, and Anica has been applying to colleges there so
we can live together and visit you and Mama on weekends."

When Anica inhaled deeply to calm her fast-beating
heart, she was surprised to discover . . . black pepper deceit,
just as Rachel had said. "You're lying, Papa. Why?"

Bojan turned to stare at her then sniffed the air himself.
"You *are*. What is the truth?"

Slamming his palms down on the table, Papa swore in several languages. "I *hate* your nose, Anica. It is too sensitive.
Who could possibly lie with you in the room? Fine. Mama
is struggling. That is truth." Both she and Bojan sniffed to
confirm it. "And it is truth you must go back."

Again, truth. But if not to help Mama . . . "Why?"

He half-stood from his chair and fished in his front pocket.
He pulled out two folded-up envelopes and tossed them

across the table. Anica reached for one and her suddenly shaking hands revealed an official government seal in the corner. "Your visa applications were denied. You and Bojan are being deported."

Her stomach sank. It had never occurred to her that they would not be accepted in this country.

"What about you?" Bojan's voice was outraged, but Anica couldn't tell why his reaction was so much stronger now than before.

Now Papa's scent and words were sad. "Mine was accepted. I have no answer why. Perhaps more mayors are needed in America than cooks or students." Just by the way he said it, Anica knew he would not be going with them. Was it because of Mama, or something more? Was the thought of a large pack of unstable bears just too much to consider leading? Was a town of an unstable other kind of animal somehow better?

Everything in the room looked normal. The table was still fine polished wood, the carpeting thick and rich, just like when they moved in. But like that first day, the world had tipped on its side. Everything was askew and disconcerting. Just a few months ago, Anica was standing in a raspberry field in Serbia, helping collect fresh berries with Mama and Samit to make jam.

America wasn't even in her mind. Rachel and Dalvin, Claire and Alek, Denis . . . even Skew, weren't even considerations. And now she'd found Tristan and liked him. She couldn't imagine life without all of them—could barely remember her life a year ago. She tried to imagine a life where she was back in the raspberry fields with no hope of friends, of travel, warring with the neighbors over a field of bushes. But couldn't. Even Luna Lake, so quiet and peaceful, felt like home now. "I don't want to go. Who can take appeals? What about mediator who helped us? She was not just Sazi official, but U.S. government person, yes?"

Papa let out a sigh. "I think of this too. I get letters a week ago. I have been trying to fix it since. I have asked Elizabeth Sutton to check. She is doing this for us, but said not to have hopes. All of America is dangerous now for refugees, and we cannot tell State Department people *why* we cannot go home, or who threatens us. That is how they decide whether to grant asylum."

Anica hadn't thought of that. The Sazi stayed in the shadows always. How could they explain that because they broke up a plot to make more shape-shifters now snake shifters wanted them dead and they had to hide here?

Bojan kicked the table leg, hard enough to move the table a foot away from Papa. "I'm going out."

She wanted to leave too, to run away. But that would not solve the problem. Patience was needed now. "Thank you for telling us, Papa. And for trying to keep us together."

But he wasn't watching her. Didn't even acknowledge her words. Instead, he watched Bojan grab his jacket and stalk out, slamming the door the same way he had when he got home. But now for a different reason.

"I am going to office," he announced after a long moment. "I will be home late. Don't wait awake."

He closed the door quietly, but it sounded loud to her in the suddenly silent house. It was probably time to do the dishes and get some rest. It had been a very long and traumatic day. But first she made a call to Rachel. Anica needed to talk to someone and she was the closest thing to a friend in town. But Rachel didn't answer and the call went to her recorder. "Can we talk tomorrow? It's important."

She was worn-out, emotionally and physically. It was like someone had turned off a switch on her back and she couldn't keep going. Her eyes kept closing as she did the dishes, making it hard to focus. Finally, she gave up when the scrubbed dishes were rinsed and she staggered down the hallway. She didn't remember hitting the bed.

CHAPTER 12

"Okay, I've blocked the connection. Let the pining begin." Amber had changed from her blue scrubs with ducks into yellow ones with cartoon mice scattered across the fabric. Apparently, she slept in them too, since they'd woken her up on a cot in the back of the clinic. She saw him looking and shrugged her shoulders as she wiped her hands on a paper towel. "Don't judge. They're comfortable and I never know when people—and I use that term loosely—are going to drop by, expecting me to jump through hoops for them."

That part wasn't worth commenting on. "I don't know why you say there will be pining. We haven't had sex." Tristan couldn't gloss over what Bobby had told him. When his friend suggested telling Amber, he had agreed. She was a noted healer and would know for certain if a mating had happened.

By the time he felt the connection break in his mind, she didn't need to confirm the mating. The echo was gone. He hadn't realized that's what it was, but ever since the fire he'd heard a hollow sound in his own mind, like tapping on a coconut while it was next to his ear. He assumed his head had been a little scrambled by the log hitting him. And in a way, he was right.

"Perhaps not. But it was stronger than you think it was. Maybe not sex, but something happened between you that locked the mating tie. I have no idea what it is with matings lately, but they're stronger than they've been in the past.

"I shared some power with her when she wasn't getting air. Would that be enough?"

Bobby let out a laugh. "If you add in the near sex in the forest, I'd say yes."

Tristan shot him a dirty look. He didn't see why Amber needed to know about that. "We didn't have sex. End of story."

Amber's thoughts might as well have been tattooed on her forehead. She didn't approve, but since it was a mating, she couldn't disapprove either. "Sharing energy, sharing spit—" She apologized with a shrug and a scent when he shot her a similar annoyed look. "Sorry. Crude but accurate. It was probably enough. Not that it really matters *how*. It just matters *that*."

"So, now what happens? It's sort of my first time being the one who's mated."

Bobby chortled. "Now, life begins to suck. You'll think of her every day. Every minute. You can't *stop* thinking about her. You throw yourself into work . . . which is sort of good, in your case. It'll keep Ahmad off your ass and you'll probably catch Lagash. We'll get the girl to safety."

"That should be easy," Amber added. "Zarko came to me today to say her visa application had been denied by the State Department. Without a declared major and with no discernable skills, plus no government trying to kill her, she's not a priority."

"So what happens to Anica?" All of a sudden it mattered. A lot, which bothered him more than he liked.

Bobby laughed again, which was really getting annoying. "And there's the mating kicking in. Having her matter will take up most of your head space until you learn to shield. Pretend she's your mom and lock the big metal door in your head."

"I know how to shield." Except he didn't *want* to shield. In fact, he wanted to know where she was right now, wanted to go to her, take her in his arms, and explore her body fully until they were both exhausted.

"Wow, has the mating kicked in." Amber fanned her hand in the air, bringing him back to the present abruptly. "Different shielding than danger, Ris. I can add a shield in, but I'll be stuck in your head for the duration. Any secrets you don't want known by the world? Or at least by the Council?"

"I'll handle my own shields, thank you." There was no need to go into the things he would rather not share with the Sazi hierarchy.

"Okay, then here's problem number two. Your new status is going to be broadcast to the whole town unless you can find a way to tamp it down in your scent."

"Peppermint soap is great for that," Bobby inserted with a raised hand. "I know just how much you'll love smelling like a candy store." He was enjoying this conversation far too much. That was likely Tristan's own fault for his constant teasing when Bobby and Asri had first gotten together.

"Is that why I was smelling mint underwater?"

Amber decided that was interesting enough to sit down

across from him on the rolling stool. "Underwater? Really? Where were you?"

"In the lake. I shifted and was swimming to clear my head after taking Anica home."

Amber turned to Bobby for confirmation. "Did you smell mint?" He shook his head, not bothering to speak. So she reached for her mobile phone in her pocket. "Let's find out where the mint comes from." She dialed a number on the phone that he couldn't see. A man answered, but she kept the phone pressed so close to her ear that he couldn't identify the voice. "When's the last time you smelled mint, any kind of mint?"

She nodded and then kept repeating, "Uh-huh. Uh-huh." Another pause and then she nodded. "Okay, thank you. Get some sleep." She pressed the red button and raised both hands with no particular scent attached. "That answers that. Anica just got done soaking in a mint-scented bubble bath. Her father remembered distinctly because his wife was allergic to the scent and it was the first time he'd smelled it since she went back to Serbia." She leaned forward until her forearms were on her knees. "You're smelling through her nose, instead of the other way around. It's a double mating, Ris. That's not a good thing for you."

Oh, he was well aware of that. "I can't afford to be mated at all. My life really doesn't allow for someone tagging along." He lived very simply, in a hut by the ocean on a tiny island off the Sumatran coast, barely more than a large rock. He didn't even own a stove, preferring to eat his fish fresh and raw. Traveling frequently, he hunted criminals for the Sazi government, with no guarantee he would survive from job to job.

"And a three-day who will need energy just to exist? No.

That's not going to work. How do we fix this?" The moment
the words were out of his mouth, he wanted to take them
back. The effort to think clearly about the girl . . . about
Anica, which was a beautiful name. Musical, like her voice.
He missed her voice in his thoughts. He put a palm to his
forehead, struggling with the warring images in his mind.
"What's happening to me?"

"Mating." "Pining." The words came from Amber and
Bobby simultaneously, along with the next word, in unison:
"Sucks."

"Mostly, it sucks because she's now a liability to you. Any
damage to her will cut into your energy. Any threat to her
will make you do anything . . . anything at all to fix it. And
from what you've told me about Lagash, he already knows
that."

I almost hate to interrupt . . . almost. "No wonder he'd
waited. Lagash was hiding in the forest, watching us kiss.
He said he *almost* hated to interrupt. Do you think he was
waiting for the mating? Could he possibly have smelled it
before anyone else could?"

Amber let out a harsh breath and the scent of her frustration filled the small room with burnt metal. "It's definitely
possible, if he knew what to smell for. He threw the power
against *both* of you. If he wasn't lying, and he *is* a local resident in disguise, he would have been here for the mediation.
She was one of the challengers in the contest to decide who
got the land in Serbia. Everyone who was here knows she's
a three-day. He might well have been curious to see if she
would be killed by his blast."

Maybe it was best to involve them after all. Ahmad
wouldn't like a Monier knowing his business, but he would
forgive quickly once Lagash was dead. "Lagash said he had

been amused that Ahmad hadn't spotted him in town and that I hadn't either. But Anica brought up that he was angry when he should have been smug because he had succeeding in hiding from us. Or at least amused, which is what he claimed."

Bobby pursed his lips and nodded. "Anica's got a good mind. We need to get her into school, train her properly. Maybe recommendations from some friends in the sciences can reverse the decision about her visa. We need to keep her here, and out of the shadows. Which means she can't become undocumented."

An alarm started beeping in Amber's pocket, a sharp, annoying sound that made her reach quickly for her phone. "Sorry, that's my medical emergency alert. Hold on." Plucking out the phone, she stared at the screen. "Crap. We've got another one."

"Another murder?"

"Alek Siska says so. He's handling nine-one-one calls tonight, and he's Wolven, so he can keep this local. Says the cook at the diner, David Haskell, has been strangled. He was found by a customer who was hoping for a late-night snack."

"The last murder victim was a waitress there. Maybe this isn't Lagash at work. Maybe it's related to the diner after all."

Bobby nodded. "I'll go with Amber to the scene and talk to the person who called it in."

Tristan stood up, feeling a little more focused. Maybe Bobby was right that he needed to keep his mind occupied to make his shielding work. "Bring the cook to the ice cream store. I can look at his wounds at the same time as the waitress's."

He left while the others were gathering Amber's medical tools. He could imagine Anica becoming a scientist. She could have a long career, even as a three-day. Tristan had always wondered why Bobby subjected himself to the schooling when he already had a natural talent with his tongue. But Amber also had gotten a formal education, becoming a medical doctor as well as a healer. Perhaps there was value in the human school system he hadn't noticed before.

He slipped behind the building to stay to the shadows, in case he was being watched by Lagash. The smoke was thicker than earlier, making it easy to stay out of sight as he headed for the basement where they'd left Paula's corpse. From the smell, the fire wasn't close by, at least not yet.

The little shop building was dark. Asylin said they hadn't had a chance to clean up the mousetraps, so it was probably best to go in the same way Anica had come out. Going to the back of the building, he looked in through the window at ground level but couldn't see through. Black plastic sheeting had been put over all the openings to help hide the new body on the floor. The windows were all locked and he hadn't thought to ask for a key. That was stupid of him.

He'd have to find another way in, which would be easier in snake form. Shedding his clothing, he was soon slithering around the base of the building, looking for likely openings. The world shifted to light and dark, black and white, which made it easier to see in the near pitch-blackness of the forest. Small mammals in the undergrowth scurried out of his way as he flicked his tongue, feeling for warm air leaking from the cold concrete foundation. He raised his body up to feel along the concrete. The roughness of the gravel skimmed across his skin. When he found what he was looking for, a small series of hissing laughs slipped out. The dryer vent. Of course.

It was short work to slide up through the hose to the edge

of the machine and then bite his way through the thin plastic-ringed sheath.

Staying along the wall leading out of the laundry room, he saw the falcon shifter sleeping fitfully in her bed. There was no need to wake her, but if she did wake he would put her in a magical hold until he finished working. Thankfully, there were no mousetraps in her home and the door between her apartment and the main shop was open a crack, so he didn't have to shift to continue toward the basement. The mousetraps all over the floor in the shop would be a trick, though.

If he thought like a snake, that was—

He looked up. While the counter was also covered with traps, there was a decorative railing that separated the pine paneling on the bottom half of the wall from the painted upper half.

Getting *to* the railing was no problem, and it was wide enough to stretch out on. But snakes didn't move in a straight line; their scales generally propelled them in an S-shaped pattern. Still, it was possible to make tiny movements slowly, like walking on a rope bridge over jagged rocks. Fortunately, he'd done that very thing before. A little nerve-wracking, but he managed it.

Once he'd slithered downstairs, he started inspecting the body of the cook. While he knew from television shows that human police preferred a body to be as fresh as possible to get their clues, it was actually easier for someone with tongue scent ability when the body was a little more . . . ripe. He decided to start with the woman's body in the walk-in first, returning to human form to pull her out into the main room before shutting the door and shifting back to snake form so he had full use of his talents.

Paula's body was in a good state for his investigation. Even though she'd been in the freezer, enough time had passed for some natural breakdown of tissue to occur, releasing scents that told of how the damage had occurred. Unfortunately, the woman's neck and chest were so damaged by tearing that determining the *type* of teeth would be difficult. He slowly slid along the body, using the taste buds embedded in his skin to try to figure out the scent of the killer. Multiple people had touched the body, so he had to first eliminate those he'd come in contact with. His own scent, along with those of Bobby, Rachel, Dalvin, and Anica, were quickly discarded. Three others had touched the body: two female, one male. Could this have been a coordinated effort to kill the woman? If so, why?

Concentrating on the wounds, he wrapped himself around Paula's neck, putting the pieces of the skin back together so he could determine the shape of the original tooth marks.

"It was strangulation." The voice made him look up sharply. The falcon the others had called Skew was standing at the foot of the stairs in human form. Flicking out his tongue, he realized one of the scents under his skin was hers.

"How so?" She didn't seem concerned that he was a snake, nor that he was slithering around on a dead body.

Moving forward, she knelt down beside him and pulled one of the dead woman's ears forward, folding it over so he could look at it. "Look at the bruising behind the ears. Someone tore out the throat after she was strangled, to hide the finger marks." She was correct. There was bruising, darkening the skin to nearly black. "And look at the eyes." Raising the body's eyelids, Skew showed him that the whites were bloodred. "There's clear evidence of asphyxiation that wouldn't be evident with animal bites."

"You've already done an exam?"

She nodded. "Of course. I'm the town's medical examiner. First death by misadventure in years."

"You seem to know your forensics. Are you trained?"

She nodded. "It wasn't my major, but I minored in forensic science. It annoyed my parents." She winked slyly. "There's no legal requirement in this state that the ME be a doctor, so I fill in."

Lights brightened the stairwell and they both turned to look as a voice called down, "Ris? You down there?" It was Bobby, but he could also smell Amber and another person, a wolf.

A second voice joined his. *Must be the wolf.* "Skew? Is everything okay? It's Alek."

The change in his companion was remarkable. It was like a switch was thrown. Her head started bobbing and her movements went from smooth and practiced to twitching. "Alek. Alek. Need more vanilla. Must get ready for customers. Ice cream for the children."

She backed up until she was pressed against the freezer door, her eyes completely vacant. Tristan was stunned. Whatever had just happened was utterly fascinating.

"Bobby? Whoever just spoke needs to say good-bye loudly and then leave. Do not let him come down here. Have him guard the door. And you and Amber should come downstairs in animal form."

There were muffled noises and then the male named Alek spoke again. He sounded confused and a little annoyed. "Okay, see you tomorrow, Skew. Have a good night."

Tristan tucked himself under the cot while footsteps sounded and then the bright metal bell dinged and the door shut. As he expected, with both his and the wolf's stimuli removed the woman stood absolutely still, barely breathing, as though in some sort of stasis.

"Now?" It was Bobby's voice.

"Okay. But slowly." He slithered out from under the cot and went on talking as though they hadn't been interrupted. "How long have you been acting as ME again?"

She blinked and looked down at him. "Since the town was formed. It must be five years now."

He let out a chuckle as the others crept down the stairs. "Probably a pretty easy gig in a town full of Sazi." He used the tip of his nose to try to get the eyelid to open. Once again, she knelt down next to him and lifted the skin to show the red eyeball.

"Not as much as you'd think. The plague has been rough on the town. We lost four children just last fall. I never even got to see them. The family just called the mayor and he disposed of them. We have to burn them, you see. Can't bury them because cemeteries have to be registered with the county. Controlled burns don't. It's hard on the families, though."

He kept his face pointed toward her but flicked his eyes to the cat and python perched on the stairs, wide-eyed and as openmouthed as was possible in that form. "By the way, we haven't been introduced. He wrapped his head and neck gently around her arm and squeezed, as was the proper custom to greet in his form. "Ris Tupo. I'm investigating for Wolven."

She squeezed his chest lightly with her palm before raising her other hand in the air and shouting to the ceiling,

"Hallelujah! No offense to you because I'm sure you're busy, but it's about damned time they sent someone here. Make sure you stop by the police station. They probably have a stack of files you need to sign off on."

"And you are?"

"Carolyn. Dr. Carolyn Archeson. The doctorate is in organic chemistry, so don't ask me for an exam." He heard Bobby suck in a sharp hissing breath, which made her turn her head. "Oh. More Wolven? Wow, you guys do descend when you finally come."

Amber smoothly lied, pretending to be her own twin sister. That was good, since she and Skew had met in human form. No telling what would set her off again. "Aspen Monier. A pleasure."

"The famous seer? Any help is welcome, of course, but do we need a seer?"

She padded down the stairs the rest of the way, her bobcat-fluffy feet making her movements absolutely silent. "I'm thinking you do at this point. And this is Bobby Mbutu."

Carolyn, formerly Skew, smiled and rose, dipping her head courteously. "I'm twice honored. You're something of a legend, Professor Mbutu. I never thought I'd get a chance to meet you. Although I did attend the European Symposium in Warsaw back in ninety-five, hoping I'd run into you."

It took a few tries for Bobby to get words out. "I've heard of your work in new reaction media. I've been looking forward to meeting you."

Tristan forced his way into Bobby's mind for a quick discussion. *You know her?*

Knew. But only by mail. I've never seen her in person. Word was she died during the snake attack.

That would be why nobody had been looking for her. He

pushed into Amber's mind next, which was difficult because
she had shields up. **Ask the man who left, Alek, to come back
and announce himself. You have to see this.**

I've linked to him before, she replied. **Hang on.**

Bobby was chatting with Carolyn about the Warsaw con-
vention they'd both attended and how they'd happened to
miss meeting each other when the bell dinged upstairs and
the door opened. The woman paused mid-word, her lips
pulled back slightly from her teeth in a half smile.

"It's just me, Skew. Forgot my jacket."

The falcon's head started bobbing and it was as though
none of them were there or had been talking. "Alek is back.
Jacket, jacket. Cold outside. Bundle up!"

Bobby's head tipped until it was completely sideways. He
was staring at Skew's leg. "That is freaky. Amber, are you
picking up the shift in scents?"

Tristan definitely was. He was flicking his tongue as
quickly as Bobby was. Amber was sniffing up and down
Carolyn's leg. It was like her scent was cooking, right on her
body. "It's subtle but very deliberate. Balsam pine to pon-
derosa, milk to cream. All with the ringing of the bell. She's
Pavlov's bird."

"How did you get her to be . . . normal?" Amber had
shifted back to human and was twisting Skew's head toward
the light to look at her pupils.

"I was examining the body. She just spoke up, said it was
strangulation, with the throat being ripped out afterward to
cover the bruising. I'd already smelled that she'd touched
the body, so I asked if she'd examined the woman. You heard
the rest." He slithered around her feet, staring at the twitching muscles. "Do you think it's hypnosis or actual repetitive
conditioning?"

"I don't know. But I'm going to find out. I'm going to take her upstairs and put her in a trance sleep and see if I can unwind whatever happened to her head." She turned her head and stared down at him. "Thank you so much for planning my overnight, Ris. Silly me—I thought I might sleep."

He would have shrugged if he had shoulders. "She's been this way for years. I don't think it probably has to be fixed tonight if you don't want to."

Bobby nudged Amber's leg with the top of his head. "She was a brilliant chemist, Amber. Now she's trapped in the mind of a parakeet. Do what you can."

"So," Tristan said as he looked from the dead body to the brain-dead live body. "It looks like more than one person in town isn't who they appear to be. Things are getting interesting."

CHAPTER 13

It wasn't quite light when Anica woke up struggling to breathe on top of the covers, still wearing the light pullover top and jeans she'd had on at dinner. The window next to the bed was cracked open, and billowing tendrils of gray were filling the room. She sat up in a fit of coughing, and shooting white lights sparkled in her vision. It felt as though she'd been beaten with sticks. Every muscle in her body hurt.

"Papa?" She couldn't smell anything over the smoke and was getting disoriented. But she knew that Papa was a heavy sleeper. If she didn't get him out of the house, he might never wake up. "Bojan? Everyone must wake up, please!"

She heard an answering cough. It wasn't deep enough for Papa, so it must be Bojan. "We must get out of house quickly. The fire nearly here."

Crawling down the hallway, she saw Bojan first, coming out of Papa's room. He shook his head. "He didn't sleep in his bed last night. I will check the bathroom and study. You check the kitchen and front of house."

Anica nodded and shook her head, trying to get her head

unfuzzy. She pulled her shirt up over her nose, trying to block some of the smoke. Her heart was pounding faster with each second. That was going to make her sick very fast. She could not help Papa if she passed out herself. Reaching out to put a hand on the wall to help guide her through the house, she noticed something startling. *There is no heat.* Could it just be smoke, but no fire? How could that be?

The kitchen and dining area were less smoky. The smoke hovered about a foot off the floor, letting her see the carpeting clearly. Papa was not in this area. "He is not in kitchen, Bojan!"

"Not in bathroom or study either!" Her brother came into view at the edge of the dining room. "I will check garage— see if ATV is in there. Maybe he did not come home last night. My phone is on charger there. I will call fire department."

She nodded. "I will check laundry area." She pointed at her wristwatch. "We will meet outside in five minutes. Yes?"

He held up his hands. He had on no watch. "But I will count seconds instead. If you are not outside when I am done counting, I *will* come back in and find you." They clasped hands and squeezed. They were family and had been through worse together. She knew she could count on him.

"And I will do the same." He leaned forward and kissed each cheek and then tousled her hair like when they were both small.

Just as he disappeared into the swirling smoke, she heard a noise. But it didn't sound like a noise that Papa would make. It was too . . . stealthy. She extended her senses in the direction of the laundry room, her eyes first, then her nose. A scent ruffled at the back of her nose, of her memory. But she couldn't remember what it was. She did as Bobby had told her; she started to peel back the layers of scents. Discarding the smoke would be easy, as it was the heaviest scent. But her brain wouldn't let her cast it aside. Until now, she'd presumed the smoke was like all the other smoke floating around town. This smoke wasn't from wood, though. This smoke was heavy, metallic. It nearly cut her skin as she inhaled. A whisper of movement at the corner of her vision might have been smoke, but her nose said it wasn't. She believed her nose more than her eyes in the predawn haze.

The laundry room was just ahead. A tension was singing through her nerves as she approached the room, her face close to the floor. Something was wrong. Then she heard a noise, close to the sound of a growling dog. She'd heard that sound before, years before. A cold washed through her that didn't fit with the warm, humid air. It made her keep very still, and when she moved it was as silent as she could make it. She watched for any movement, kept bringing in smoke-filled air to scent with small breaths. She couldn't keep up breathing that way for long. She'd hyperventilate. But that wasn't her concern right now.

When the attack came, she was expecting it. But even knowing it was coming couldn't prepare her for the speed and ferocity of the body that landed on her back. Anica tried to turn over, to face her attacker, but the woman . . . yes, definitely a woman from the scent of perfume, countered, kept her face from being seen. The fragrance was expensive, something from Paris that was strong with the smell of exotic flowers. But she was far more than just a woman.

She was a shifter and, much more important, a *viper*.

Anica dipped her shoulder and rolled fast, forcing the woman to either let her go or follow her into the roll. The woman let herself be rolled, keeping her arms around Anica's neck, tightening with a strength that screamed *alpha*. Anica grabbed the arm that was throttling her throat and dug in her nails, while simultaneously turning her head to bite hard into the soft flesh in the crook of the woman's arm. The attacker cried out in pain and slapped her on the side of the head hard enough for Anica to see stars.

But she let go enough for Anica to pull in a great gulp of air near the floor, while the attacker's lungs had filled with smoke. She started coughing, hard enough that Anica was able to pull away. She reached back to grab on to the woman's shirt to keep her close and then used all her strength to slam her head and shoulders up and back. Her skull connected with the woman's face. The sound of bone meeting bone went in her ears and echoed in her head. The shirt ripped with a wet, sucking sound. A wave of dizziness swept through Anica's head, but she pulled away sharply before the woman could recover. She dropped the scrap of yellow fabric and scrambled for purchase on the carpeting, digging in her fingernails to pull out of the woman's reach for her.

"Bojan!" She didn't know if he heard her, or if he was able to help, but she didn't hear him trying to get back in to the house.

The growling hiss that sounded behind her gave her fresh incentive to get away. The skin-crawling scent of angry viper made her heart pound until the walls of the house turned to stone and the haze of smoke turned to feces-scented water vapor. She turned her head because she couldn't help herself. Her body froze and she stared in horrid fascination as the dark-haired woman's body narrowed, pale honeyed arms folding in and disappearing under scales that were nearly the same golden. When the hood of skin opened with a snap, the flow of magic stabbed at her, so strong it felt like venom burning her flesh.

The snake's head lunged forward, trying to impale her with poisoned fangs. Anica screamed and scrambled to get away, her fingers and sneakers digging for purchase. She leaped forward, just barely ahead of the teeth. One fang got caught in her shoe sole, tearing the shoe off her foot. But she didn't feel any pain in the foot, so she kept moving. She reached for the door to the garage, where Bojan had just gone through. A splat of venom landed on the wall next to her, smelling of cobra. She closed her eyes automatically. She couldn't afford to be blinded.

The door was locked! She turned the knob over and over in a panic, while the sound of fast-moving scales made her lash out with her foot. It met empty air. She couldn't afford to look back or search for another exit. The house, formerly the home of the police chief of the town, was intended to be a makeshift jail to imprison rogue shifters when they couldn't get the person into the jail in time. All the doors were heavy, steel-core security doors, meant for alpha shifters to open. But she wasn't an alpha.

The snake was close. Too close, but she had slowed down, enjoying the chase. The oranges smell from the snake was tainted, coated with thick, oily venom that corrupted everything Anica thought of as *happy*. She called on every ounce of strength, from deep down in her stomach, and slammed her body against the door. The shock wave made her whole body vibrate and sting. A deep dent appeared in the steel. She hit it again as the snake stopped. The tiny series of hisses, laughter at her panic with a wet and hollow sound, infuriated Anica.

"You will *never* have me!" She spit the words with eyes

closed, like the snake had spit at her. She risked a glance back. The blob of her saliva traveled across the tiled floor of the laundry room and hit the snake in the face. The snake let out another hiss—this one high-pitched, her mouth open wide under angry eyes. But Anica didn't care if she was angry. Even if Anica would die today, she would not give the snake the satisfaction of showing fear. "Go back to hell, where you belong!"

As Anica threw her entire body weight into the door one last time, the frame finally gave way. Bojan was on the floor of the empty garage, his wavy black hair matted with red. A metal baseball bat lay on the concrete next to him, covered with blood. She slammed the door shut behind her, but the latch was broken, so it bounced and hung wrong on the hinges. Reaching down, she felt his heart beating erratically. Blood pooled around his head, frightening Anica until she remembered that head wounds bled much. Once, when she was a child, a bale of hay Papa and Samit were lifting into the hayloft had slipped and thrown her against one of the stall doors. She had bled horribly even though she hadn't felt dizzy at all and Mama had sewed up the injury with only four tiny stitches.

Anica had no idea where the switch was that would open the garage door—she never went in or out this way. Even if she could escape, she wouldn't leave her brother behind, and she couldn't carry him. She looked for his phone but could not spot it. Had he called the fire department? Was anyone coming? Her heart was pounding, panicked.

The time for running is gone. It is time to face my fears.

Her mind cleared and her pulse calmed. She picked up the bat. It wasn't much of a weapon for long range but could inflict a lot of damage if she charged the woman.

The side of the fangs.

The thought came into her head almost unbidden, but she realized it was exactly what she needed to do. She remembered one of the snakes from the cave when he broke a fang. He had been disoriented for several minutes. A successful blow might disable her attacker long enough for both Anica and her brother to get away. She heard the slithering of scales across the tile and then the sting of magic as the snake contemplated the door.

Holding the bat under her arm, she dragged Bojan to the far side of the big metal refrigerator, where he was protected from a fast attack. There was really nowhere to hide for long. Looking around the garage, she noticed several cans of wasp spray. Papa hated wasps from years back. They would chase him around the raspberry patch, where anyone else could pick the berries in peace. Tiny stinging insects were his only real phobia, so there were several full cans on the shelf. She quietly picked each one up until she found a full one. If the snake came in, she'd find out what it felt like to have poison spit at her!

But the snake was smart. Instead of a frontal assault, she sent her magic into the room ahead of her. Anica felt her muscles freeze in place. She couldn't move at all. The wasp spray was locked in one hand. The bat in the other. But both of them may as well have been in a different house for the good they did her.

The door began to creak open, the bent hinges struggling to work properly. She saw the tongue slide in first, flicking pale and pink into the air as her heart began to pound in her temples. As the head moved through the narrow gap, the slitted golden eyes fixed on her. The rest of the shifter's snake body eased through the opening without hesitation. Anica was no threat; try as she might, her muscles refused to function. The snake ignored her, instead following the trail of blood to where Bojan lay in a heap behind her. He was helpless!

I must move. I must! *Help me!*

As the snake made a long S curve toward her brother, Anica tightened her grasp on the bat, realizing suddenly that she *could* tighten her fingers. Adrenaline raced through every nerve; each muscle and her skin began to tingle, the hairs standing on end so completely she could see them as an almost electric blue sheen on top of her skin.

The bindings of what felt like steel began to bend, like the door had. She took a step forward, then another. It hurt like fire. Every muscle felt like it was being rubbed raw by sandpaper. But she couldn't just let the snake kill Bojan. Already she was raised up over his still form, hood extended.

Using every ounce of willpower she could summon, she opened her mouth and screamed, "Get away from my brother!" The snake turned like lightning and Anica's bat hit her right in the mouth. It wasn't hard enough to break her tooth, but it stunned her for a moment. The viper's magic increased in response, slowing Anica even more. But she pushed through, just as she'd pushed herself to escape the cave, twelve years ago.

It felt like her chest was going to explode from the inside, and her lungs burned, just trying to catch a breath. The snake flicked her tongue rapidly and suddenly the black slits in the golden eyes narrowed like a bright light had been shown in them. Anica smelled fear for the first time, just before she brought the bat down again—this time on the tip of the snake's tail. As with stubbing a pinky toe or getting a thorn in a paw, she'd learned that the smallest spot was the most delicate.

The snake screamed then, with a human voice. The scream wasn't as high-pitched as she'd expected from a woman. The cobra fled back into the house, and though she wanted to, Anica didn't dare follow. She had to stay with Bojan. She used a bottle of water Papa kept in the refrigerator to clean the blood off Bojan's head. There was a wide gash in his scalp.

While she was carefully probing the wound, she heard a voice at the other end of the house. "Anica!" Was it Tristan? It was! She could feel his presence in her mind again.

"Be careful, Tristan!" she called out as loud as she could. "There is viper in house! A woman snake!"

"Bojan! Anica!" It was Papa! "Where are you?"

"Papa! Tristan! We're in the garage." She put Bojan's head gently on the floor and raced to the door, yanking it open. She didn't worry about the snake anymore. The men could handle her, if she was still in the house.

Papa raced toward Anica, his arms open wide. Tristan was just behind, his face worried. She wasn't sure who to run to, but Papa reached her first and pulled her into a tight hug that reminded her of his animal form.

Tristan stopped just behind. She hugged Papa but looked at Tristan over her father's shoulder and held out a hand. He touched it quickly and then slipped into her mind.

Are you okay?

She nodded, and smiled at him. **I am well. Bojan is hurt, but he will heal. He is alpha.**

His brow furrowed and he smelled worried, but she wasn't sure why. She'd just told him she felt fine. Actually, she felt better than fine. Good, really. It seemed long ago that she'd woken hurting so much. And even the pain from fighting against the snake's magic seemed gone.

"Anica," Papa said, pulling her to arm's length, away from Tristan's hand. Papa smelled both worried and guilty. "You say there is snake. I smell it when I come in. Where did it come from? Where did it go?"

She didn't have an answer for him. "I wake and house is filled with smoke. We . . . Bojan and I . . . call for you and when do you do not answer, we look for you to make sure you are safe." She pointed to where Bojan was still unconscious. Tristan moved to squat down beside him.

The sour, bitter scent of Papa's guilt was overwhelming. "I should have been here. I should have been protecting you. Again, I have failed you. And Bojan." She followed her father's gaze to where Tristan was helping Bojan sit up. She could feel the push of magic he was using to heal the wound on her brother's head. It wasn't healing magic, but it was strong enough to mend the flesh. He would probably have a scar, but he would live to have one.

She put a hand on Papa's cheek, rough with thick, unshaven hair. She turned his face to meet hers. She couldn't help but notice the swollen nose and heavy, dark bruising under reddened eyes. He was exhausted. "No, Papa. No. You do not have to protect me." He tightened his grip on her arm and she patted his cheek. "I love that you wish to." She pointed to the door. "But the snake? I fight her and she runs. *She* runs. I do not. You have taught me to be strong. You did not fail me."

Anica turned her head to a new smell. More people were arriving. "Hello? Anyone here?" It was the doctor's voice, but Anica also smelled Bobby with her. It actually excited her, because there was so much to smell here and she didn't quite know where to start.

"Excuse me, Papa." She gave him a quick hug and gave Tristan a fast kiss on her way to the front door. It surprised him, but she could feel that he didn't object. The pair had remained outside the door, only each poking a head in to call their arrival. It was very courteous of them, so she was too. She held the door and waved them in as Mama had taught her, with a short curtsy. "Please, come in. It is nice to have guests who do not sneak in and try to kill me."

Bobby's tongue was already flicking as Tristan came to stand near her, close enough that the exotic spice of his scent surrounded her, soaked into her skin. "Yeah, I smell the viper. Female king cobra. And I haven't smelled a single snake until this second . . . present company excepted."

Tristan put a hand on her shoulder and pulled her close, to nestle against his chest. "She fought off the snake with a baseball bat. There's blood in two spots in the garage and spit venom in at least one. We should be able to find the shifter who attacked the family fairly quickly." He motioned with his head behind them. "If the good doctor could check on Anica's brother, I'm sure he'd appreciate it. He was unconscious with a bad head wound. I got him awake, but I'll bet he has a nasty headache."

She nodded. "I'm on it." Then the doctor looked at her with a strangely amused expression. "I take it Anica doesn't require any healing?"

Anica wasn't sure why that would amuse her. "I am well. I was very sore when I woke up, but it was just stiffness."

Even Bobby had a quirk of a smile. "I'm sure you're feeling better now." The amusement of the two was making

Tristan annoyed, judging by the burnt-metal smell wafting through the smoke. Which reminded her!

She looked at Bobby, who might share her excitement. "The smoke in the house now is not same smoke as when I woke! There was much more and it smelled of metal."

He turned his attention from Tristan to her. "What sort of metal?"

Anica let out a frustrated breath. "That is problem. I do not know so many metals. But it is not steel or aluminum or copper. I have smelled those all recently, when you say to smell things. So I smell copper pipes in bathroom and metal of refrigerator and stove and pots when I am cooking. Cold and hot make the metal smell different!"

This time, his smile went with the pride smell. "Yes, they do. I'm glad you're studying on your own. So . . . not a common metal. Where did you smell it the strongest? In what room?"

She tried to think back. "It was when I first smell snake. So in hallway on way to laundry."

Tristan let out a slight cough. "I'm going to find some fans and get the rest of this smoke out of here."

"There are fans in the bedrooms and on the ceilings. But there is smoke outside too, yes?"

Bobby waved his hand in agreement. "Don't clear out the smells until I finish with the scene, okay? Check the outside perimeter. See if the snake left a trail."

Tristan gave a curt nod and went out on the front porch. Like at Paula's house, he took off his shirt and stood very still with arms raised.

"Excuse me," she asked Bobby, "but what does he do, to stand like that? He is very pretty, but I do not understand this way to smell for trail." "Very pretty" was an understatement. Every muscle stood out in sharp relief under his skin. He reminded Anica of the models she saw in expensive magazines who sold swimming things in photos. For just a moment, he turned and their eyes met through the window before he shut his again. Her whole body felt woozy just from a look. Never had other boyfriends made her feel so . . . wobbly on her feet, yet tight and flush all over.

Bobby was already flicking his tongue around the hallway and spoke to her in a distracted way. "Kraits smell with their skin . . . *all* of their skin. Where you have only the tissues in your nose that can absorb and identify scent, every pore of his body can absorb and identify. You can smell better in your animal form, but imagine if every hair on your body as a bear was a separate, distinct nose." He touched a spot on the wall, brushing the paint with his fingers and flicking his tongue. "The more skin he exposes, the bigger his . . . *nose*."

Anica stared out through the blinds on the window. Tristan had moved from the porch to stand on the front path. He would walk a step, then stand with eyes shut. Then turn and take another step. She wondered first what sort of bear a *crake* was and then what it would feel like to smell with her shoulder or finger or—"What is it like to smell with tongue?" She noticed he was tasting the air very high on the wall. "You are not smelling in right place. I *crawl* down hall . . . below smoke."

Bobby turned his head. "But smoke, like heat, *rises*. What you smelled at the floor earlier is on the top of the wall or the ceiling now. That's why you found air near the floor. For crime scenes, we look for where things *go*. Where blood splatters, where particles fall, where scents stick."

Oh! That made very good sense!

"And for smelling with my tongue, I don't know that I can compare it to a nose. I've never had one . . . not to smell with, anyway. But I can tell you that when I eat, I don't get the luxury of tasting blends. You can eat a piece of cake and taste *cake*. I eat cake and I taste flour and butter and egg. Each taste is distinct by itself. I really hate anything processed, because I don't like the taste of the chemicals."

She wasn't really sure what to say to that, except, "I do like cake. I would be sad to not taste it anymore." He just shrugged. She watched him looking up, and then thought of what he said. To look where things *go*. It reminded her of the fight and how she bit the woman. "When we fight, before she shift, I bite her and rip her shirt." She started looking around the floor and there—"Here is piece of shirt I rip. Will this help you?" She picked up the piece of golden fabric. It clung to her fingers. "It is silk." She reached down and smelled it. "This is the perfume she was wearing, and you can still smell the metal smoke." She handed it up to Bobby, who flicked his tongue all along the surface but left no wet spots that would say his tongue had been there.

"Wait. This is *terbium*. But I don't smell any insulation burning."

"I do not know this . . . is it a metal? You say insulation. Is it in walls? Was the house really on fire? I did not smell any fire. Only smoke." She looked up and around. There was a pattern of black smoke on the ceiling, but she didn't see anything that looked burnt.

"Terbium is used in fluorescent lightbulbs and televisions to create yellow and orange color. It's used in a lot of other things too, but in tiny little amounts. It's a rare earth metal but isn't found in pure form in nature. The thing is, there's too much of it on this tiny scrap of fabric. This is more terbium than you would normally find in a whole room of flat screens."

"Then why you say insulation? It is not in walls?"

He flicked a glance down at her. "Since it's *inside* bulbs or screens, I would expect to smell the insulation covering the wiring—"

He paused long enough that she looked up to see his reddish-golden slitted eyes watching her calmly. But she could hear his heart beating faster and his smell had anticipation, as though he was willing her to work it out for herself. "I have never smell this metal before, even when I have dropped long bulb and it breaks. So it must only smell when hot. If wiring is burnt or hot, then bulbs break and we smell the terbium? So not just where things go, but what causes them to go we must look for?"

Again the scent of pride from his dark skin and what she realized was a rare smile. He patted her head. "Exactly. But there aren't any burnt bulbs here and no hot wiring."

"So where does terbium come from?" She knew little about metals, but he said *rare* and *tiny* and there was already too much for a small scrap of shirt. And far too much smoke she'd smelled. "Metal comes from stone, yes? We have only lived here a short time. Could there be such stone in house that burn?"

Bobby clapped her on the shoulder so firmly that she nearly fell over. "A good question. I think we need to find out."

Papa came in from the garage. "You find where this snake went, Agent?"

Bobby shook his head. "Tristan is outside looking for that. I'm trying to find out why she was here at all."

Papa nodded thoughtfully. "I have wonder this too. An-ica has never hurt fly, and Bojan is gentle soul. Samit . . . yes. I could see him angering someone enough to attack. But not my other children. Why come here in night? Attack my children? Was she looking for *me*? I know no snakes, and there are no snakes in town. Except you, of course." He paused and shook his head. His scent was troubled, chaotic, and Bobby waited until he found the words. "But I must say this, even though I do not like to say it. Please know that." Bobby nodded, but he was frowning. "You are first snake in town since I come here, other than snake councilman and his guards. Did you come here alone? I do not see you come to town."

Papa was asking if he brought the attacker *with* him? It made sense, for a snake to come with another snake, and for a man to come with a woman. But why would he do that? To Anica's surprise, Bobby didn't react with anger. "Thank you for your honesty. I do understand your concern, but I did come here alone." Papa accepted his words, but his nose wasn't as good as hers. Bobby was lying. *Should I tell Papa?* She didn't know. Everyone acted like he was an important man, honest and trusted. He was smart. But evil men could be smart too. She needed to talk to someone *she* trusted first. But she would be keeping a close eye on him.

She turned her head as she smelled Bojan come into the house from the garage. His face lit up with a smile when he saw her and he opened his arms wide to greet her. "Anica!" She raced to him and let him envelop her in a hug. "Papa tells me you smash snake with *bat*?!" He laughed when she nodded. "You are *mean* little bear."

That made her smile. The doctor had healed him well for him to be laughing. "You were hurt. She slithered to you, was going to bite you. It was bad enough little bear bit you. I do not want snake for a brother."

She didn't mean to say it loud, but Bobby heard and let out an annoyed sigh. "I understand your anger, Anica, but not all snakes are bad. There are good snakes in the world too."

Turning her head, she didn't leave her brother's side. "I know you believe this, and I *want* to believe you too. But I have seen only two good snakes in my short time as Sazi. Ahmad and Tuli are good snakes. When they help us, after the mediation, find the cave where I was turned, they fight their own kind to protect *bears*. Ahmad's anger is real for poor bear children. I could smell it myself. Never would I have believed that before I see, so it is possible, and I hope you are right that there are others."

Bobby's face showed a knowledge he wasn't willing to share and his scent was muddied with too many other smells. She would need time for her head to sort them. "There are others, closer than you may think."

CHAPTER 14

Tristan was trying hard to concentrate on what Bobby had asked him to do. The problem was, he knew who the attacker was and that was making it difficult to focus. Because the simple answer was, if he could find Lagash he would find the woman too, because she was his mate. Not only that, she was likely the reason Ahmad had sent him here. It wasn't Lagash Ahmad had smelled when he arrived.

It was Ahmad's own sister.

Ahmad and Tristan had both thought her dead. But then, they'd thought Lagash dead too. If Ahmad had stopped to think about it, he would have realized it himself. But the fact that he couldn't root out Enheduanna in such a small town meant they both had incredibly clever disguises.

Tristan didn't know the oldest of Sargon's daughters very well. Mostly, she'd kept to the temples—she was the high priestess. But Enheduanna was a prolific and brilliant writer, of both songs and epic poems, and Tristan had read nearly everything she'd written back then.

What an odd pairing, Lagash and Enheduanna, the warrior

and the poet. But the cosmos had an odd sense of humor when it came to matings.

Such as his own.

What the hell am I going to do about Anica? How could he be mated to an attack victim . . . one who hated snakes with completely justified passion?

He'd thought he could shield her out. They hadn't had sex. Not really. He *should* be able to block the connection. It should be possible for her to remain blissfully unaware and he could move on to complete his mission and go home.

But that plan had failed miserably. Bobby had found it hilarious when he'd been awakened by the feel of his magic being sucked away to deal with Anica's crisis. When he'd taken Bobby's advice and dropped his shields, he'd known instantly what the crisis *was* and had rushed to find her father and bring him home.

I'm pretty sure Zarko knew I was lying about how I knew his children were in danger. But he didn't question it. He'd just told Tristan to get in the ATV and they'd raced to get here.

"You okay?" Amber's voice made him jump. She noticed and apologized. "Sorry. Didn't realize you were concentrating."

He shook his head and lowered his arms, reaching down to pick up his shirt. "That's okay. I was concentrating on the wrong things anyway."

Her answer was noncommittal. "Ah." They stood there for a moment, breathing in the smoky air before she finally spoke again. "I suggest telling her." She was serious, and there was a concern there that was surprising, considering she really didn't like him.

It wasn't her decision. "Noted."

Another pause before she spoke. "So there's another snake in town?"

"Yes, and it's a real concern. I think I need to do some more looking around town and then talk to Ahmad before I discuss what I found with anyone else."

The abrupt stink of annoyed cat flooded his pores on one side. "Not acceptable. Tell me and I'll decide whether the full Council needs to know."

He turned and looked down at the diminutive bobcat. He didn't really worry if she was annoyed. He'd never met a Monier he couldn't handle, including her vicious, unstable mother. "I don't answer to you. I don't even answer to the Council. An old friend called in a *favor*. I answer to him alone. But if you want to try to convince Ahmad that I should tell the Council, feel free. Or hey, Bobby's right here. He's a fine investigator. Let him figure it out and tell Charles. But see, there's a problem. Finding and killing Lagash would be relatively easy. I could go through town and slaughter the whole population in the middle of the night and it would be done. One of the people here is him. A simple fire would destroy the evidence and barely raise a human eyebrow in a state covered with wildfires." She winced when he said that, and her anger ratcheted up even more. A high-pitched growl escaped her.

He let out a harsh laugh. "Be pissed at me if you want. I could care less. You know it's the truth. What I want to know, what *Ahmad* wants to know, is, what is he up to? *Why* is Lagash in Luna Lake? Why integrate and live quietly for a decade? Why suddenly kill a waitress and blow up her house just when I arrive? Something deeper is going on and it's been going on for a very long time." He paused to let it sink in. "Lagash was Sargon's cupbearer, Amber. He was Sargon's *planner.* His war planner, his schemer, the one who made the bodies of Sargon's enemies disappear. Akede became an empire because of *Lagash*, not Sargon. Of the two, I would much rather face Sargon."

Her entire body stilled, and he couldn't even hear her heart beating. "You're serious." Her words were a whisper, as though she didn't want to say it too loud.

"No," he said with sarcasm dripping from his voice and skin, "I'm just here for fun. I will probably die doing this, Amber. Ahmad and I are both aware that this is likely a suicide mission. I'm doing it because I know what Lagash is capable of, how dangerous he is to both Sazi and humans. Right now, I need to figure out why Lagash wants Anica and her brother dead. Because make no mistake . . . no matter who did the actual job, he planned it."

The next words out of her mouth dropped his jaw, because it was something he hadn't considered. "Maybe his plan was simply to kill your mate. In a new mating, it could easily kill you too. Clean and simple way to get rid of you without confrontation."

It was clean and simple. Almost *too* clean. "Possibly, but there's an equal chance it would drive me insane with grief and make me impossible to defeat." He shook his head. "No. There's something deeper at work. I just need to figure it out." He tapped his fingers against his blue jeans. "I need to interview this family . . . see what threat they could possibly pose to someone like Lagash."

Amber had given in. He could sense it in his skin. She sighed and said, "Dalvin still has the mediation files. He planned to turn them over to Charles when he arrives next week. Read them first. It'll give you a lot of background on the family and cut down the number of questions you need to ask." She paused. "I'll be talking to Charles tonight. Should I tell him to prepare for battle when he comes?"

Tristan considered that. Charles was a hell of a fighter but was likely out of practice. Formerly known as Sasha, the Great Bear of the North, he was one of the oldest Sazi in the world, and one of the few who had been worshiped as a god. Could Charles take Lagash, one-on-one? In his youth, absolutely. Without breaking a sweat. Possibly even today. But—

"Lagash never fights alone. He's always preferred sneak attacks and overwhelming force. It's how Sargon became an emperor instead of just a minor tribal leader."

If Lagash wasn't alone, it could easily be a trap. "If he knows *you're* here, he knows Charles isn't far behind. That he hasn't run means he isn't worried, which means he has a plan. It might not be wise for Charles to come right now. He barely survived the plague. There's no guarantee he would survive another dose. Or something worse—"

That made her nervous. Bobby had told him that Amber had nearly drained herself permanently while healing Charles. She was still powerful, but she wasn't the healer she had once been. The whole damned Council had become watercolor versions of the original oil paintings he remembered. "Let me look over what he has. And speaking of Dalvin, he probably needs to keep an eye on the brother. Zarko can take care of himself."

Amber used the back of her hand to push back her hair several times, looking for all the world like she was grooming in animal form. "What about Anica? Mating or no, she's a three-day. She's damned lucky she survived an attack like this. I still can't believe she survived being thrown into a *house*. That impact was the equivalent of falling off a ten-story building. But I checked her out. She's fine. More than fine, actually. She's in perfect health."

He knew. Tristan couldn't help but look back at the house. He could *feel* her, right at the edge of his senses. "Can you watch her? I don't like to ask, but . . . I don't dare keep her with me."

She nodded. "She can stay with me at the apartments until Charles arrives. But just so you know . . . Zarko told me both of the kids were denied visas. They'll be returning to Serbia unless we can find someone at a level to help her. We lost a *lot* of people at the federal level during the attacks. It's been hard to rig the system like we used to." That actually might not be a bad thing. Lagash would have no reason to chase Anica to Serbia, and perhaps that much distance would allow him to break the tie. She would be safe, could be happy. He looked over to see Amber watching him. "I know that smile, Ris. Speaking from experience, mating ties don't work that way." He'd been smiling? "You can't just send her away and have it all disappear. It sneaks up on you, overwhelms you."

"You escaped your mating tie. Charles is your *choice*, not your mate."

She replied in a soft voice that had iron bindings wrapped tightly around, "And every day . . . every *single* day I have to fight the urge to run to the man I'm mated to . . . Raphael. Or to kill myself." She let him get a glimpse at the pain just below the surface of her skin. Her hands were clenched into fists and the tension extended into the muscles of her forearms until they disappeared beneath the soft tan and gold shirt. Her voice lowered to a whisper. "It sneaks in, Ris. As quiet as the night . . . and as relentless as the tide." Pain was carved in the lines of her face, in the hollows beneath her eyes. "You're strong. But not strong enough."

"Hey, you guys okay?" Bobby walked toward them, his movements tentative. He might not be able to see her face, but he could probably smell the open wound in her soul. Then, like a cloud had passed to reveal the sun, her face was normal again. A calm illusion.

"Just going over the clues. Did you find anything new inside?"

Bobby had good intuition, but he also respected boundaries. His eyes took on an expression of disinterest in their business. "Does a bomb count?"

"What!?" Tristan turned and started forward. How did he not feel her panic?

The taller man let out a small chuckle and put a restraining hand on his shoulder. "Easy, boy. The intruder didn't have time to arm it. It's likely that's what Anica interrupted. It was in the dryer. Nobody probably would have noticed it until they came to investigate the murders. I have no doubt that's what she'd planned for Bojan and Anica."

This wasn't making any sense. "But why try a second murder, less than a day after the first? She had to know we would be watching for a pattern. And for a bomb."

Bobby shrugged. "This was a woman. The first was a man. Maybe they're unrelated."

Except when they weren't. His nephew-in-law paused and stared at him long enough his inner eyelids blinked up at the same time the outer ones blinked down. One of the things Tristan liked best about Bobby was his brain. And one of the things he hated about him was the same thing. "You're lying to me, Ris. Spill."

He tried to brush it off. "How can I be lying to you? I haven't said anything."

"Less than nothing, I'd say." Now Amber was watching him too. "Your scent has vanished and you only do that when you're hiding something. Your glands were the source of the Wolven cologne, if you recall, which means we both recognize when it's used."

"And I'll repeat again what I already told you. I report to *Ahmad*. He gets first shot at any information I've found. But it's all right there for you to find too." He waved at the house. "Have at it."

Bobby blinked and put his hands on his hips. He laughed then, a sound of pure joy. His snow-white teeth were nearly blinding. "A race to the finish it is, then. You have your experience and I have my training. But we face the final threat together. Your word." He held out one broad hand, his golden watch flashing in the morning sun. Amber let out a snort and a scent of angry cat that said she wasn't at all pleased by the turn of events.

Tristan took the offered hand of his python cohort. "If I have any say in when that happens."

Shaking her head in resignation, Amber walked back toward the front door. "I'll talk to Zarko about new sleeping arrangements for the duration of this . . . *mess*." She turned so she was staring at them, walking backward in her high-heeled short boots. "By the way, we're a little short of beds in town. That means you and Bobby get to sleep here with Anica's *papa*, Ris. Have fun!" She laughed all the way through the door and slammed it shut before either of them could object.

CHAPTER 15

I am glad I can stay with you again, Rachel," Anica said as she unpacked her toiletries onto the counter. "And thank you for the clothes. I will be careful with them. This time."

"Happy to have you!" her friend called from the next room. "And don't worry about it. I put all your clothes in the washer downstairs to get rid of the smoky smell. Dalvin told me down there that he and Bojan will be bunking in Alek's apartment and Amber will be just down the hall in Tammy's old place. Anyone trying to get at you will have to get through a bunch of pretty tough alphas to do it." Rachel stood in the doorway and leaned against the jamb. Her hair was longer than the last time Anica stayed here, nearly to her shoulders. It brushed the collar of the burgundy satin shirt that made her skin glow. Rachel was a very good dresser. It always made Anica feel a little self-conscious about her functional but plain wardrobe. "Hey, can I ask you something?"

Anica nodded. "Of course."

"What's up between Bojan and Scott? He has a hell of a shiner."

She stopped unpacking her shirts and looked up, confused. "I do not know this word, 'shiner.'"

"Black eye. Someone punched Scott. He wouldn't say who, but I think it might have been Bojan."

Anica let out a breath. She wasn't sure if she should betray her brother's confidence, but Rachel was very smart and she knew Scott very well. But Anica lowered her voice, just to be safe. She motioned for Rachel to come in the room and sit next to her on the quilted bedspread that had a bridal ring pattern in a pretty shade of blue and white. "Bojan did hit Scott. He was angry, but I think it is not Scott he is angry with, but himself."

Rachel likewise whispered, keeping her head close to Anica's. Her hair smelled like mint, which would have made her smile at a different time. "What's up? I thought they were friends."

"Yes," Anica conceded. "But Scott maybe thinks it is more? He kissed Bojan. Like *boyfriend*. Bojan . . . he has never thought of himself for such a thing."

Rachel's jaw dropped so far, her mouth was a wide o. She covered it with a hand before speaking from behind her palm. Her voice lowered even further until it was an astonished hiss. "Holy shit, are you kidding me?" There wasn't a need to respond, so Anica just shrugged. Rachel leaned back on the bed and seemed to be sorting through events in her head. "But it actually makes a lot of sense."

Now Anica nodded agreement. She turned to where she could look at Rachel and the other woman mirrored her motion, each of them putting a knee on the bed with the other foot on the floor for balance. "It does to me as well.

Bojan has always been very . . . sensitive for a man. He has
many more friends who are girls than boys when he is young.
Samit always had friends who were rough, masculine. They
race cars, watch rugby, fistfight for fun. Bojan's friends
cook and write poetry and hate to watch fights." She raised
a finger, not wanting to give Rachel the wrong impression.
"Bojan *can* fight. He is very strong. But he fights to *defend*.
Other mothers in town, they ask Bojan to walk their daughters
home or take them to festivals, for protection. Never would
they ask Samit that. He was who girls needed protection
from. You see?"

Rachel had been witness to that side of Samit, so she
didn't have to go into detail. She had seen Samit at his worst,
when he went rogue and tried to kill her with a rifle. "Yeah,
I get that. Scott has really been enjoying hanging out with
Bojan. They have a lot in common. This past month has been
the happiest I've seen him in . . . forever." All of a sudden,
Rachel smelled sad, like she realized, as Anica had, that
the two men could be throwing away their own happiness in
exchange for silly pride.

It made Anica shake her head with frustration. "Bojan
too. I tell him this when he is so angry, with swollen fist.
I tell him I fear that Samit tease him so much, for whole
life, that he would never consider another man to be someone to . . . be happy with." She picked up the last item from
the suitcase, the novel she was reading, and looked at the
cover, where two people were embracing with need in their
eyes. Why could it *not* be two men, instead of a man and
woman, who saw each other in that way?

"Well, that explains why when Dalvin suggested Bojan
room with Scott he snapped at him and told him to mind
his own business. Dalvin couldn't figure out what made him

so mad." Rachel stood up. "We need to get them together. For their own good."

Anica winced. "I do not think this is such a good idea. Bojan can be stubborn."

Rachel walked to the doorway and tapped a finger on the painted wood trim. "Scott's like that too, trust me. But I'll think of something." She spun on her heels and nearly skipped from the room. "I'll get some dinner started and then you can tell me about that hottie, Tristan."

Anica opened her mouth to respond, but Rachel was already in the kitchen. She bent down and flipped her hair over her head and bound it in a yellow band. When she stood up, it floated over her head like a pom-pom. "His scent is all over your neck. I can't wait to hear how his spit wound up in your *ear.*"

Heat rose into Anica's face and even made the tops of her ears hot, which made Rachel laugh lightly. Anica remembered that Bojan had interrupted her bath before she could finish scrubbing with the mint. And she'd hugged Papa. He didn't say anything, but oh! Tristan was going to be sleeping there. She should warn him. Of course, it might already be too late. She didn't worry that they would hurt each other, but there could be much yelling.

It might be good to talk to Rachel, especially since her stomach was sick with the thought that Papa would make Tristan angry enough to leave. Yes, she would tell her. She needed to say some of it out loud, and not just in her mind.

There was a knock on the door and Anica presumed it would be Amber. "I'll get it." She walked to the front door and opened it. But instead of the bobcat doctor, it was Claire Sanchez. She hadn't seen Claire in nearly two weeks! She reached out and gave the other woman a quick hug. "Claire! It is good to see you."

"Hey, girls. I didn't realize you two were back to rooming together."

Rachel let out a little squeal and ran across the room to give the blond Texas wolf a big hug. "You look *great*, girl! Come in, come in! The sorority meeting is complete. How was the trip across the Bering Strait? Did you find the island? How's Alek? Did you find Sonya? Did you get to eat fresh crabs?" Her words were spilling over themselves to get out. Claire laughed and came inside. Anica shut the door behind her.

When she sat down on the couch, Rachel returned to the kitchen and opened the refrigerator. Anica noticed Claire's face was burnt and her lips still chapped from the harsh ocean winds. "You have been on the ocean for many hours. Your skin is very red."

Claire touched her face gingerly and nodded. "We just flew in from the coast this morning. It should be healed by tomorrow. But yeah, I should have worn a face mask like Alek did. But I grew up in Kansas and Texas. I'd never seen glaciers! I wanted to have the experience of standing on the bow watching the icebergs while we were at full steam. It was totally worth it."

"Ooo!" Anica said, sitting down next to her on the brown-and-green-patterned couch. "I have never seen icebergs. Always we would take boat from Dubrovnik when Papa wanted to fish. The Adriatic Sea had many storms that would chap my skin, but never were there icebergs to make it worth pain!"

Rachel came back and handed them bottles of soda.

"Sorry, I'm out of liquor. The grocery is totally empty. Your papa needs to send someone shopping in Spokane pretty damned quick. I'm down to crackers and tuna."

Anica winced. "That will be difficult. There is no money. Papa has been trying to find ways to pay for food for the people. He has such worry about it. He has been paying from the money we travel with to feed the older people. But do not worry. When the moon is full, we will do big hunt and fill freezers. But there is no more food until then."

Rachel's jaw dropped, while Claire's shut tight, causing one of the cracks on her lips to break open. A spot of blood pooled in the crack and grew to fill it. "Are you kidding? That's more than a *week*!" Rachel asked with outrage making her voice harsh. "What about all of the Council members who have been wandering through here? There isn't any money *anywhere*?"

Anica shook her head sadly, staring down at her fingers as she twisted the fabric of her pale blue cotton top. "I should probably not say, but Papa has already borrowed all he can from Council, just to pay off the debts to the food stores the town already had when the former mayor died. The doctor has given much money of her own for last month's food run. We must find other ways to get money or town will have to close down and people move to other towns."

Claire let out a small sigh. "The Tedford pack gave too. We don't have much, though. We own our land and raise our food, so the only money we get is during hunting season. We're strapped."

Rachel fell back in her chair. "Well, hell. I have no idea where to get a job around here. It's not like there's a help wanted section of the bulletin board at the Community

Center. And even if there was . . . they get their money from the same place. It's robbing Peter to pay Paul."

Anica couldn't help but agree. "Papa is looking to see whether there are computer jobs elsewhere that could be done here, without travel, since only a very few residents could keep a full-time job without sick days for moon." She took a deep breath. "But let us not talk of sad things." Patting Claire's hand, she tried to put happy in her scent. "Tell us of icebergs and finding Alek's sister, yes?"

Claire held up her index finger. "Actually, before we do that, let me run upstairs for a second." She jumped up and quickly left the apartment, leaving the door open. Anica could hear her footsteps as she ran up the stairs. It was only moments before they returned down again and Claire lugged in three stretched-tight plastic grocery bags. "Alek and I did a major shopping run on the way back because I emptied all my cupboards before we left. It's mostly healthy, with some junk food thrown in, but I'll be happy to share. I figured it was this or eat at the *diner*, and I'd really rather avoid Paula."

Anica looked at Rachel, who blanched and winced. "What?" Claire asked. "Has she whacked out again? Do I need to sleep in wolf form for a few days so she doesn't jump me?"

Another wave of sadness hit Anica and her eyes teared up. "No. You do not need to fear anymore. Paula was killed yesterday."

Claire nearly dropped the bags in her hands and did set them down rapidly before sitting down again. "Oh, Anica. I'm so sorry."

No, she wasn't. The pepper scent was strong in the air. Like Rachel, Claire didn't like Paula. "That is *kind* of you to say." Anica could hear her own words come out raspy, harsh, and brimming with the scent of lie, just as Claire's words had.

Claire winced at her anger. Her blue eyes showed a flash of sorrow and her scent finally turned misty, at least with regret. "Okay, you're right. I'm not sorry. Well, I'm *sort of* sorry." That was at least the truth. "I'm sorry for *you*, because you seemed to get along. But I'm not surprised, I guess is what I mean. Paula made enemies easier than friends."

Anica rubbed at her runny nose. "This is true. I hear of many people who do not like her. But I *do*." She blinked back tears. "And I will miss her. She did not deserve to die like that."

Claire reached forward and touched her hand, more curious now than sad. But Anica couldn't expect so much anger between them to simply disappear. "What happened?"

Rachel shrugged and sat forward, reached for the grocery bags, and rose to take them to the kitchen. "Nobody knows yet. Her throat was ripped up and there was a *lot* of blood. But the house is rubble now, so we might never know for sure."

"Oh, wow! I didn't realize the fires had gotten that close to town. We had to detour a long way to get here. But it didn't seem to have dropped into the valley."

Anica shook her head. "Not burn down. Blew up. There was a bomb in house. We almost explode with it."

Now Claire gasped as Rachel confirmed the details from the kitchen. She looked over the top of the refrigerator door. "Yep. Anica was the big hero yesterday. She *smelled* the bomb and got us all out. Me and Dalvin and Bobby, plus the already-dead Paula."

"Wow! You guys had a busy day. I don't see a bunch of

human police, so I presume you stowed the body some-where?"

"The basement at Polar Pops," Rachel said with a nod. Then she looked at the contents of the final bag and let out a small, nearly silent cheer. "Milk! And eggs! And *wine*! Oh, you are the *best*, Claire. We're having breakfast, Anica."

"Yes, good. I like chicken eggs, however you cook them."

Rachel let out a chuckle. "*Chicken* eggs? As opposed to what? Ostrich?"

Now Anica could finally let out a small laugh, but she could feel her eyes burning. She didn't doubt they were red. "Duck. We had many ducks when I am little. The eggs are very good, and *big*." She paused, not sure whether Rachel was supposed to know, or Claire. But Rachel was there yesterday, so she deserved to know. "You should also know. There was second bomb, today. At *my* home."

Rachel froze, halfway from the kitchen with three filled glasses of orange juice. "And it didn't occur to you to *lead* with that information when you got here?"

Anica held up her hands. "There were so many things, in so short a time—"

Rachel started to return to the kitchen. "You two talk. I can hear from here. I'll get breakfast started."

Claire wasn't sure what to say for a long moment. Then she reached a hand out, flipping her fingers while staring at the glasses. "I think we should start with one of these. It sounds like this story could go on for a while."

It did.

By the time Anica finished telling them about the morning and previous night, the breakfast plates were empty and her throat was sore from talking.

"Wow," Rachel finally said from her curled-up position in

the brown recliner that was big enough to fit Papa and her both, "it's . . . been a wild couple of days for you."

"Oh," she added after pouring the last bit of pink wine down her throat. She raised her glass at them. "I forget one thing. Papa tell Bojan and I that our visa applications are denied. So all of this?" She snapped her fingers on the other hand, frustration and anger finally rising to the surface. "None of it really matters. I must go back to Serbia." She tightened her grasp on the juice glass, staring at the clock on the wall that was ticking away her time here, and let out a small yelp when the glass exploded in her hand. The pain was immediate, sharp. Her attention flicked to Rachel. "I'm sorry. I did not mean to break your glass." She just wasn't sure if she'd intended to hurt herself.

Anica started to stand up, but there was glass everywhere. She wasn't sure where to move that it wouldn't cut the couch or her clothes.

The other women smelled more sad than surprised at the broken glass. "Don't move," Claire said. "I'll get a trash can."

Rachel also got out of her chair and leaned over to pry open Anica's closed fist. Streaks of red that smelled of copper began rolling down her palm to land on her jeans. Once again, she couldn't feel the pain when her hand should be throbbing. Rachel plucked several pieces of glass from her hand and turned to carefully set them on the top of the table near her knees. "You're bleeding, sweetie. Try not to dig them in deeper." When her friend turned back to get the next, smaller shard, they both watched as the skin began to mend. The glass slowly rose out of her palm as if a magnet were pulling it toward the ceiling. "Whoa. Claire, come look at this."

Carrying a white plastic trash can, the third woman came

over, and they all watched all the glass shards, big and small, begin to rise up and out of Anica's skin, falling over to land in her palm. Soon only the red stains on the glass were evidence she'd ever been cut. Claire shook her head. "If I didn't know you were a three-day, I'd swear you were alphic. That's *exactly* what happens to me when I get stabbed by something."

Anica took a deep breath and admitted one of the things she'd wanted to talk to Rachel about. "I think it is Tristan. When we hit the wall after meeting the bad man, it was like this. For first few seconds, I hurt like nothing I have ever felt. So many things felt broken. Then, minutes later, woof! I felt no pain, even though I know I *should* hurt. The next morning, I hurt again, but then it fades, like never there."

That interested Claire. She looked at her very seriously. "Do you feel strange when you're near him? Like you can't take your eyes off him? Can you hear him in your head?"

Anica nodded. "He is very pretty, but it's more than that. It is like I cannot help myself, even when other, more important things are happening. I only hear him in head when he talks to me."

Rachel began to pick up the pieces of glass and drop them in the trash can. "Ooo. You're thinking they're mated? Can it happen that quick?"

Claire moved the trash bin closer and looked at her askance as she reached down to pick up some shards that had fallen to the floor. "Uh, yeah. It did for me, and for you too, if you remember. Alek got hooked to me when he gave me mouth-to-mouth, before I'd ever seen his face, and Dalvin got hooked to you in a crisis, right?" Then she looked at Anica. "Any crisis happen with you and this Tristan?"

"*Before* bad man?" When they nodded, she sighed. "When

I am not able to breathe from smell in forest—" Rachel let out a short laugh that made Claire's brows rise. "Tristan is at hospital. When doctor went to find medicine, Tristan stays with me, helps me breathe."

"And there's the smoking gun," Rachel said. "I should have thought of that myself. I saw Tristan leaving the hospital with your father when I got there."

"No," Anica replied. "There was no gun. He just helped me breathe with magic. He asked permission to enter my mind to talk to me because I could not speak. He helped me tell doctor what was wrong."

Rachel gave her a small smile and touched her arm. "A *smoking gun* only smokes after it fires. Finding a gun that's smoking means it's the likely reason a bullet was found."

One of the things she liked best about Rachel was her ability to explain things in a way that made sense without being condescending. It was why she trusted her not to lie or tease her. "So my healing like this and being able to speak into Tristan's mind are the bullets and Tristan helping me is the gun?"

Rachel bumped shoulders with her as she stood, and then looked at Claire. "Told you she was bright. Here, let me get the hand vacuum for the rest of the glass."

The front door opened. Amber walked in. "Everyone getting settled in here? Oh, Claire. I saw Alek earlier but didn't ask—how was the trip?"

"Y'know," Rachel said as she turned to look at the doctor with a slightly annoyed expression. "A lot of people *knock* before they walk in someone's home."

"Bodyguards don't knock. It sort of warns the bad guys if they're already inside."

"You are our bodyguard?" Anica was a little surprised.

The doctor did not seem like someone who used violence. She was petite and even her animal form was small. "Can you fight?"

Claire let out a burst of surprised laughter that she quickly stifled with a hand over her mouth. Amber put one hand on her hip and raised a single reddish-gold eyebrow at the Wolven agent. "Does the thought of me fighting amuse you, Agent?"

She quickly shook her head. Her scent was shocked at the idea, but Anica wasn't sure why. "Good God no! The exact opposite, in fact. When I was training at Wolven Academy, Lucas always told me that the obstacle course was designed to your abilities. It took me close to a *year* to make some of those jumps. Lucas said you used to spar with him when you were in town. If you're still alive, you're *good*. Frankly, if I can ever become as good a *bodyguard* as you, I'll be thrilled."

The bobcat doctor dipped her head, in both acknowledgment and gratitude. A beam of sunlight made her hair glow like a flaming halo. "While I was very annoyed with Lucas that he kept you hidden from even me, you've proved yourself to be fairly competent as a bodyguard yourself."

"Okay, okay," Rachel said with a roll of her eyes that made Anica smile, "the mutual admiration society is getting a little too sweet for my taste. Let's talk about specifics. Why does Anica need a bodyguard to begin with? Who are we watching out for?" She scratched at the back of her head, making the pom-pom of hair bounce like she was on a trampoline.

"The quick answer is, we don't know." Amber shrugged one shoulder, not looking terribly concerned. "We're not actually positive Anica is a target. This may have nothing to do with her. Or her brother or father, or even that particular house. *That's* what we need to figure out."

Anica brushed off the last bits of glass from her pants and stood up. "I am not a good investigator, but I have ideas. May I say?"

Amber nodded and closed the door behind her. "Let's have it. I'm open to ideas." She walked a few steps and sat down in the recliner that Rachel had vacated. If Rachel had seemed swallowed by it, Amber seemed to fill it completely and comfortably.

All eyes were on Anica. If it had been anyone except these three women, she might have frozen. But they had been nothing but kind to her, supportive, so she took a deep breath and spoke. "Part of this I must talk to think, yes? So please hear what I am trying to say when I may not say it well."

Rachel nodded, sitting down on the couch next to her. "It's okay. We get it."

She nodded and stared at the table for coffee at her knees. She found that staring at glass—the flickering light and ghostly reflections of the ticking clock and people—helped her focus. "Bobby tell me to look where things *go* and how they came to be there." Nobody spoke, interrupted, so she continued, "Tristan came to be here because snake councilman, Ahmad, tell him there is dangerous man here. There *is* dangerous man and he admitted he has been here since Ahmad is here. All people were checked by Dalvin and other Wolven man. But other Wolven man is also bad man, so we don't know if he lies."

Amber leaned forward. "You're *right*. Tamir could have been bought. He could have known Lagash was already here."

"Lagash! Yes, that is name Tristan tells me. But no, I do

not think Tamir is working for him. He is little bad man. Lagash is *big* bad man. Tristan fears him and he is not afraid of Sargon. I was very afraid of Sargon, so I must trust Tristan on what defines 'bad.'"

Claire and Rachel had similar dropped jaws in the glass reflection and their scents were stunned. "Tristan *knew* Sargon and *wasn't* afraid of him?" When Amber nodded, Rachel took a deep breath but didn't let it out for a long time. When she did, it was slow, like air leaking from a balloon until it was spent and limp.

"Who is this Tristan? I don't think I've ever seen that name in the Wolven files." Claire seemed more confused than concerned. She was interested and listening closely. Her attention was so complete that if it weren't for the glass Anica might have been unable to continue.

"You wouldn't have," Amber said, almost offhand. "He's been off-grid for centuries. He's a very, and I stress this word, *dangerous* man. Ris . . . or Tristan, was an assassin—the person certain Council members would call in to make people disappear. He never failed, was never seen, never scented, never caught. Nobody really knows why he stopped. Almost everyone, myself included, thought he'd died or been killed when he tried to eliminate someone who was finally better than him. But he's here now and we have to deal with that. *All* of us."

She decided to ask the question, because Amber was likely to be the only person who would know the true answer. "Am I mated to him?" She didn't really understand what it meant, but she needed to know.

Amber shook her head. "No. You're not. At least, not yet. Maybe not ever. But *he* is mated to *you*. And I have to tell you, that terrifies me."

"Why?" She really wanted to know. "He is not a bad man. Not like Lagash or even like Tamir. Perhaps dangerous, yes. Like Dalvin is dangerous, or Papa. But not bad."

The bark of a laugh was the doctor's response. "You are so young, Anica. Tristan is not the right man for you. You need to leave, disappear, and never let him find you. It's too dangerous for you to stay here. . . . I don't know if I can even explain it to you."

She shrugged. "Then do not try to explain. You have lived long, and I know I must respect that. But I have not lived at all yet." Anger rose into her and she raised her eyes to meet the doctor's, even if Mama would consider it rude. "I tire of everyone who tells me what is right thing for *me*." Saying the words out loud made all the pain of a decade fill her like dark, thick fluid. Her mind flashed to a lifetime of lowered eyes, quiet obedience—

"Anica, you need to understand—" The doctor's eyes were glowing golden with power. Anica felt the power try to surround her, tame her, but she threw it off with a wave of her hand. Blue power flashed against golden and the room lit up like a festival. But she didn't feel festive.

She snapped, finally snapped, and it felt so good to raise her voice, to yell the pain into the air. "No! *You* understand! Mama tell me how to live when I am little and I obey. But obeying is what makes me target to be taken by the snakes. The snakes tell me to obey and I do. Then they hurt me, rip open my flesh, make me into something I hate! But then . . . like a dog to bell, I fall back into obedience to Papa, who tells me to make the others into bears. Where once, just *once* in my life, I was the equal of Papa and Mama that was taken away too! Then other bears tell me I must move . . . give up what little left of me. Now government tells me I must go back, now that all of what was me is gone there."

The others seemed to be stunned into silence and it was only then that she realized she'd stood and was pacing around the room, like a trapped animal. Well, she *felt* like a trapped animal. "It was only when I finally refused to obey that I was able to escape the caves and find my way home. It was only when I refused to obey that I found men to love, even for a little while, and became a woman. It was only when I refused to give away our home that Bosnians were forced to go to mediator.

"I tire of it all!" She found herself in the farthest corner of the kitchen, surrounded by cabinets, with nowhere left to go. She slapped her recently injured palm down on the counter and felt no pain. "No. No more. It is time for *me* to tell me. I *refuse* to leave. Maybe I mate with Tristan. Or I do not. I might go to college, or perhaps become famous. But please do not tell me I am foolish, or young or stupid. I am all of them, and none of them."

"You go, girl." Rachel's voice was a whisper, and there were shining tears in her eyes.

Amber let out a great sigh that came from deep in her stomach. "Josette told me you would have to find your own way. All of you. I was sent here to watch . . . things unfold. The future is a tricky thing, though. Every time I think I'm doing the right thing, it turns out to be the wrong thing.

"I hate seers and all their—*our*—manipulation too. I hate, like you hate, being told what to do. So . . . fine. Do what you think is best. I won't interfere. I hope I never have to attend your funeral, though. Because Tristan will be bound by the mating to try to save you, no matter how dangerous things get. Your choices could drain him, kill him. I don't really care if he dies. He's earned that a thousand times over. But then you'll die too. He's already healing you, and it's not without cost to him. The more you're hurt, the weaker he'll grow. Lagash likely knows that."

Hearing that calmed Anica down the rest of the way. She knew so little about mating! She returned to the living room, where the others watched her carefully. "I did not think of Lagash hurting me to hurt Tristan. I do not feel when he hurts. What does that mean?"

The bobcat doctor sighed. "Mating is very complicated, but the short version is when a mating is one-sided, the mated one gives—power, magic, devotion. Usually, a weaker Sazi is mated to a stronger one, and the stronger one doesn't need the power or magic, and doesn't understand, or return, the devotion. So the impact on the mated one is minimal, other than emotionally, which is hard. You can probably shut him out of your thoughts pretty easy, but he will drown in yours. In a double mating, everything is shared and damage to one is damage to both, mental, emotional, and physical. I can tell Tristan is mated to you because he's healing you and can smell things you smell. Pretty classic signs." Now she stared at Anica with intent eyes that weren't glowing but were fascinated. "What I don't know is whether you're mated to him. I think Lagash is trying to find that out now. Testing you both."

It made sense. Sort of. "But that does not explain Paula's death or the bomb. Tristan is not mated to *her*. Does not even know her and was not in the room where bomb was, and Lagash couldn't know I would be there. But I see past time in Tristan's mind, when Lagash wants to turn all humans to Sazi, with him as king. Tristan says Lagash is a planner.

Years would mean nothing, yes? Decades are hours. Only ten years has he been here . . . just a few hours for one like you. True?"

Amber reluctantly nodded. Anica could smell her anger, but it was tempered, biding its time. "True. A decade is nothing, barely the equivalent of breakfast to lunch for you."

Anica didn't want to invoke that anger, but she needed to speak, to work it out in her own mind. "So, there is no need to kill a waitress. Unless she knows something or has something. And there is no reason for woman to kill Bojan and I unless we know something or have something." She paused, looking at each of the women in turn. "Or she *thinks* we know or have something."

Rachel started tapping her fingers on her thigh, which she always did when she was trying to sort something out. The fresh paint on her nails, nearly matching her shirt, but with a little more purple, added a chemical scent to the air as her fingers moved. "We were all at Paula's this morning. Maybe we picked up something, or saw something that we don't know we saw."

Amber wanted the answers. Her eyes were bright with curiosity, her body coiled in the chair like she was ready to spring on any hint of an answer to the mystery. "Tristan is going through the mediation files right now, looking at your history. Maybe this isn't about Luna Lake at all, but about Serbia."

Anica shook her head. That made no sense to her. "But again . . . why Paula? Lagash has to have been here for whole time Luna Lake has been here. Only residents were allowed to stay during mediation. So either my bomb was mistake, or hers was."

"Or," added Claire, the word lilting up with new information, "there's something at *both* houses he can't afford to

have more eyes on. Until I came to town, nobody in Wolven had been here. Dani Williams made a point of telling
me they had been abandoned by the Council. For a whole
decade. The mayor and police chief were too involved in
their own dirty plotting to notice something happening right
under their noses. But now there are Wolven agents, Council members, people from his past who could actually recognize him, or sniff him out. Maybe it's time to bury the
evidence . . . whatever that may be."

Anica liked that idea and so did Rachel. Her eyes lit up and
her head began to move in tiny nods. Even Amber began to
nod, but then the cloves in her scent burned away into metallic frustration. "But evidence of *what*? That's the part we
don't know. And it needs to stop here. If Lagash is truly here
and not even Ahmad can recognize him, then the disguise is
so perfect nobody else will find him if he leaves and another
decade or century could pass before the plan unfolds."

I need to see you. Can you get away? Tristan's voice filled
Anica's mind like a balloon that was suddenly near to burst-
ing. She tried to give no sign of it, other than rubbing her
temples, because it really did hurt when he intruded so
abruptly. She couldn't think of any reason why she couldn't
leave for a moment. The conversation had stalled. They all
needed some time to try to organize all the ideas.

"I am going to go put clothes in dryer downstairs and
check on Bojan. I need to think, to remember for a few moments." She spoke it in her mind at the same time, hoping
Tristan could hear.

"Sure," Rachel said, waving a hand toward the door. "You
know where it is. I'll clean up the dishes and we'll figure out
what to do next. You want anything to eat, Amber? We just
finished."

"I'd take a couple slices of toast," Amber said. Her words were casual, but her eyes were intent on Anica. She could feel the bobcat's gaze burning into her. But the doctor didn't say a word.

Anica left the apartment, letting the coolness of the dimly lit hallway calm her down. But her heart was beating too fast, as she was wondering what Tristan would need so urgently that he couldn't come to the door and talk in front of the others.

She raced down the stairs, feeling out with her senses and her nose to see if she was being followed. As far as she could tell, she was alone in the stairwell. Anticipation replaced worry in her stomach, making the tight worry settle into something that was a different sort of tight.

The laundry room was nothing special, just four plain white washers and four dryers along opposite walls. She'd been in it before, during the mediation, helping Rachel wash and fold towels and sheets. The room was empty. *Well, I may as well put the laundry in the dryer.* She opened the washer and the rough, stale scent of lingering smoke erupted from inside. It made her realize the whole house was going to smell just as stale when she returned. It would take much cleaning to get the smell of snake out. Shutting the lid again, she set the washer to run a second time, but this time on hot. While it filled, she added some of the liquid soap that was on the shelf above. Just as she closed the lid again, her pulse sped. Tristan's exotic spice scent was just behind her, so close, she could feel the rustle of his clothing against her skin.

When his head lowered to nestle next to her ear, his hands moved to slide along her waist. She would have sucked in a sharp breath if only she could breathe. Power poured over her, soaked into her skin like lotion after a shower as he blew lightly against her neck. Light shivers made the hair stand up on her arms and legs but then became something far deeper inside and she remembered Claire's words—*Do you feel strange when you're near him?*

This would qualify as strange. She'd experienced the giddy sensation of arousal before and the hunger that led to sex from boys in her teens and, as she grew older, men. But never before had she felt magic in sweeping waves that licked at every nerve, stole her breath, and made her dizzy and crazy with need. Her hands covered his and pulled them around her. She wanted to feel the lines of muscles against her back, the cool strength of his body surrounding her, in her. He stepped forward, pressing her against the equally chilled metal of the washer, sandwiching her in cold, so that her body responded with more heat. Her breath finally came out in a trembling rush just as the water turned off and the agitator vibrated the whole machine. The combination of sensations made her feel sweaty and flustered. One word was heard by her ears and her mind simultaneously. *"Anica."*

"Tristan," she whispered in reply; it sounded like begging. His whole body shuddered and he heaved, trying to catch his breath. He held her like that for a long moment and then leaned back, shook his head, and released her abruptly.

The sudden lack of pressure and cold made it hard to stand. Tristan was swallowing repeatedly, his throat working rhythmically as though trying to recover from nearly drowning. His eyes were glazed and blazing with blue fire. Even now, she could feel the attachment of the magic, like a wet sheet covering her, suctioned against her skin. She wasn't positive she could peel it away if she tried. She started forward, to wrap her arms around him to feel that sensation again, but he held up a hand and stepped back a pace, putting a shaky hand against the wall. "Don't. Please. I thought I could control this, but I'm not sure I can. I don't know if I can stop and this is not the place."

He was serious. She could see his pulse pounding so hard that the vein in his neck was throbbing. She wondered what else might be, and dropped her eyes.

Tristan let out a low chuckle that brought heat to her face. "You don't have to wonder. My whole body is feeling it."

"Is this why you wanted to see me? To see if you could control yourself?" She wasn't sure whether to feel happy or insulted. He moved all the way across the small room and leaned against the dryers.

"No." His laugh wasn't so much erotic and needy now as it was edging toward hysterical. "No . . . *this* didn't happen until I saw you. Apparently, being able to see you, to smell your scent, is tougher than I'd expected. I was fine this morning. But when you cut yourself—" He shook his head, fast and hard, as though to clear his mind. "You pulled on me and I tried to stop the flow, tried to cut it off. But I couldn't . . . and then I didn't want to."

Now Amber's words came back—*He's already healing you, and it's not without cost to him. The more you're hurt, the weaker he'll grow.*

"I am very sorry. I cut myself on a glass, and then Amber made me angry." Anica looked down at her hand, now healed and without even a scar to show the event had happened. "I did not mean to involve you. But I don't know how *not* to. I was angry and it just . . . happened. I just learn from Amber what is causing this." She *was* sorry. Whatever was happening to him wasn't with his consent. That was obvious by the panicked look on his face and the heavy jaw-tightening scent of fear that filled the room. To have him be afraid of her, when he *wasn't* afraid of Sargon, made her wonder what sort of magic this *mating* was. She needed to find out much more about how to protect him—and herself. But for now, what she was doing was no better than stealing, and she wasn't a thief. "I will be more careful in the future. You should not have to protect me."

He nodded, but it was a lie. He didn't believe her and how could she blame him? She had no idea how to control it. "Okay. Thank you." She started again to step toward him, to comfort him and try to ease his fear, but he held up his hand. "That's close enough. I can manage this distance for the moment."

She stopped, nodding, but realized it was actually hard *not* to walk toward him. The room seemed to slide out of focus until he was the only thing clear in her vision. She reached out and grabbed on to a metal rod attached to the wall that supported a wooden dowel to hang clothes hangers. Feeling the metal under her hand helped ground her and the room became clear again. "Again, I am sorry. What is your question?"

"When you were in the forest, what were you smelling when the attack happened . . . a tree, a plant, ashes?"

She thought back. "I was trying to find your pack." That memory made her suddenly annoyed, which helped clear her mind. "You tell me to go the wrong way! Why do you do that?" Pointing at her face, she challenged him. "I tell you when we meet that I have very good nose. Your pack is still out there because you lied to me."

His scent took on the dusty dryness of the desert at high sun, which she knew meant he was embarrassed. Some of the magic attaching them together severed, tiny strands unraveling like a failed row of knitting. "I did lie to you. I'm sorry for that. But before I knew there would be people who would recognize me, I'd planned to investigate undercover. You only know me as Tristan, but that's my undercover name."

That made her smile, because he didn't really understand how much she could overhear when he was in her head. "I know you as all names that come to your head. You are Risten, and Adika, Tulus, and Pawura. But I like 'Tristan' best, so I call you that. It is a nice name." She cocked her head as an image came into her head. "It is interesting. When I say 'Pawura,' you think of yourself different—with darker skin and black hair, and always carrying a long bow, like for archery. When I say 'Adika,' you are fairer, but not as fair as now, with reddish hair. Can you change how you look, even to you? Is that how Lagash is hiding? Even to him he looks different? But how do you change your *smell*?"

He balled his hand into a fist and banged it against the white-painted metal of the dryer. It wasn't hard enough to dent the metal, but it rocked the whole machine back a little. "The things you're seeing are very dangerous, Anica. There are things in my past that I don't want you to see in my memories."

She didn't know what to say to that. The images just appeared, like twilight dreams that she couldn't control. "I am not looking for things. They just appear in my mind and I know they are not my thoughts." She paused, not wanting him to be angry. "I have not told anyone what I see. They are private, like reading someone's diary."

He ran his fingers through his hair in a practiced movement. She doubted he would even remember doing it. His frustration shredded the rest of the magic and she was back fully in her own skin. It was strangely unnerving. "Back to the scent. What specifically were you smelling?"

"The ground." She remembered it distinctly. "Someone was following you. I could smell their footprints over the top of yours and I worried about it because they smelled dangerous. I don't know how to better describe it. It was something in the footsteps, in the ashes." She started to take a step but then stopped and gripped the steel bar tighter. "I can take you back there."

He shook his head, a burst of panic in his scent. "I'll go back to the forest and find it. I don't want you to get anywhere near whatever it was again." He was not lying, but this time it was not fear that rose from him at being close to her. It was worry that she could be hurt. It made her feel warm inside that it would matter to him.

There was another option, but she didn't really want to bring it up, considering his fear. Still, it would be foolish not to say it, considering the fear everyone seemed to have about Lagash. "Can you look in my mind? I remember smells very well, even if I don't know what name to put with it."

He considered that, staring at her with narrowed eyes and suspicion. But he wasn't suspicious of her. Not really. It was what he might find in her mind, or more that he might not be able to get back out. "It'll still be there later if I need to find it."

She nodded as he backed out of the room, clearly shaken. She didn't try to follow, although she wanted to so badly it made her skin hurt. The room seemed suddenly cold, emptier than when she arrived. Having him leave was like a bandage was being ripped off and cold air hitting a wound.

She kept holding on to her metal bar, and in time the empty, needy sensation passed. By the time she felt confident she was herself again and could leave the room without trying to track his scent, the washer was done a second time. As she picked the clothes out of the washer, one of her socks dropped back behind. It was one of her favorite socks, bought by Mama in New York on their way here for the mediation. It was covered with sparkling gold threads. She put the clothing back in the washer and pulled the washer away from the wall. To her surprise, there was a hole in the wall, big enough to crawl through. It went back into the rock as far as she could see and she could feel a light breeze coming through that smelled of outside. But there wasn't much smoke, so she presumed there was a cover over wherever it came out. She would have to ask Rachel about it.

She was just putting the clothes in the dryer when she heard quick footfalls coming down the stairs. Rachel's voice preceded her body by just a few seconds. "Anica? You down here? What's taking so long?"

Throwing in a dryer softener sheet, she shut the door and turned on the tumbler. "The smoke scent wasn't gone. I started the washer over."

Her friend stood by the door, leaning on the metal hinges. Her eyes were twinkling and a half smile quirked the corners of her lips. "Smells like you had plenty to keep you busy down here."

Oh, no! Once again, everyone would be able to smell that Tristan had been near her. She *hated* that she could never have secrets. Letting out a sigh, she turned to face her friend. "Tristan is troubled by the mating. He cannot control his attraction to me and is afraid. So he comes and touches me, holds me, but then is angry and leaves. It is very confusing and I wonder if I should be angry too."

"Ah." That one word held the wisdom of experience. "The

panic is a guy thing. It's not your fault and you have to try not to be insulted." She raised her hand, like when a teacher would ask a question in class. "Been there. Although"— she lowered her hand and waggled her head from side to side—"it was Claire who fought her mating, not Alek, so maybe it's not just a guy thing. I think it's whoever has control issues."

Rachel was very good at helping her focus. "What are *control issues*?"

" 'Someone who can't follow' I guess is the best description. They have to be in control of whatever situation they're in. Larissa had control issues. Tamir had control issues. See? You and I, we're okay following someone we trust. Alek too. Even Amber can follow orders, although she probably wouldn't have to, being as powerful as she apparently is. Claire told me that the head of Wolven told her to not get involved in taking down the mayor here, and she did it. But Claire really struggles with following orders. She does it, but you can tell it grates on her."

That made a lot of sense. Larissa Grebo was a very willful woman. She had deceived Anica, tried to kill her. Kill her! All because she had been turned into Sazi. If that was what "control issues" meant, Anica understood immediately. Samit was like that too. She tried to think of Tristan by comparison. "Yes, I can see what you say. Tristan needs to have his own way and is powerful enough to get his way. Now he cannot and fears that loss of control. I understand."

Rachel came farther in the room and sat down on one of the chairs next to the wall. "Dalvin told me that Tristan told him—so take what you will from it—that Ahmad considered him annoying. Think about that. *Ahmad* considered him annoying, but Tristan's still alive."

Papa had talked much of the snake councilman, and when they traveled together to Serbia Anica found him to be very cold and distant. He was demanding and expected everyone to wait on him, including Papa! It was very seldom that Papa used bad language, but she had heard him muttering swears nearly every time he encountered the snake councilman. As for Anica, she truly hadn't been sure he wouldn't turn on them all once they got to the caves, and it seemed to her that everyone had been somewhat surprised when he'd followed through.

Only the tiger councilman, Rabi, had been completely confident in Ahmad.

"Ahmad would not stand for anyone being annoying *to* him." She couldn't help but chuckle as a memory popped into her head. "Do you remember the owner of the café in Zlatibor who refused to let Ahmad's guards search the kitchen for fresh mice or rats?"

Rachel burst out laughing. "O. M. G.! I thought that man was going to come *unglued*! I didn't have to speak the language to know what he was saying. Just the sputtering and red face at the hint he would have rodents in his kitchen was enough. It was sort of a shame he kicked us out and locked the door. The food had smelled pretty good."

It was nice she had shared an adventure with Rachel. They had been able to become very close. "I must agree with what you say. If Ahmad puts up with Tristan, and *only* holds grudge, Tristan is, as Amber says, a dangerous man. And probably has what you say—*control issues*."

Rachel stood and came over to give her a quick hug before leaning on the machine beside Anica. "Give him some time. He's going to have to come to terms with the mating by himself. Even now, Dalvin sort of freaks out when we have the mental connection. His mom says it took his dad a couple of years to get used to it. If you're mated back to him, it'll be worse. Or that's what I hear." She shrugged. "It's okay. There's time. Don't rush. Lust is a sprint. Love is a marathon."

Love. It was not a word she would use to describe how she felt about the blond bear. But it had only been two short days. "Is it bad that I do not feel love for Tristan? Everyone says word 'mating' like it is very special and important. But I know so little about him. He is so secretive. I do not even know where he comes from, or who his family is. How could I love a man I do not know?"

Rachel's jaw dropped. "Bad? Oh, lord no! Sweetie, it's only been two *days.* How could you feel anything for him? Mating doesn't trump love and love takes time. I've known Dalvin since I was six. And I don't think even Claire and Alek are really in *love.* They're definitely in lust, though. I think mating only enhances the feelings when love happens." She paused and then let out a short laugh that was equal parts surprised and annoyed. "Frankly, I'm amazed you even *like* Tristan. I think he's sort of a jerk. No, I like what you said upstairs better. *You* get to decide what's right for you. Make him come looking for you. Don't go chasing him."

That made sense to Anica. "He said if he wishes to find me, he would. I think for now, I will let him. I will find Bojan and talk to him. Maybe it *is* time to go home to Serbia. I will miss America, and you, but there is much worry and heartache here. For us and for Papa and Mama."

"I feel you, girl. I'm looking forward to going home to Detroit too. Scared, but anxious too. I'm just trying to wrap up things here with the Kragans and Dani. I'm supposed to separate myself from their parliament so I can join Dalvin's group back home. It's a slow process, cutting ties to this place. Not just the magic, but the people." She looked around the room and lightly bounced her fist on top of the dryer, like pounding on a drum. "Lots of stuff changing here. I wouldn't be surprised if the whole town shuts down after we leave. With Alek and Denis moving to be closer to Sonya—"

"Oh! I did not hear what happen on island. They *did* find their sister?" She opened the door of the dryer to stop it. A lightweight pink shirt was close enough to dry to wear. She stripped off the shirt that smelled of Tristan and tossed it across the room. It bounced off the open lid of one of the washers and dropped inside, while Rachel let out a little chuckle. Anica felt a little embarrassed, but she had to be practical. "I do not want Papa to smell Tristan close to me again so soon. I could explain one time. Two becomes more difficult."

"I get that. I'd probably do the same if it was my father and he could smell things like yours. Anyway, Alek and Claire *might* have found Sonya. The problem is the girl they found doesn't, or at least *says* she doesn't, remember much about when she was little, and the translator wasn't able to speak English as well as they'd hoped. Claire thought there was something fishy about the whole thing, but Alek was convinced. Amber says she knows of a seer who can see the past and can dig through memories to find out what's real. It's called *hindsight*. I don't know about that, but I do know Denis is *not* going to be happy about moving. I think he was hoping they could move to a city when they left here, not to an even smaller town on a remote island in the middle of the ocean. I don't see him handling it very well."

Anica had opened her mouth to reply when a low-pitched

siren began to wail. It rose in volume and pitch until it made her ears hurt. She covered them with her hands and shouted over the sound, "What is that noise?!"

Rachel looked suddenly concerned. She moved to the wall and looked up through the window. "Tornado siren. We need to go upstairs and see what's happening."

That didn't make much sense. "If it is tornado, shouldn't we stay here under the ground where it is safe?"

Rachel grabbed her elbow and pulled her out the door. "It's not a tornado. It's just a tornado *siren*. It's how the police and mayor alert the whole town at once. We hardly ever get tornadoes up here, but the siren can be heard all the way out at the lake. Everyone can know there's a problem at once. I can't see anything outside through the smoke. But they wouldn't use it unless there was a big problem, so we need to find out what it is."

"Should we go out by tunnel?"

That stopped Rachel. She glanced at the very washer Anica had pulled back. "How do you know about that?"

"A sock fell back there. Where does it go?"

"It comes out in the forest. Forget you saw it. It's complicated. We need to use the stairs." Rachel took the stairs two at a time, while Anica followed behind more slowly, wondering about her friend's dismissal of what she'd found and watching for signs of trouble. Rachel opened the door to her apartment, but Amber and Claire were gone. So were Bojan, Scott, and Dalvin next door. Anica followed Rachel at a sprint to the front door and then down the steps.

Frantic activity had transformed the already-busy courtyard into something close to a riot. "Go, go, go!" A man in a fireman's yellow jacket and a helmet with a large gold shield on the front slapped the top of a jeep crowded with people.

The back of his jacket was covered with thick gray dust. Noticing the young women, he pointed at them, shouting to be heard over the wailing siren, "You two—find a vehicle! The town's evacuating. We have ten minutes, tops, before the fire turns this place to ash."

Anica didn't even need to inhale to smell the growing fire from the north. The heat pressed against her like a wall that made her eyeballs hot and dry. She looked around, searching for people she knew, but everyone was a stranger, most of them smelling fully human.

"Holy crap!" Rachel grabbed Anica's arm, holding her tightly for a moment. "C'mon. We need to stay together and find your father and brother and my alphas. Bitty and her brothers are powerful, but they're old and they don't move too fast anymore, at least with their legs." Rachel turned in a circle, hopping up in the air. "Damn it! It looks like someone already took my car. I knew I shouldn't have left the keys in it."

It was hard for Anica to see through the wave of people. It felt like the airport in New York City, where everyone except her seemed to have been taught a special dance to get through the crowds. Even Papa and Mama had been able to spin and dance past people with their bags, while Anica was constantly stepping on feet, or being stepped on, or getting bumped or knocked into a wall.

She tried to stay with Rachel, but they were separated in seconds. Pushed by the crowds back to the apartment building, Anica climbed the steps to be able to look over people's heads. She searched for Rachel's bright shirt and pom-pom of dark fuzzy hair, but her friend was nowhere to be seen.

Tristan, however, was easier to spot, or maybe it was just that she could smell him even over the smoke. He'd changed clothes and was dressed head to foot in colors that nearly were the same shade as the log buildings around him. Even the stocking hat on his head matched. Most people ignored him, especially because he was moving toward the fire. Why would he do that?

She watched until she was sure he was out of the crowd and edged around the back of the buildings until she could see him again. The wind created by the fire blew his scent toward her, so she was able to stay out of sight as she trailed him past the police department, the town hall, and the post office. He seemed to be heading for the diner.

When her nose detected a new scent, near the ground, Anica stopped short. It was the same perfume her attacker had worn at the house. The problem was the wind was getting so strong that the perfume could have come from a long distance away. But why was it at ground level? Was the woman in snake form again?

She lowered her head so she was bent nearly double. The air was clearer closer to the dirt, so it was easier to track the scent for long moments, until it disappeared. By the time she looked up again, Tristan was long gone. And so were most of the people in the center of town. She was between the diner and post office, out of sight.

Alone.

She tried to think, but the ever-growing roaring sound in the distance, louder even than the siren, made it hard to focus. The sky began to turn orange, then red, as the air heated and the smoke became a choking cloud. She started coughing and dropped to the ground near the foundation of the post office. It was coming too fast. She wasn't even sure where to go to get out of the way of the firestorm.

"What the hell are you doing here?!" Anica's head snapped

around to see Tristan and Bobby. It was obvious they were planning something together. The dark man from South Africa—no, wait; Amber had told her it was Mozambique where he came from—was dressed in black cargo pants and a patterned shirt like hunters wear. Tristan was furious, but his anger wasn't mad anger; it was fear anger, born of worry. "Are you trying to get yourself killed?"

"No! I just lost track of—"

Bobby grabbed her arm and then Tristan's, so tight she could feel the pulse of his magic like fingers digging under her skin. The feeling of panic overwhelmed her. She tried to pull away but couldn't break free of the magic. "It doesn't matter why. We've got to get out of here!"

He pulled her up and they all ran, at a pace that made her legs feel like rubber. The fire was closing in on two sides now, forcing them to move away from the main road. She pointed to their right, already struggling to breathe through the smoke and heat. "We can make it to the lake! The water is deep and cold."

"We don't have much choice!" Bobby yelled over the roar that had drowned out the siren. Anica had never run so fast in her life. The landscape blurred and then she was being pulled along in the two men's wake. It didn't even feel like her feet were touching the ground.

When the familiar boat dock came into view, they were ahead of the flames, but just barely. The hollow sound of the wooden dock under their feet echoed as they pounded toward the water, then gave way to sudden silence as dry land ran out. "Fill your lungs!" Tristan didn't need to say it, because Anica was already pulling in a great breath, filling her chest to nearly overflowing. The three of them hit the water hard, arm in arm. The two men pulled her down deeper into the water. It was hard to swim with her pants and shoes on, but she didn't want to risk taking them off. Fish flashed past silver in the corner of her vision, just far enough ahead that she couldn't tell what sort of fish they were. And without being able to inhale, she couldn't smell. It wasn't until they leveled out and the red glow of the surface no longer brought heat that she noticed the strange way the men were swimming. Like fish. They didn't kick their legs like she did, so their clothing didn't slow them at all. Their whole bodies were moving like big fish, side to side. It was both elegant and soothing. They effortlessly moved down to skim the bottom. The longer they were under, the tighter her chest was getting. She could hold her breath a long time, but Tristan and Bobby weren't even trying to surface for air.

The tightness soon turned to burning in her lungs. She had to get air soon. She started to pull away from the men, heading toward the surface. Even if there was fire above, she should be able to get a sip of air and then dive back under. Tristan shook his head and dug his fingers into her arm, pulling her farther down. He pointed ahead to an odd structure, like a large container covered with window screen. She pushed a thought into his head.

I have to breathe, Tristan! I can't go any farther.

Trust me. It seemed Bobby was also headed toward the container with purpose. In seconds, she realized why. There was a scuba tank and face mask attached to the container! Why in the world was there an air tank at the bottom of the lake? Did the men put it there, knowing they were going to need it?

Tristan put the mask over her face and she gratefully took several breaths of clean air, blowing the old air out through her nose. Once she had her lungs full again, she nodded and he handed the mask to Bobby, who did the same. Only after they had both gotten air did Tristan take the mask. When he put the mask back on the container, he smiled at her, his teeth surprisingly white in the blueness of the water.

She heard, or perhaps felt, a rumbling that surrounded them, vibrated through her body for a few seconds. The fish began to panic around her, swimming around as though searching for cover as the red above intensified, seemed to try to burn the very water.

They stayed underwater long minutes, sharing the air in careful sips, until the red above turned to yellow and then to light blue. When they finally surfaced, the landscape was oddly patchy. Some trees were charred to sticks, while others just a few feet away were barely singed. Smoke was thick in the air, hovering like fog just inches above the water. Hot ash blew sideways, like snow in a winter blizzard, and stuck to her skin and hair, and even her eyes, like glue. Anica ducked under the water to clear her vision. Tiny flames dotted the beach where grass had once grown, making the shore look like a vast campground for fairies. She looked in the direction of town and sniffed the wind. There was barely a hint of the acrid black smoke that wiring and paint made. Had the town somehow survived the fire? And what about the people? "Do you think everyone made it away?"

Bobby nodded as they bobbed in the water, which was warm like a bath. "I think so. We had already evacuated the fringe houses. I was just coming back to town when the siren started. We've been keeping an eye on the Forest Service reports all morning and started moving people when the fire jumped the road to the north."

"The perfumed lady snake had been right where you

found me. I was trying to track her smell when you pulled me away. Now that fire is past, I must go back to find it again."

Tristan let out a harsh breath. "Anica, I don't want you chasing this. It has nothing to do with you."

Bobby pursed his lips and raised his brows but wisely stayed silent and began to swim for shore. She spun in the water and stared at Tristan with rising anger. "Has nothing to do with me? She tried to *kill* me. And Bojan. Yes, I will chase her. I will chase her and find her and then—"

He interrupted her, splashing his palm down on the surface of the lake, causing a spray of water to shoot into the air. "Then *what*, Anica? You have no idea who you're dealing with. These are vicious people . . . ancient and powerful. You're nothing but cannon fodder to them, a mosquito to be slapped and brushed away."

If he thought that was a way to make her back down, he didn't understand her very well. He tried to push his way into her head and wrap his magic around her to keep her still, but she did not want him there, so, though he knocked on the door, she did not open. Instead, she used her voice so he would *hear* her outrage.

"Do you not think I *know* they are vicious?" Anica wanted to scream at him, but instead, she kept her voice low and quiet, which seemed to unnerve him more. "I have scars of evil like theirs . . . many of them." She stretched her sopping-wet shirt, pulling the neck to reveal the ragged scars down her collarbone that had dug deep into the tissue of her breast—daily reminders of the bears who nearly killed her. Not a day went by that she didn't look in the mirror and feel angry.

"You see? So I know. And yes, they are ancient, and

powerful. But I am powerful too. I am stubborn and do not give in, or give up." He was frowning now, his mouth a tight line under narrowed eyes. "Mosquitoes are quick, Tristan. And also vicious. Even the greatest of animals fears the tiny mosquito. They prey on things larger than them and can *kill* . . . kill with the tiniest bit of their spit." She turned her head and spit, then hit herself on the chest with her palm, just like he had done with the water. "So I am *proud* to be mosquito. I am not easy to slap . . . and do not think I can be easily brushed away."

Instead of waiting for him to decide how to yell at her next, she started to swim to shore. He was more than welcome to chase Lagash. She wanted to get back to town to check on their house and to try to find the snake's perfume scent. Lagash was not who she wanted to find. He was not a woman and he had not hit Bojan with a bat.

"Anica!" he called to her as she swam, but she didn't answer. *"Anica!"* She dove underwater so she didn't have to listen to him. When he reached out with his magic, she pushed it away and kept swimming, holding her breath as long as she could.

She made it on one breath underwater to the shore. When she got out of the water on the scorched beach, Tristan was already there. She hadn't even seen him swim past her! Bobby was stomping out the doll campfires with his boots. Tristan grabbed her arm, but not hard like when the fire was coming. "I can force this, you know. I can put a magic hold on you until this is over so you don't get hurt." The surface of his face was angry, but it was a lie. The undercurrent, just beneath the surface, was worry, fear.

She pulled her arm away and he didn't stop her. But his eyes started to glow blue and the push of magic pressed against her skin. She couldn't help but stare at his face, those eyes, with surprise and anger in return. "Does this mating thing make you stupid?" The glow in his eyes dimmed the slightest amount. She smelled oranges rising over the smoke, but it was not hers, or Tristan's. Bobby was listening and commenting without a word. But he was amused. "Or is being mated to me so horrible that you *want* to die?"

The questions seemed to take the wind completely out of him. It was obvious from his scent that he didn't know exactly how to reply, so she continued, "Each time you attach to me you are weaker. You have said so yourself. So either your brain does not work right and you do not know you will die, or you do not *care* that you will die if you face this bad man, which insults me." He blinked, then blinked again, and his jaw opened, but no sound came out.

Bobby didn't turn around to face them, but he did clear his throat. "Interesting note in the mediation files, Ris: Anica's culture requires a challenge battle for insults." He smiled when Tristan glared at him. But then Bobby's face grew more serious. "But more important, if you intention-ally go into battle while mated and it kills your mate, it's a death sentence."

She raised her brows and crossed her arms over her chest to watch him process that. Seconds passed while his cloth-ing slowly turned gray from the ash settling on him and his face turned gray from Bobby's words. He could tell his friend was not lying and she certainly wasn't going to dispute the first part, because it was true. "I do not intend to chase your bad man. He has done me no harm. But the woman snake, she has harmed me and my family. I do not ask your help, but I will find her to bring justice to my family."

Bobby sighed. "Not that simple, Anica. Same rules apply.

You can't intentionally go into battle and risk Ris. Since he's mated to *you*, your death could actually kill him."

Now it was her turn to stare openmouthed at the snake. Smoke rose all around him from the fires he had tamped out. It blended with the golden power that rose around him to make him hazy and indistinct. She had to blink and rub the tears in her eyes brought on by the stinging. "How can you stop legitimate justice for a wrong? Your *job* is to do justice!"

He walked closer, stomping on one last smoldering fire and flipping some wet dirt over the sputtering flame. "Exactly. *My* job is to do justice. Not yours. You are welcome to track her. But if you find something, you come to me or Alek or Amber. You don't get to go off half-cocked and take her down yourself."

"But Tristan *can*?!"

Bobby raised his hands, like it was out of his control. "Official sanction for war crimes. Lagash has a long history of . . . well, choose your high crime and he's done it."

"You can't kill the woman." Tristan's voice was quiet, subdued. "Even I can't and I have no idea what I'm going to do with Lagash because of it."

"Wait." Bobby turned to him. "What?"

"You might as well both know," Tristan said with a sigh. "I recognized the snake's scent at Anica's house." He rubbed the bridge of his nose and smeared the soot, causing streaks of pale skin to show through. "She's Ahmad's older sister."

Bobby walked closer to them, until he was close enough that had he flicked his tongue he would have hit Tristan's nose. "Ahmad doesn't have any siblings."

"He used to. Five or six I knew of. Everyone presumed Enheduanna was long dead. Of course, we thought Lagash was, as well. He was mated to her, which is where some of his power comes from, so I'm shocked it's her. I guess I assumed he'd drained her dry long ago. But I know her smell. And I can assure you that no matter what she's done, Ahmad will never allow her to die."

"Are you fucking *kidding* me?" Bobby reached down and picked up a rock that should have taken two hands to pick up. He threw it into the water with enough force that it looked like a stick of dynamite had been tossed in instead. "That means we can't kill him either, if they're mated."

"But he can kill us? How is that fair?" Neither man answered her, but they both had similar sour expressions. Some days, Anica hated having to play by the rules, when nobody else seemed to care about them. "Then at least we can *find* them. We can catch them and give them to Ahmad. If he breaks rules, nobody will care. Yes?"

That actually made Bobby think. "A few will care, but I don't know they'll punish him. It's probably as close to a solution as we're going to find."

She turned her head suddenly to a distant sound. Lifting her head, she tried to smell what went with the noise, but there was too much ash in the air. "I hear something." She pointed to a stand of trees that was only partially burnt. "It sounds like someone yelling."

Bobby and Tristan turned their heads, tried to listen. But the crackling, hissing sound of the fire was still too loud. Tristan shook his head. "Which way?"

She pointed and Bobby took off at a trot in that direction. Before Tristan followed him, Anica put a hand on his arm. "This is not over. Okay? We must talk."

He didn't respond before turning to follow Bobby, but she smelled such a flurry of emotions, even if they talked, she wasn't sure he would be able to talk reasonably. She broke into a run. Too much was happening. The thought of talking with him when he was not ready made her tired. If she was lucky, it would only be like Papa and he would calm down and listen logically. Or it could be worse, like trying to talk sense to Samit when he was angry.

She would have to approach it carefully. Or not at all. She wasn't sure a relationship with Tristan was worth chasing if he didn't consider her smart enough or strong enough to deal with her own problems. Even Papa, for all his worry, had considered her strong enough to fight Larissa. Had the two families not chosen to decide the boundary issue with the Ascension challenge, she would have been allowed to fight in animal form.

Anica heard the sound again, and sprinted past the two men, cutting right hard to match the sound. Then her nose picked up the scent. It was Bojan! Her speed increased at about the same moment as Bobby and Tristan caught the smell. "Bojan! Where are you?"

"Anica! Here!" She turned in her trajectory and found Bojan near the base of the mountain. His shoulder was pressed flush against the stone as though he was reaching for something. "Help me! Scott is trapped." He pulled his arm back and Anica came close to the small opening between the fallen boulders, which was just barely wide enough to fit an arm in.

She tried to see in, but it was too dark. "Scott? Are you okay?"

His voice was distant, tinny, like it was traveling a long distance inside the hole. "No. My wing's trapped in the rocks. If Bojan shifts me back to human, the rock will move and probably rip my arm right off." Anica put her nose right against the rock and inhaled. It was definitely Scott and he was in much pain.

Bobby touched Bojan on the shoulder. "What happened? How did you get here? You were on the first truck out of town."

Her brother shook his head. "I don't want to talk about it."

That was not the answer the Wolven investigator wanted and, frankly, not the one that Anica wanted either. She wanted to know why Bojan had risked his life to come to the middle of a forest fire. Smoke still rose from the skeletons of massive pines all around him. He was covered with ash, the soot thick enough on his face that it looked like the makeup rock stars wear. She could smell burnt hair but couldn't tell where under the gray. "You need to tell me," Bobby said, his voice flat and serious. "We'll get him out of there, but I have to make sure you didn't *put* him there." Bojan looked at her and Bobby noticed. He put a hand on his arm and turned him away. "Let's talk about this over here." Bojan went, but he kept looking back over his shoulder. The scents of worry and fear were strong, but there was guilt there too—thick and oily enough to stick to the inside of her nose.

Bojan, what have you done?

Tristan had squatted down next to the hole and was feeling inside with one arm. He called down the hole, "Do you know how far down you fell?" He turned to her and lowered his voice. "What's the boy's name again?"

"Scott." She felt helpless. The rock was so large. Bigger than the delivery truck that used to take their raspberries to market. "Can you move it? Can you move the rock and get him out?"

"Scott? Do you know how far down you are?"

The tiny voice inside the stone replied, "It was a cave before the entrance collapsed. I don't know for sure, but maybe twenty feet." So that was the rumbling they felt under the water. It had probably been loud, but with everyone gone for the fire, nobody was here to help. Tristan took a deep breath and let it out slow before shaking his head.

She didn't like what that said to her, so she tapped him, and questioned with her eyes, so not to worry Scott. Tristan put a hand over the hole and whispered, "I don't know. Look up." He motioned with his head. When she did, all she saw was more mountain . . . a big pile of rocks. She shrugged, not sure what she was supposed to see.

"The rock that fell is a base stone. It's holding up everything above it. When it fell, everything else shifted. If we move it, the whole mountainside could come down in a rock avalanche that could bury half of the valley, including Luna Lake."

The knot of worry in her stomach grew until it felt like something in her insides was chewing its way out of her body.

CHAPTER 16

his was the very reason why Tristan had abandoned humanity. So many problems. So many emotions. Anica and her brother wore their worry and fear on the surface of their skin. While her brother was just worried for his friend, Anica was worried for everyone. He could feel it pressing against him, burrowing under his skin so deep he couldn't ignore it. Worse, Anica was a doer. Her first thought was to fix problems, to take the weight of them on herself, without want of glory or money, but just to make things right. He could feel that too and both hated it and was refreshed by it. He used to be the same way, but time and experience had beaten it out of him. Too many failures, not enough appreciation for the wounds and scars earned for others. Scars like Anica's. He'd been shocked by the deep claw marks she'd revealed. How she'd survived the attack he couldn't imagine. They'd tried to claw out her heart, and given the size of her body, they should have succeeded.

Proud, tough, determined, and sentimental: a dangerous combination . . . for many reasons.

"Stay still down there. Try not to move around. We'll see

what we can do to get you out." Tristan could feel the man's desperate hope waft from the hole, accompanied by a scent that said he knew he was doomed. Tristan was pretty sure he was. There was only one way to know for sure. "Hey, toss me your flashlight."

Bobby reached down to open one of the pockets on his pant legs. "No guarantee it'll work. I didn't bring the water-resistant one."

"Scott, are there multiple entrances into the mountain?" Tristan asked.

"Yes! There's a whole network of caves. But this one doesn't connect with the others and I don't feel any air moving except from this hole."

Okay, that was a problem he hadn't anticipated. The opening in front of him was barely big enough for him to slither through. But if this was the only air hole, he'd be blocking it for as long as it took him to reach the trapped man. He passed the flashlight to Anica.

"Take this apart and dry everything as best you can. I'm going to see if there's another way in." She nodded and set to work. Tristan addressed his fellow snake again. "Bobby. Scuba or Amber. Your choice. He'll need either air or magic to keep breathing while I try this."

Bobby looked at him, then at the hole, then back again. From his expression, he wondered if Tristan had lost his mind. "You can't be serious—"

"You have a better idea? One of us has to go look and, let's face it, you won't fit."

Bobby could squeeze himself into some pretty small spaces, but even in python form he was too big to fit into the gap. "It'll have to be Amber. You and the scuba hose won't fit at the same time."

Anica had moved next to her brother, the only dry one of the lot of them, and was using the inside hem of his shirt to sop up water from inside the flashlight. The look she gave him was mostly confused, with a thread of nervousness. "How will you get down to him without making hole bigger and causing more rocks to fall?"

He stared at her. With her nose, she had to know he wasn't really a bear. But the fact that she had to ask at all meant neither Bobby nor Amber had told her directly. "I think you know the answer to that." Instead of saying the word out loud—"snake"—he instead thought of hunting with his family when he was young. A dozen of them, blue and black bands shimmering with magic in the water, diving peacefully among the coral and grass, searching for eels and young fish. Then, weighted down with their meals, slithering up onto the shore to rest and sun themselves on the warm rocks.

He couldn't tell if she was watching the memory in his mind, but her brow furrowed and she stopped putting the flashlight back together. She walked toward him, until she was nearly touching him. Finally, she spoke. "Another lie. You cannot be both bear and snake."

But who was lying? He stared at her long enough that she looked away. She *knew*. Maybe not the whole truth, but part of her knew he wasn't a bear. "People have thought I've been different things at different times. What you can see or smell can be tricked. Illusion magic can be very powerful. But what's in my mind is real."

She shrugged one shoulder, not believing him, then focused on the batteries, inspecting every inch of them before sliding them back into the body of the unit. "Unless you lie to yourself too. If you believe it real . . . remember it that way . . . isn't it still a lie?"

Was it?

How much of his past was shaded by how he remembered an event? Did it matter what was real or just how he interpreted it at the time?

"Let's get Scott out and safe and then we can talk. Okay?" She nodded, just once, her eyes cold and distant, then handed him the flashlight. He was not at all surprised that it worked when he pressed the button. Anica was nothing if not thorough.

"I like Scott and he is important to Bojan. Do what you can. I will not ask how." She paused and then turned away. "But I cannot watch." She strode away and to stand beside Bobby and Bojan, her back to Tristan.

He was surprised how much that bothered him.

Yes, she had a bad history with snakes. Yet why did he have to *prove* himself as a snake when he hadn't had to as a bear? Her prejudice, no matter how well deserved, told him that he would do whatever he had to do to end the mating cleanly. He'd spent most of his life alone and been fine. He didn't need the emotional stress of fitting someone into his life.

He put up mental shields like he was back in Sargon's court, where Nasil and his priests could invade his mind and torture him at will. His mental walls were solid stone to keep his mind clear and free of influence. He felt the connection with Anica sever, leaving him alone in his own mind. It was harder than he expected to maintain, and a little unnerving to realize how accustomed he'd gotten to having someone share his head and how odd it felt to be by himself.

Shaking off the sensation, he pulled his arms out of the sleeves of his shirt and concentrated on shifting. His arms melded into his body, which then narrowed until he was able to wriggle out of the neck of his shirt. His legs joined into one mass, then smoothed out until he could slither freely. He picked up the flashlight in his teeth and easily climbed the seemingly smooth rock, grasping the microfractures in the stone with his scales. Fingers were so clumsy for climbing. He never understood why humans liked to climb freehanded.

Tristan shined the flashlight into the hole and set it down while most of his body was still outside. "Scott?"

"Still here," came the faint reply.

"You're going to have to hold your breath for a few minutes. I'm going to try to get to you and it's going to block this hole."

There was a pause while he sorted that out. "Okay. But . . . it's a little tight on space in here. I don't know that there's really room for even another owl. Or how you're going to get in here. But I can hold my breath for about two minutes underwater."

Two minutes. That wasn't nearly enough time to negotiate a safe path through the crevice. But he'd have to try. "Just breathe slow and shallow. Hopefully, there's air coming in from more than just this entry." Without turning his attention, he called out behind him, "Bobby, send someone to get Amber. I might need you here and she might be needed for Scott!"

Without waiting for an answer, he picked up the flashlight in his teeth again and entered the hole. Thankfully, the crevice was wide enough to allow the flashlight passage—at least, so far. He was entirely within the mountain now, even to the tip of his tail. His senses narrowed to the sensation of rock under his scales and watching for the next turn in the narrow passage. He made four nearly ninety-degree turns in three dimensions in the first three feet. Tristan began to feel a little like a pretzel and it was getting hard to keep moving forward. His skin was being rubbed raw all over by the rough stone—unavoidable in such tight quarters but painful. There was no reason to stop to heal himself, so he was just going to have to put up with it. His best hope was to speed up.

"Hey! I can see the light!" Scott's voice was excited, but then he coughed. "Little hard to breathe, though."

Scott wasn't the only one struggling to breathe. Tristan was starting to think he should have backed in. He could hold his breath well, but the rock was squeezing the air out of him.

The flashlight got stuck, jarring Tristan to a halt.

Oh, this isn't good. He wasn't positive he could back up at this point.

"You're through," Scott said, sounding more tired than he had just seconds before. "I can see the flashlight. But there's a sliver of rock in the way. You'll have to break it to get it through."

Tristan's mouth was dry and sore from being held open so long; it wasn't easy to release his grip on the flashlight and it took a moment before he could speak. "You'll have to grab it from your side and pull it through. It's too narrow in here for me to get any leverage."

"I don't know that I can reach it, but I'll try." Tristan heard a fluttering and talons scratching ahead of him. A second later, the flashlight flew backward and cracked him right between the eyes. Both his head and the torch bounced off the roof of the crevice, showering his face and eyes with a shower of rock dust. Blinking rapidly, he let out a swear and spit dirt until his mouth was clear. *Right now it would be good to have fingers.*

"Shit!" Scott said. "I'm sorry. I missed. Push it forward and I'll try again."

Sighing, Tristan moved the flashlight back into position.

It took two more tries, and a guaranteed black eye later, before Scott was able to catch the front of the flashlight and yank it through the hole, breaking off a chunk of rock in the process. Now that he had a light to shoot for, Tristan began to ease through the hole.

Scott didn't exactly react to him with a hero's welcome. "What the hell!? A *snake*!" He began to beat at Tristan's head with his good wing and bite at his back with his beak. "Shit, shit, shit! Get out!"

"For God's sake, Scott, stop!" Tristan threw out a wave of magic that froze the owl in place. If Scott closed those claws around Tristan's body, it wouldn't kill him, but it would hurt. The owl's eyes were wide and panicked in the light from the flashlight at his feet. "I'm Tristan. Okay?" He released just a bit of the magic so the owl's head could move.

"But you're a *bear*."

"Or not," he replied as he slid the rest of his body into the tight space. Air flooded through behind him and he took a grateful breath. Scott was right that it was tight quarters. It was a narrow space, but at least there was a tall ceiling. He moved around to where he could get a good look at Scott's wing.

Scott's head vibrated and his breathing was fast, nearly hyperventilating as Tristan moved his body to where he could see. "Dude, your slithering is seriously creepy. I have nightmares about shit like this. Couldn't even finish watching *Snakes on a Plane* on video."

"Suck it up . . . *dude*." He said it around the flashlight, so the sarcasm wasn't quite as effective as he'd like. But the owl got it, letting out an annoyed sound that was close to a hoot, but too human for the proper regalness. "I'm trying to get you out of here." Locating a nearly flat rock, Tristan positioned the flashlight so it shined on the trapped wing. The rock pinning Scott in place wasn't all that big, but it was tightly jammed among a dozen others.

He agreed with Scott that pulling out the injured arm could collapse the whole area. The wing was sideways and Scott's collarbone was probably dislocated. That he hadn't mentioned the pain was a little surprising. Tristan nosed gently around the wing, confirming that it was solidly trapped all the way up to the bone. Grabbing one of the feathers with his mouth, he tried to pull it out from underneath. No luck. But he wondered if the reverse was true. He decided to treat it like a joke, to lighten the mood a little. "Hey, I'm not familiar enough with bird shifters. If I pull your feathers out of your wing, will you have fingers when you shift?"

"Don't even fucking *joke* about that!" The outrage in the owl's voice was answer enough. Tristan let out a little hissing snicker. In the next moment, the fear in Scott's scent decreased a little, replaced by anger. "You know I'll have fingers, but it would rip out my fingernails. Amber was right. You *are* an asshole."

"So I'm told. But I'm what you've got, so have a little respect."

The owl took a deep breath; Tristan could tell his heart was beating a mile a minute. "Could you *please* loosen your magic? I've got a little phobia about being held. Bad memories of the old alphas doing sick stuff to me back when I was the Omega. I don't want to combine that with my existing snake phobia, if it's okay."

Scott was an *omega*? How was that possible? After all, he was in owl form more than a week before the full moon. "Did someone shift you today?"

He bobbed his head several times. "Bojan. We had a fight earlier today. He was apologizing by shifting me so I could ride the heat currents as the fire passed. It was stupid, I know, but I've never flown in the daytime before. Rachel said it was amazing and I thought, with the rising hot air, I could fly really high. Then the fire shifted and we had to take cover. I'm not sure how the cave-in happened."

"Sorry," Tristan said. "I didn't know about your phobia. I'll lighten up, but you have to try not to freak out, okay?"

"Okay. Yeah. I'll stay calm."

Tristan released Scott and pulled his power inside him. It was like holding his breath, but down deep in his stomach. "Is that better?"

Scott took a deep breath, his beak as close to the entry hole as he could manage. "It'll do for now. But I'll be glad to get out of here. You do have a plan, right?"

Drawing a deep breath of his own, Tristan looked around the small space, searching for options. "Not yet, but I'm working on one. You might want to close your eyes. To avoid future nightmares."

The owl turned his head sharply, to where he was nearly looking down at his own tail feathers. "Just let me know when I can look again."

Tristan began to climb the walls of the space, once again carrying the flashlight in his mouth. About two feet up, he found a second, larger opening. The owl would have to crouch, but he might be able to wiggle out if the opening led to the outside. It seemed unlikely—Tristan hadn't seen any sign of a second exit and there was no flow of air, so he'd have to follow it to see where it led. He called down to Scott, letting him know, and ended by asking, "You gonna be okay if I leave?"

"Yeah. Just make sure you come back." His voice was a little shaky, but Tristan got it. Dying alone, trapped in a cave, would be a bad way to go.

The flashlight only lit up the opening to the first turn, if it was a turn at all. Only one way to find out. He took a deep breath and slithered into the hole.

CHAPTER 17

Anica sat on the ground next to Bojan, waiting. Tristan had blocked himself off so thoroughly that she couldn't feel him at all, and despite what Tristan had said, Bobby had gone to get Amber himself. The cell phones weren't working. No signal at all and he couldn't reach her telepathically. That worried him, so he'd gone to make sure she was okay. Anica was more concerned about Scott and Tristan.

"Why did you come to the forest during a fire, Brother? You could have been killed."

"I could ask the same thing of you, Sister." He used his shirt to wipe off most of the black from his face and snorted out gobs of dark-stained mucus from his nose. "Two men now you are involved with?"

She snorted too, but not from the ash. "Not even one. He is a snake, Bojan. A *snake* is mated to me. I have no wish to be involved with him. He lied to me, more than once. Snakes cannot be trusted."

Bojan turned to look at her, alarm plain in his face and scent. "Then can he be trusted to help Scott?"

Anica sighed and sat down on the ground near a tree that was spared by the fire. "Yes, he can be trusted to help Scott. He is, I think, a good man. But he is a snake. And he lies."

Bojan looked at her with an odd expression. "He is snake, and he lies, but is a good man? You make no sense, Anica."

It didn't make any sense to her either. "He is a good *man*, when he is a man. And perhaps when he is bear, he is also good."

"Ohhhh," her brother said with a lilt to the word that said he thought he understood but probably didn't. "So snakes are simply evil? All snakes, everywhere . . . because of the few who hurt you. Is that right?" She didn't answer, so he prodded further. "What if you had turned snake, instead of bear, in attacks? Both bit you. Would that form on the full moon change your brain . . . your *heart* to be evil too?"

She blew out a harsh breath and stared at the ground. "Don't be stupid. Of course not."

"Hmm," he said. "Just checking." Walking to the crevice in the rockfall, he called, "Scott? You are okay?"

Eventually a soft reply came: "Yeah. My wing really hurts, though."

Bojan closed his eyes and put his hand on the rock next to the crevice. Emotions filled his scent and Anica had to work to separate the smells. *There is fear, and sorrow, guilt and anger and*—a smell she hadn't smelled from him before. It was one she recognized. Just not from Bojan. Cinnamon and sugar and nutmeg. Cookie spices. "It will be fine," he whispered, his head pressed against the rock. Then he repeated, louder, so Scott could hear, "It will be fine. We'll get you out of there."

"Bojan?" Her brother froze at the suspicious tone in her voice but didn't turn his head. "How is Scott in owl form?

You say at Paula's home you are not able to change me. How can you change Scott? He has been this pack's Omega, like I am ours."

Bojan shook his head. "I do not know. Scott asked weeks ago if I could shift him so he could fly at night. He likes to fly when he doesn't *have* to . . . you know, to hunt. He doesn't like to hunt, but must. His bird insists, like my bear does. I tried, and I could change him. I was surprised how it was easy." Turning to face her, he leaned back against the stone and wrapped his arms around himself. He smiled softly, looking up at the sky, a bright azure blue through the smoke.

"Today, he is angry with me for hitting him. We yelled much in truck when we were leaving town. When the truck stopped to turn onto the main road, he jumped out and ran. I followed, telling him not to be stupid. Then he shifted and flew, without me changing him. I do not know how. Soon we are trapped by flames and must run to the caves."

"How are you not trapped too?"

He shook his head, the scent of guilt and shame overpowering even the smoke in the air.

"Bojan . . . " She had to voice the same question that Bobby had: "Did you *intend* to trap him?"

His sudden anger, the strength of it, surprised her. "*No!* Anica, I would never . . ." He paused and then sighed. "We moved back into the cave as the fire passed. It was smoky, so we went deeper to where the air was clear. We talked instead of yelling, trying to find if we could still be friends. While we talk, he shifted back to human." He paused again, uncomfortable, looking at everything except her. "I am not thinking when he does that he will be naked. I was . . . attracted."

She abruptly understood. "Oh."

"He knows that I am, and kisses me again before I can think. I panicked, pulled away before I . . . before *we* can—" He cleared his throat. "I tried to leave cave, but he followed, grabbed my arm. I shifted him back to owl so I do not have to look at him that way. That is when I hear rumbling.

"I grab his wing to pull him out, but he is angry for me shifting him. He pushes me away very hard and then falling rock separates us." Bojan fell silent for a moment, looking at the sky. "He likes to fly. When he flies very high, so high I can barely see him in the night sky, he feels powerful. Not like an omega. It makes him happy."

"You like it when he is happy, yes?" Bojan might not be at peace with himself, but he was at least not angry with Scott anymore.

He tilted his head and then shrugged. "Of course. That is what friends do." Anica knew it was more than friendship between her brother and Scott. She wasn't sure Bojan would let himself realize it.

A crunching of charred branches caught her attention. She was expecting Bobby or Amber but found herself looking at an old man in a red plaid wool shirt and tattered worker pants. Heavy canvas, like the men back home wore. He was smiling at her, but not with the smile of a friend. She'd seen him before but couldn't remember where.

"Hello," she said, trying to keep her tone neutral as she got to her feet. Flaring her nostrils brought a shock of recognition. He made the footprints! The footprints that had followed Tristan two days ago.

"Hello, Anica."

She narrowed her eyes. "Have we met?"

That smile again, filled with menace, and age. Not just the

age that went with his gray hair and stooped body, but time that spanned centuries. She knew the smile from last night and from Tristan's mind, in the stone building. "Not formally. But I know who you are. I know *what* you are."

Anica moved closer to Bojan, carefully. She took his arm, digging her nails into his skin to keep him still, and quiet. The man was Lagash. Whatever his form now, she knew that. Her brother read her scent and didn't try to puff his chest like Samit would have.

With a press of thought, she tried to reach Tristan in her mind, but he was blocking her. She was no match for Lagash, nor was Bojan. *Cannon fodder*, Tristan had said, and now his words made sense. Her muscles began to tremble as she was gripped by a sort of fear she'd never felt before. Even stronger than when she'd been in the caves, before the bears attacked—because it was not just her, but her brother and the others she feared for. It numbed her, robbed her of the ability to think. But she had to—had to think, had to protect herself and her brother, somehow. "Amber is coming, and Bobby. You can't defeat them both."

He put frail, wrinkled hands on his hips, amused. The hands were a lie, like Tristan's bear. His real form was what she saw last night, when his muscles were thick and powerful and magic had radiated from him in a stinging cloud. She knew he was only showing a fraction of his true magic now. "A Monier and a Mbutu. A good challenge but, really, sparring partners only. Not a real fight."

"Why bother me, or my brother? Why try to kill us? We can't possibly be a threat to you."

But maybe she could be. Anica concentrated on gathering as much scent as she could. She smelled mint . . . no, not mint. The medicine Mama used to put on Bojan's chest when he was sick and couldn't breathe well. Menthol! The strong scent covered many others. She started to take small snuffles, like she did in her animal form, coaxing the layers apart. Pine was next, but not real pine—the pine of cheap green trees that her teacher in primary school had hung from his car mirror. Another layer, another scent. The railroad tie smell. What had Tristan called it? Oh, yes . . . creosote! She pulled in the scents as quickly as she could, hoping that maybe if they were killed at least there would be enough evidence to bring him to justice. The final scent was right next to his skin, a lingering memory of a real scent. It was the perfume of the lady snake. Should she make that bluff? Was it worth the risk to let him know she might actually be a threat?

"Maybe it is Enheduanna who thinks we are a threat?"

He smiled, bright enough to make her think the teeth were store-bought, like Grandfather's, but she knew better and her chest hurt with the knowledge, with the memory of flying through the air and hitting a house hard enough to shatter her bones. "A three-day baby bear and her man-loving brother. It seemed unlikely to me too. Yet she's never been wrong before." He shook his head, the smile no less dangerous, but more amused now. "Facing you without Ris Tupo at your side, though, I think perhaps she *was* wrong."

He turned to leave. Relief surged through her; she gasped for air as her legs went rubbery under her.

Then Lagash said, "But why take the risk?"

Her enemy turned with a speed and elegance that didn't match his human form. She pulled Bojan down and to the side as Lagash threw power at them in a wave that should have killed them both, squashing them into tiny bug puddles. The magic struck the rock; an instant later, a great rumbling began deep in the ground, like when she was underwater.

Panic and pain surged through Anica's mind as Bojan screamed, "Scott!"

The rumbling continued as the old man put a hand next to his mouth and mock-whispered, "I wasn't aiming for you, little girl. So much more fun to kill your mates. Two at once . . . a good day for the bad guys."

He raised his hand again. There was a flash of light.

Then blackness.

CHAPTER 18

Fear clawed at Tristan's stomach. Anica was terrified, in horrible danger. She'd tried to reach him, but he'd shut her out. Now he couldn't reach her at all.

Whatever had shaken the mountain made rocks rain down on him. One particularly large stone landed on the flashlight, breaking the bulb and trapping the tip of his nose, though not for long. He needed to find out what had happened outside. There was barely enough room to slither past the new rock, but he managed to squeeze through, back to the main, but now much more narrow, corridor.

Anica? He opened his mind, but she wasn't there. He felt his heart pound. He needed to get out *now*. It was a tight fit, but he managed to turn around and start back to Scott.

"Tristan! Hey, Tristan, you okay?" He could feel the other man's excitement as he negotiated the now-rock-strewn path. More sharp stones cut through his scales, but that didn't matter right now. "Hey! I can see light. Is that you?"

"No, it's not. The flashlight is toast. Where do you see the light?"

"In the same direction you went. But it's faint."

Tristan blinked. It did seem lighter in the tunnel—he could see individual rocks and feel air flowing. Damned if the explosion, whatever it was, hadn't opened a new rift. "You're right. There's a new way out."

The detour led to an opening a long way up the mountain from where he'd entered. He could climb down, but Scott probably couldn't fly with his damaged wing, even if he could get the owl freed. He didn't dare try to heal him fully. It would take too much magic that he might need to defend all of them. Still, out was out, and Tristan could probably help the man to the ground with minimal damage. He looked around, trying to get his bearings. He couldn't see the lake, or Anica or Bojan. But he could smell magic. It was Lagash. His heart began to race.

Another tremor made dust rain down on him again. First things first. Who knew how much time was left before the whole mountain collapsed?

He quickly made his way back to the trapped owl. "Okay, we have one shot at this. You ready?"

Scott blinked his massive yellow eyes and took a shuddering breath. "This is going to hurt, isn't it?"

"Like a son of a bitch. No guarantees either."

The owl looked at him and then at the faint light above. He fluffed his feathers until he looked like a child's toy. He lowered his head and dug his talons into the dirt, cracking the rock below. "Let's do it. Take the fingernails if you have to. They'll grow back."

Tristan wriggled around Scott until most of his body was under the rock pinning the man's wing. "I lift, you pull, and then get the hell up to the light. Don't stop. Don't look back. Just move forward. Fly, claw, or pull yourself with your beak. Just get out. Understood?"

The owl's nod was curt, tight. "Understood." It seemed to Tristan that Scott knew what he hadn't said—that it was likely only one of them would get out alive.

Tristan wedged himself under the lip of the stone and began to draw on the magic inside him. He had to focus the magic precisely or the stone might crack and crush them both. Physics always trumped magic. "Three . . . two . . ." Scott tensed, leaning forward and pulling on his damaged wing. His other wing rose and his claws dug for purchase.

"One!" Tristan lifted the rock, using as much magic as he dared. The stone rose only a few inches. Scott pulled hard, screaming as his feathers tore across the tips and his shoulder pulled out of its socket.

The rock began to crack. "Go, go, *go!*"

Scott did as ordered. He clawed at the ledge, flapping his good wing to get some air, and finally made it onto the shelf above, mostly using his beak to pull himself up. It wasn't elegant, but it was effective.

Half the stone dropped squarely onto Tristan's chest. He might have enough magic left to lift it once more, but he didn't want to risk it until Scott was out. Even now, his power was holding the weight of nearly the entire mountain just to keep the stone from crushing him. Every nerve in his body screamed in agony and his magic drained rapidly away.

This was Lagash's fault. All of this was his fault. Tristan's anger surged, giving him the strength he needed to pull the last ounce of power from his battered body. How long had it been since he'd been in such pain? He remembered the lash and the rod, the fangs in his side, his legs. He remembered every injury Lagash had caused him.

If that man had laid so much as a finger on Anica—

You can only punish him if you make it out of here.

"I'm out! Tristan! I made it out. C'mon. Hurry!" Scott's voice seemed to come from a thousand miles away.

Taking what might be his last deep breath, Tristan screamed in defiance and shoved the stone up with muscle and magic. It cracked, then shattered, and the world around him started to collapse in on itself.

As he raced upward, his scales grabbed every ounce of purchase and on the wall. Just as he reached the shelf, it gave way and he started to fall.

Tristan! Anica's voice was like a bright light in his mind, giving him speed and purpose. He raced into the sunlight, wrapped himself around Scott's feathered form, and flung both of them into the air, mere seconds before the crevice collapsed.

Looking down was a mistake. It was a *long* way to the ground. Scott muttered softly as they started to fall, "Oh, this is going to hurt."

The owl instinctively tried to open his wing to glide, but Tristan kept a tight hold around him. "Don't try to fly. All you'll do is spin us out of control with your bad wing."

The owl kept struggling. "But we won't *die*. I can fly better with one wing than you can with none."

Tristan tried to throw out a net of magic to soften their landing—simply because *landing* sounded better than crashing—but he was so exhausted from the tunnel and whatever Anica had been forced to fight off that he realized Scott was right. They were going to land *hard*.

Scott let out a piercing screech that was better suited to a barn owl than a snowy as the ground rushed up to meet them. To both men's surprise, there was an answering screech. A massive falcon dove upon them, out of the smoke. Wide talons wrapped around Tristan's body and all he could do was tighten his grip on Scott, who let out an audible grunt. No doubt his wing was in a lot of pain. He got points for not bitching.

There was a moment of whiplash that jerked Tristan's head as the falcon dropped several feet before she opened and began to flap her massive wings. Not until the second flap did Tristan realize who their savior was. Then he managed to croak out, "Thank you for your help, Carolyn."

Gliding down to the lakeshore, she fluttered in place long enough to drop Tristan and Scott onto the soft grass before landing herself. "Of course. It's a Sazi's duty to lend assistance to Wolven."

Scott was struggling to keep his balance with the bad wing, staggering in a sort of circle while his feathers dragged in the mud. "Who's Carolyn? This is—" Tristan lashed out with his tail and knocked the owl's feet from under him, sending him sprawling—anything to keep Scott from finishing his thought. Tristan kept talking.

"As I was saying, *Dr. Archeson*, I greatly appreciate the assistance. If I might ask a favor, I could use some help studying an unusual mineral specimen we discovered nearby." Scott blinked as the bird he knew as Skew responded with a completely different personality.

"Of course. There are some very interesting minerals in the county. Some of the things I've found locally could change everything. Come by my lab later and bring the specimen. I'll take a look at it." She tapped the top of his head with her wing. "And no more base jumping with prisoners, okay?"

"I can assure you, I have no plans to try that stunt again." That was absolutely true. "I'll stop by your lab later."

She took off in a flurry of wing beats, leaving Scott sitting

back on his tail feathers, both literally and figuratively.
"What the hell?! What did you do to Skew? I know that's
her . . . but that is *not* her. Even her voice is different."

Tristan shifted, being careful to give the appearance of
clothing. The last thing he needed was to have one of the
volunteer firefighters call the police about a naked man in
the middle of a forest fire. "That's one of the things I plan
to find out." He jumped to the side quickly when his bare
feet landed on a pile of embers. He was really looking forward to putting on some shoes. The illusion of boots didn't
stop the fire from scorching his skin. "You see, the question isn't what I did to Skew, but what someone else did to
Carolyn Archeson to *make* her Skew."

Scott blinked large golden eyes at him and his beak
opened. "*Make* her Skew?"

"Tristan! You are okay?" Anica ran toward them with
Bojan hot on her heels. She was safe! The sight of her made
his chest pound like he'd been running a marathon. He
started to walk toward her, needing to touch her, smell her.
She stopped short, her scent uncertain, angry. She was carrying the clothing he'd slithered out of. "We see bird catch
you in air. Did she hurt you?" There was worry under the
anger, and concern. But when she held out his clothing she
would not look him in the eye, and she snatched her hands
away before their skin touched.

"Your wing. It is broken?" Bojan, overwhelmed with
worry and concern, and a warmth that was deeper than bud-
dies normally felt for each other, squatted down next to
Scott, then called, "Doctor! Come please and help."

Tristan spotted Bobby and Amber making their way
through the smoking remains of brush and trees. He busied
himself with putting on the clothing Anica had handed him.

"Wish we could have gotten here sooner," Bobby said as Amber rushed to Scott's side. "Too many humans around to shift or use magic while the fire was close. Too many questions later." Yeah, Tristan had seen what flames looked like when he'd tried to use magic around them. Tall columns of bright blue that looked like a gigantic propane flame. You could see it for miles and arson investigators would descend on the area.

"Okay, Scott," Amber said after looking over the wing, "I think you'll be a lot more comfortable if I put you in stasis for this." The owl nodded gratefully. Bojan's scent said he was confused and nervous, so the healer explained, looking reassuringly at him, "Stasis is a magical form of anesthesia. He'll be asleep when I set the arm." She waved the rest of them off. "I'll need a little room, please. Bojan can help me."

Touching Tristan's sleeve to get his attention, Anica said, "May we speak?"

Tristan nodded. As they walked off together, he put a hand on the small of her back, just to touch her. A brush of electricity at the contact made the hairs on his arm stand on end and a tumble of tension tighten his gut. Anica started and jumped a step ahead with a gasp. Her arms rose to cross across her chest.

From behind, Tristan heard Bobby's voice in his head. **Don't force it. That'll only make things worse.** Tristan gave Anica some room.

Once they were standing at the water's edge, Anica turned. "Your phone rang while you were in the cave. I saw on the display that it was Ahmad, so I answered it. I know I should not look at your phone, but no other phones have signal, so I am surprised when I see call and am hoping we can use to get help." Tristan didn't bother to mention it was a satellite phone that had a signal whether or not the towers were working.

Bobby's mouth dropped open at about the same time as his own did. Bobby spoke first, proving he'd been listening in on Tristan's brain. *Damn it!* Tristan slammed down his shields, which a week ago wouldn't have taken nearly as much effort. "Why would you think it was okay to talk to a *councilman*? You know he's the snake councilman, right?"

She shrugged, her scent unconcerned and a touch confused. "Of course. But I know him . . . and Tuli. We traveled together for days in a small car across Serbia. Ahmad sent you both here. If anything happened to Tristan while he was trying to save Scott, Ahmad would want to know what he had found out."

Tristan wasn't sure whether to feel annoyed, impressed, or terrified. "What did you tell him?"

Another shrug, along with a blink. "Everything. I told him of the fires and the bombs, Paula and Lagash. And his sister. He was surprised, and concerned."

No doubt. "What does he want me to do?"

Anica reached into her pocket and held out his cell phone. "Call him. He said he would talk to only you . . . if you survived."

That sounded like Ahmad. Bobby waved at him with the back of his hand as he pulled a second satellite phone from a leather case on his belt. It made Tristan wonder why he hadn't used it to contact Amber. She should have one as well. "Go. Talk to your boss. I'll talk to mine."

Anica didn't move as he started to dial. She just stared at him, her thoughts hidden, or maybe just too confused to be coherent. But her scent wasn't as shielded. She was annoyed, angry, and a dozen other things—he wasn't sure exactly what she was feeling. Those large dark eyes were sad. He didn't want to see her sad.

He had to turn away.

His call was answered before the first ring ended, but the person on the other end remained silent. "Ahmad."

"You survived." There was no surprise in the voice, just an acknowledgment. He heard a whisper in the background, a female, but not Tuli. "And the boy?"

The way he said it made it sound like Scott was a child. "The *man's* shoulder is dislocated, the arm likely broken. But he'll live."

A pause and a muttered conversation to the side. It would do no good to ask who was listening in. Ahmad would just tell him to go to hell. "Find a private place and tell me everything."

Tristan looked around. The closest thing to privacy was a public bathroom made of concrete blocks on the other side of the lake. "I'll call back." He disconnected without saying good-bye. Nearby, Bobby was listening intently. Tristan could just make out the hushed voice coming through the speaker: Lucas, the head of Wolven. As Tristan approached, Bobby turned his head slightly, acknowledging him. Tristan pointed at the bathroom. "I'll be over there." The snake shifter nodded.

As he passed Anica, he could smell the flurry of her emotions. She reached out as though she were going to touch him, then pulled back at the last moment. It was a struggle not to stop, to gather her close and take her with him, keep her safe. Keep her close.

Even when he got to the bathroom, he positioned himself where he could keep a watch on her through the high opening in the painted blocks.

She turned, as though she could feel him staring at her, and locked eyes with him. *What is she thinking? Why is she angry when she already knew I wasn't a bear? Or did she?*

"Risten! Perhatian!" The bellowing voice from the phone in his hand cut through his daze. He nearly dropped it. That was something his mother used to say, in Indonesian, telling him to pay attention. But it wasn't his mother's voice. It was Ahmad's. *I don't even remember dialing.* He inhaled, trying to focus. The sharp, unpleasant scent of dirty concrete, old graffiti, and stale urine that was soaking into his pores made him shudder and walk around to the other side of the building and the entrance to the ladies' side, which stank less. *Why are ladies' rooms always cleaner?*

His name and a string of hissing curses sounded again from the device in his hand. He raised it to his ear. This was not going to be a pleasant conversation.

CHAPTER 19

Why it is so much harder to think with Tristan close enough to touch? Anica tried to focus on what Tuli had taught her by phone in their conversation. She could count on one hand the number of times she'd spoken with Ahmad's wife, even including their time together in Serbia. Tuli was a woman of action, not words. But Tuli had taken the phone from her husband's hand earlier when Anica had asked about mating and they had talked, the woman's voice softening to sound almost maternal.

"Don't listen to Ahmad. Of course it's possible for a snake to be mated to a bear. I . . ." Her voice became distant, as though she was holding her hand over the phone, and then the language changed to one Anica didn't understand. There was a loud crash that made her pull the phone away from her ear, before Tuli's voice came back on the line. "Apologies. I had to explain to my husband why he's an idiot."

It made Anica smile. Very few people would likely still be alive after that. It made her ask the other woman a question: "Is Tristan a good man?" Ahmad was a good man—tough, hard, unrelenting. But underneath, he was good.

There was a pause and then a reply of sorts. "He's very good at what he does. Is that what you mean?"

It was, and it wasn't. "I had always thought when I found a man interested in me that he would be strong, but thoughtful, and that he would trust me and support me and want the best for me. A *good* man . . . like Ahmad. Is he?"

Tuli had answered at length; Anica would need to think much about what the older woman had said. Then the snake councilman's voice had replaced Tuli's with a final warning: "Fear is a thief, Anica. It steals strength. Do not weaken Risten with fear or worry. He is strong and capable like you are strong and capable. I have seen you both face danger, impossible odds, and live. If you wish to have a future with Ris, let him be who he is and insist you be who you are. But you must let him do what he was sent there for. Risten is who other snakes fear. Remember that."

He'd hung up then without saying good-bye, as she'd seen him do in Serbia also. She'd thought about the conversation for long minutes while she'd waited to see whether Tristan and Scott would survive. She thought about the impossible odds of finding her prison again and taking down the cell of evil snakes and bears who had turned her.

She *had* survived.

When the mountain had started to rumble a second time and panic had blown open the door in her head once more, she had to keep Ahmad's words in her head: *Risten is who other snakes fear.*

He had to be able to concentrate, so she shut the door again, her heart pounding with a panic he couldn't afford to feel. It had been hard to do that when she saw his black-and-blue-banded form, wrapped around the fluffy white owl, burst into the air from a place high on the stone wall. Snakes could not fly, and neither could a bird with a broken wing.

He is strong and capable.

Bobby and Amber arrived just as Skew had caught the escapees in mid-air and then it was a race to see who would get to their landing site first. That Anica had arrived first surprised her, considering who she was racing against. Then when she'd seen Tristan, she felt awkward. Part of her wanted to hug him, another part to hit him. She didn't want to distract him, and was also still angry about his lies.

So she did nothing . . . and he noticed.

When he'd touched her back, the physical pleasure had nearly overwhelmed her. Every nerve in her body had been awakened at once, making her stumble and nearly fall over. She'd had to fight to keep the door closed, as though a hurricane were on the other side. But Tristan hadn't pushed beyond his natural magic, thank goodness. In fact, he'd pulled back further into himself, making it easier to keep the door shut.

While everyone was busy and her head was briefly clear, she had time to think. It had been the first time since before she arrived at Rachel's. She sneezed and she raised her hand up to cover her nose. When she pulled her hand away, there were smears of wet in the ash and soot covering her entire body like paste. *Things keep happening too fast. Every new thing is piling on top of the old. There is no time to process a single event.*

She looked at her hands again. *A single event.* That was the answer.

She looked around her quickly and saw Bobby just finishing his phone call. She quickly moved close to him and pulled on his sleeve. "We must hurry to town . . . before people return. I just think of way to find Lagash."

That made him turn so quickly he nearly elbowed her in the head. "What? How?"

"Things happen very quickly, keep us off-balance. Yes?" When he nodded, she continued, "But he could not predict big fire from north and he has just attacked me and Bojan. *After* fire." She smeared her finger through the same paste covering his dark skin and held up her finger for him to see. This time, she waited for him to think of it.

He did. "His will be the only footprints *on top* of the ash."

"And fingerprints. Perhaps he was foolish enough to go to his own home. And even if not, he will be the only person at the safe place—"

Now Bobby was smiling. He finished her thought, "With fresh ash on his boot. At least the same kind of ash, in the same quantities, that burned here."

"But we will need *time*. There is much to smell and I must clean my nose. It is very plugged."

"I can handle that." He patted her on the shoulder and then gave her arm a squeeze. "You definitely need to join Wolven after college. You have promise." His confidence made her smile. Perhaps there was one more snake she could trust. He pulled his phone out again and wandered off to make another call.

She stared at her shoes, then placed a tentative foot in a nearby patch of fresh ash, noting the pattern of the bottom of her shoe. She took off her shoe, balancing on one foot while she smelled the sole. But the ash was hard to sort out. It just smelled burnt.

"What are you doing?" Tristan's voice behind her startled her, throwing her off-balance. He immediately reached forward to steady her. The contact of his hand on her bare arm caused a wind to spring up around her, blowing back her hair and causing actual sparks in the air. He instantly let her go and began to rub his hand against his pant leg, staring at her with a look that approached fear but smelled of desire.

Anica tried to catch her breath after putting her stocking foot on the ground to keep her balance. Once again, her insides were liquid from his touch. "I was trying to sort out smells of ash on ground." Bobby strode up, speaking before he really stopped to take a breath.

"Okay, I talked to Zarko. He's going to do a head count of the residents and call me back with the names of anyone missing. Everyone in town was taken to the high school in Republic. Nobody is going to be allowed to leave until the evacuation order is lifted, and I've just made sure that won't be until tomorrow. So, we have the rest of today, at a minimum."

Amber walked up to them, pulling off a pair of plastic gloves. "I'll take Scott and Bojan to the shelter. Too many people saw them jump off the truck. It'll be noticed if they don't turn up. You don't need any search parties out here." The doctor then nodded her way. "Anica probably should go with us. Her father will be worried if she's here alone with two men."

Anica's stomach dropped. Amber was right, of course. Papa would be frantic and would go to any lengths to make sure she wasn't left alone all night with two strangers. "But my nose is needed here." She turned to Bobby, asking silently for his help. "Isn't that right?"

Bobby was wavering. She could tell. But it was Tristan who came up with an answer: "Lagash must think I'm dead, or he would have stayed around to finish me off." He turned to her. "What did he say before he left?"

It was Bojan who answered, from where he knelt beside Scott's unconscious form. "He threw lightning at us, like in superhero movie. When we ducked, and looked up, surprised we were still alive, he said he hadn't been aiming for us. It was *more fun* to kill our mates."

Anica remembered it, and it made her furious how cavalier he was about it. "Yes, and he said it was a good day for the bad guys."

Tristan nodded and Bobby gave him a knowing look before speaking. "He thinks you're dead and so are Anica and Bojan because you're mated and not alphic. We can use that."

Amber was nodding, and Anica could almost see the wheels spinning in her head. "I can use my link to the owl parliament to make it seem like everyone is devastated at your loss. I'll call Zarko and prepare him. I hope he can pull off being grief stricken."

Bojan looked at her and shook his head. "Papa is not good actor. It would make more sense for him to race out and want to check to see if it is a lie."

She agreed. "If it was real, he would leave, like he did for Samit."

"That's true," Amber agreed. "Everyone in town will remember that he showed up the minute we caught Samit after he was faking going rogue."

Bobby's eyebrows dropped. "I thought I saw in the report that he *did* go rogue."

"Later," Anica amended. "At first, he was pretending, to throw blame on the Kasuns." Bobby shook his head, and she had to shrug. "It is complicated." She turned to look at Tristan. "You know Lagash. Would he want to go with Papa to watch the pain he causes, or would he gloat in private?"

Tristan raised his brows and the scent of sugar and cloves managed to break through her stuffy nose enough so she could recognize his pride in her. He crossed his arms over his chest and thought for a moment, tapping his finger on his opposite forearm. "Neither one, actually. He's a planner. He got his satisfaction at the time. He would be relaxed, calm. But I think Enheduanna would be distressed at his calm. She never had a stomach for killing."

Amber nodded. "So we're looking for a husband and wife spatting or avoiding each other." When Tristan nodded, so did she. "I'll start to put out the word. I'll leave it to you all to keep watch on Scott." She then addressed Bojan directly: "Just put him in a bed. He'll wake up naturally in the morning. Notify me right away if there's any change." Then she pointed her finger at each of them in turn. "And all of you, watch each other's backs. If we're wrong and Lagash is *not* masquerading as someone in town, then he's likely still here and could be a danger to the five of you."

"Six," Anica corrected automatically, and the others stared at her. "Skew is still here somewhere." Then something occurred to her. "Could Skew be Enheduanna? Being married to a madman could make someone go mad themselves. Why did she suddenly appear to help Tristan and Scott? How could she know they needed help unless she was part of it?"

"Good point," Bobby said. "We'll have to keep an eye out for her. If we find her, we can put her in the jail for safekeeping. And, if Lagash is her mate, he'll be drawn to rescue her."

So, Skew was either a potential victim or an enemy and they had no idea which one, or where she was. "I know her scent. I've been in the sweet shop many times. I can find her.

The hard part will be keeping my nose up instead of down. She could be in any tree or on any rooftop. I have never search for a bird before."

Tristan moved closer to her. Electricity lit up the ash in the air between them like tiny fireflies. "I have. And so has Bobby. One of us will always stay with you, keeping you safe."

Bojan let out a small growl as he stared at the tiny flickers of magic between them. "Papa will not like this. I do not either."

Amber raised her hand. "I'll explain it to Zarko. There are a number of things I need to discuss with your father . . . and mother, if we can reach her. This is only a tiny part of the shocks he's going to have tonight." She touched Bojan's arm. "I trust Bobby and Ris. She'll be safe. And I trust *you* to keep Scott safe." Bojan stopped growling. He still smelled nervous, but he glanced at his friend and let out a sigh of resignation.

Amber began to repack her medical bag. "I talked to Charles earlier. He told me everything he remembers about Lagash, and from what I heard, he's at his most dangerous after dark. Nobody searches alone or wanders outside, especially when night hits. Direct orders. Remember," she said, standing up and putting the straps of the bag on like a backpack, "there's no rush. This is an opportunity, not a deadline. Don't risk your lives."

Anica had to fight not to laugh as Amber took off at an easy trot toward the road. Her warning was no laughing matter, but it was far too late to worry about risk.

CHAPTER 20

With mixed emotions Tristan watched Amber leave. "I'll help Bojan carry Scott to the Williams house, in case Enheduanna is there. She was able to get into the Petrovic house with ease, so she or Lagash might have keys to everyone's home."

"They might also *be* the Williamses. Remember, we had just left the Williams house when Lagash appeared." Anica let out a snort.

That wasn't something he had considered, and he should have. He had to figure out how to get his head straight again and back on the hunt.

"What do you think, Bobby? I don't know if there's a safe place in town to keep someone as vulnerable as Scott."

Bobby tapped one booted foot on the ground. "I vote for the Petrovic house. I don't know anything about the Williams house or what fortifications it has. But the fortifications at the Petrovics' are impressive and I've been in the home and know its smells. I'll be able to smell if anything is out of place since we were there last. So, at least for now, we stay together."

Stripping off his shirt, Tristan motioned for Bobby and Bojan to do the same. "We can make a stretcher for Scott with our shirts and some of these unburnt branches. It'll be easier than trying to carry him without touching his wing. Bojan, can you keep holding his form? His feathers will protect him from falling ash better as we head into where the trees are still smoldering."

Anica's brother nodded. His face was drawn, the skin sagging from overexertion. Tristan had seen that look before, in troops who had been fighting too long. "I am getting tired," the young man said, "but I will keep holding him. I do not wish to risk either of you losing power if you have to protect us later."

Anica also stripped off her shirt, revealing what had once been a lacy white bra, now covered with smudges of gray and black. The sight of her made his heart pound and he had to look away, to focus on the stretcher, which he was struggling to make fit the tall man. "You need a fourth shirt. If you will shift me, I will not need mine, and my nose will be better for searching for Lagash."

He looked at Bobby hopefully, but the python shifter let out an amused snort and waved away the idea with his hands. "Oh, no. No way do I want to be tied to another man's mate. That's a recipe for a mating challenge. You have no way of knowing how you'd react to feeling my magic slide under your automatic defenses, and I don't want to find out."

A mating challenge. He hadn't seen one of those for better than a century, but he remembered it well. Two friends, mated to the same alphic female. The men had beaten each other nearly to death before one gave up and slithered out of the nest to pine to death. He'd refused to eat, to sleep, to drink even a drop of water. It had taken weeks for him to

die: a slow, ugly suicide over what Tristan had believed to
be a ridiculous reason.

How ridiculous was it now? "I'm sure I'd be fine. We
haven't fully mated."

Now Bobby let out a laugh, his teeth more a baring of
fangs than a smile. "Really? Let's test that theory." Before
Tristan could move, he'd moved over to Anica, put his arm
around her bare shoulders, and begun to flick his tongue
softly against her hair.

Anica twitched and tried to pull away, but Bobby just
pulled her closer, putting his other bare arm around her.
Something welled up in Tristan's stomach. His chest started
to heave for air, like he couldn't breathe. He hissed, long and
low, and took a step forward as Anica struggled under
Bobby's grip. She pushed against his chest, protesting in
word and scent. "Bobby! What are you doing?"

A red film slid down over Tristan's vision, like the fire had
started all over again. He flicked his tongue out, his muscles tensing as he watched for an opening to the snake's weak
spot, near the back of his neck.

Before he could take another step forward, Bobby released Anica, so abruptly that it was as though they'd never
touched. "And there's your answer," he said calmly. "No way
am I getting my magic anywhere close to her."

Anica backed away from both of them, her eyes wide.
"You are not going to fight, are you?"

"No," Tristan was able to finally gasp out. "No. We're not
going to fight." The statement felt like a lie, because it was
taking every ounce of his willpower to hold himself steady.
He tightened his fingers into fists, the fingernails digging
deep into his palms.

Bobby pointed toward town. "Go. Finish the mating

process, just like I had to. It's only because you're not fully mated that you're reacting like this. I wanted to kill Nikoli for daring to touch a woman who had already been his lover for years. I can't afford for you to be less than at your best if we do run into Lagash. We'll guard the house."

"You won't be able to help yourself, even in times when you shouldn't." Anica's voice was nearly a whisper, and Bojan looked stricken. But her scent wasn't fear or worry. It was the light, clean ozone of realization and calm.

"What are you talking about?"

Bojan looked from Anica to Tristan, then took his sister's hand. The contact between siblings didn't make Tristan see red, and he was grateful for that. Bojan kissed her hand lightly. "Go, and let it be a choice, not a fate."

She kissed his fist in return. "Nor a thing of shame, but of hope and strength." Bojan's smile was more shaky than hers, but he nodded and tightened his grip on her hand for a moment before letting go and returning to the stretcher.

Anica's footsteps were light and confident as she and Tristan walked back to town. "Shift me," she said in what sounded like a seductive whisper. A shudder passed over his skin as he complied, easing magic over her until her fur flowed. He couldn't help but touch the brown fur to see if it had the same texture as her hair. Her whole body shook when he did, like shedding water after a swim. She quickly moved out of reach, leaving her clothing on the ground for him to pick up. "But not now. We have work first, yes? We think no more of what others say we *must* do. We will do as we choose, when we choose."

She bounded into the distance, letting him decide whether to follow. It was an easy decision—he really had no other options. Instead of heading toward town with Bobby and

Bojan, Anica went back to the cave where Scott had been stuck. Tristan caught up as she was sniffing the ground carefully. "Why are we here instead of going to town?"

"I know where Lagash stands when he attacks Bojan and me. Knowing what kind of footprint he left and following his prints seems good place to start. Yes?"

It was, and he was an idiot for not thinking of it. He ran his fingers through his hair and let out a frustrated breath. "My head is really not in the game right now. I apologize." But that was going to change, right now.

"It is difficult for me as well. But I must try. He says to me and Bojan that Enheduanna is seer and she tells him that Bojan and I are a danger. That is why he must attack us. But then he does not. He must be smart, but that was stupid. He could have easily killed us. Why leave us alive?"

That was a very good question. A plan within a plan, perhaps? "Lagash was always good at shifting on the fly." When Anica cocked her head, questioning, and smelled curious, he explained further. "He could change plans quickly to adapt to a new situation, even while a current plan was in progress. But I had no idea Enheduanna was a seer. That might explain how they stayed hidden from the entire Council and Wolven for so long. It also explains why he abandoned Sargon and went underground."

Anica's nose came up from the ground, the black tip covered with fine gray ash. "Or perhaps he does not abandon, but divide to conquer. This is tactic of many good generals, yes?" He must have looked surprised, because she raised one shoulder in a shrug. "Papa studies dead generals for fun. He likes smart men, so he reads books on their lives, learns how they planned."

Divide to conquer. Sargon and Lagash didn't mind a long

game. They were both willing to wait generations for a plan to unfurl. And with a seer at their command . . . he remembered Ahmad talking about his father's seers. But why wouldn't Ahmad mention Enheduanna was one of them? "I think I'm starting to see why the seer considered you a threat, Anica."

A burst of desert heat said she was embarrassed, since she couldn't blush with fur. "I am like Papa. I like to read and have always liked mysteries. I learn English by reading Nancy Drew books. When I am little girl, I think, 'I am going to become famous detective when I grow up.' Is silly, I know. But later I know that just solving mystery is not enough. I must try to help people not kill to begin with."

He wasn't sure who Nancy Drew was, but he didn't think Anica's ambition was silly at all. "You have the head, and Bobby thinks you have the talent."

She looked up at him, her eyes like deep pools of endless black. "What do *you* think?"

He shrugged, not sure what to say. "I don't know that it matters what *I* think."

"Well." She lowered her nose to snuffle at a large boot print with distinctive diamond-shaped markings. "If we are to be mated, and are tied as one like marriage, then you *would* have say in what I do. Yes?" She didn't smell like she liked that idea. It came with anger attached, but he didn't know why.

Tied as one like marriage. It wasn't something that had really occurred to him until she said it. "Where I come from, the women make their own choices." That made her scent move from spicy to fruity. "My mother chose to be a mother. She raised many children and that was what she wanted. My brothers and sisters were mostly fighters. They would fight against whoever was trying to occupy our country at a given time. But someone was *always* trying to occupy, and because of that, I don't have any siblings left."

"Oh. I am sorry for you. So—"

He wasn't really answering her question. He knew that but wasn't sure what she wanted to hear. "I really don't get involved in what other people want to do. It's none of my business. I've mostly kept to myself for years, which is why I'm still alive. I have a certain *reputation* as a hunter and killer. I suppose it's true, since that seems to be what I've always done and I'm good at it."

"So you are assassin?" Her voice and scent said she didn't believe it. "I have met assassins. They are dangerous, and you know immediately. You do not seem like one." She put her head down and snuffled the next print. "This boot does not smell like boot at Williams house. Did you notice?"

He did notice it, and had already catalogued it in his head without really thinking about it. But scents could lie. "Did he appear as he did there? In the same clothing?"

She shook her head. "No, he appeared as old man . . . white skin with gray hair. I felt like I recognized him, but I don't know all people in town yet. It smelled like Lagash in air, so I ignore body appearance." She tapped the ground. "But not same smell in print. It is odd."

"That part isn't odd at all. Not to me. Appearance by magic is intended to change everything. You can't just look like one person and smell like another. The disguise has to encompass all of the senses to work in the Sazi world. *That* is why I can do what I do."

She sat down and stared up at him again, those eyes far

too big for a bear face. "So what I see in your head is true? Each name you are known has different face, scent . . . everything? Then this face is lie too?"

It was digging too far inside now. She had seen things she shouldn't have. Yet he answered before he could stop himself, "Yes . . . and no. I *am* Tristan Davies. There is no other Tristan Davies out in the world that I'm just appearing to be. I was also Justin Davies, who everyone believes is Tristan's father. I lived for a dozen years as the father to establish myself before Justin sold his house to his only son and moved to Florida. I can slip into an identity like other people slip into a favorite shirt."

"I see." And he could tell she did. But she didn't like it. "So you lie for a living? Like spy? How can people trust you?"

He started answering before he really thought. Something deep inside *needed* her to understand him. It was both terrifying and liberating to say it out loud after so long. "Not a spy. Not really, anyway . . . and I've never needed anyone to trust me. I'm the Council's enforcer, or one of them. There are several of us who hunt the worst of the worst—the shifters who are serial killers or mass murderers. I'm not called up often, so I just live my life, moving from place to place and skin to skin, waiting for the next call to rid the world of another murderer. Either for the human government where I live, or for the Council. Each identity is important because it can get me close to a target. That's why I didn't want you to find my backpack. It had several passports inside, more identities than I normally carry with me. But I really had been heading back to Kansas from Canada when Ahmad called me."

"And Lagash is the same, changing people like shirts while he plots?"

That was the best explanation he had at the moment. "I think so. I didn't realize we were the same, but I suppose we are. I don't, or *didn't*, think Enheduanna had that gift. She was a late turn and not terribly powerful. Or so I thought. That's why I was surprised she's still alive."

Anica was staring into the distance. She lowered her voice to a harsh whisper. "Then how is she able to do *that*?" She pointed and Tristan spun. The smoke was thicker in that direction and the natural slope of the land created a small gully that likely funneled water to the lake during rains. Blinking repeatedly to push away the fine film that was protecting his eyes from stinging, he followed her finger to what looked very much like the head of a king cobra slithering along just below the rise, away from town and downwind enough that he couldn't catch the scent. *How indeed?* It was full daylight and not close enough to the moon to let her change herself. So either Lagash forced her change, or she really *was* alphic, or that *wasn't* Ahmad's sister and there was another snake in town.

He touched her arm, intending to follow the snake. Maybe it would lead back to Lagash's lair. He leaned down next to her so-soft ear that twitched when he whispered, "You go stay with Bojan and Bobby at the house. I'm going to follow the snake."

Her furred nose lifted and brushed his lips. He didn't move away as she replied, "Then I go with you. Amber say nobody searches alone. Yes?"

"She didn't mean me. She meant *you*."

Anica let out a small snort and the snake paused. Anica lowered to the ground while Tristan stepped behind a tree. She replied into his mind, her voice carrying a sarcasm that surprised him, **She say it to five people. She does not say, "But no,** only four of you must obey Charles." He is great bear, yes? Bigger than Ahmad?

Technically, that was true. An order from Charles did beat out an order from Ahmad. But he didn't want to be the one to have explain that to the snake councilman.

Their target flicked its tongue and looked around in a circle, which likely didn't do it any good given the thickening smoke. It was becoming increasingly difficult for even Tristan to smell anything other than burnt wood. His pores felt so clogged that it was like he was blind and he hated even sticking out his tongue to taste the air. Finally, after a long moment when his muscles tensed and readied for a fight if necessary, the snake continued on.

He put a hand on Anica's shoulder and pressed down. Stay here. He let out a soft hiss to try to press home the point that he was in charge, but Anica wasn't impressed. She just blinked and sniffed, and shook off his hand, then started to carefully pad through the trees after the snake, keeping just out of sight. He could put her in a hold, but she'd be defenseless unless he carried her along.

He thought back to them talking earlier. How was it possible the snake didn't know they were there? The woods were mostly silent except for the distant crackling of the fire. I think we're being led into a trap.

Anica tipped her head, an acknowledgment that was completely devoid of fear. He found that both refreshing and disturbing in someone so young. It reminded him a great deal of himself, as well as his grandniece, Asri. No wonder Bobby was enchanted by this little bear. And maybe not just Bobby.

Possibly. But why bother to lure us somewhere *more* remote that could not be done here?

It was a good point.

By the time they walked to a point where they could remain hidden but still see into the gully, the snake had disappeared up into the rolling clouds of smoke that seemed to
be settling here from higher up the mountain. It was getting
harder to breathe shallowly enough that he didn't cough.

He shook his head and touched Anica's shoulder to stop
her from starting into the narrow water pathway. **If we follow
into the heavy smoke, we'll start coughing and become an easy
target for the cobra to spit poison before we can see it.**

Anica paused, considering. Then she sighed. **It is good advice. But I hate getting so close and then walking away.**

He understood completely. **Still, I would rather walk away
than give away every advantage in a fight.**

She nodded and turned away from the gully while he
watched the smoke carefully, looking for any movement in
the swirling white wall. By extending his magic just a touch,
he was able to tie himself to her so that she could watch
forward and he could keep facing the gully to watch their
backs until they got to clearer air.

He stopped abruptly when she did, her body suddenly
tense, nearly vibrating. **Another snake. This one is not cobra.** He turned, following where she was gesturing with
her nose. He caught just the tail of a second snake heading
into the smoke. This tail had circular rings and a row of
rattles.

We need to get back to town. Now. Two against one was decent odds with a snake. Two against two was not. He needed
to talk to Bobby and possibly Ahmad. He didn't know of any
rattlers who lived in Washington, so either this was one of
the firefighters, or something Lagash had been planning was
beginning.

This time, she didn't hesitate. **I must clean my nose. My eyes are not as good. I should have smelled snake before I saw.**

He should have too and he wondered why even now he couldn't smell it. Sazi rattlers had a very distinct odor, like cucumbers soaking in vinegar. He should be able to smell it over the smoke. That he couldn't, even when he tried, bothered him.

A lot.

CHAPTER 21

Anica was never so glad to get inside solid walls. After meeting up with Bobby and Bojan, they decided to go to the apartment building instead of the Petrovics' home. Rachel had showed her the defenses the building had, and she made sure the bars were locked on the outside windows and doors before she went in. She took a sniff downstairs, toward the laundry room, but smelled no snakes. She even locked that door, just to be safe.

Her own house didn't have a basement, or many tools. But the apartment building did, and she supposed snakes would know how best to fight other snakes. Anica helped Bojan take Scott to finish his healing in his own apartment. She encouraged Bojan to try to get some sleep as well. Her exhausted brother could barely stand while giving her a warm hug and promising to rest. Then Anica had retreated to Rachel's apartment. Thankfully, the key in her pocket hadn't come out during her swim or when she'd shifted out of her clothes.

Tristan had wanted to talk to Bobby privately, and while a part of her understood they were both police and had many things to discuss, they were also both snakes and having even more of them in town was making her increasingly uneasy.

Too, she was worried about Papa and Rachel and the others, but her cell phone had no signal, so she could not check. Neither of the snakes had offered to let her use theirs and she was reluctant to draw attention to herself by asking.

Walking through the town had felt very strange with nobody there. What remained of the diner smoldered, with only one partial wall still standing. The windows of the post office had shattered, leaving blackened glass in a wide arc around the building. Polar Pops was untouched, but Skew was nowhere to be found. Yet all the mousetraps and their projectiles had been removed. Paula and the cook remained at peace in the freezer in the basement, their skin a chalky white, with the dull red of her neck wounds.

Why nothing else burned was a mystery, but Anica was glad most of the town had been spared.

Her stomach growled audibly as she locked the door behind her. She leaned on the door for a moment, closed her eyes, and sighed. She was emotionally and physically wrung out and she stank of smoke. She tried to decide which need to fill first.

The gurgling noises from her stomach made the decision for her. It had been hours since the light breakfast Rachel had made. She grabbed a tissue from a box on the kitchen counter and blew black goo from her nose as she walked to the refrigerator. It took two more blows before she could start to smell anything other than burnt wood and grass.

A lower shelf held a package of sliced turkey and one of sliced cheese. A half loaf of bread sat in a clear plastic container next to the stove. The sight of her fingers, black with soot against the bright yellow of the meat package, forced her to stop.

Streaks of black turned into gray bubbles under the running water from the sink as she soaped her fingers and nails and then her hands until there was a clean line to her wrists and she at least felt like she wouldn't be eating ash.

The first bite of sandwich dispelled that idea, reminding her that her nose wasn't the only thing that was clogged. She spit out the gritty bread, then put the sandwich down on a paper towel. A glass of water helped clear her mouth, especially when she swirled it around and spit into the sink. She wondered about brushing her teeth as well, then decided to do that later. She drank a second glassful of water before returning to her sandwich.

A knock on the door made her wary, but a quick sniff from her newly cleaned nose identified the visitors as Tristan and Bobby. She walked across the living room, sandwich in hand, and noticed a dark print on the white paint from her butt and shoulders when she'd leaned. She sighed and opened the door. After swallowing another amazingly tasty bite of the simple fare, she asked, "Is there any more sign of the snakes?"

They both shook their heads. Bobby's face was sour as he said, "Nothing. But I can't smell for shit through all the smoke."

Standing back to let them pass, she closed and locked the door behind them. Noticing them staring longingly at her sandwich, Anica waved them toward the kitchen. Rachel's apartment wasn't her home, so she didn't feel compelled to treat them as guests and prepare a meal. "Please. Eat. And thank Claire when you see her next. She filled the icebox just this morning."

She decided to sit down on the couch instead of the chairs, since it wouldn't show the soot as badly. Closing her eyes, she relaxed to the homey sounds of running water, clinking cutlery and plates. A shaking, crunching sound made her open them. Tristan was holding out a bag of chips, offering her some. She had no plate but took a handful anyway. He sat down beside her and put a glass of milk on the table in front of her, which would be the perfect complement to the turkey once she had a free hand.

They ate without speaking, the men each devouring two sandwiches to her one, along with a half-dozen pickles that she'd forgotten were in the door of the refrigerator.

"Oh, man, I needed that. And I normally don't even *like* turkey," Bobby said, leaning back in the dark brown chair that seemed too small for his big frame.

Tristan nodded. "I do like turkey, so my tongue is very happy." He bumped her with his shoulder. "You look exhausted, Anica. Why don't you get some sleep? We'll keep watch. We all need some rest before we start hunting snakes."

She'd known one of the risks of stopping, after all the events of the day, would be that her body would refuse to move again. She could barely keep her eyes open, so she just nodded. "Shower first, then bed."

Tiredness showed in Bobby's movements as he stood. "I'll take first watch." He grabbed a chair from the kitchen table and carried it to the door. "This should be uncomfortable enough to keep me awake in the hallway. Any chance there's a phone charger around? I should probably call Asri and a few other people."

"I think there is charger in kitchen, but I do not know for what phone." She tried to remember where she'd seen Rachel put the phone cord. After rummaging around in several drawers in the kitchen, she'd found several with different connector ends, and brought them out for Bobby. "Will one of these fit?"

The third one did. "Now I just have to find an outlet in the hallway. I think there's one by the stairs, which isn't a bad spot to keep watch and talk."

"I had no signal, so I don't know who you can talk to."

He held up his phone and smiled, confirming what Tristan had said. "Satellite phone. Doesn't rely on towers. As long as our eye in the sky isn't hit by a meteor, I'll have a signal." He waved the charger. "Reliable electricity is our real challenge." Carrying the metal and vinyl-padded chair, he left. When the door shut, a tension she'd forgotten returned. Tristan was watching her—she could feel his gaze like pressure against her skin, smell the spice that seemed to intensify with desire.

"Do you mind if I shower first? I am very . . . itchy." Anica's voice caught and she coughed, suddenly uncomfortable. She realized that she wanted to shower with him, to feel the pounding water against her skin as he touched her and she touched him. But the images in her mind were of looking down *at* her under the water. That was when she realized the door in her head had slipped open. She wasn't sure whose thoughts she was thinking. *Should I close the door or leave it open?*

She looked at Tristan. His hands were balled into fists and a fine trembling made his skin vibrate. His blue eyes were panicked. He didn't look like a man who wanted to be thinking what he was. She turned away, walked down the hallway, and felt his eyes scanning her body as she did. He'd seen her nearly naked, yet had been a gentleman. Part of her wanted to tease him, but she didn't wish to make his desire worse.

Or did she? *Choice. What happens next must be my choice. And his. But I have decided. He is a good man.*

That was part of what she'd talked to Tuli about earlier. Good men. "Ris can be good. Of course, I've only known him for bits and pieces of time. You have to realize he's lived a long life, for many centuries. As have I. I've only run into him from time to time, in different eras." The snake shifter had paused, seeming to really consider the question.

"I've seen him be a warrior and a leader who has inspired people. The people he has chosen as underlings have had talent and brains. He has come to trust Ahmad and has supported and followed him even when that wasn't easy. I've watched him protect lesser beings and be angry at injustice. But . . . like many warriors and leaders, my husband included, Ris can sometimes be an ass—thoughtless, impatient, callous.

"He can be dangerous, and can kill without emotion. I've seen him relish the death of an enemy, but I've also seen pain in his eyes when an innocent suffers. He is not always kind, but he can be. Yes, very much like Ahmad, now that I think of it. I believe he has loved, but has never mated before. So I really don't have any idea how he'll manage being mated to someone so young."

"I'm not that young. I'm twenty-four."

Tuli had laughed, a light chuckle. "Once you've added a zero to the back of that, we'll talk again."

Two hundred forty? Was that even possible? "Could I live that long? Truly?"

"With Ris mated to you? Absolutely. You'll gain a tremendous amount of power just from his magic and if you're double mated—which you likely won't find out until you have sex with him—you'll gain even more. By the way, if you're double mated you won't be able to resist having sex. You'll want him so badly, your skin will hurt. You won't be able to stop thinking about it, even at times when you shouldn't."

"It does now . . . hurt." She'd felt heat rise to her face as she said this out loud, especially because her brother was standing right there. Bojan had listened intently to the conversation, likely gathering information for his own situation. "I cannot get him out of my mind. Literally. I can hear his thoughts, feel his feelings. I can't not hear what's happening to him. Even now, I can feel the sensation of him wriggling through rock. It makes my skin crawl.

"He's a snake and he lied to me, but I fear for him, and worry, and want him." She'd let out an exasperated breath. "Tuli, I only just met him. Just two days ago. I was just nearly killed, the killer could be lurking nearby even now, and Tristan might be crushed by rocks any second. It makes no sense to think of sex right now. But I can't seem to help it!"

The other woman had sighed, as though she'd felt the same thing. "That's mating for you. It makes no sense. High emotion makes it stronger, so dangerous situations are actually when you think about sex more."

Anica closed the door to the bathroom but didn't lock it. It was a pretty space, decorated in silver and gray. The items on the small counter matched the fluffy towels, from the toothbrush holder to the soap dish and even the covered cotton ball container. Turning on the water, she made it as hot as possible to cut through the sweat and soot. A glance in the mirror made her wonder why Tristan felt any desire at all.

She was filthy, grimy . . . her hair stringy and hanging in clumps. *Yuck.*

After undressing, she stepped under the water. She felt him move closer to the door, inhale the steam that carried her scent around the doorframe. His desire to touch her overwhelmed her, making her nearly stagger. As she scrubbed her hair and soaped her skin with fragrant citrus soap and a poofy white sponge, it was as though his hands were smoothing the lather along her body. Her own hunger began to rise as she scrubbed the day off. She wanted him to open the door and join her under the pounding water. But he didn't, even as she intentionally touched her nipples and then between her legs. Her desire grew, but still he held back. The battle inside him pushed against her own mind and made her want him even more. Magic began to fill the air like a sparkling cloud of blue-white glitter in the steam.

Once she was clean, she brushed the knots out of her hair and wrapped one of the massive bath sheets around herself, nearly twice, before tucking the end in to hold it closed. Tristan was concentrating on each tiny act she was doing, even to brushing her teeth, so he didn't think about the nude body under the towel. Every action she did was echoed in her mind, the mundane motions turned into a reverse striptease that was making him crazy. Yet still he fought opening the door to claim her.

So she did it for him. But the sight of him when she did made her stop and reconsider. He was hanging on to his control by teeth and toenails, his eyes wide and bright with magic, his breath coming in tiny gasps from desperate need. Even his hands were clenched into tight fists, the knuckles white from effort. So, instead of dropping the towel and inviting him to take her, she stepped past him. "Your turn."

He nodded gratefully and nearly leaped into the room before shutting the door.

She waited . . . until the water started and she could hear, smell the soap. Then Anica opened the door and stepped inside.

He froze behind the shower curtain. "You need to leave. Before—"

She removed her towel and carefully hung it on the rack. "No. You needed to prove to yourself that you could defeat desire. You did. You wanted to protect me from something you did not believe you could control. You did. Now, it is *my* choice and your choice. Not a requirement, but a wish, between two adults, two *humans*, not just their animals."

He paused, so close she could reach forward and touch him except for the thin plastic sheet. The glitter was in the air again, even more powerful this close, and her body was tight with need. "I don't think you understand who I really am."

That was true. "Then show me. Open this curtain and show me the *real* you. I wish to have you now, to feel you inside me and give you pleasure. But only whoever you are in truth."

The shadow of his body behind the curtain changed, so quickly that it might have been her imagination. But she didn't imagine that the hand that reached out to grasp the edge of the shower curtain was different—the skin darker, the hand smaller, more slender.

When he pulled back the curtain, she didn't gasp. She'd seen him before, in Tristan's mind. His hair was jet-black and wavy, his eyes the dark gray of a stormy sea lit with intense blue fire. The lines at the edges of his eyes and mouth told her he had smiled more often in his life than frowned.

She reached out, touched the creases in his face, and felt his power surge through her, quicken her body. Her skin vibrated with electricity that made her shiver and her nipples harden instantly.

His cock did too. She moved from his face to grasp it and he moaned, nearly falling back against the wall. He reached for her, pulled her into the shower, and kissed her. It was a frantic, desperate kiss that poured all of his desire down her throat. Feeling his muscles envelop her made her wet, swollen with need, so that when he reached between them and began to slide himself inside her she lifted one leg, putting her foot on the edge of the tub, and leaned back against the wall, to ease his way. She was a little afraid she'd slip, but he braced one foot back against the front of the small enclosure, not as much a bathtub as a shower stall, keeping them solidly balanced.

It was an awkward first joining, but it felt completely right—to be under water for their first time. The hot water pounded down on her head as he cupped her butt cheeks and slammed into her. He filled her completely, to nearly overflowing, and her muscles contracted around him so tight she wanted to scream. But she could only whimper as his mouth found her neck, sucking and licking at the same speed as his hands clutched at her ass, while his constantly moving chest made her breasts so swollen and heavy that she couldn't help herself as she exploded into climax. There were too many sensations, too soon, and while she didn't scream out her ecstasy, it was only because his mouth suddenly moved to cover hers, his tongue in the way of any sound escaping.

One hand moved, slipped between them to quickly rub her clitoris while she climaxed, taking her even higher, to where firefly sparkles appeared in her vision. Her heart was beating so fast she was afraid it would leap out of her chest.

Yet he kept up the same pace, moving in and out of her in something approaching a frenzy, unrelenting, intensifying the sight-stealing sensations that gripped her, plunged her into a place she'd never been before. She began to push her hips against him just as hard, until his breathing grew ragged. She pulled her mouth away from his to whisper, "Your turn."

He shook his head. "Not here." He pulled himself out of her and let the water pour down on them while he toyed with her breasts, feeling the weight of them and teasing the nipples until her insides began to clench again.

Tristan stepped out of the tub and pulled her along until they were standing in front of the sink. "I want you to see your eyes as you go over again." He spread her legs and entered her from behind and the different angle in the already-swollen passage made her gasp and clutch the edge of the counter from the sheer pleasure. She could see her expression in the mirror and the glow of magic that made her eyes look like opals in the sunlight.

Once again, he reached his hands around, this time squeezing her breast with one hand while the other returned to rub her clit. His mouth moved to her neck and she couldn't seem to shut her eyes while she watched the entire scene. Her chest began to heave for air. Then, like moments before, her insides began to clench around the length and width of his cock as he moved in and out of her, faster and faster with each second. The smells of sex and magic, combined with Tristan's exotic spices, nearly made her pass out.

When she climaxed again, she understood why he wanted her to watch. Her eyes looked like captive stars. The sight should have terrified her, but it didn't, because his eyes were the same, glowing with an inner fire that joined them, and when he finally let go and allowed his climax to claim him even their skin was glowing with white light. The door in her mind became a chasm that pulled her into the fire. It gripped her body and mind in something that "climax" couldn't begin to describe. She was open to him, and he to her, and she didn't know that the door could ever be closed again.

"Dear Gods," was all he could whisper before he pulled himself out of her. She felt the heat as he spilled himself onto her back. Then he collapsed onto her, pushing her forward so abruptly that she nearly hit her head on the mirror.

While they both remembered how to breathe, he let out a gasping sort of chuckle. "I think we're going to need another shower."

CHAPTER 22

Anica slid out from underneath Tristan's arm, the weight of it telling her he was in deep slumber. After yet another session of lovemaking once they'd made it to the bedroom, she wasn't surprised.

She padded to the bathroom and saw the mess they'd left behind, and sensed the smells that even now pulled at her. When she returned to the bed after using the toilet, she intended to lie back down. But she was fully awake and he looked so peaceful sleeping. Her mind still struggled to grasp that the dark hair and deeply tanned skin on the white pillow were of the same man she'd seen for the past two days. Should she still think of him as Tristan? *No. He is Ris. I like him better this way. It is the honest him.*

He rolled over then, into the spot where she'd lain, revealing the tattoo of ocean waves that was the only reminder of the blond-haired, blue-eyed Tristan. But he still felt the same in her head. The sensation was quiet now, a light pressure like hair or jewelry that was there but not noticed unless she thought about it.

She was beginning to learn to shield. Another lesson from

Tuli that she'd sorely needed. Bojan too had learned while waiting for word from their mates inside the mountain.

"Shielding will help," Tuli had told her. "Has anyone taught you how?"

She'd glanced at Bojan, who pursed his lips and shook his head. "No," Anica replied for them both. If he was mated to Scott, as she was starting to believe, then this might help him too.

"Concentrate very hard. Think about Ris. Then use your finger to point to the spot on your head where you can feel him strongest. Tell me when you have that spot."

Anica had closed her eyes and thought, really thought. It took only seconds to feel the slithering sensation all along her body and for her mind to see the black and blue bands of his snake form in her head. When she opened her eyes, her finger was pointed just behind her left ear.

It was still where she felt him in her mind.

"Behind my left ear," she'd told the snake mate of Ahmad. "Does that mean something?"

"No. It doesn't matter where it is. You just need to know. Now, imagine a whole row of doors. Different kinds of doors, like you are standing in a store trying to decide which kind to buy. There are wooden ones and metal ones in different colors and doors like bank vaults and others with screens. Can you seem them all?"

She could. Her mind flashed on every door she'd ever seen. The steel door where she lived now with tiny panes of thick, beveled glass set higher than her eyes could see out, and the home where she'd grown up, painted white, and the black steel door, painted with scrolls and flowers, with the heavy crank lock at the bank. "Yes. I can see many doors."

"Now, choose the one you want to hide behind. For danger, choose steel. When you want the attachment to him, pick a screen door or a Dutch door, where half opens."

"Now is danger. Tristan is in danger, but it's not danger I can fix or help with. I'm scared and it makes it worse that I can feel everything."

"Then steel. Put the door on top of the spot in your head. That hole in your head is a doorway. Imagine a frame around it where you can replace the doors at will." Tuli's voice was like a lifeline to grab on to for both her and Bojan. If her brother was feeling Scott's situation like she was feeling Tristan's, then he was feeling the pain of his arm trapped in the rock and the panic of the darkness. When she looked at her brother's face, she knew . . . just knew that he was.

"Put the door in your hand and put your hand on the spot on your head where you feel that attachment. Then push the door closed. It will be difficult to shut the first time, as though the hinges are rusty. You will have to push very hard to move the door. But keep trying. Work the hinges back and forth by pressing and releasing the pressure of your hand." She paused. "Close your eyes and shut the door now. Hard."

Anica had done as she was instructed, and so had Bojan. Their hands were in different spots. Hers was behind her left ear. Bojan's was on his forehead. When she closed her eyes and pushed on the spot, it had felt much like Tuli had said. Rusty . . . but even more like there was air pressure behind it keeping the door from closing. She kept pushing and releasing her hand on her ear until finally something similar to a bubble of air popped in her ear and the door closed. "I closed it!" She blinked her eyes.

Opening it, fully, while they'd made love, had been the most amazing experience of her life.

She swallowed at the memory, and realized her mouth was dry, her throat still raw from the smoke. But the rest of her felt healed, loose, and limber—even though she knew she should be sore everywhere. *This, the healing and the mind joining, is part of mating I will not mind.* But what about the rest? She wasn't sure how she felt about Ris. While her body wanted him, even now desiring to turn him over and straddle him—to feel him fill her and take her to that place again—her mind slipped back to a conversation with Mama, years ago, when she was positive she was in love with a boy at school. She'd been only fifteen and Mikhail had paid much attention to her. He brought her flowers to school, and carried her books and bought her lunch. He'd been funny and sweet, and she'd gushed to Mama about him.

"What do you know about him?" Mama had asked it while holding her hands and smiling.

Anica remembered she'd told her everything she knew, which wasn't much. Everything she knew was appearance . . . how he dressed, what his classes were, who his family was. The deepest thing she knew, once Mama had started to press, was that they liked the same bands and both hated the taste of coffee.

"Love," Mama had told her, "includes those things. You are on the right path. But love is so much more. It is knowing their pain and their hopes. It is wanting them to succeed, but helping them soothe their failures." She went on to tell Anica how she'd known the moment she realized she was in love with Papa. Their marriage had been arranged by the families and she'd only seen him at a distance. They'd never even met.

He had snuck out of his house the day before the wedding to talk to her. She'd crawled out her window and they'd run down to sit on a bench by the small pond, where he'd laid bare his soul. He'd told her of his hopes and dreams and beliefs for hours. And he told her of raspberries. "By the time he was done telling me about raspberries," Mama had said, "each tiny seed, the reason for the little hairs, why the baskets had holes, they were no longer just a tasty fruit to me. They were his *world* . . . To be surrounded by tall, healthy bushes in the perfect soil that he could sell to the world was his greatest dream. And he wanted to share that dream with another dreamer." Mama had smiled. "When I saw that look, I knew. It was as though a big bell in my chest I didn't know was there had finally been rung, and it changed me—in minutes."

Anica remembered thinking that Mikhail was nice and sweet, but she felt no such bell for the boy. She'd waited, and dated him, but no bell ever rang.

When she'd come home crying, finally giving up on her first love, Mama had hugged her and patted her and said, "It doesn't always happen quickly. But remember, you must either share a dream or be willing to follow the other person's. I had no big dreams before Papa. I didn't want to change the world like he did. But I wanted it *for* him. I wanted to be part of his dream and I could be happy."

They had been happy, for many years. Anica wasn't sure if the family could recover from Mama's betrayal, but she knew Papa wanted to because he still talked of raspberries and every time he spoke of the farm, of his precious raspberry dream, he still said "we."

Could there be a *we* for her and Ris?

"I don't know," came his voice from the bed. "Tell me your dreams."

She started, not even realizing he'd woken up. "You heard

all that . . . in my head?" He nodded lightly and patted the bed.

She sat down cross-legged on the covers, facing him in the darkness, and he sat up under the sheet and blanket, poofing the pillows behind him for a backrest. While she would have liked to turn on the light, they needed to be sure that nobody realized they were there. The bathroom had been safe because there were no windows. His voice was soft and quiet to match the darkness.

"Just so you know, I wasn't listening intentionally. It's like overhearing something said in the kitchen when you're in the living room. You've never had to shield your mind, so you still have to think about it. The shields will slip at first. I've forgotten what it's like to have that luxury. Too many years of being on the defense. But it's difficult for me to shield from you now."

"Have you always had to be defensive? Have you always been a hunter?"

He shook his head. "Telling you about my life would make me wallow in the pain again. I'd rather hear what you dream of. Happy things. Like your mother, I have no big dreams. Maybe I can be part of yours."

"What I dream of now isn't what I used to dream of." She waggled her head. "Well, in a way, it is. When I was little, and human, and after I wanted to be Nancy Drew, I wanted to grow up and work for the United Nations, finding ways for people not to fight. There has always been fighting in my country, since I was born, and I wanted to help bring peace. There's so much tension, always barricades and troops. But then I was taken, tortured, turned, and my dreams changed."

He frowned and reached out to touch her hand. "Show me. Think of it."

She shook her head. "Like you, I do not wish to wallow in pain again." He seemed sad and . . . like he wanted to share his own memories but wanted to spare her the horror. Then she remembered when Rachel had mentally shared her struggle to get out of her own cave, far away in a place called Texas. The memory had been like being there, the sights, the sounds, the smells. Unlike Anica's damp cave behind a waterfall, Rachel's cave had been in a desert, surrounded by sand and cactus and birds instead of bears to slash open her skin. But the fear and pain had been the same. And having the owl shifter share a similar past had been . . . rejuvenating. So she nodded, wrapped her fingers around his, and let him into her memories. Perhaps her showing would give him the courage to unburden himself of some of his pain.

She closed her eyes and thought back to the day when she'd been coming home from school, carrying a brand-new textbook about geography, and been snatched off her feet, pulled into a covered truck, and hit over the head. She remembered so clearly the last thing she saw before she blacked out was the new textbook, lying in the mud, and it had made her angry.

She woke in chains, surrounded by screams and the smell of death, and the anger gave way to fear. But the anger never truly went away.

Ris's hand tightened on hers as she remembered the days and weeks filled with cuts and scratches and skin rubbed raw from struggling against chains, of trying to stay quiet and small so she wouldn't be noticed. His tight grip kept her grounded as she recalled the taste of moldy bread and stale river water that gave her stomachaches, and hearing the never-ending screams that turned to roars. They still haunted her dreams. But worst was never, *never* getting the smell of blood and sweat and bear shit out of her nose. "Maybe that was why I was cursed with such a sensitive nose as a bear— because I hated smelling so much." She sighed, opening her eyes to see her own pain reflected in his black eyes, like a dark mirror. "I decided that day that nobody else should have to suffer through that. That is why when Rachel helped me remember the place I had to go back and clean out the nest. But is it terrible of me that I didn't want to stay and help the children put their lives back together? I want to fight the bad snakes and bears, make them feel pain and free the cap-tors, but the nightmares, the memories . . . I don't think I can make them go away. That's their own battle, like it has been mine."

She was surprised to see a small smile come to his face. But it was sad, haunted. "You remind me of my sister, Umi. Everyone said she was too tiny to have such a great fire in her chest, with a heart too big for the defenseless. But she was a warrior unmatched in skill and she fought with such ferocity, and viciousness, that even the rumor she was in a battle would send enemies running." He opened his mind to her and she saw Umi, seeming so small and childlike, her long black hair tied in a braid that touched the backs of her knees as she lifted a sword as tall as she to lay waste to a half-dozen men a meter or more taller than she. Ris smiled broader, a light chuckle moving his chest. "She would con-stantly argue with my brother, Mako, who was our healer, because she would strike to maim or kill, rather than wound. He would ask her to be more gentle, to try to salvage their lives. She would say, 'Why in the world would I want to leave an enemy with the ability to fight again, Mako? Everywhere I go, I'm surrounded by friends . . . because there are no enemies left.' "

In Ris's mind, she saw Umi's smile and Mako's frown, and it made her sad she would never meet them. "It is very sad you have no femily left. They seem to have been good people."

He shrugged. "Fighters always risk the next fight. Healers give away their strength to keep the fighters going. But the stronger you are, the stronger the opponents sent against you. Eventually, you'll fall. It's one of the reasons I hunt, instead of fight. My venom is fatal, no matter where I bite them, or when. I'm fine with sneaking up when they're sleeping. In fact, I prefer it. It's why I'm still alive and my siblings aren't."

"So you do not fight fair?" That seemed just . . . *wrong*. "It makes you no better than the bad men."

His reply was unapologetic, his humor gone like a flash. "I'm sent against the worst of the worst, Anica—those who have slaughtered countless lives, who have killed and raped and tortured for their own pleasure. The Council doesn't lay down a death sentence lightly. Only Sargon himself received a sentence . . . none of his followers did. Including those who held you. Even after what you saw in my memory, Lagash doesn't have a formal sentence. Do you truly believe those who have been judged as so evil as deserving to die also deserve *fairness*?"

She had to think about that. The snakes and bears they had fought in the cave where she was held prisoner had died by her own hand, and by the hands of the others with her. Yet they had not been convicted, or sentenced. She had also snuck up on them, let Ahmad use her in a ruse to get inside to further sneak up. Why had they not been tried, when they were known torturers and kidnappers? "There should be more death sentences."

The moment she said it, she knew the comment made no sense based on her own words earlier. But it did make him laugh again and he pulled her into a sudden hug. "I don't think we disagree on that. It's why Ahmad sent me to investigate. This is a hunting mission only, to find out what Lagash is up to, so he can go to the Council for a verdict. And if you can petition the Council for even more verdicts, I'll be happy to carry them out. I've been a little bored lately."

He kissed the top of her head, nuzzling his nose in her hair. She was hoping he would keep nuzzling, but lower, but something pulled his attention away. His body tensed and she turned as he pushed her away to ease away from under the covers. She looked where he was staring, out the window, to where two women were walking in the empty town. *Two?*

Anica likewise slid off the bed, careful to make no sound, and joined Ris at the window. One of the women was Skew and she was in chains . . . her wrists and ankles burdened by iron braces. But who was the other? Then the woman's head turned and Anica caught sight of her face. "I have seen her before," she whispered. "But I do not know her name. She cooks meals for the prisoners. When Denis was in jail, I visited him and she brought supper."

"Is she married?" Ris's voice was deep, deeply angry at the same sight of the falcon who had saved him stumbling in the ash while the other woman prodded her to stand.

Anica nodded. "To the postmaster." And then she remembered him, always at the edge of everything. Protesting their being in town at the first meeting with the negotiator, jeering from the edge of the crowd during the Ascension challenge, refusing to leave the post office to fight the fires with the others. In fact, there wasn't a time of day she hadn't seen him there. She'd even wondered why a post office would be open at night when she had seen lights on after eating in the diner. "We need to go to post office. I remember once I asked Paula why he worked such strange hours for a government place, she had said, 'Fred does what Fred does. It's best not to ask too many questions about him.'"

Anica was chilled at Ris's next statement: "Maybe Paula broke her own rule." He motioned her backward and pulled her into his arms. "Don't move." He began to slide his bare chest against her back. His skin was slick with something that wasn't sweat. It flowed over her like lotion, to be sucked into her pores. He even ran his hands over her face and chest. But when she touched her skin, it was dry. Not even damp.

"What did you do to me?"

He grinned at her and leaned over her shoulder to give the tip of her nose a quick kiss. "Made you invisible. Get dressed while I go do the same to the others."

Wait. He was going to rub his naked body over Bobby? She had no idea what the other man's reaction would be to that. Ris gave her butt a light swat that made her jump. "Get your mind out of the gutter. I'll put it on a towel for them."

"What is *it*?"

"My people secrete an oil in their skin that can make scents disappear. Bobby created a cologne from it for Wolven agents to use. It's why we're such effective hunters. And we have some hunting to do, so get dressed, little warrior. Time to fight the bad snakes and free the captives."

The way he said that, with equal amounts of bravado and

confidence, made her feel . . . odd. He wasn't apologizing for
what he was about to do, or trying to convince her to stay
down, as before. She went to the dresser and opened it
before remembering all of her clothes were downstairs in
the dryer. Going out the door and across the hall, she started
pulling some of Rachel's clothes out of her dresser. She could
ask forgiveness later. As she hurriedly put on the clothing,
she thought back to Ris's words.

Something had changed.

She found him in the bathroom, where he was rubbing
himself down as though drying himself after a shower. But
he looked like Tristan again. He was wearing the illusion like
a shirt over his true self. One only she, and perhaps Bobby
and Ahmad, had ever seen underneath. "I am to fight as
well? That is okay?"

His shoulder moved in what might be a shrug. Or not.
"Pretty sure I couldn't stop you, could I?"

She didn't respond, but he was probably right. She liked
Skew and didn't want her to be hurt. He walked past her,
causing a few small sparks that snapped against her skin like
after scuffing across a carpeting. He opened the closet door
and smelled surprised and happy as he whispered, "Hey,
men's clothes. I can actually wear something clean."

"Those must be Dalvin's. He's been staying here."

He put on a pair of too-tall pants and a long-sleeved shirt
before digging around in the dressers. Not finding what he
wanted, he rushed to the kitchen with preternatural speed.
He pulled several of the knives out of the wooden block on
the counter, feeling the balance and slashing the air.

But instead of putting them in the pockets on the pant legs
as she expected, he handed one to her, hilt first. "Put this

somewhere it won't cut you. If you have to attack, don't stab. Make long cuts that will open wider as it tries to slither."

She didn't have a chance to respond before he rolled up the pant legs so he wouldn't trip and raced out into the hallway. "Don't forget the key."

Oh! Yes, the door key. She had to return to the bathroom and dug through her pant pockets before retrieving the key and putting it in her pocket. She didn't know what to do with the knife. There weren't any pockets that if she had to bend over she wouldn't cut herself. She finally went to Rachel's closet and pulled out a pair of hiking boots. They were a little big, but a second pair of socks fixed that.

She heard Ris's voice just as she was tucking the knife in the laces, with the edge underneath the metal lace guides so it wouldn't cut the laces as she walked. The tip was pointing at the floor. She hoped she wouldn't trip. "Anica, hurry. We need to get on their trail."

In the dim hallway, lit only by the emergency exit lights by the stairs, she found Bojan and Scott coming out of Scott's apartment. The owl shifter looked tired but was moving without a limp and was rolling his shoulder, almost experimentally. Judging by his scent, he was surprised he wasn't more injured. "You are well?" She was concerned about him. She liked Scott quite a bit and hoped he might someday become part of her family.

He nodded, glancing at Bojan, his scent a combination of guilt and anger, with a splash of warm cookie spice that was likely the aftermath of the fulfilled desire that lingered on his skin . . . and Bojan's. "I honestly have no idea what I am right now."

Ris tossed the oiled towel at him, hitting him in the face

on the way past and down the hallway. "Mated, by the smell. Rub this all over yourself, so it's not so obvious."

The tall blond's face went white as a sheet, then beet red. He gratefully turned away and rubbed his face and arms with the towel, handing it to Bojan when he was done.

Anica touched her brother's arm. He looked a little lost but was trying to be strong. So much like Papa. "No shame, Brother. Remember?"

He nodded, but she could still smell his negative emotions. They vanished in an instant when he rubbed his skin with the towel. She leaned close to him to sniff, but all the scent was gone. "That is very good oil. How long does it last?"

Bobby came bounding up the stairs and down the hallway. "At least until morning, in its pure concentrate." He grabbed the towel and proceeded to rub it over his own face and arms, his scents disappearing like magic. But she supposed it *was* magic. "Sorry. I lost them in the smoke. It's like they just dis-a-damn-ppeared. No tracks, no scent."

"We're going to have to be careful leaving the building," he continued. "You can see the front of this building from almost anywhere. Even the smoke won't help. Lagash is powerful enough to see right through that."

Scott held up his hand. "If you're right, and it's Fred and Betty Birch—which I'm still trying to wrap my head around— then there's nowhere in town we can sneak up on him. He's the postmaster. He's been in every house, walked every path, knows . . . everything. About everyone. He's the keeper of the mail. We have no decent Internet, so the mail is our connection to the world. I've always known he's opened our mail. It's hard to hide an envelope being resealed. If the mail is delayed, is it just crappy service, or is he hiding it from us? We've never known." He let out a snort. "I've always just considered him *quirky*. That stupid old hat, the cherry tobacco smell that wrecks your nose—"

Wait! That was it! "I am allergic to tobacco!" It all made sense now.

The men just shrugged. "Okay," Bobby said. "Is that important?"

She smiled. "Yes. It is *very* important. That is what I smell in boot step in the forest . . . from person who was following Ris. It caused my chest to choke. Papa had a friend who smoked a pipe. He had to stop coming to house because I could not breathe. But he never smoked cherry tobacco. Just regular."

"And the cherry scent isn't actually cherry, but a combination of chemicals you don't know the names for." She could tell Bobby understood.

"So I know now, for sure, it was Lagash, who is wearing a Fred shirt."

Ris smirked and had to hide it behind his hand. The others looked confused. Then Ris cleared his throat. "I think we need to split up. We need two good noses. Anica and I will go to the post office. I doubt they took Carolyn—*Skew* there. It's too obvious. But maybe we can find out what they're up to. The three of you can track her and the woman . . . Betty, did you say?" Scott nodded. Ris put his hand on Anica's arm and a wave of warmth swept through her that wasn't desire but could go there without much effort.

"That still leaves the problem of getting out of the building without being seen by him or his spies," Bobby said. "And if there's a rattlesnake in town, he has spies."

"We could go out tunnel. Maybe he would not watch there."

Bobby and Ris asked, nearly simultaneously, "What tunnel?"

Scott frowned, saying, just like Rachel had earlier, "How do you know about that?"

"I find it," Anica said. "In basement. Why is it secret?"

The owl shifter said nothing, just blinked. Ris asked the obvious question: "Are there more tunnels around town? Should we be looking underground for whatever is going on?"

Still the owl said nothing. Looking concerned, Bojan touched Scott on the arm, then looked at Bobby. "His mind, it is as if something is blocking it—something thick and sticky, like tar."

"He was well until I mention tunnel," Anica said ruefully. "Rachel does same thing when I ask earlier. I think maybe we go into tunnel ourselves and not ask anymore?"

Ris nodded. "Zarko told me that the original buildings in town were intended to be forts, to hold off snake attacks. All decent forts, throughout history, have had a way to escape if the walls are breached. Maybe what you found it an escape tunnel.

"Bobby and I will check it out first in animal form. Make sure there are no booby traps or cave-ins." The two men nodded and they started down the stairway.

"Perhaps you should stay behind with Scott. I don't know how he would react if he sees us enter the tunnel. You might try to do something comforting with him," she added. "Maybe cooking. Scott is sensitive to smells. Not as much as me, but he likes to sniff herbs."

Bojan nodded. "True. I burned some incense while he was sleeping. It gives me a headache, but he likes the smell." He turned to his friend, who Anica supposed now needed to be considered his boyfriend or partner—or maybe just *mate*—and clapped him on the shoulder. "Let's go cook some dinner, Scott."

The taller man didn't respond, just kept blinking. Worried, Anica took his other arm and helped Bojan turn him around and get him back into his apartment. She'd never been in Scott's apartment before. It was nice, better decorated than Rachel's, with black metal and glass furniture and paintings of different birds in flight. Everything was as coordinated as though a decorator had planned the room. Small splashes of deep burgundy in the black and white pillows matched bits of the background in the paintings, and geometric-patterned throw rugs covered the same older carpeting that was in Rachel's home.

Anica could smell the incense Bojan had mentioned. It had a nice, soothing scent, but the longer she smelled it, the more her nose sorted the smells. Some of the odors were herbs that Bojan used in food, like lemongrass, nutmeg, and cinnamon. There was a citrus smell, like orange peel. But down at the very bottom was a scent she'd smelled very recently. It made her immediately pull Scott and Bojan out of the room.

"Anica! What are you doing?" Her brother's voice was too loud—she put a finger to her lips as she took the key to Rachel's apartment out of her pocket. "Stay very quiet and take Scott to Rachel's. I think there is something wrong with that incense. It has much terbium in it, and I do not know why."

"What is *terbium*?"

She didn't have time to explain it. She had to get Bobby. "Please. Just do as I ask. Let me get Bobby and he can explain it better."

Looking puzzled, he stared back at the now-closed apartment door. "Have I hurt him? He burns this incense all the time."

She didn't know. She just knew she needed to get Bobby. His tongue was as sensitive as her nose and his brain knew more than hers. "I do not know. Please. Just do it." She ran down the stairs, nearly tripping at the corner.

The washer was still pulled back from the wall when she entered the laundry room, and Bobby's and Ris's clothing was folded and stacked on the closed lid. She inspected the hole in the wall, looking more carefully at the construction. It was definitely intentionally built. Concrete had been poured around the entrance and back inside for the first few yards. Then it turned rocky and sloped up, probably toward the forest floor. She cupped her hands around her mouth and called softly, "Bobby? Ris? Can you come back, please?"

There was no answer, and she couldn't hear any sound from the tunnel. Perhaps using her mind would be better.

Ris? No response. She couldn't even feel him in her head and wasn't certain when he'd broken contact. The door between them had been closed, from his side. When she tried to get into his mind, a flash of intense pain made her cry out and drop to her knees, pressing her hands to her temples. A second flash made her see stars and then she saw nothing at all.

CHAPTER 23

hat's a tunnel, all right. Why do you suppose there's
no cover over it?"

Ris crouched down next to Bobby and stared down into
the black hole. "I suppose the washer is *sort of* a cover, but
yeah, I would have expected something a little more permanent. There's not even a frame for a cover. I wonder how
often they have to bug bomb down here?"

Bobby chuckled. "Half of the complex is birds. Who says
they bother? Maybe it's sort of a free vending machine for
the residents."

Ris couldn't help but smile. "You've gotten a really dark
sense of humor from mating with Asri. You didn't used to
be this sarcastic. I sort of like it."

"Not Asri. Too much time undercover working on the
fringes of the Mafia. It's sort of contagious. Blame Tony and
his crew."

"I haven't met many of them. I try to avoid conflicts of
interest." Meeting people might mean he would like them
and it was harder to kill people he liked.

"Yeah. It's sort of screwed me a few times. Thankfully,

I only have to investigate, not enforce. One of these days, I'm going to have to make that choice. Now that things are starting to normalize more, maybe we can get back to just regular enforcement, instead of this cold-war standoff."

"It's tough to close the lid to that particular box, old friend. Even in humankind, prejudice runs deep. For our kind, it's even harder. The human mind has to overcome the natural prey instincts and natural enemies built into our animals." His emotions in a turmoil, he shut the connection with Anica. It would be hard for her to understand what it was like to grow up as a snake. "For all his faults, Sargon was a unifier. While I don't agree with his goals, it's tough to have always been the fall guy for every wrong committed in the world. Snakes have always gotten a bad rap as inherently evil. It becomes a self-fulfilling prophecy."

Bobby let out a slow hiss of annoyance. "No, it doesn't, Ris. It's just a lazy man's excuse to give in to base instincts. Anyone can *want* to do bad things. But no animal on this earth is evil by nature. Only the supposedly *superior* men can lay claim to true evil. It's why Sargon had to be stopped, and why Lagash has to be. They say all the pretty things that people want to hear that make them feel special, while making them believe that bad acts and the pain they cause are some sort of demented prize."

He was right, and Ris knew it. Rather than argue, he started to pull off his clothes to explore the tunnel. "It's just hard to be a guardian of good, y'know? That's why I dropped out of the rat race altogether. Back on my island, time goes by and nothing changes. But Anica has big dreams. She wants to rid the world of evil. In a way, it's sort of funny. You're the do-gooder, and Asri always wanted to leave the world to its own devices. Anica and I are the reverse. Has Asri corrupted you with her world view, or have you infected her to want to be a savior?"

"I think the kids infected her more than I could," Bobby said with a small smile as he kicked off his shoes and started to pull off the socks underneath. "She's given up on wanting to escape the world. Now she wants a safe world for them. Both of our kinds were nearly extinct, mostly because we ignored the evil around us for too long. I wouldn't want to get in her way of keeping our kids safe."

Ris tried to imagine Anica as a mother. Whether they wound up being his own children, or someone else's, she would be one fierce mama bear. "I've never thought about being a father. Not sure I want to think about it."

Bobby shifted to snake form, wider and taller than Ris's own animal body. He slithered into the opening of the tunnel. "Don't try. No matter what you expect, it won't be. It's been amazing and horrible in turns. But I wouldn't go back and change anything, even if I could."

There wasn't much more to say than that. Ris had met Bobby and Asri's children. They had great potential, if taught good morals now, to be the next generation to fill Wolven and the Council. His oldest son, Joseph, might someday challenge Ahmad himself to become head of the snakes. Provided the world survived long enough to see him become an adult.

The tunnel was wide and tall enough that it could be navigated in either human or animal form. Animal form would be easier, though, since the sharp rocks under his scales would be tough on knees. They moved quickly and silently up the slope until they reached a wooden roof that smelled smoky. "How far do you think we are from the building?"

Bobby kept his voice down, turning his head so they were

inches apart. "Maybe fifty yards. But I don't recall seeing anything that might be a hatch from the surface. So I'll be interested to see what happens when we open this."

"Okay, I'm skinnier. How about you shift back and lift the top just a bit and I'll slither through."

Bobby nodded and changed position so that when he shifted he was lying on his back under the roof. He pushed up lightly and Ris watched as his muscles tensed, stopped by something. "It's heavy. Maybe we didn't see it because it's buried or covered by something." He pushed again, this time using his considerable strength, and Ris felt him add magic to the pressure. The lid started to move. Dirt and leaves, then ash, began to rain down on them, As soon as Ris saw a large enough opening, he slithered through.

Into a trap.

The first set of fangs entered square in the top of his head, causing his warning to Bobby to be half of the word: "Tra—!"

It was a rattlesnake, by the feel of the venom. Fortunately, Ris's skin was tough enough that barely a tenth of what a normal strike would inject actually hit his system and the snake's fangs bounced off the edge of the rocks covering the escape tunnel. It hurt, though, enough that he felt the pain blast open the door between him and Anica. She screamed and he closed the door more tightly. But not before a second strike hit him in the opposite side. He heard Lagash's voice, from a distance: "Did you really believe I thought you were dead? Do you think I'm stupid?"

"No," he replied. "But do you think I am?" He slammed his own fangs into his two attackers, pumping venom from the back of his jaws. His fangs were small, his bite likely not even noticed by the two snakes, who didn't even register his movements. But that was his strength, because at the regular dose his venom wouldn't begin to affect them for a few minutes. They would simply die and not even know why.

He put his shields up as tight as they would go and moved more quickly after the first two attacks, becoming a blur along the ash. His coloring wasn't to his advantage in the ash, but rolling and swirling to raise a cloud of ash would hide his movements for a few seconds and, he hoped, cover his distinctive bands.

Most rattlesnakes didn't climb trees, but as a krait Ris regularly climbed the underwater corals. He slithered up one of the trees, the pain in his head and side making it a challenge. But he needed to be able to look down, to count how many followers Lagash had brought with him. He looked across the small clearing to see Bobby had done the same. The enemy snakes kept moving, the diamond patterns of their scales blending into the scenery so well that he couldn't find them under the layer of smoke. Some enforcers had second sight and could see the blaze of magic rise from their prey, knowing their position no matter what their cover.

But what fun would that be?

Seeing a spot of movement, he launched himself out of the tree and landed right on a cobra. It wasn't Lagash, but it was male. He wrapped himself tightly around the other snake. They swayed and dipped in an almost elegant dance, each looking for an opening. But Ris's magic was stronger and he forced the snake to the ground before slamming his fangs right into the snake's brain with as much venom as he could spare. The effect was immediate. The cobra tensed, letting out a hissing scream, and then lay silent.

"As dangerous as ever, I see." Lagash's voice came from his left and he flung himself toward the sound. Lagash was just as fast, so Ris caught only air. A loop of magic dropped over him, an attempt to freeze him in place.

The twitching in his forehead and side was enough, given how his power had been sapped by recent events, that it might just work.

"Young lady, please wake up!" Anica opened her eyes and found an elderly woman kneeling over her in the laundry room—the woman who had been holding Skew in chains! She smelled strongly of cobra. Moving as quickly as she could, Anica felt for the knife in her boot and slashed out with it, catching the woman in the thigh. The old shifter screamed and fell back. Anica scrambled to her feet and ran up the stairs.

"Wait!" the woman called after her. "I need to talk to you."

I'll just bet you do. "Sorry, not interested in talking."

"But I can tell you how to defeat my husband!" Slowing, Anica ducked into a small alcove where she could watch both the staircase and the first-floor hallway. There was no window or door in the alcove, so she was as safe as she was going to get for the moment.

"Why would you do that?" She tried to remember what she knew about Betty Birch. Not much, really. She rarely went about in public. Anica had only seen her a few times, always delivering food to the jail. "What is Lagash planning?"

There was a pause, and the scent of surprise. "So," came the disembodied voice. "You know."

"I also know you are Ahmad's sister. Why would you not tell *him* about your husband when he is here?" She kept the knife in her hand, practicing slicing the way Ris had said so it would be instinctive if she had to do it.

Anica couldn't feel Ris in her head—he had closed the door again and she knew she would only be a distraction. But she hated not knowing what was happening to him.

"Because he's the one who sold me into slavery to Lagash in the first place. I just want to escape." There was deep bitterness in the words, and the scent that came with it on the breeze from the lower floor matched the tone.

Why would Ahmad do that? She didn't believe it, but there was no lie in the air. If it was true, Enheduanna could be a valuable ally. But how could Anica believe the woman? "You're his wife. And his mate. How can you be his slave too? I see you beside him and never in bindings."

Enheduanna's laugh had a hysterical edge. "He's mated *to* me. He controls everything I do. He can implant thoughts in my head, make me think and do things I don't want to do. The only reason I can think right now is because he's in a battle. As soon as he's done killing whoever dared challenge him, he'll be back and I'll be *sick* again. He keeps me so weak by draining my magic that all I can do is lay in bed most days.

"Everyone in town believes I have a horrible disease. Since he insists I cook for him, I always cook too much, so at least I have to give away the food. He lets me do that, maybe to tempt me with a glimpse of freedom. Maybe to let the town see how much *in love* we are. It's not much, but I have a few minutes where he isn't watching me."

Killing whoever dared challenge him. That could be Bobby and Ris. "How do we kill him? Tell me now or I will wring the information from you." She stepped out of the alcove, her knife at the ready, and started down the stairs.

Enheduanna sighed. "Maybe that would be easiest. Just kill me and be done with it. I've been alive so very long and

I hate that man so much!" There was such venom in her voice that Anica had to see if her expression matched. Perhaps it was a trap, but her instincts told her it wasn't.

She made it to the bottom of the stairs and dipped her head out just enough to see the room. Enheduanna sat on the chair, almost primly, wearing her Betty shirt. "Let me see your real self."

The woman shrugged helplessly. "That would require energy. I don't have any. I might as well be human for the power I have right now. He keeps me in this form so I have no strength." She lifted one skinny arm and pushed her sleeve up. The skin underneath was floppy and hanging from her bones, like she was malnourished. "Look what he has done to me."

"You lie," Anica said, remembering what she'd seen from her window even though the woman's scent was clear of the black pepper of lying. "I saw you pushing Skew, in chains. You had strength then, because she was fighting back. Where is she? Tell me that, and if she is safe, perhaps I will help you."

"She's in her lab. Where Fred—sorry, Lagash—keeps her locked up and working when she's not serving ice cream to the children. I was forced to put her in chains because she is becoming wary. We are running out of the drug. If only they knew their treats were laced with drugs. It makes me so angry! Innocent children becoming pawns to him. I am fed up."

Anica stepped fully into the room. "I've eaten that ice cream. What sort of drugs? What do they do?"

"It makes people open to . . . *suggestion*. It's just a mineral. It probably won't hurt them if nobody uses magic on them."

Things were clicking together in Anica's brain. "It is the

terbium, isn't it? You were covered in it when you attacked me in my home. For that, and for hurting my brother, I should kill you."

The pale woman nodded, her face and scent miserable. It was becoming more difficult to doubt the old woman. As much as she distrusted the words, Anica's nose had never lied to her. "Yes. I know. I didn't want to. Fred made me get the boxes of rocks out of the safe in your garage. He couldn't be seen going to the house. I was just leaving when your brother surprised me. Zarko has been suspicious of him ever since he found out Fred was making false reports about you and your brother, so I haven't been able to get into the house to retrieve them."

Anica felt her eyes open wider. No wonder their visas were denied! Who would suspect a neutral government employee, with no history of knowing them, of lying? She wondered if the government thought she was a terrorist. "Then why go to our house at all?"

"That's where Van used to keep the rocks he mined," Enheduanna replied. "With all the firefighters, Fred couldn't go out and dig in the forest, but he had promised deliveries and had to get them sent."

Deliveries? "He was mailing terbium? I didn't think you could mail important rocks with minerals. Isn't that not allowed?"

The other woman nodded. "Yes. That's why we made it into something that could be shipped and used easily."

The last piece of the puzzle sank home. "Incense. You made it into sticks of incense."

A burst of scent, like rotten celery, rose into the air. Anica had no idea what emotion that was.

"How did you know?"

"I can smell very good. Why are people not supposed to speak of the tunnels?"

"Betty" shook her head. "I have no idea what's in Fred's head about that. Maybe that's how the snakes will get in when they come."

If nobody was supposed to talk about the tunnels, maybe they weren't supposed to think about them or check them either. Recalling Ris's words made her shiver. *I'm fine with sneaking up when they're sleeping. In fact, I prefer it.* If snakes took over the town, they would have the whole forest to mine. They would be able to make more and more of the drug to control other people. It was even worse than what she'd seen in Ris's memory, because people would go willingly to their death, or to be turned.

"Where is Skew?" Was she being forced to help Lagash plan this? Or was she a willing participant?

"The lab is under the post office. In a hidden room under the stamp vault."

How would she get into a *vault*? As though Enheduanna could read her mind, she shook her head. "Lagash has the only key. But Carolyn is safe. She just thinks she's making medicine for children. Her mind is so muddy from the drug that she doesn't know where she is most of the time. Fred was very angry that Ris broke through the conditioning on Skew. But he'd only instructed her to act like the Skew everyone knows to *residents*.

So that was why she acted very different when her family first arrived. Until they moved in and became actual residents, Skew wasn't sure how to treat them. "How do we fight Lagash, then? I can take the key from him once he's dead."

Now the old woman smiled, and there was darkness at the edges of her eyes. "Please do. The problem with working with chemicals is that they can be your undoing. He had an accident a few years ago. You probably noticed he has scars on one hand. Those are real scars, not illusion. Terbium burns. Magic makes the pain flare and burn hotter. He had the mineral dust all over him, and when he slapped me for making dinner too slow the dust caught fire from the stove. Water only made it worse. He had to pour baking soda on his hand to put out the flame."

While Anica wasn't surprised Lagash hit his wife, the casual way she said it made her twitch. It just made her want to hurt him even more. Whether or not the Council had ordered it. "Where would I find enough terbium to use on him?"

The other woman shrugged. "It's all in the vault now, except for what's left in your house. You and your brother came home too soon, so I could only take about half the boxes. I haven't been able to get back inside to get the rest."

There was little time. She tentatively felt along the magic line to Ris, who was fighting for his life against the ancient cobra. But what to do with his mate while she went out to try to help?

"Bojan!" she called as loudly as she could, and soon heard his footsteps coming down the stairs.

She pointed at the woman in the basement. "That is the snake who attacked you." Bojan's eyes narrowed and he unconsciously reached up to touch the place where she'd hit him with the baseball bat. "She may have just saved us all, so please don't kill her yet. Just keep her here. I have to go back to our house."

He didn't argue with her, just took the knife from her hand and kept staring at the snake shifter. Enheduanna sat, unmoving, blood dripping onto the concrete floor from the wound in her leg. That it wasn't healing gave more credence to what she claimed. But it could be a lie too.

Anica reached out mentally—there was someone other than Ris she could reach that way: her sorority sister. *Rachel! I need your help. Bring Claire and come back to town. Hurry!* Maybe she should ask for more help. Amber was strong, and so were Alek and Dalvin. But the two women shared Anica's desire to prevent another slave camp.

Ha! I knew you couldn't be dead! The clear, bell-like tones of Rachel's mental voice burst into her mind and made her smile. *What do we need to bring?*

The only thing that came to her mind was, *Hammers. Big, strong hammers.*

She needed to make a lot more terbium dust, and fast.

CHAPTER 24

*R*is moved quickly to the side, avoiding another spit of venom. The first two rattlesnakes lay dead from his bite, but now the others were avoiding him. He had to bring them closer, but every time he tried to slither toward one, another would strike at him. "On your six, Bobby!"

Bobby was taking on the snakes on the perimeter, slowly squeezing the life out of them. He was immune to most venoms after working in Wolven so long. He took constant doses of all manner of vaccines to keep up his immunity. So all they could really do was try to bleed him to death while he strangled them, one by one. Now he slapped his tail out fast and hard, catching the small cobra right in the face, knocking out both teeth. It wouldn't put him out of the fight for long, but he would have to grow back the fangs before he could bite again. It would give them a few minutes while he slithered off to heal.

While it might seem random to someone watching, Ris and Bobby were very carefully guiding the fight toward the mountain. Eventually, if they survived, Lagash would have his back to a wall and then they could attack in unison. The cobra likely knew it, though, so he was making sure to keep in the open. They could really use one more fighter to keep up the pressure, but Ris didn't dare call anyone else who had never fought with the two of them, or fought a lot of snakes, before.

Amber might be able to do it. She could jump fast enough that Lagash would likely never lay a fang on her. But Ris would die a slow, horrible death if he let the Chief Justice's mate get killed in a fight.

Spotting an opening on Lagash, Ris took it, moving like a blur among the trees. He opened his mouth and struck, simultaneously throwing a noose of power over the serpent to hold him still.

"Ris! Move left!" It was yet another trap and he wasn't fast enough. Lagash struck as well, his powerful jaws slicing through his skin. Ris screamed as the venom hit his system.

Bobby was there in an instant, wrapping his coils around the cobra's mouth, keeping it shut. But fangs weren't the only thing Lagash could bring to bear. His tail was a magical whip that could slice skin just as easily. The python shifter grunted in pain as one coil was ripped open. Lagash slipped free in the instant of hesitation and reared back to bite. "I grow tired of your interference!" Ris's lower body wasn't working as fast as before, as the powerful venom began to affect his muscles. He wasn't sure he was going to be able to get out of the way in time.

But instead of biting, the snake screamed as a small dark, furry form yanked him away. *Anica?!*

Before the snake could strike the bear, a pair of owls, one snowy white and glowing with power, and the other brown but seeming more golden from a halo of magic, descended from a tree, pouring some sort of silver substance all over the snake. It stuck like it was glued to his scales. A small red wolf came next. She smelled like the female Wolven agent he'd met earlier, Claire. She head-butted the snake, throwing him further off-balance. Finally came Bojan, in human form, carrying a chunk of wood that was blazing with an oddly colored flame.

Bojan threw the torch at Lagash, who screamed as the silvery substance caught fire. He began to roll in the ash, but the fire wouldn't go out. He began to glow less and less, as though he was throwing his magic away.

"The problem, Husband, is when you're all out of magic, who is to say I will give it *back*?"

Ris turned to see Betty Birch standing in the trees. As he watched, she began to shift forms, becoming first a cobra and then Enheduanna—the young long-haired, brown-skinned woman he remembered from Sargon's court. Then she returned to cobra form and slithered over to her mate to watch him burn.

Hurrying to Ris, Anica stood over him protectively, lashing out with her massive claws as Lagash's snakes came at her. They bit at her but didn't seem to be able to reach her skin through her thick brown fur. He wanted to help her, but his muscles twitched and spasmed and refused to co-operate. **You *are* helping. I am borrowing your magic. But I will stop taking it when the fight is done.**

Enheduanna lashed out with fangs and magic at Lagash, who was screaming in pain. "It is *over*! No more will I endure your beatings, or your fangs, or your attacks against innocent children." The magic acted like gasoline and the silver flame enveloped him, grew into a pillar of fire that was taller than the treetops.

"Betrayer! Evil witch!" As fast as lightning, the cobra lashed out, wrapping his mate in flames. She screamed and Anica reacted instantly.

"No!" The bear threw herself into the fire and pulled the smaller cobra out of her mate's grasp. The brown owl sank talons into Lagash's skin, pulling him in the opposite direction, trying to force him to loosen his coils. The night stank of burning flesh and feathers and fur and all Ris could do was watch and open himself to whatever she needed to take. He was having a hard time breathing as she fought against the fire and Lagash's power and almost didn't register it when Bojan began to drag him away from the blaze.

"Anica!" her brother screamed. "Let her go. You'll burn up!"

She began to jerk backward, like a dog tugging on a rope. **He . . . will . . . not . . . hurt her . . . anymore!** Ris was flooded with images that could only have come from Enheduanna's mind, of the pain and torture Lagash had inflicted on her for centuries.

Yanking free of Bojan's grip, not caring if Lagash's poison spread throughout his body, Ris launched himself toward the battle. The heat of the fire hit him like a blast furnace. For some reason, Anica, Enheduanna, and the owl weren't burning as fast as Lagash.

Or him.

Get out of the fire, Ris. We soaked ourselves in flame retardant from one of the plane dumps.

But he couldn't. Not until he did one thing. He was the hunter. Lagash was his prey.

Tristan could feel his skin crackling and a scream burst out of him. Anica jerked, wrapped her whole body around his, releasing Enheduanna at last. Tristan leaped up and struck high, taking Anica, still wrapped protectively around him, toward Lagash. His fangs struck home directly in Lagash's eyes. He put every ounce of venom he had left into the bite, then fell back, spent.

Bobby and Claire took up Anica's battle and pulled Enheduanna out of Lagash's grasp as he began to falter, slumping down from the poison and flames. The trees began to blaze again as the new fire took hold.

Anica was holding Tristan tight in her furred arms. Her fur was charred, but she did not seem to be seriously injured. "Do not die, Ris. I will not let you die!"

Between the cobra and rattlesnake venom and the fire, he wasn't sure surviving was an option. "Is he . . . dead?"

When Anica shifted position to look, Ris was able to see past her to a long line of char that which might have appeared to be a log if a person didn't look too close. But there was only one log, not two. They had managed to free Ahmad's sister. He would be pleased.

Ris was wheezing now, struggling to breathe in the smoky air, and his insides felt swollen and tight, threatening to burst through tissue-paper skin.

"Hang in there, Ris." Bobby, with his human face, came to kneel over him. "I think we've got enough power left to pump into you to keep you going."

He flicked out a tongue that was one long wound. He could taste blood as the skin flaked and cracked. "Keep Anica safe. Okay? She'll probably be fine when I'm gone."

The last thing he saw as his eyes were shutting and his breath was easing from his chest one last time was a flash of orange and yellow that might have been the sun rising.

CHAPTER 25

Anica stood at the edge of the lake, anxiously watching the water. She prayed that Ris had survived, but Amber had intentionally cut their mating link while she tried to heal him. The bobcat had been furious when she'd leaped into the clearing, both because of the injuries she had to deal with and because she had been left out of the plan to take on Lagash.

It had been hours since Bobby and Amber, wearing scuba gear, had taken Ris down into the lake. Anica hadn't realized how tied to the water kraits were. They lived their entire life in the water.

Finally, she couldn't take it anymore. She stripped off her shoes and pants and dove under the water, feeling her way through the cold darkness, searching for the spark of magic in him. She spotted bubbles just when she was running out of air. He was floating motionless and Amber's face, through the scuba mask, looked worried. Suddenly Anica didn't care that Ris was a snake anymore. He was *Ris* and she wanted to be with him, learn of his life, share her dream with him.

She wrapped herself around him and held him tight

against her skin. His body was cool, like it had been when she first met him. His heartbeat was there, but barely, a thready pulsing against her chest. Reaching inside herself, she pushed what little magic she had into him. It wasn't enough. If even Amber's magic wasn't enough, what could she do?

Bobby handed her the breathing mask, but she didn't want it. He had to force it into her mouth. She took a breath, almost grudgingly. **You are my family. You cannot die.**

That's when it occurred to her. He *was* family. And her family was strong. She took another deep breath and looked inside herself. There was a tie to Bojan and to Papa and, further out, Mama—her whole sloth. She reached out, asking . . . *begging* them to help save Ris. Bojan was first, joined quickly by Scott. Papa's reaction was surprise, then worry, then acceptance of two new bear sloth members, who weren't bears at all. Mama's face came to her mind, her heart desperate to have her family back. She would give anything, risk everything, to have Papa back among the raspberries. She heard her mother's voice, soft and heartbroken: **Please, come home to me, my love.**

They all gave willingly, pushing power into her, and then into Ris, while she floated and hoped. *Ris!* **Come home to me!** She used Tuli's advice and threw open the door, ripped at the edges until it was not just a house door, but a barn door that she threw wide open. The sloth's magic poured through the doorway like floodwater. His eyes opened, the slitted pupils growing wide and round. His mouth opened and she held her breath, shoved the oxygen mouthpiece between his fangs, and released his chest with her other arm to help him inhale.

He sucked at the air, even though his mouth wasn't really

suited. When he began to breathe regularly, she moved him in the water, like helping a fish back to life after it was caught on a hook. Amber had healed his skin and the fresh scales glowed with opalescent brilliance, lighting up the water around them all.

Why am I in the water? What happened? Why are there all these voices in my head with yours?

She smiled, and felt the bubbles tickle as they floated up around her head. Bobby pointed up and she helped Ris swim to the surface. Once they broke into the air and he took his first unaided breath since the previous night, Amber shifted him back to human and he treaded water, looking around the smoky landscape. Luna Lake had survived, but the town hadn't. It was a smoking ruin thanks to the magical blaze started by Lagash's death. At least nobody but Sazi were around to see the blue flames.

But the people had survived, including Enheduanna. She was free and, like Rachel had said after they made it back to the shelter, she was now the fourth sorority sister. With her help, there would be many more in the future. Enheduanna knew the location of all of the rest of the slave camps, and now that she was no longer under Lagash's control she would help them clear out the nests and help her brother bind the remaining snakes to him so they could do good without fear. Someday maybe all snakes would be good. Like Ris was good. Of course, he was part bear, so he had a head start.

"You are part of my sloth now, Ris . . . my femily. The voices in your head are Mama and Papa and your new brothers. Perhaps they are not warriors like Umi or Mako. But they are yours now. Like I am yours. And when you are

DENIED 349

healed, we are going home. Mama is wanting to meeting my new mate. And Bojan's."

Amber added, "I've eaten with her family, Ris. I suggest bringing salmon to dinner instead of wine. A *lot* of salmon."

Anica laughed. After a moment, so did Ris.